Praise for
Virginia is for Mysteries: Volume II

"The second volume of *Virginia is for Mysteries* is another entertaining adventure travelogue taking you across one of the U.S.'s most scenic states, with Mayhem and Revenge your traveling companions and Malice serving as your travel guide. From Jamestown to Luray Caverns, and from a gritty Thelma and Louise-style tale of loyalty and friendship to witty tips for disposing of a troublesome office mate—I think you'll enjoy this road trip."
—G.M. Malliet
Agatha Award Winning Author of the St. Just and Max Tudor Mysteries

"Relentlessly suspenseful and completely engaging! You don't have to be from Virginia to delight in this terrific collection of twisty and clever mysteries."
—Hank Phillippi Ryan,
Agatha, Anthony, Macavity and Mary Higgins Clark
Award Winning Author

"Mystery fans will find a lot to love about *Virginia is for Mysteries II*."
—Mary Burton
New York Times and USA Today Bestselling Author

"*Virginia is for Mysteries Volume II* offers a sparkling selection of stories packed with passion, jealousy, and vengeance, in the past and the present. Carefully detailed with evocative settings from Richmond to Roanoke, the Luray Caverns to Williamsburg and Jamestown, these tales prove that when it comes to murder, there's always something new in the Old Dominion. I loved it!"
—Ellen Byerrum
Author of The Crime of Fashion Mysteries

"A deliciously wicked mix of mysteries, with plenty of Southern 'charm' —Virginia style."
—Mollie Cox Bryan,
Author of the Agatha-nominated Cumberland Creek Mysteries

"*Virginia is for Mysteries Volume II* is a collection of smart, sassy, and spine-tingling tales."
—**Ellery Adams,**
New York Times Bestselling Author of *The Books by the Bay*
Mysteries, Charmed Pie Shoppe Mysteries, and Book Retreat Mysteries

"Whether you've lived in Virginia or just driven through, you'll find familiar settings in this dark and twisty anthology. From wine shops to college campuses, these nineteen short stories will take you on a trip you won't soon forget!"
—**Diane Vallere,**
Nationally Bestselling Author of the Material Witness, Madison Night,
and Style & Error Mysteries

"From revenge to the supernatural and everything in between, this fabulous collection of tales from the Old Dominion will keep you turning pages into the wee hours. I loved every single story!"
—**LynDee Walker,**
Agatha Award-Nominated Author of *Cover Shot*

"From classic whodunits to light romance and historicals, *Virginia is for Mysteries Volume II* is a wild ride of deadly deeds crisscrossing the Commonwealth. Anyone who has traveled across Virginia will love the familiar and cherished settings, from the Blue Ridge to the Chesapeake Bay."
—**Leah St. James,**
Award-winning Author of Romance and Suspense

"*Virginia is for Mysteries Volume II* is an amazing collection of mystery short stories – something for every mystery-loving reader. Contemporary or historical, even blood-chilling, but always entertaining – each of these mysteries kept me guessing until the end. The familiar Virginia locations were such a plus!"
—**Grace Greene,**
USA Today Bestselling Author,
Author of the Emerald Isle, NC Series and Virginia Country Roads Series

"They are back with great tales situated across the Commonwealth. A wonderful read for anyone interested in places for mystery."
—**Tina Glasneck,**
Author of the Spark before Dying Series

"Diabolical, creative plots and absolutely wicked solutions abound! Cunning endings you didn't see coming and tales so well-crafted one might believe they're reading actual Virginia history. These clever stories prove there are almost no limits to the things women will do for their friends—or to their enemies! The authors of this anthology have outdone themselves again. *Virginia is for Mysteries II* will leave you impatient for volume III."
—**P. J. Woods,**
Author of *The Hour To Reap*

"Buckle your seatbelt for a thrilling tour of the Commonwealth—from Tidewater to the Blue Ridge, from Richmond to Roanoke—with this cool collection of cleverly crafted crime stories!"
—**Alan Orloff,**
Agatha-nominated Author of *Running from the Past*

"From Virginia's wine country and the Shenandoah Valley to Fort Monroe, the Dismal Swamp and points beyond, the second volume of *Virginia is for Mysteries* offers a stunning collection of mysteries by Virginia's premier mystery writers that features rich characters, complex plots, beautiful descriptions and the rich heritage of the Commonwealth. Truly the best short-story mystery available."
—**Judith Lucci,**
Author of the Alex Destephano Medical Thrillers
and Michaela McPherson Mysteries

"I'm a transplanted Virginian and reading the nifty short stories in Virginia is for Mysteries made me want to take a road trip home. There are wonderful things to do and see in Virginia. If you're a mystery lover, you'll want to use this anthology as your guidebook."
—**Frankie Y. Bailey,**
Author of the Lizzie Stuart and Hannah McCabe Mysteries

"Murder and mystery lurk behind every hairpin turn of Virginia's winding country roads. This collection is an entertaining guide to the Old Dominion's dark past and present.

There is no shortage of ways to die in Virginia. Whether it is in an amusement park, a swamp, a luxury hotel, or a hurricane, you can't beat the Commonwealth for dramatic locations to meet your end. Let this collection be your travel guide to some great places and creative ways to die in the Old Dominion."

—Christopher Semtner
Curator, Edgar Allan Poe Museum

"What a delight I found reading *Virginia is for Mysteries II*, an anthology of short mysteries compiled and edited by Sisters in Crime. From the first story to the last, mystery after mystery, one thought occurred: "How does Virginia keep producing so many fine authors?" No matter, I suspect. Just sink in and enjoy these fine stories. A true pleasure. *Virginia is for Mysteries II* is one stop shopping for the mystery lover."

—Susan Wingate
Amazon Bestseller and triple award-winner for *The Deer Effect*

"These 19 authors take the reader on a dark trip through Virginia's past and present while introducing a wealth of uncommon criminals and sleuths. *Virginia is for Mysteries Volume II* reveals there's much more to the genre than the classic whodunit and that sometimes the bad guy can turn into the hero of the story. For the person who wants to discover all the things that a mystery can be, this anthology is the answer."

—Bill Blume,
Author of *Gidion's Hunt*

"This collection of Virginia mysteries is fast-paced, creepy, and fun."

—Sheri Reynolds,
#1 New York Times bestselling author of *The Rapture of Canaan,*
***The Homespun Wisdom of Myrtle T Cribb* and four other novels.**

"Nothing says success better than Volume II."

—Jean Loxley-Barnard, Publisher
The Shopper, Doctor to Doctor Magazine, Main Street - The Business Magazine

Virginia is for Mysteries: Volume II

by Meriah Lysistrata Crawford, Adele Gardner,
Debbiann Holmes, Maria Hudgins, Teresa Inge,
Maggie King, Kristin Kisska, C.B. Lane,
Vivian Lawry, Michael McGowan,
Kathleen Mix, Jayne Ormerod, Yvonne Saxon,
Rosemary Shomaker, Rosemary Stevens,
Linda Thornburg, Heather Weidner,
Lee A. Wells, Ken Wingate

ISBN 978-1-63393-149-7

Published by

 köehlerbooks™

210 60th Street
Virginia Beach, VA 23451
212-574-7939
www.koehlerbooks.com

Virginia is for Mysteries

VOLUME II

An Anthology of Mysteries Set in and Around Virginia

Meriah Lysistrata Crawford — Adele Gardner
Debbiann Holmes — Maria Hudgins
Teresa Inge — Maggie King
Kristin Kisska — C.B. Lane
Vivian Lawry — Michael McGowan
Kathleen Mix — Jayne Ormerod
Yvonne Saxon — Rosemary Shomaker
Rosemary Stevens — Linda Thornburg
Heather Weidner — Lee A. Wells — Ken Wingate

VIRGINIA BEACH
CAPE CHARLES

Introduction

The idea for *Virginia is for Mysteries* came about when Teresa Inge, a member of the Mystery by the Sea, Sisters in Crime chapter discussed writing an anthology with the Mystery by the Sea and Central Virginia chapters at the Library of Virginia's Literary Festival in 2011. With a lot of work and creativity, Koehler Books published *Virginia is for Mysteries* in 2013.

Set in and around Virginia, each of the seventeen stories featured a Virginia landmark, from the Cape Henry Lighthouse to Richmond's Hollywood Cemetery.

The original fourteen authors embarked on an adventure that included a standing-room-only panel at the Virginia Festival of the Book, the Poe Birthday Bash, Suffolk Mystery Authors Festival, and RavenCon. As authors crisscrossed Virginia, North Carolina, and Maryland, they met many mystery lovers.

And now they are back with more authors and nineteen new stories, set in even more Virginia locations!

Teresa Inge and Heather Weidner
Anthology Coordinators

TABLE OF CONTENTS

4   COMING CLEAN — Meriah Lysistrata Crawford

22   THE WITCHES' BRIDGE — Adele Gardner

32   MURDER IN THE NAME OF LOVE —
Debbiann Holmes

48   A MYSTERY AT LURAY CAVERNS — Maria Hudgins

62   CORKED FOR MURDER — Teresa Inge

76   REUNION IN SHOCKOE SLIP — Maggie King

92   A COLONIAL GRAVE — Kristin Kisska

110   DEATH IN THE GREAT DISMAL — C. B. Lane

124   WAR AND MURDER AT NIMROD HALL —
Vivian Lawry

142   A HOUSE ON JEFFERSON STREET —
Michael McGowan

156   THE TANGLED WEB — Kathleen Mix

170   IT'S WINE O'CLOCK SOMEWHERE — Jayne Ormerod

188   CAPE CHARLES COFFEE CAPER — Yvonne Saxon

196   ARTIFACTS OF A FRIENDSHIP —
Rosemary Shomaker

212   DOWN BY THE RIVER — Rosemary Stevens

230   USED — Linda Thornburg

244   SPRING CLEANING — Heather Weidner

252   BIKES, BOATS AND BERRIES — Lee A. Wells

268   WITHIN THIS CIRCLE — Ken Wingate

Virginia is for Mysteries: Volume II Story Locations

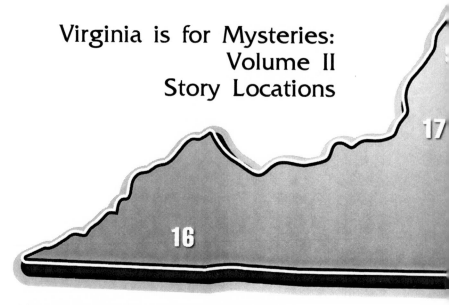

1 I-95 Corridor/Richmond, Va
   Coming Clean by Meriah Lysistrata
   Crawford

2 Busch Gardens Williamsburg
   1 Busch Gardens Boulevard,
   Williamsburg, Va 23185
   The Witches' Bridge by Adele Gardner

3 Virginia Beach Oceanfront
   31st Street,
   Virginia Beach, Va 23451
   Murder in the Name of Love
   by Debbiann Holmes

4 Luray Caverns
   101 Cave Hill Rd,
   Luray, Va 22835
   A Mystery at Luray Caverns
   by Maria Hudgins

5 Battlefield Boulevard
   Chesapeake, Va 23322
   Corked for Murder by Teresa Inge

6 Fountain Bookstore
   1312 E Cary St.,
   Richmond, Va 23219
   Reunion in Shockoe Slip
   by Maggie King

7 Colonial Williamsburg
   Thomas Everard House
   214 Palace Green St.,
   Williamsburg, VA 23185
   A Colonial Grave by Kristin Kisska

8 Great Dismal Swamp National
   Wildlife Refuge
   3100 Desert Rd.,
   Suffolk, Va 23434
   Death in the Great Dismal by C. B. Lane

9 Nimrod Hall
   216 Nimrod Drive,
   Millboro, Va 24460
   War and Murder at Nimrod Hall
   by Vivian Lawry

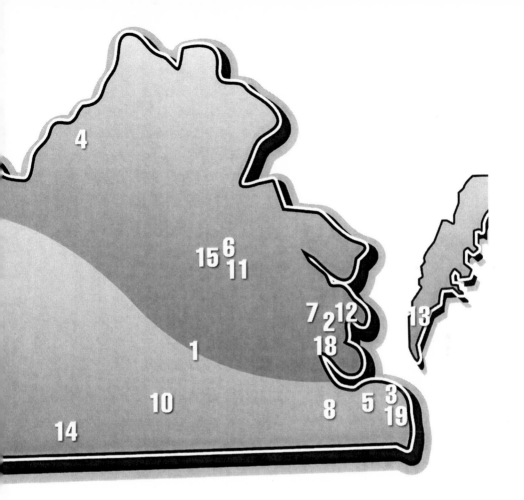

10   Brunswick County, Va 23843
     A House on Jefferson Street by
     Michael McGowan

11   Near the Airport
     Richmond, Va 23250
     The Tangled Web by Kathleen Mix

12   Yorktown, Va 23690
     It's Wine O'clock Somewhere
     by Jayne Ormerod

13   Cape Charles Historic District
     Cape Charles, Va 23310
     Cape Charles Coffee Caper
     by Yvonne Saxon

14   Prestwould Plantation
     429 Prestwould Drive,
     Clarksville, Va 23927
     Artifacts of a Friendship
     by Rosemary Shomaker

15   James River
     4301 Riverside Dr,
     Richmond, Va 23219
     Down by the River by Rosemary Stevens

16   Barter Theatre
     127 W. Main St.,
     Abingdon, Va 24210
     Used by Linda Thornburg

17   Mill Mountain
     Roanoke, Va 24016
     Spring Cleaning by Heather Weidner

18   Jamestown Ferry
     Jamestown, Va 23081
     Bikes, Boats and Berries by Lee A. Wells

19   Virginia Museum of Contemporary Art
     2200 Parks Avenue,
     Virginia Beach, Va 23451
     Within this Circle by Ken Wingate

COMING CLEAN

By Meriah Lysistrata Crawford

"ROAD TRIP?" ANDREA ASKED as I climbed into her car a little before one.

We'd planned to spend Friday afternoon together since I had the day off and she didn't work on Fridays, but hadn't decided on anything specific in advance.

"Heck yeah," I said. "Where to?"

Andrea shrugged and pulled away from the curb as I buckled up. "South?"

I smiled. "My favorite direction. Onward!"

She smiled a bit stiffly and turned on the radio, both of which were uncharacteristic.

"Hey," I said. "Wassup?"

She shook her head. "Rough week. Let's just drive for a while, okay?"

"Sure." I sat back to watch the world go by.

Andrea headed northwest on East Broad toward downtown Richmond, then turned onto I-95 South. We were outside the city in minutes, passing the huge Philip Morris tower with its cigarette brand names painted on the side, and then long stretches of trees interrupted by billboards. Another twenty minutes and a shopping mall later, the sign for I-85 came up.

"What's that way?" she asked, pointing at the sign.

"No idea. Atlanta, maybe? Yeah. And Raleigh, I think. Only, not in that order."

She nodded and took the exit, and we angled inland.

Three and a half hours later, we were still going, still listening to the radio, and not talking. My brain had switched to autopilot, and I'd just been gazing at the scenery, thinking fondly of road trips during my childhood when we played car games, sang goofy songs, and called out unusual license plates. But finally my stomach started grumbling, so I suggested we find dinner. I figured that would be a good time to talk, too.

We ended up, fifteen minutes later, at a Cracker Barrel in Salisbury, North Carolina.

After Andrea parked the car, she leaned back in her seat and sat for a moment, both of us a little stunned by the silence and stillness.

"Sherri, you always said you'd help me if I was in trouble."

"Of course." I reached over and squeezed her forearm. "You know I'll do anything I can to help."

She and I had been close since sixth grade when we discovered a shared love of reading, a hatred of peanut butter and jelly, and the skill to cut school without getting caught. Now, at forty-six, we'd been through the usual tragedies and triumphs together—emergency room runs, my divorce, her mom's death, chest pains, poison ivy, kidney stones, and on and on. We'd helped each other survive them all. I couldn't imagine anything I wouldn't do for her.

She nodded. "Okay. So, let's eat."

"But—wait."

Andrea let out a giddy laugh. "C'mon! Food now, talk later. Me *hug-ree!*"

That was what her son Aiden had said as a child when he was hungry, and it had become one of our inside jokes. I smiled and went along, as always.

After we made our way through the dizzying array of tchotchkes, candles, and T-shirts in the gift shop, we settled at a table near the front windows and ordered. And then I tried, tried, tried to get Andrea to tell me what was going on. She wouldn't.

"Too many people around," she said, which was fair.

Instead, she talked about her crazy sister and her jailbird uncle. Her daughter's success in high school and her son's progress in the Marines. Her neighbor's nasty, howling dog and her cat Lulu's prowess as a hunter of houseflies. She talked about her volunteer work at the Poe Museum. She asked for my opinion of the latest round of *American Idol* contestants, but I hadn't been watching.

When we were done, I paid the bill since we were using her gas, and we got on the road again. We were still heading south, still blasting the tunes—and still not talking. This went on for so long that I finally gathered we weren't going home that night.

"Where are we headed?" I asked.

"South," she said.

"Yeah, I noticed, but you could have warned me to pack a bag or something." I said it lightly because it didn't bother me particularly. I like spontaneous trips—was thrilled, actually, to be doing something different. But still . . .

"You're always complaining that you don't get out of town enough."

"True."

"Well, then."

So, on we drove. I offered to take the wheel a few times—especially when she started to yawn. Each time she declined—maybe afraid I'd get back on the highway headed north. But I didn't have plans for the weekend. I was in the clear until nine Monday morning, when I was due at work. And it would not be a tragedy if I had to call in sick. I hated that damn place.

At a little past eleven, I pointed out a billboard advertising a hotel seven miles away, near Hogansville, Georgia. She nodded and I leaned back, and we were quiet except for the bland '90s music on the radio. I decided I would insist on driving when we got started in the morning, and we'd damn well find a different station to listen to.

We stopped at a drug store off the exit, and I grabbed some essentials. My road-numbed brain finally noticed that Andrea was following idly in my wake, not picking anything off the shelves.

"Why aren't you—" and then it hit me. "Andrea! You packed a bag, didn't you?"

She looked sheepish and shrugged.

"Bitch," I said, shaking my head. I was annoyed, but too tired to be angry. She didn't do it with malice or even selfishness, really—she just wanted to make sure I didn't make waves or thwart her plans. I was the last one to complain that she wasn't perfect, though, so I just paid for my purchases, and we stumbled back to the car.

Once we arrived at the hotel, Andrea grabbed her bag from under a blanket on the floor behind her seat, and then we checked in. She paid for the room from an envelope full of cash. She was the queen of credit cards—always trying to earn points for miles—so it struck me as odd, but I figured her husband, Bobby, or her mom had given her some cash, and she was just going to use it rather than waste time hitting the bank to deposit it.

All I really cared about by then was grabbing a shower, brushing my teeth, and getting to bed. Andrea brushed first, and then I took over the bathroom for a while, and by the time I got out, she was already asleep—or pretending to be—in the bed near the windows. She was clearly avoiding my questions, and it was starting to worry me—a lot. In the morning, I would make sure we talked before we got on the road.

— 🖤 —

Despite my best intentions, I found myself back in the passenger seat the next morning, heading south again, looking for a restaurant. Still no answers, and I was starting to add *peeved* to *worried*.

I'd pressed her to talk, but all she said was, "Sweetie, I need to eat first. You know how I am in the morning. It's all a big ol' fog until I get some coffee and a big plate of something greasy."

Breakfast had always been her favorite meal. I was more a dinner person. Give me a yogurt or some fruit, and I was a happy camper until noon. But I was still a bit dazed from the drive the day before, so I let it go. It was easier to sit back and wait, let her do her thing. She was a force of nature sometimes, like a herd of cattle stampeding.

We spent almost an hour at an IHOP not far off the highway. Andrea spent the entire meal talking about reunions, picnics, and trips to Virginia Beach. Three-bean salad and deviled eggs, cold fried chicken and Rice Krispy squares, fresh steamed shrimp and corn dripping with butter. Volleyball, Frisbee, and even skinny-dipping after an evening of surprisingly tolerable box wine and penny poker. I'd been there for most of it, and it was great to reminisce. I forgot, sometimes, just how much fun we'd had together.

That's when I realized something had to be *really* wrong.

This wasn't just a lighthearted trip down memory lane. She was trying to cement our ties because she was going to drop something big on me. Something huge.

This time, I didn't bother asking her in the restaurant. I reached for the check when we were done, but she took it, paid in cash again, and we left. But when we got to the parking lot, I slid between her and the driver's door and said, "Enough, Andrea. Stop. It's time."

"But I—"

"*No.*"

We locked eyes for a minute as she considered her options, but she finally sighed, slumped, and looked away. I had won— but I was pretty sure I was going to regret it.

She looked around cautiously. "Okay, but we should get in the car. I need to show you something."

I held my hands out for the keys and stood there, immobile, until she handed them over.

I climbed behind the wheel and adjusted the seat and mirrors. It was a relief to feel as though I had some kind of control again—even if only briefly.

Andrea climbed in on the other side, and I turned to face her. After a moment, she opened the top three buttons of her blouse. She slid the fabric aside and showed me: a huge, black bruise above her left breast, disappearing down into her bra. She had a look on her face like she was lost, and I felt a deep rage.

"There are others, too," she said. "Not, you know, where they'd be obvious. Not where they'd be visible, normally."

"Son of a bitch. That *bastard*."

Barry. I'd always disliked him. He was nasty, condescending. But this?

"How long has he been doing this? Did you call the police?"

"Just . . . just in the last couple of months."

"Why didn't you tell me? I could have helped."

"I . . . I was afraid you might hurt him."

"You're damn right I'd have hurt him! I would have driven over that son of a bitch with my car."

She wrung her hands, playing with her finger where her wedding ring used to be. She had lost it three years earlier while gardening. Barry rented a metal detector and found the ring after three hours of searching, and he insisted she leave it at home in her jewelry box after that. The ring had belonged to his mother, and he said he wouldn't risk letting her lose "Momma's ring" again. *Asshole.*

I tried to calm down—or at least sound calm. I asked again if she'd called the police, though I was sure I already knew the answer.

She shook her head.

"Well, we can call them now. We can show them the bruises. They'll arrest him. Everything will be okay."

She was shaking her head before I was through.

"Why not?"

She whispered. "He's gone."

"Gone?" I asked. "Gone where?"

She squeezed her eyes closed and spoke even more softly. "In the trunk."

"What?"

She turned her head, looking toward the rear of the car.

Oh, my God. The trunk. Barry's in the trunk.

"Oh, God, Andrea . . . Oh, God." I leaned forward and closed my eyes, resting my forehead on the steering wheel. "Why?"

"He kept hitting me," she said. "I just . . . I just couldn't . . . I shot him."

"With what?"

"His gun. The .38 that he keeps in his bedside table."

"You were in the bedroom?"

"No, outside. In the garage. You see, he was out of beer. He'd told me the night before to get more beer, but I was already half asleep when he said it, and I didn't remember. And I had to get his drycleaning, and Katie had her college orientation that I had to take her to—"

"Okay," I said, cutting her off. "So that's why he hit you? He was mad about the beer?"

She nodded. "Shouldn't we . . . ?" She looked around the lot, as if afraid someone might think our continued presence was suspicious.

And then it occurred to me: we were in full sun and it was getting warm outside, and there was a body decomposing in the trunk. As soon as I thought of it, I noticed a faint smell.

I started the car, cranked up the air conditioning, and headed south on a road that paralleled the highway. I still thought there must be some way out of this, for both of us. There must be.

"Why did you have the gun? Why wasn't it in the table?"

"I . . . when he yelled for me to come downstairs . . ."

"You knew he was angry."

"Furious."

"So you grabbed the gun before going downstairs?"

"Yes."

Fuck. Was it self-defense or premeditation? My mind raced.

Setting aside the issue of the road trip, of course, which was a whole huge problem by itself. But what if we just drove on home, put the corpse back in the garage, and called the police? Could we still get out of this?

"Does anyone else know?"

She shook her head and I felt a moment of relief, but then she said, "They'll have noticed he's missing by now, though."

"They?"

"Well, he had a barbeque today—at his cousin's house in Powhatan. And you know he never misses those. *Never.*"

I shook my head and made myself ease my grip on the steering wheel and slow the car. "Okay. Did you clean up?"

"Yes. With bleach and everything."

"Rags?"

"Paper towels. They're in a bag." She nodded toward the back of the car.

On the one hand, it was good she'd cleaned up. On the other, it all looked very calculating.

We talked some more about who knew what and when. Most of it was bad: she'd never discussed the abuse—whether psychological or physical—with anyone; both kids were out of the way that weekend, and it could be argued that she'd had a hand in that; and the way she'd cleaned up and even packed a bag before our trip; it would be hard, if not impossible, to successfully argue self-defense. I was her friend, and I knew Barry was a dick, but I still had problems with what she'd done.

"Sweetie," I said gently, "why didn't you call the police? Either before you went downstairs, or after he attacked you? After you shot him, I mean?"

"Does it really matter now?"

"Maybe not, but I want to know."

"I just couldn't stand it anymore." Her voice grew quiet again as she gazed off into the distance. "It wasn't just how he treated me. He was always good to the kids, you know? Gentle. Not always so good at praising them, but I was always there for that. But, Katie—"

Katie was her oldest, just starting college at Virginia Commonwealth University in the fall.

"Well, Katie wants to be an artist. And she's *so* good—you've seen her work."

I had, and she was truly talented. Her pencil drawings delivered not just realism, but emotion. Joy, grief, fear, love—it was an incredible gift.

"Barry wanted her to get a degree in something practical. The more she resisted, the more he just—" her voice cracked, "the more he tore her down. And I realized—he was saying the same exact things he'd said to me over the years. Quiet things, at first. Sneaky things, like 'I know you think you have a lot of skill with those drawings of yours, but a lot of people have skill. And you need a whole lot of luck and connections and money to make it as an artist. Do you really think you have those? You know you don't.' And recently, he'd moved on to things like, 'We're not going to support you in this idiotic quest to make a living with a bunch of damn doodles on paper, missy. You need to get a real job. Make something of yourself.' And, oh, Sherri, how she'd cry!"

Andrea finished with a sob, and I found a quiet place to pull over in the shade and held her as she cried. The car shuddered gently with the effort of keeping the cool air flowing, and it felt like all three of us were shaking together, knocked off course by this mess we shared.

Finally, she pulled back and tried to compose herself. I wiped away some tears of my own and wished I could undo the last two days. If only she'd—well, if only she'd done so many things differently, like never dated that dirt bag to begin with.

Much as I loved Andrea and felt for her pain, I admit I briefly thought about making a phone call and extricating myself. If I called a lawyer and got some advice and then turned her in, I could get out of it with my freedom intact. If I kept on driving south, it was anyone's guess where any of us would end up. But I didn't really have a choice. She was closer than family. I was going to see this through with her, wherever it led.

"So," I said, finally, "do you have a plan?"

She cleared her throat and then looked back at the road.

"I've heard Costa Rica is nice."

"You want to take a corpse to Costa Rica?" I said, more loudly than I had intended.

She grimaced and shrank a bit in her seat. "No," she whispered. "I thought we could, you know, find a quiet place and . . ."

I took her hand and squeezed it gently.

"Okay, that's . . . well, I don't know if *good idea* is the way to put it, but I suppose we do need to take care of that." I frowned and tried to remember what little I knew about forensics from TV shows. Some of them were documentaries, so they ought to be accurate. I didn't remember a whole lot, though. It would be ideal to drop him in a big hole, but the chances of us being able to dig one without witnesses weren't so good. Finding a hole to put him in was risky, too, for a variety of reasons. Maybe we could find a place where an alligator would eat him. Do they eat corpses? Ugh.

And then I thought of Gracie. She was a sweet old lady who had worked with my grandmother at a department store right out of high school and had been the best of friends for life. Even after Grandma died six years earlier, I'd kept in touch, mostly through holiday cards and phone calls on her birthday and Christmas. She always invited me to visit, and I always said I would try, but Tallahassee was a long way to go, and I didn't get a lot of vacation time. But if Andrea and I stopped in for a brief visit, that would be a good enough excuse for us to be down there, wouldn't it?

I pulled out my cell and checked the map and realized we were actually pretty close. Another four or five hours of driving— carefully and at the speed limit—and we could be there. The map showed a huge national forest nearby—Apalachicola. It was, no doubt, filled with swamps and alligators. *Perfect!*

I pulled the car back on the road and shared my plan with

Andrea, who agreed it sounded like a good bet, so I called Gracie. As I expected, Gracie was pleased to hear from me and elated that I was going to be in her area and wanted to visit. I told her we'd arrive the next day. Gracie promised to have her guest room made up for us—and no, I told her, we didn't mind sharing at all.

"Why tomorrow?" Andrea asked when I got off the phone.

I turned onto Hamilton Road, heading for 185 South. "We need to get there and take care of the body before going to her house. I don't know if you'd noticed, but there's a bit of an odor. We'll need to clean and try to air the trunk out a bit, or she'll be in there with Lysol and a vacuum within minutes of our arriving. Besides, it would be rude to show up with so little notice. She'd think it was very odd. Heck, she probably already does."

Andrea nodded.

And then I wondered—Andrea's phone hadn't rung once.

"Do you have your cell with you?"

She shook her head. "I left it in the bedroom, with Barry's."

I groaned.

"What?"

"People will be worried. They'll think something happened to both of you!"

She shrugged.

I felt a rush of anger and almost snapped at her. We were both tense and getting tenser. We had to just stay focused. I pulled out my phone and handed it to her.

"Can you remove the battery?"

"Why?"

"Well, it will make it harder to find him if they figure this out. At least, I think it will."

She pulled the battery out and slid them both back into my bag, and then she wrinkled her nose and pressed her hand to her stomach. "Ugh."

"I know." The smell was becoming more obvious, but there was nothing to do but keep going. I found an on-ramp and we got back on the highway. Every time we passed a cop—which was pretty often—both of us tensed up and stared straight ahead. There'd be no hope for either of us if we got caught now. No hope at all.

We stopped for lunch in Bainbridge, Georgia, parking the car under a tree in an empty bank lot well away from the restaurant. I'd have liked to eat in the car, but the smell was too much. In fact, it was starting to worry me.

After we ate, while Andrea was paying with cash, which I thought was a useless ploy, I stopped in a store nearby and grabbed some sport-scent spray sunscreen. I stopped at the back of the car and sprayed it on my arms, making sure to get plenty of it on the trunk, even spraying some of it along the gap between the lid and the car. It would make sense to open it and spray inside, but I just could not do it.

Andrea sprayed some on, too, and as we climbed in, we sprayed the back seat for good measure. We could tell anyone who still noticed the smell that we left a bag of trash in the trunk for too long. It was all we could do for the time being—and it did really help. Another couple months later, in the middle of summer, it would have been impossible. Good timing, I guess.

As we passed through a town called Havana, we angled southwest to avoid Tallahassee. Call me paranoid, but I didn't want to risk Gracie seeing us before we were supposed to get there. We found a visitors center, grabbed maps and brochures, and pored through them. Finally, we found a good spot: the Mud Swamp/New River Wilderness.

We arrived at the park in early afternoon. It was a Saturday, and there were a fair number of cars. We kept rolling, with Andrea navigating and me watching for any signs of people following us or, worse, smelling us.

We soon found a smaller road and turned right. Andrea said if we kept going, there'd be a river off to the side. Before long, we reached what we both judged was about the right place. There were plenty of trees and brush, no other cars—at least for the moment—and good access to the river.

I gingerly backed the car into a narrow slot between trees that looked as if it had been used for parking before. We climbed out, stretched, and then stood and listened. There were bugs, of course, and lots of them. Birds sang. Small animals rustled in the leaves. Every so often, in the distance, we could hear vehicles, but no one came our way for at least a few minutes.

We were both batting furiously at mosquitoes, and we looked at each other and said, "Bug spray."

"We're idiots," I said.

"Yeah, no kidding." Andrea slapped a mosquito on her arm. "Should we wait, or . . ."

"Ideally, I suppose, we would do a few days of driving around to see what happens and when, but we don't have the time." Already, we'd both moved away from the car without even thinking about it. There was still a faint scent of sunscreen—and the pungent odor of death.

"Okay," I said. "Let's just do it."

Andrea's eyes were wide. Neither of us wanted to have anything to do with this. And, like an idiot, I found myself thinking, *If you had just told me, we could have dumped him in a Virginia swamp when he was still fresh.* But the thought was useless. I shook my head, clearing it away.

"Okay. Right." I popped the trunk and opened it. "Oh . . . God."

The stench. The maggots and flies. The bright-goddamn-blue tarp.

"Andrea, Jesus!"

"What?"

"Blue? That's damn subtle."

"Well, I thought it would be dark, I guess. And that was all I had!"

"Gaahhhh. Damn." I looked around, watching for movement. There could be a flock of bird watchers behind any given cluster of trees, or a busload of camera-laden tourists coming around a turn at any minute. No way to know—and it was too late to wait any longer.

"Okay, come on. Grab an end."

"Oh, honey," she said, looking pale green. "I don't know if I can."

"Andrea, your scumbag former husband was not a small man. I can't do this by myself."

"Oh, dear Lord," she said and stepped forward to help.

We gathered up the edges of the tarp and started pulling. There was a hideous squishing sound as the body shifted.

Andrea dropped her end of the tarp, lurched to the side, and lost what was left of her lunch on a tree trunk. I'd been barely holding on myself—watching her vomit was beyond my limit. I spun around and did the same.

When I was done heaving, I grabbed our water bottles from the car and handed hers to her while we paused to clean up and try to settle our stomachs. A gentle breeze picked up and helped ease the stink, though not by much. "Ready?" I asked.

She nodded. We tossed our bottles into the car and grabbed the tarp again, this time moving more quickly. It took all our strength, groaning at the effort while trying not to inhale, but we hauled him out and thudded him down on the ground. She started to let go.

"No, no, don't let—don't let anything drip out."

She nodded and, after a quick scan of the road, we started pulling him across the ground toward the river, just two hundred feet or so from where we stood. The tarp, at least, made dragging him fairly easy, except for the roots and branches on the ground. We eased down a gentle embankment, both of us starting to sink into the soft ground. Finally, we reached the water's edge.

"Here?" she asked.

I looked back toward the road, but couldn't see it through the dense canopy and underbrush. I'd have been happier farther away, but the longer we lingered with our blue tarp, the more likely it was that someone would see us. I scanned for people again and then nodded. We both grabbed one side of the tarp and rolled him out. He splashed gently into the water, and I realized he was nude.

"His clothing?" I asked.

"He was wearing one of his orange Virginia Tech T-shirts and white shorts. I figured—"

"Yeah, okay." Smart move—but, again, something that would look bad in court. I hoped to God we'd never find out just how bad.

Barry was mostly submerged, but he seemed to be snagged on a submerged tree limb. I grabbed a branch and tried to lever him further out into the water, but quickly gave up. It was what it was. It didn't make sense for me to get soaked trying to hide him better. Did it?

I grabbed some branches from the ground nearby and tossed them over the parts of his body that stuck out. Then I stood and gazed at him for a moment, trying to absorb the fact that he was really dead. In all honesty, I'd never thought they were especially good together. I never let myself think much about it, because he was Andrea's husband and I had to support her. Now that I knew the truth about how he'd treated her, I could hardly mourn his passing. But this? Had he deserved this? Did his family deserve this?

I shook my head to clear my thoughts again.

We rinsed the tarp in the river, shaking off maggots and blood clots, then folded it, and hustled back to the car.

"Oh, geez," Andrea said.

"Yeah." The stench was still powerful. "Next time, wrap the body better."

She gaped at me and started giggling. I did, too, and then we both seemed to realize it was more shock than humor and quieted down. I stuffed the tarp into the trash bag that held the paper towels, clothing, and other stuff she'd used to clean up, and then stared in horror at the trunk. He had leaked—a lot.

"Do you think we can clean it?" she asked.

"What it really needs is a good fire," I said. "Or, in other words, probably not."

"What do we do?"

"Hell if I know."

We could probably find someone to clean it, but then there'd be a record. We could plausibly argue that it was from a dead animal—like a pet dog or something—but why would we let it rot in there? And what if they took a sample?

"We need to get on the road right now," I said. I sprayed some more sunscreen in there and slammed the lid shut, and we both used some hand sanitizer.

And then I was driving again. And wouldn't you know it, about ten seconds later, a minivan full of what looked like intoxicated college students whipped past us, almost running us off the road.

After I was done cursing, Andrea said, "It's okay, they missed us."

"Yeah, but if they hadn't? Think the police wouldn't notice

the smell?"

"They might not find him," she said.

"They'd get dogs in here. They'd find him. And regardless, they could get DNA from the trunk."

"Oh."

Andrea was, it was turning out, either more of an optimist than I'd thought, or in deep denial. Maybe that was better, though, because I felt like my entire world was threatening to collapse under me, and that felt pretty horrible.

We drove south, heading out of the park, aiming for a town called Carrabelle. Andrea turned up her '90s music again and I let her, glad we didn't have to talk for a while. It gave me time to think, and to plan—and to scratch my bug bites.

An hour and a half later, we reached the edge of town. We hit a store and grabbed cleaning supplies, plus food, anti-itch lotion, and two bottles of white wine to help ease our stress. I also stopped in a beachwear shop and bought some T-shirts and shorts and a hat. I was out of cash, but I saw no point in avoiding the inevitable, so I used my credit card for the first time. It made me feel exposed, but what else could I do?

We again sprayed the trunk as covertly as we could, and I put my battery back into my phone. No messages.

I located a small motel with cabins, and called ahead to be sure they had space. When I asked for a quiet spot, they agreeably offered an end unit, which was perfect.

And then I told Andrea my plan.

"No, no, no!" she said.

"Why not?"

"I can't possibly talk to Barry's sister. She'll know I'm lying. She'll hear it in my voice! No!"

"Okay, okay." I sighed. "How about if I call her?"

"And say what?"

"That you're upset because you fought. That you don't want to talk to anyone right now, but I wanted to let someone know you're okay and I couldn't reach Barry."

She thought about it and agreed, albeit reluctantly, so I called.

Gwen seemed surprised but glad to hear from me, but she was very worried. Barry and Andrea were missing. I explained about Andrea and expressed concern about Barry. I asked how long he'd been missing and if they'd called the police yet.

"Should we?"

"Well," I said, "you know how he is when he's angry and he drinks. What if he drove somewhere? What if he's hurt?"

"Oh, my. Maybe I *should* call," Gwen said.

"Of course, he could just be sleeping it off in a motel somewhere."

She gasped. "Oh! Oh, he'd be so angry if she sent the police after him."

"Would he? Well, whatever you think is best."

Gwen decided not to call just yet. She agreed to let me know if Barry turned up and said she would let everyone know Andrea was out of town with me.

Next, Andrea and I both left messages at work, saying we'd be out on Monday—a friend was having a crisis and we'd had to go out of town. *Sorry!*

And off we went to check into our cabin for the afternoon. It was a sweet little place on the water—clean and comfortable, and with stunning views. We parked the car on the far side of the cabin, and then spent hours cleaning the bejeesus out of the trunk.

Both of us sprayed and scrubbed as if our lives depended on it, which they did. It was grim, foul work, but we labored quickly and thoroughly together, as we always had. And we discussed our jobs and our families and our plans for the future, as if there was no question about whether or not we would have one.

Was the cleaning job good enough? Not really. Not if we were suspects. We just had to hope it wouldn't come to that. But by the time we were done, I was pretty sure it would pass a visual and olfactory inspection.

Finally, we packed everything into two layers of trash bags and took them to the already-overflowing dumpster nearby. I lifted the lid and some other bags so she could tuck our trash underneath, and then we trooped back to the cabin together.

"Dibs on the shower," I said as we neared the building, remembering there was only one.

"Shit," she said. "You always do that."

"Not my fault I'm smarter," I said, sticking my tongue out at her.

"You smell worse, too."

"Bitch," I said.

"Skank."

We laughed—and it was real this time. Was it going to be okay? It was way too soon to tell, but we'd done our best. Together, like always.

Happy Halloween!

THE WITCHES' BRIDGE

BY ADELE GARDNER

Adele Gardner

HALLOWEEN TURNED BUSCH GARDENS Williamsburg into a carnival of frights. Each year, Howl-O-Scream felt scarier than ever. Susan stood on the bridge that led into the witches' camp, where the trip-trap of human feet triggered bloodcurdling screams. The tree-lined bridge spanned a stream whose gurgling depths disappeared into darkness. Occasionally, the ribbon of Halloween revelers snapped, leaving Susan alone on the bridge where her friend Holly had died six years ago today—Halloween Sunday, 2004.

Susan leaned out over the rail, gripping it tightly. She stared intently at the glistening tips of protruding stones and the froth of the waterfall sliding past. From the slope above, running feet emerged from the witches' woods. "Hey, lady, are you going to jump?" Two teenage boys loped past, laughing. As they crossed the right point, the bridge shrieked. One kid laughed a curse. Susan stood alone.

"Holly," she whispered. "Holly, can you hear me? It's tonight, sweetheart. It's finally Halloween Sunday again."

The trial had been agonizing. As the only witness to the crime, Susan had burned with shame as the defense team dragged out secrets and speculated about motives, accusing her of everything from being jealous of Brant to being jealous of Holly. The defense lawyers had pointed out how plain Susan was, even ugly without makeup, and accused her of both bitter envy and lesbianism. They'd even dissected her divorce.

It was true, of course, that she'd loved Holly, but not that way. Since the divorce, Susan had cherished her friends even more. Since second grade, Holly had been the best of friends, someone whose love and loyalty Susan could trust when her husband's failed.

Since they were girls together, they'd made special plans for Halloween—parties and haunted tours, spooky poetry readings, and ghost hunting. They'd first met at the school Halloween party, and it was this enthusiasm that cemented their friendship after school at each other's houses as they created books of ghosts and drawings of black cats. They loved witches best of all—black silhouettes against the moonlit sky, riding twig-crooked brooms, their black cats arching to spring and scratch out eyes. At eight, the girls' highest ambition had been to become witches themselves, with crooked hats to mirror the sickle moon they flew beside. They'd written witch haiku and limericks that they called spells, and even made a witches' pact of friendship, dripping blood from pricked thumbs into a pot of boiling water over the stove's gas flame. This, Holly's idea, felt dangerous, rash—thrilling and scary with forever.

They'd shared more than Halloween, of course, dancing to Holly's mom's '70s LPs, playing in the treehouse, acting out their favorite television shows, and, later, laughing about boys. They remained best friends through high school, despite Holly's growing mania for makeup and making out with jocks who never treated her right. But Susan loved Holly enough to put up with all the embarrassing public displays, though she far preferred the time they spent alone.

Six years ago tonight, when Holly told her that Brant would be joining them at the park, Susan had tried to object.

"It's Halloween. Our special day."

To include Brant in their private moment felt like a betrayal. She knew what Brant was like—what an evening in his company would mean. She'd gone to the park with them a few times, putting up with Brant's aggressive and possessive shenanigans for Holly's sake, though she'd urged Holly privately to kick him out. But Halloween meant too much to squander on Brant's macho tomfoolery. He did his best to spoil the fun for everyone.

But Holly had been adamant. "He goes where I go." And the evening had quickly gone sour, between Brant's teasing antics and harassment of the costumed staff and Holly's deliberately sexy shrieks. The monsters went out of their way to scare the beautiful girl with the round, laughing cheeks and eyes that gleamed with each new thrill. They wanted to see the lusty swell of her breasts as she threw back that long chestnut hair and screamed. Sometimes Brant beat them to the punch, yelling in her ear to make her jump or goosing her as he laughed wickedly. When a bloody vampire surprised her and she cowered against Brant, he shoved her protectively aside and roared threats till the monster melted away.

It disgusted Susan, who walked behind them through one wasted maze after another. At last, they emerged from another haunted house ruined by Brant's sarcastic, cajoling wisecracks.

Holly's laughter goaded him on.

"I'm going to explore the park by myself," Susan said. "I'll meet you later at the witches' caravan."

Holly shrugged as if it didn't matter. As Susan walked off, she thought she heard Holly say with a low laugh, "Thank God we got rid of Ms. Sourpuss." But the warped carnival music, revelers' shrieks, and growls of the spooks were so loud, she couldn't tell for sure.

Susan put it behind her and threw herself into the Halloween spirit, cringing so the spooks would jump out to get her. Sometimes they passed her over for pretty girls, but it served the ghouls right when, as often as not, the beauty laughed or made bored comments to her boyfriend. Susan did it right; she shrieked and scampered at a skeleton's sudden lunge. Once they caught on, they followed her through the maze—more and more of them. They tilted their eyeless skulls, their movements stiff with lack of cartilage. Their finger bones clutched after her, till she ran screaming into the night. Sometimes she stumbled in surprise, lifting one leg like a pawing horse before starting to run, their deep chuckles following her into the darkness. Only under the arc lights did her grin escape.

Alone, Susan could slip through the crowds in half the time, weaving around clumps of friends and families with strollers. She toured maze after maze, again and again. Near closing time, her regret caught up with her. Halloween was almost over, and she'd spent most of their favorite holiday without her friend. Remembering their first Halloween as kids when they'd pretended to be witches, she made her way toward the Witches' Bridge.

Susan passed other stragglers whose leisurely pace said that they, too, wanted to milk the final moments. Trees darkened the approach to the bridge, and a blind curve meant hidden monsters could scare a screamer twice. Tired home-goers grew sparse on the paths. The creepy music sounded louder as the park emptied, that eerie music piping into the dim, dead place.

The boards of the bridge were smooth from many crossings. The sides dropped away into a moist, gurgling darkness. As Susan neared, mist shot up over the bridge, accompanied by a sepulchral laugh from underneath. As the mist parted, Susan saw Holly and Brant embracing on the bridge.

Brant's back was to her, and Holly didn't seem to see her. Holly laughed at Brant's mutter. The curling ends of her long chestnut locks swung freely, brushing her shoulders, while his crew cut was so short it was hard to see the color of his hair. Her round hips pressed his narrow ones, both of them in jeans. His biceps bulged under a thin, green T-shirt.

Susan stepped back. Holly looked up. Holding Susan's eyes, she whispered in Brant's ear.

Her own ears burning, Susan started walking away. Then Holly shrieked. Susan glanced back. Brant had lifted Holly into his arms like a bride and tossed her up. Staggering slightly, Brant crooned. "So you want to go home? Without me?"

Holly screamed—a pleased, haunted-house squeal. "Let me down!"

"You think you're getting off that easily?" he chuckled tenderly.

Holly kicked the air. He staggered again under her weight.

Susan froze. For a joke, it was too dangerous. With each toss, he lurched closer to the rail. Holly clung to his neck and started pleading, "Brant, let me down, oh, please God, let me go!"

Susan looked up and down the bridge. No one else was in sight or within hearing range, with that blasted music. Far ahead, the last walkers didn't look back.

Holly stopped kicking; she clung to Brant's neck.

"Please, baby, put me down!" Her hair fell over his shoulder.

"Come on, you know you like it," he chuckled. His waist pressed the rail as muscles bunched across his back.

"Help!" Holly shrieked. Over Brant's shoulder, her eyes

sought her best friend.

Susan took a step toward them, arms outstretched, readying herself to make a grab—could she catch Holly without making things worse? There were guards in the park—even a few local police. But they'd never get here in time.

Holly's back hung over open space. Susan checked her fists to be sure her thumbs were outside the way Daddy taught her. She ran toward Brant's back.

"Hey!" she bellowed.

Brant whirled. His face convulsed as he saw Susan. With a spastic jerk, he dropped Holly over the rail.

Holly's gasp hung in the air. No time to scream. In an instant, the splash ended in a terrible crunch. Susan thought inanely of trolls grinding bones.

She ran to the rail. Brant stood there, frozen, his face an unreadable mask. Holly was gone.

Susan cursed him and ran for the cops. When they returned, Brant still waited on the bridge, staring over the rail at the water with glazed eyes. It took the rescue team some time to retrieve Holly's remains.

— 👧 —

At the trial, Brant's defense lawyers painted Susan as an obsessive stalker who'd figuratively suffocated Holly and hated Brant for his influence on her. According to Brant, Susan would have accused him of anything; she was always badmouthing him to Holly, trying to turn her against him. Susan clearly had a chip on her shoulder, and Holly was sweet as pie unless she'd been talking to Susan, after which she'd suddenly come home with a laundry list of complaints. Brant had claimed he hadn't seen Holly since they entered the park—that she'd gone off with her friend. He'd finally caught up with them just in time to see Susan push Holly off the bridge.

But security cameras showed Holly and Brant walking toward the bridge, wrapped in each other's arms. Staff and attendees from haunted houses all over the park remembered Brant's obnoxious behavior and Holly's beauty. They remembered the way the couple had been all over each other. Then Brant tried to claim it was an "accident," that Holly had been so startled by the recorded screams on the bridge she'd tripped and fallen over the side. In response, the police proved the railing was chest-high on Holly and difficult to climb.

Gruesome crime scene photos showed Holly's body shattered on the rocks, her bones poking through twisted limbs. The medical examiner described lungs filled with blood and water. The grisly evidence silenced Brant and cemented the case in the jury's mind.

Finally the police unearthed emails Brant sent Holly a month before her death, threatening to kill them both. He said he'd had enough of interfering friends who sapped her time and swayed her against him. He was only happy in the moments when she truly loved him. In some innocent moment of happiness, he'd make sure they died together like Bonnie and Clyde. They'd be together forever. It would look like an accident, but he wanted her to know. "I'd go to the grave with you, baby." Holly's reply sounded truly scared. She demanded he stay away from her. Brant's wheedling, insistent replies laughed it off as a joke. He said she'd made too much of it. He promised if she gave him another chance she wouldn't be sorry. But events proved otherwise.

In the end, Susan got justice for Holly at the risk of her dignity, her reputation, and possibly her life if Brant got free. But Brant's conviction, even his execution, couldn't bring Holly back.

Each year, Susan returned to the park, wishing with all her heart for an impossible reunion with Holly, oppressed by the thought of what she'd failed to do. Halloween itself had fallen during the week when the park was closed until Halloween Friday in 2008. Brant was still making appeals.

Susan found herself at the bridge rail, talking earnestly to Holly while the spooks swirled all around. She felt as though her friend were listening, a ghostly presence as faint but as real as the wind upon her cheek.

For Halloween Saturday in 2009, Susan had done her research. Her voice trembled with excitement as she spoke the words that should free her friend. Fog rose to surround her; the green lights from the foot of the bridge shone through it in a blurry haze. In the blindness, she felt Holly's cold, clammy hand upon her wrist. But the fog blew away with the same acrid aftertaste as that generated by the park's machines. Susan stood on the bridge alone, feeling useless and lost, as bewildered as she'd been when Holly first went over the side.

But 2010 brought new hope. Halloween fell on Sunday once more, just like when Holly died. Though the fall in Eastern Virginia had been warm and bright as usual with cheery blue skies, Halloween dawned crisp and cold, with fog shrouding an orange sun in a visible reminder of the powerful change in the year. Susan felt calm, certain. The conditions were right. This time, she would free Holly's spirit. *Third time's the charm,* she thought. And within moments, Holly's killer would be dead.

"His last appeal fell through," Susan told Holly. "I guess he finally accepted what he did to you," she choked, then continued raggedly, "He never did say he was sorry. But he asked to be executed tonight at the same time you fell. His request was granted. They told me I could watch, but I'd rather be here with you."

Brant's execution alone couldn't bring Holly back. But Halloween had its own magic and power. And tonight she had a whole park full of Halloween believers to back her up, lending strength with their screams. Even the scoffers added weight by participation.

"We'll be witches at last," Susan told Holly with a shaky laugh. When the moon was high, she performed the simplest ritual of all. One nick to the thumb, and blood fell into the roiling water where Holly's blood had pooled six years before. Their childhood spell revived with all the strength of a friend's belief and the wild magic of Halloween.

Susan leaned over the dark water.

"You're free now, Holly! He's dead!"

Her eyes filled with tears. The park's generated mist coalesced under the bridge and rose, glowing purple in the Halloween lights as it engulfed the walkers around her. Their startled protests sounded muffled. They bumped into one another and laughed.

Susan put her head down on her arms on the wooden rail. Her long hair tickled her arms. Why was she such a coward? Why hadn't she saved her friend?

The wind brushed her neck. Her arms felt wet. When she wiped her eyes, she felt dizzy.

Why was the ground so far away?

A new fog crept up over the railing. Susan felt stretched between earth and heaven—like a bridge, her soul spanning a road born of witches' blood. Holly? These last few years, she'd felt her friend's presence, slumbering, waiting for the right moment. Now, her chest hurt as Holly drew breath inside her. The fog formed a phosphorescent face—not decayed, not broken, but dark with pain.

Susan opened her arms to Holly.

"At last," Holly whispered, her breath as cold as mist. "I've waited. To tell you."

The green-shot fog embraced Susan, filling her sight. Thrilled, Susan felt her feet lifting from the ground. "Holly—I've missed you—"

The mist vanished. Susan's stomach dropped with terror and fluttering delight as she hung suspended—flying!

Then Brant's face leered up at her, his crew cut so close she could see his scalp through gold stubble. She yelped and clutched his neck, the only thing to hold. He murmured soothingly, "I got you, babe," with a wicked smile.

She shrieked; he laughed. He tossed her again, his arms strong and solid, though he pretended his knees buckled under her weight, and let her fall a little more. She sobbed, terror like a knife at her throat, but the thrill in her belly was expansive and warm.

Across the bridge, she saw her friend Susan—her old self—standing like a ghost, her face shocked and pale. Watching over Brant's shoulder, Holly-Susan laughed inside and ratcheted up the screams, putting a new note of terror in her voice. True to form, Brant smacked his lips at the lusty quaver in her cries.

Brant didn't know Susan stood there. Holly pleaded with her eyes. Susan thought so little of Brant. This would be amusing. Let the big lunk be scared for a change!

Susan. Best friend for so long. Suffocating devotion. Yet Holly had regretted the instant when she'd let her annoyance slip into mockery. Susan could be cloying, but that was due to them being as close as sisters, so close Susan felt she had a say in how Holly lived her life. In truth, Holly did feel humiliated sometimes by the public ownership Brant demanded—their lascivious spectacles. But he was exciting and dangerous to deny. His recklessness was a breath of fresh air after Susan's overprotective cocoon. For one nasty moment, the imp of the perverse had seized her outside that maze. Playing up to Brant, she'd insulted Susan *sotto voce*. She saw the pain in Susan's stiff back and hated the deed. But Susan would get over it. She'd forgive, without ever admitting she'd heard. Holly blamed Brant for inciting the whole thing.

So, when she'd seen her friend hesitating at the edge of the bridge, she'd whispered in Brant's ear, "I'm riding home with Susan."

Inside Holly, Susan's heart swelled with joy. She cried out in Holly's mind, "Yes!"

Holly's back crawled where Brant held her so near the edge. He bent his knees suddenly, and she felt her heart stop. He caught her, chortling, "Oops!"

"Help!" Holly screamed.

Past-Susan's determination solidified. Her mouth hardened. Her eyes flashed. Riding inside her friend, now-Susan saw that Holly knew her friend would battle demons—go to the ends of the earth. That past-Susan would fight Brant.

In that instant, from Holly's vantage point, Susan saw it. Breaking through the fog in her head and the light, ghostly pressure of the wind on her neck, Susan sobbed.

"Holly, no! I didn't."

Behind her, a whisper trailed her neck in dewdrops.

"Yes. You did. But it's too late now for regrets. My boyfriend's dead. And so am I. You killed us both."

Trapped inside Holly—in Brant's arms—Susan shrieked as her determined past-self ran up purposefully.

"Witch sisters," Holly crooned. "Halloween night. You said you came for a reunion. Our special day."

Past-Susan yelled. Brant shied like a colt. His burden slipped. He whirled, his arms lifting, providing accidental boost.

Holly-Susan flew—hung for a moment, buoyed up in cold, dead arms.

Behind her, the bridge shrieked lustily, then burst into maniacal laughter and dragged them over the side and into a watery embrace.

They tumbled down, shrieking along with the bridge, in perfect harmony with Halloween.

MURDER IN THE NAME OF LOVE

By Debbiann Holmes

BEING A MURDER-MYSTERY WRITER has its perks. I was a single mom. My three year old, Chloe, was the love of my life, but I struggled to keep us afloat. Writing doesn't make much money until you are famous, that is. My first self-published novel was making its way out to the public, but that takes time. Only avid mystery readers who loved to soak up new books by new authors would recognize me. Taking care of the hotel guests at the Virginia Beach oceanfront was my steady source of income for now. This time my job was going to boost my writing career. I was getting access to someone who was not only famous, but also a person of interest in a recent murder.

The four-star hotel at 31st street on the Boardwalk, with its view of a King Neptune statue sculpted by Paul DiPasquale below, was luxurious. I'd learned only that morning that Mr. Robert Peale, an actor in a recent blockbuster movie, was staying at the hotel. And I was the maid assigned to his room. He was under *house arrest* so to speak, suspected of murdering his best friend and co-star, Johnston Towne. The police hadn't charged him, officially, but they told him to stay in the area until he was no longer a suspect.

Rumor had it that Peale and Towne had been fighting over a girl. Something went seriously wrong, and Towne ended up dead. I was intrigued. Who was the girl? Why did the murder take place on the set of their new movie at Fort Monroe? Why were there no witnesses? It wasn't as if famous actors could go out on their own without an entourage of fans and bodyguards. I was excited—and a little bit scared.

My heart raced. I adjusted the collar of my uniform. In the mirror, wide, brown eyes looked back at me under a fringe of dark lashes. I tucked a wayward brown curl back into the bun pulled tight to the back of my head, but gave up after several tries. I swiped a little more lipstick across my bottom lip before turning away from the looking glass. I grabbed the cart of towels, soaps, and linens, and headed towards the elevator.

As I headed down the eleventh-floor hallway to Mr. Peale's room, I noted the bodyguards beside his door. They checked my cart as I waited, then nodded their approval that I could go in. One asked my name, and I choked out, "Sandra Den." I cleared my throat, squashing the overwhelming sense of fear. Writing mysteries was one thing, but being in a room with a suspected killer was different. The bodyguard announced my entry as he opened the door and closed it behind me. I was momentarily blinded by sunlight pouring into the room.

"Please, come in." I recognized the voice. After all, his movies were popular with women of all ages. My heart pounded, more because I was meeting a suspected murderer than a movie star.

I moved farther into the room. "I will only be a few moments. Would you like to have your linens changed?"

"Yes, please."

He rose from the table where he was sitting, dropping a pen onto the paper on the desk. He was taller than I'd imagined, and more handsome, too. He could be Robert Patterson's twin. I tried to swallow around the sudden knot in my throat. I did what any good employee would and started to change the bed linen. It was awkward. Usually the occupants weren't in the room when I cleaned. But this wasn't a usual situation. He had nowhere else he could go due to the crush of fans.

Peale leaned casually against the dresser.

"So," he said, "what's the weather like today?"

Really? The weather? I chuckled a bit as I replied. "Hot and sticky, as it usually is this time of year."

"You are laughing at me."

"I'm sorry, Mr. Peale."

"No, don't be sorry. I find you refreshing. And the name is Robert."

"It was wrong of me to laugh. It's just that I found it odd you would ask about the weather. You don't have to converse with me. I'm just the hired help."

It was his turn to laugh. I looked up at him.

"You are indeed refreshing. So, hired help, what can one do to escape both bodyguards and cops when in Virginia Beach."

I finished making the bed and walked to the cart, grabbing towels for the bathroom.

"Well, for starters, cooperate with the police."

He stood in front of me, blocking my path.

"What makes you think I'm not cooperating?

"I don't know. It may be a guess, but you are still here, aren't you? And the movie is done, isn't it?"

"Do you think I am capable of murdering my co-star and friend?"

My spine stiffened "I don't know you."

"Sure you do. Everyone knows me. If you have been alive for the past five years, you know all about me."

"I know your character on screen, yes, or what the tabloids say about you. But I don't know you."

He let me pass. "I like you. You're frank with me, you're not blown away by my status, and you're smart."

I removed the soiled towels and replaced them with new ones.

"How do you know I'm smart?"

"Because," he chuckled, "you aren't afraid to speak your mind. It's not something I come across every day. Women are usually too busy falling all over me."

"So," I asked blatantly, "did you do it? Did you kill your co-star?"

"No."

The answer was strong. No hint of regret or fear. I don't know why, but I wanted to believe him.

"I want you to help me."

"Me? I don't understand."

"You are a new mystery writer, right? Or do I have the wrong Sandra Den?

"You've heard of me?"

"I'm an avid reader of mysteries, especially new emerging authors."

"I'm flattered."

He laughed, and I realized the irony.

"Look, you would know the clues, what to look for. We could solve this together. We could find the real killer and clear my name."

"What about the bodyguards and undercover cops following your every move?"

"You help me slip out of this room, we go to Fort Monroe, and we investigate. Come on, it'll be fun, and you'll get a real mystery you can write about."

My guard went up. *What if he really is a killer? What if I help him escape and he eludes the police or worse, murders me?*

Robert read my mind. He placed his hands on my forearms as he gazed down into my eyes.

"I'm not a killer. You won't regret it. I promise."

I liked to think I had a sixth sense when it came to people. After all, I'd seen right through my fiancé's' lies years ago when he cheated on me after I gave birth to Chloe. Robert dropped his hands as he waited for my reply. I wasn't sure if I was quite yet sold on the idea that he was innocent, but it was getting harder to believe he was a killer.

"Okay, but we play by my rules. I'll come back at the end of my shift and get you out of here. But, I'll bring a close friend of mine from the local newspaper.

"Do you trust this friend?"

"Yes," I answered. "I'd trust him with my life."

I returned around five. Nick, my friend from the paper, waited outside the room as I pushed the cleaning cart through the door.

Robert was waiting, wearing dark jeans and a shirt, with a cap pulled low over his head. "How are you going to get me past the guards?"

I laughed at the way he called them *the guards*.

"I have a plan."

I listened at the door. Nick told the bodyguards he saw teenage girls around the corner of the stairwell, apparently stalking. One bodyguard left to shoo away what he assumed were Robert's fans. Nick occupied the other bodyguard as he talked about his life as a reporter and how difficult it was to talk to people who protect the stars.

"Guess I'd better get going," Nick said loudly to the other guard, giving me the sign we should get going.

I grabbed Robert by the arm.

"Now . . . and move fast."

He crawled into the laundry hamper and I easily pushed the cart through the door. Nick assisted by getting it into the elevator.

I slid into the elevator behind the cart just as the other bodyguard was coming back from the stairwell.

After sneaking Robert into the maid's changing room, I pulled off my uniform, wearing a T-shirt and shorts underneath. I grabbed my purse.

"Let's go."

We jumped into my car and waited for Nick, who showed up minutes later.

Nick laughed. "We did it!"

I laughed too as I pulled out of the parking lot and headed to the highway.

After introductions, Nick was quick to let Robert know that this was no field trip.

"Don't get smart and try anything stupid. I'm trained in martial arts." Nick nodded at me. "She's not bad at protecting herself as well. I've seen her take down a man twice her size."

Robert nodded his head. "I just want to solve this thing and get on with my life. Let's go solve a murder."

Fort Monroe was beautiful at sunset. We parked near the lighthouse, and then trekked by foot to the stone building where the murder had taken place. Police tape sealed off the spot. We surveyed the area, remaining quiet as we moved around the perimeter looking for clues.

"Okay, Robert. Were you here when it happened?" Nick asked.

"I was here earlier in the day. We had an argument after the shoot, which got pretty heated until the bodyguards got in between us. I wasn't here when he got shot though."

"And you don't have an alibi?"

Robert shook his head. "I had sneaked away from the bodyguards. I do that sometimes."

"The fight was over a girl?" I asked.

"It was, but not like you think. Johnston thought I was seeing his girlfriend, Alice, behind his back. I wasn't, but it wasn't from a lack of her trying. He was too blind to the type of girl she is. Alice isn't very, um, dedicated to their relationship, if you get what I mean."

"She was making a play for you?" Nick asked.

"She was making a play for anything that moved. She's needy and clingy, not my type at all."

I turned to Nick. "Have you talked with her yet?"

"She'd talk to anyone who showed an interest in her story. She seems to enjoy the attention and the fact that she's making headline news. The police have ruled her out as a suspect, but told her not to leave town in case they had further questions."

"That's exactly why we need to take a second look at her," I said.

I knew women like her. They made better actors than the real ones.

I turned to Robert. "Why aren't you cooperating with the police?"

"I am, but that doesn't mean that I'm still not a suspect."

"But you trust me?"

Robert shrugged his shoulders. I didn't know how I felt about his response, but it made me cautious. Maybe he was guilty. Maybe he was just playing me and hoping he'd get a chance to slip away. I kept my guard up as we split from Nick to search the area.

I spotted something away from the sectioned-off area. I walked towards it as Robert followed close behind me. I bent down to up a piece of red silk. Holding it between my fingers, I turned around and bumped into Robert.

He grabbed my arms to steady me. I panicked, not sure why. Nick called out. "Everything okay over there?"

Robert dropped his arms and I hollered back.

"Come take a look at this!"

Nick ran over.

"You okay?"

"Yeah," I stuttered a bit. "I was just being clumsy. Wonder if this could be anything of interest?"

Robert looked over our shoulder.

"Wait! Alice was here that day we were on the set. She was wearing a red silk dress."

"Let's go find Alice and see if we can get a look at her dress," Nick said to me.

We thought it best if Robert returned to his room before the bodyguards discovered his absence, so we took him back to the hotel. Nick said he'd wait in the car as we pulled into the parking garage.

As we waited for the elevator, Robert moved closer to me. I looked up in surprise.

"It's better if we look like a couple coming into the hotel . . . less suspicious."

I nodded as it made sense, but my breath caught in my throat. I thought of how he grabbed me when we were at Fort Monroe. *Was it to steady me or something else?*

The elevator arrived and Robert suddenly pulled me in close, I looked up in surprise, and he kissed me. At first, I struggled and then relaxed as a feeling I hadn't had in a long time took over. I leaned in and kissed back. After what seemed like an eternity, Robert pulled back, smiling. I blushed.

Robert explained. "Someone was coming off the elevator, and I didn't want them to recognize me. Sorry, I acted on impulse."

"I knew that." I wasn't about to admit that I'd had no idea why he kissed me or why I reacted that way to his kiss.

As we walked into the elevator, Robert said the bodyguards were used to him sneaking out, so he would just walk back in. I watched as the numbers escalated until we reached his floor. Neither of us spoke, each wrapped up in our own thoughts. When we reached eleven, Robert walked out first and took off his disguise of hat and glasses.

"Hey, how did you get past us?" The bodyguards asked as they turned a slight shade of red.

Robert smiled, "I have my ways, gentlemen." Without explaining further he held the door for me as he grabbed my arm to force me into his room. Before I could run back out, Robert was blocking my path. He locked the door.

I was nervous again. He could be very dangerous; he could steal my heart.

"I see no reason you need to rush out." Robert explained as he casually took my arm and moved me into the room.

He waited for me to sit. With my options limited, I chose the chair at the table where he'd been writing earlier.

"Don't run off. I'm just going to freshen up." He went into the bathroom and closed the door.

I remembered he had been writing when I first entered his room earlier that day. I looked down and started to read.

My dear Alice, it started. *We know what happened. I know what you are thinking.*

I jumped up as Robert came back into the room. I'd wish I'd been able to read more or to grab the letter and take it with me. With Robert in the room, that wasn't about to happen. I tried to think of a distraction.

"Do you have anything to drink?" I asked.

Robert moved to the stocked refrigerator and took out a soda. He grabbed a cup off the counter above it to fill with ice. I tried to glance down at the desk but with no luck.

"Alcohol or not?"

"Better not." I replied. "Thanks."

He poured it and handed me the cup. I took it as he reached behind me and flipped shut the notebook. He smiled as he turned to me.

"Are we going to talk about what happened?"

"What?" I wasn't sure if he was talking about the murder or the kiss.

"You like me."

"I hardly know you."

"But you like me."

I moved away to put some distance between us. He frowned. I had to know.

"Did you do it?"

"I've already told you the answer. You're stalling. What was that between us, downstairs?"

I made my way to the door.

"I better leave. Thanks . . . for the drink."

I rushed out before he could say anything.

So many questions ran through my head as Nick and I drove to Alice's home. *Is Robert guilty? What's in that letter? Why is Alice's dress torn? Who is she protecting, or is she?* And the question that bothered me most of all, *Why did I respond to Robert's kiss?*

At Alice's home, Nick rang the doorbell. We were met by a lovely, tiny blonde. She was breathtaking. I had no doubt Johnston would be jealous of other men, especially if she showed an interest in them.

Alice motioned us in. As we entered the living room, Nick made small talk before he said he had more questions for an article he was writing about the murder. I made the excuse of needing to use the bathroom. Before the bathroom, there was a staircase. I quietly made my way to the second floor and found her bedroom. I searched the hamper and underneath the bed with no luck. Where would someone hide something if they didn't want to look suspicious? A piece of red all the way in the back of the closet caught my eye.

The dress was hanging there, hidden in plain sight. When I pulled it off the hanger, I noticed a tear in the shoulder. And a large dark stain on the front. I heard Alice calling to Nick as she headed up the stairs saying she'd be right back with the ring that Johnston had proposed with. I stuffed the dress in my purse and hid behind the closet door. Alice walked in the bedroom, and I could hear her opening a drawer. My heart raced as she walked over to the closet. I tried to sink further into the side. An arm reached in and grabbed a box on the top shelf. She took something out and then replaced the box. She walked out. I peeked around the corner to make sure the coast was clear and crept back down the stairs.

As I approached the living room, I overheard her say to Nick, "I was here at home when it happened. Robert felt our relationship was getting too close so we agreed to cool it for a while. Robert loved me though, and everyone knew it. It was a matter of time before things would blow up between those two. Johnston was very possessive of me."

She had no alibi. She stated she was home by herself when it happened. Tears rolled down her face as she said that although their relationship was over, she still felt sorry for Johnston. She had given Nick a card that she had received from Johnston the day before his death. I leaned over his shoulder and read. *You are my life, Alice. Without you in it, there is no reason for me to live.*

As we left, Nick said he may return for more of the story if anything else came up. She smiled and stated she would love to assist in any way that she could. It was clear she was enjoying the attention.

"What do you make of her?" Nick asked.

"I don't know, but I found this." I pulled the dress from my purse. "I'd guess that this would be of interest to the police since it was still in her possession, and it was possibly the dress she was wearing that day. There is a large stain on the front, and the torn piece off the shoulder could match what we found earlier."

Nick agreed and said he would take it in to the police. It wasn't unusual for a reporter to be snooping around where he shouldn't be. It may be something important or nothing at all. Nick dropped me off at my place as he headed over to the station with the dress and the scrap of material that we had found. He stated he would let me know if he got wind of any new developments on the story.

Several days passed. Nick let me know that the police had called Alice back in for more questioning. We could only surmise that the dress created new evidence that warranted another look at Alice.

Alice, looking to make front line news, called Nick and asked if he wanted to hear even more details. If he would accompany her to the police station, he could interview her on the way.

As she drove, Nick took out his recorder.

"Why did Robert and Johnston fight that evening?"

Alice wiped tears as she spoke.

"Johnston found out that I was seeing Robert. "

"Oh, really? Robert told us that he wasn't interested in you."

She looked flustered for a moment.

"Robert is lying. He was jealous of my relationship with Johnston. That's probably why he killed him."

"So you think Robert is guilty?"

"Well . . . ," she hesitated for a moment. "Yes, I think he is." She concentrated on the road ahead without looking at Nick.

"Were you there when they had the fight?"

"No, of course not."

"Then tell my why the red dress you were seen wearing at the set that day has Johnston's blood all over it."

She fell silent as she looked at Nick, clearly shocked he knew about the dress.

"I went there after he didn't come home. I saw him lying there in his blood. I hugged him close as I cried over him. I was distraught. I called the police immediately and then left before they arrived."

Nick leaned forward.

"Why didn't you tell me this before?"

"I thought I'd be a suspect."

"You were a suspect anyway. Why didn't you tell the police about the dress? If you weren't guilty, why not just turn in the evidence?"

"I didn't want to be accused of murdering him." Her voice rose as sweat beaded on her brow. "His blood was all over me. I knew how it would look."

"So, Robert killed him, and he has no blood at all on his clothes? But you didn't kill him, and you do?"

"I don't know why Robert doesn't have any blood on his clothes. Maybe he ditched them."

"They searched him thoroughly. There was no blood, Alice."

"Well, maybe there was someone else. I don't know. I arrived after he'd already been shot. Why are you asking me? Aren't you the investigative reporter? "

Nick called me with an update after Alice didn't leave the station that afternoon.

"Well?" I asked him.

"They are holding her for now. She withheld evidence. But I don't know. She's tricky and she lies, but I don't think she's capable of murder."

"So it's back to Robert?" My heart sank.

"I'm afraid so."

I hung up, distraught. I wasn't convinced it was Robert. I wasn't sure if it was how I felt for him that made me think that or not, but the way he had stated he wasn't the killer made me want to prove him right.

I made a list of all possible suspects. Robert, Alice, a crazed fan, a bodyguard, an unrelated person. The list could be endless. I called Nick back, and we went through my list.

"What about bodyguards? Which one was on duty that night?"

Nick gave me the name of both bodyguards on duty that night. One of them was John Stanton. I told Nick I'd be in touch. I had an idea. I made another quick call to my friend and co-worker who was scheduled for work that day and switched shifts with her. She readily agreed because it was a night shift.

At the hotel, I changed into my uniform and headed back up to Robert's room. A policeman was standing guard by the door in addition to the bodyguard. It may be there were new developments from Alice's story. He checked the hotel employee schedule.

"It doesn't list you on the schedule this evening, Miss Den."

"Maria called in sick. I'm her fill-in. The hotel didn't advise you?"

"No, they didn't. So you won't mind that I verify that, right?"

"No problem." I smiled.

He confirmed with management the change in staffing, then opened the door to Robert's room and announced my arrival to Robert. I pushed the cart through the door as it closed behind me. Robert looked worn out.

"Are you feeling okay?"

"I'm better now that you are here. How'd it go with Alice?"

"They are holding her now because of the evidence that she withheld." I changed the topic. "Just curious, which bodyguard was on duty that night?"

"It was John, the guy out there tonight. He's been preoccupied these past few months. I just found a convenient time while he was on the phone, and I was able to get past him."

I made a mental note to check on John's whereabouts that night.

"When I was here earlier, I noticed a letter you were writing."
I figured that if curiosity killed the cat, then asking outright
would be a step in the right direction.

"I didn't expect anyone to see that except Alice."

I sat next to him on the bed and asked softly, "What was it
about?"

"I just wanted her to get the picture. She and I were not a
couple, nor would we ever be."

"That's all?"

"Does there have to be more?" Robert leaned in. I knew he
wanted to kiss me, but I moved away and walked back towards my
cart. I couldn't make this more complicated than it was already.

"I need to go. I need to see if there is some way we can clear
your name."

"So you do believe me!" Robert smiled.

"I don't know. I know I don't want it to be you."

I walked out, hoping that I was placing my trust in someone
who wasn't a murderer.

I finished the rest of my rounds for the evening. Nick met
me back at the apartment, and as Chloe slept, we poured over
all the details.

"Does John have an alibi?" I asked.

"The bodyguard? Why?"

"I don't want to rule anyone out."

"No record of an alibi."

"Can you get in to talk to the detective at the station again?
I have a hunch."

I'd filled Nick in on my hunch so he would be well prepared
to provide details to the police.

Some days later, Nick was able to get another interview with
Alice. She sank into the chair across from him.

"Do you want to tell me about John, Robert's bodyguard?"
Nick asked her.

"There isn't anything to tell." She looked scared.

"You don't want to tell me how you have been seeing a lot of
him. You two have been in conversations a lot over the past few
months."

She started to cry.

"I swear I wouldn't hurt him."

"Hurt who?" Nick asked as he leaned forward in his chair.

"John."

"You were there when John killed Johnston, weren't you? You were protecting John because you were in love with him, aren't you?"

Alice broke down in tears as she nodded.

"I'm so sorry, John!" She muttered into the room.

The police arranged for someone to pick up John. Nick gave me the heads up that an arrest was imminent, and we headed over to the hotel to tell Robert the good news. Nick looked over at me.

"How'd you figure it out?"

"Robert told me John was distracted lately, and we both heard how Alice liked to play around. She had the hidden dress, and John had no alibi. It was a lucky guess; Alice did all the rest."

"If you ever want a job on the paper, just let me know. You'd make a good investigative reporter."

I opened the car door as we got to the hotel and looked back at Nick.

"No thanks, Nick. I think I'll stick to writing books. Now, let's go make a movie star a true star."

We headed to Robert's room as a smile broke across my face. I couldn't wait to tell Robert he had been cleared.

A MYSTERY AT LURAY CAVERNS

By Maria Hudgins

THE TEENAGER IN AN orange polo shirt led her group of twenty tourists into the underworld of Luray Caverns, down a walkway illuminated by recessed lights, around stalagmites, and past glassy pools. She froze when she heard the scream from behind.

"Blood!"

The twenty visitors—old and young, fat and thin—melded into an impenetrable mass around the source of the scream. Waving her flashlight like a weapon, she shouted, "Let me through!"

A few seconds later, her beam found the reason for the alarm. A stalactite close to the paved path dripped a bright crimson liquid from its tip and into a shallow pool. A thin red line wiggled down its wavy surface, like an artery in a stone leg. It looked thicker than water and oozed more than flowed. The teenager's arms and legs turned cold. *What should I do?* she thought. *My training didn't cover this.*

She directed her flashlight's beam up and up until it disappeared into the darkness. She could see no hole, no clue as to the source. Stalactites all through the caverns dripped clear water continuously, and the guide couldn't recall ever actually looking at this particular formation. Illuminating the little pool below, she saw it was bright red as well.

Several of her charges began whimpering. A woman fell against her, slithering down, but was caught by someone else before she hit the floor. The guide told herself, *Take charge and do the right thing.*

"Well! This is certainly unusual! I don't think this is normal, y'all."

"Oohh!" the prostrate woman, now struggling to her feet, moaned.

"If you would all just move along the path—that's right—move along, please—I need to make a call."

Staying near the back of the group, the guide herded them forward to a wide spot in the walkway, pulled a walkie-talkie from her belt, and called her superior in the ticket booth above. The manager relayed the message to other guides, who quickly escorted all visitors currently underground to the exit. New admissions were halted pending a decision on what to do next. Within minutes, guides and cave officials gathered around the strange dripping stalactite and shook their heads. One particularly reckless employee stuck his finger under it before anyone in charge could stop him, caught a drop, and tasted it.

"Blood. Definitely blood."

— 🧛 —

Geologist Rachel Elkins got the call in her lab at nearby James Madison University. "Would you repeat that?" She had had weird calls before, but this took the cake. The caller announced that a stalactite in Luray was dripping blood. She mimed a small giggle toward a co-worker bent over a polarizing microscope.

"It's probably iron oxide," she told the caller. "Blood does taste like iron, you know. Some people say it tastes like copper, but since you say it's red, I'll go with iron oxide as the most likely culprit."

"Oh, come on! Bright red?" Caverns Director Herb Foshee fired back.

Rachel couldn't insult the man's intelligence by explaining about dissolved iron and cave water. He already knew.

"No, not bright red. I'll come out and see what we're dealing with."

The thirty-five mile trip up I-81 and US 211 to Luray Caverns took Rachel from rolling hills and farmland across the sandstone of Massanutten Mountain and into the limestone bedrock of Luray. The parking lot at the Caverns stood almost empty except for the cars of lingering rubberneckers, probably hoping to hear something ghoulish about the blood-dripping stalactite. Rachel parked, marched past the deserted ticket booth, and followed the waiting guide into the bowels of the earth. A dozen employees, just hanging around now that the attraction was closed, nodded to her as she passed.

Using a flash, Rachel took photos of the stalactite. This ranked high among the strangest things she'd ever seen. It gave her the shivers. She climbed around the path, searching for a vantage point from which she could see the top of the stalactite more clearly. It hung from the ceiling at a spot that didn't have a visible hole nearby, but she reasoned there might be one on the side she couldn't see. Rachel knew the water in caves often wound through cracks and hollows, this way and that, and emerged far away from its source. Oddly the red liquid wasn't getting diluted much by ground water along its way. And it was bright red.

She pulled a hand-held GPS from her backpack, and then, embarrassed, sneaked it back in when she realized it wouldn't work underground. How could she establish an accurate location? Did the Caverns have a 3-D map? She might well need to trace this spot to another directly above it on the surface.

She rummaged through her pack, found an empty sample bottle, and filled it with the red liquid from the little pool. On a microscope slide, she collected one drop directly from the tip of the stalactite, covered it with a thin glass, and snapped it into a tiny plastic case.

"You say someone already tasted this?"

Director Foshee was standing right behind her.

"Yes, he said it was blood. Tasted like blood."

"That wasn't a smart thing to do. What if it was poison?"

"What next?" The director ignored her mild rebuke and looked around at the deserted walkways above and below. "We can't keep visitors out long. We're losing thousands of dollars every hour we stay closed!"

Rachel considered the next logical step. She held up the sample bottle.

"I'll get this tested, and I'll have an answer for you by morning. If it's something harmless, you can re-open tomorrow, but I'll still want to tape off this area. If it's blood, the next question will be human or animal? If animal, why? Is material from a slaughterhouse seeping in? . . . If it's human blood, we'll have to notify law enforcement."

"The sheriff," Foshee said, rolling his eyes slightly.

"Right." Rachel's heart fluttered when she recalled the local sheriff was Jude Brown, her high school true love. He was married now.

"Dear Lord, let it not be human," the director said. "That'll shut us down for a week."

— 🎎 —

Back at her lab in the university, Rachel quickly determined the sample was blood and only slightly diluted with water. Oddly, the red blood cells were intact, but she attributed this to the buffering effect of the calcium carbonate in cave water. In pure water the cells would have exploded and spilled their contents. Now she needed to find out if it was human or something else. She called a friend in JMU's Biology Department.

Carrying her sample to the biology wing, she talked a graduate student acquaintance into doing a test immediately. It was after five o'clock, and he sighed deeply but acquiesced.

"Tests positive," he said, studying a strip of membrane from a test kit.

"Human? Are you sure?" This was not what Rachel wanted to hear.

"Primate," he said. "Could be human, gorilla, monkey, chimpanzee, bush baby, lemur, or orangutan."

"Given the location, I think we can assume it's human."

— 🎎 —

Driving home, Rachel called the sheriff's office and waited, heart pounding, while a sergeant went to look for Sheriff Jude Brown. Her last words to him, some ten years ago, had been, "I never want to see you again." Maybe he had forgotten by now. The sergeant returned to the phone and told her the sheriff had already left for the day. He gave her Jude's cell number. She took a deep breath and dialed it.

"Rachel? Good to hear you!"

Jude sounded older, but she still recognized his voice. She

explained the situation at the Caverns. He asked her to meet him there. He didn't want to wait until morning. Meanwhile, she called Director Foshee and explained that he would likely have to keep Luray closed. He was not pleased, but he agreed to meet her and Sheriff Brown at the cave entrance.

It was past seven o'clock when Rachel arrived. She waited on the stone wall outside the ticket area until a car with the seal of the sheriff's office on its door drove up.

She remembered Jude's determined gait as she watched him walk toward her. He was heavier than the last time she'd seen him, which had been a mere two lips away on her front door step after senior prom. As soon as his blue eyes locked on hers, she knew she wasn't prepared for this. He took her hands in his. She looked down to break the eye contact and recognized those hands, those slightly-too-short nails. Deep breath. *I can do this.*

Director Foshee unlocked the door through which hundreds of tourists passed every day and flipped a switch. Like some outlandishly baroque cathedral, the cavernous space came to life. The spot they sought was a hundred yards in and down. Jude Brown stood in front of the blood-dripping stalactite and looked up, squinting. "Human blood. You're sure?"

"Primate for sure," Rachel said. "But given the scarcity of non-human primates in the area, I think we can assume it's human." Her heart felt back to normal now. This was business and an ugly business at that. "That's *what* it is. Now we have to find out *who* and *where* and *why.*"

"How long will I have to keep the visitors out?" Foshee asked.

"Don't know yet." Jude stepped back and looked up. "I need to examine the top of that—what is it? Stalactite or stalagmite? I always forget."

"Stalactite," the director answered. "And you can't go up there. You'd destroy thousands of years of growth on everything you stepped on."

"I have to," Jude said. "Do I need to get a warrant, or can we do this like civilized people?"

Both men bristled, and Rachel saw potential trouble.

"Can we go back up and talk it over? This is going to take planning."

They settled in a small office near the gift shop. Rachel took the lead, asking Foshee, "We need to know where the blood is coming from, and for that we need a three-dimensional map of the caverns. Do you have one?"

"I have a large one in my office, not for general distribution, but I'll get it for you."

While they waited for the director's return, the former high school sweethearts talked.

"We need to locate the spot on the surface directly above that stalactite," Rachel said. "Since GPS won't work underground, we may need to get UGPS equipment, and I think we can arrange that through the JMU Geology Department."

"What's UGPS?" Jude asked.

"Underground Global Positioning System."

He frowned. "Didn't know there was such thing."

"If we can pinpoint the source, we'll likely find a body."

"No way," Jude said.

"Why not?" Rachel had already imagined a body, a knife inserted in its chest, lying on the ground, and a trickle of blood winding into a hole and disappearing.

"Dead bodies don't bleed."

She just stared at him. He always used to do this. He loved to make her feel like an idiot.

"Wounded people bleed. When the heart stops, bleeding stops."

"Still, there must have been a wounded person at the source sometime. Lying there, bleeding out, for how long? This person may have eventually died, and the body may be still there."

He raised both hands to silence her. "Possibly. But we can't assume a crime has been committed." He paused. "Someone was injured. Caught in an animal trap? Fell on his own gun? Fell on his own knife? Attacked by a bear? Whatever. He bled all over the place, and the blood found its way into a hole and . . . well . . . ended up here."

"Then what? We're talking about a lot of blood."

Jude shrugged. "No one's been reported missing."

"Could be a hiker. Not necessarily a local person. Someone who hasn't been missed yet."

"But how much blood are we talking about, really? Must be

a lot, to be dripping all the way down inside the cave, but still like . . ." Jude paused, his eyebrows knitted. "Like pure blood."

"What are you suggesting?"

"I wonder if we might find our source *inside* the cave."

"Oh my God!"

"When was the blood discovered?"

"About two, I think."

"So a number of groups had already done the whole tour, start to finish?" He pushed back, tipping his chair onto its back legs and looked at her a bit longer than necessary. "Then we can assume there's no body lying in the cavern proper or someone would have noticed it."

"I'm not so sure," she said. "There are large spaces, yards and yards from the walkway, and huge formations that a whole bunch of corpses could be lying behind, and no one would see them unless they went where they're not supposed to go."

Jude laughed. *Same old laugh.* He rocked his chair back and forth, staring at the floor and then quickly looked up.

"I'm thinking this may be a practical joke," he said.

"A joke? Why?"

"Because I can't imagine a body bleeding continuously like that." He paused. "How about this? Some joker brings a bag of blood from the hospital or wherever, dumps it into a hole he knows leads down into the cave. Don't hospitals put something in the blood they store to keep it from clotting up?"

"I don't know."

Herb Foshee reappeared with a large, rolled-up sheet of paper and spread it out on the desk. This diagram of Luray Caverns showed all the main cavities and formations. It looked a bit like an ant farm, but with more depth and more layers. With his finger on the paper he traced the walkway, from the entrance to the approximate location of the bloody stalactite.

Rachel saw several small cavities and veins within the bedrock between this spot and the surface.

"We need to get the exact location. That means UGPS. I'll go to work on borrowing it, first thing tomorrow."

Back outside, the director bade them goodbye and promised to return bright and early the next morning. Jude took off for the hills behind the visitor center, and Rachel followed. He stopped at one point, turned and looked back on the valley, now dotted with streetlights, stoplights, and creeping headlights.

"You're still Rachel Elkins, eh? Never married, or do you keep your maiden name for professional reasons?"

"I'm single. Too busy to do much dating." She turned and, like him, stared out toward the valley.

"I was married for a few years—to Jen Williams. You remember her?"

She remembered. Of course she remembered. *Did he say was?*"

"We divorced a couple of years ago."

She knew he was looking at her, waiting for her to return his stare or to say something that would give him an opening to lead the conversation in a more personal direction. She wasn't about to make it that easy for him.

"There's a lot of that going around," she said. "Look! Trees! Nothing but trees up here. How will we ever find the right spot in this jungle?"

—— 🎎 ——

It took three workers and a truckload of technology to set up the Underground GPS equipment Rachel borrowed from a local mining company. She lugged a big cylindrical transmitter to the foot of the bloody stalactite and set it up according to instructions. Blood still dripped, but now it looked more pink than red. She returned to the surface and joined Jude Brown, who was watching from a mossy boulder above the roof of the visitor center. The entire area of interest was nothing but forest. Off to the south stood a house and barn with white-painted fences and a few grazing horses. "Whose farm is that?" she asked.

"George Brown's."

"Any relation?"

"Cousin."

Small world, she thought. But in these parts, everyone was related to everyone else, and family histories went back generations. Her own family, the Elkinses, had lived here since before the Civil War.

"Got it!" one of the technicians shouted.

Rachel and Jude approached and found the workers had jammed a wooden post into the ground on the spot that lay directly above the bloody stalactite. A perfectly ordinary spot covered with a thick layer of pine needles and oak leaves. That was okay. Rachel didn't expect to find an opening at this exact spot, but she did hope to find one fairly nearby. She dismissed the technicians to gather their equipment and return it to the mining company. Jude wanted to call in some of his own men to help in the search for an opening, but Rachel begged him to wait a bit.

"Before we let this whole area get trampled, let's look around, just us."

Jude looked at her, tilted his head, smiled, and Rachel knew he had read more into her statement than she had intended. Starting at the post, they moved in a clockwise spiral out, veering around trees and stepping over decayed logs.

When they found it, it wasn't hard to recognize—the spot where the battle had taken place. It was a horrible scene. Blood spatters lay all over an area the size of a large living room. Leaves were trampled, bathed in blood now dried. Boulders and tree trunks sprayed with blood. Rachel found some loose change among the flattened leaves, as if it had flown from the pocket of a combatant. Poking through broken twigs and leaves with a stick, she lifted out a white athletic sock, bloody and swarming with bugs.

"A man's sock." She dropped it.

"We need to leave now before we compromise the scene," Jude said. "The forensic guys will have a hissy-fit if we mess things up."

Rachel started walking, obeying his order, but she stopped after traveling no more than a few yards. She spotted a rock, also blood-spattered, but it hung over an opening just large enough to stick a hand in. She poked at it with her stick and shifted a mass of powder-dry pine needles. There lay a tooth. She picked it up and found that it had a single root, broken, and a white composite filling on one side. Someone's front tooth, she thought, unless the foxes in the area had their own dentist.

"Leave it," Jude said, tugging at her sleeve. Something in his voice sounded strange.

— 🙎 —

Rachel was no longer welcome at the site, and Jude's demeanor changed. For the next couple of days, forensic people worked. Rachel drove up once to look but wasn't admitted beyond the yellow tape. Beyond the fact that they had traced the path of the blood into a small cavity underground, Jude would tell her nothing. No body was found, and no one was reported missing.

She couldn't let it drop. She did still have the blood sample, and she talked a friend in the biochemistry department into analyzing. It contained a small amount of warfarin, an anti-clotting agent, which might explain why it kept flowing. She could get the sample's DNA analyzed, of course, but she assumed the forensic people were already doing that—not that they'd tell her anything when they did.

Her mind went back to the farm adjoining the woods. She consulted the university's Geology Department's *Page County Property Map* and discovered most of the woods belonged with the farm—and both belonged to George C. Brown. Jude had mentioned that he was distantly related. More Internet snooping in Ancestry and People Finder sites revealed that George C. and Jude were third cousins. Their great-grandfathers were brothers.

The household of George C, aged sixty-two, comprised of Anna Sue, aged sixty, and Joshua, aged thirty-five. *Thirty-five? A son? Still living at home?* She wanted to call Jude and ask him, but he had been acting so strangely, she hesitated. What reason could she give him for wanting to know? Was this grown man a troublemaker? A ne'er-do-well? Was it any of her business?

She checked online for an arrest record. Nothing.

She checked a local news site and discovered Anna Sue Brown had died on Feb 23, 2014. A household of three had, a few months earlier, been reduced to two. *Was Anna Sue's death natural?* If not for the time span—this was August—she'd wonder if the blood was Anna Sue's. Rachel sat back in her office chair and closed her eyes. The area of woodland where they had found the bloody scene was on Luray Caverns' property, but it was separated from the adjoining land of George C. Brown only by a split rail fence.

She needed to talk to someone who knew the Brown family. Fortunately, in this part of Virginia, the "six degrees of separation" rule was more like four degrees—or three. Back to the *Page County Property Map*, then to *University Faculty and Students*. She found three students whose home addresses were quite close to the Brown farm. One of these, a sophomore girl, agreed to meet Rachel for coffee at the student center. A bubbly little thing, she did know the Browns, and she didn't question Rachel's hastily explained need to know. She loved to talk.

"Poor old George and Anna Sue. They have this son, Josh, who's—well, there's something wrong with him. He's like retarded—I mean mentally challenged—and plus, I've heard he gets violent. He threw his mother down the stairs one time, and he's attacked his father. They say George has always wanted to put him into a home or something, but Anna Sue won't hear of it. So they do the best they can, I guess."

"Have you ever been to their home?" Rachel asked, setting her coffee cup down.

"My sister and I used to go over and ride their horses sometimes. They were both so sweet. Anna Sue and George, I mean. Not Josh. You never saw him. I think Anna Sue wished she had girls like us."

"It must have been a grim life, living with a son who might turn violent at any time," Rachel said.

"What do you mean, "must have been?"

"You don't know? Anna Sue died last winter," Rachel said.

The girl's eyes widened. "Oh, no. I didn't know that."

— 🂠 —

Now Rachel had to call Jude. When she asked him if he'd considered George Brown as a possible suspect, Rachel got the strong impression that Jude didn't want to hear it. Was he protecting the family reputation? How could he *not* have considered the Caverns' nearest neighbor? After Rachael's call, Jude was forced to consider it. His last meeting with his cousin George had ended on a sour note. Josh had gotten loose and killed a neighbor's calf. George paid for the calf, but Jude told him, straight out, that this wasn't a permanent solution. Josh was a grown man now, and George and Anna Sue were growing old. This sort of thing would keep happening, and it might well get worse. George had cried when he told Jude how strongly Anna Sue hated the idea of sending their son away. He agreed that something had to be done but begged for a little more time. Anna Sue was dead now, so what was holding George up?

Jude drove out to the farm directly after he hung up from talking to Rachel. He found George at home, but not Joshua. Where was Joshua? Missing. Why hadn't George reported him missing? He'd wandered off before, George reminded him, but he always came back. While the two men talked in George's parlor room, the old farmer's gaze kept wandering out a north window. Toward the barn.

Jude put his men to work in the barn and its surroundings. They found Joshua's body, covered by several feet of debris, in an old abandoned well some thirty yards from the barn.

The complete story came out in hours of questioning at sheriff's headquarters.

Before Anna Sue died, George promised her he wouldn't put Josh in a home, and he had tried his best to comply with her wishes. But he couldn't handle his strong, unpredictable son. That awful day, George had found Josh wandering through the woods on Luray Caverns property. Josh refused to return home and attacked his father. George had simply lost it, attacking with the ferocity of years of pent-up rage.

CORKED FOR MURDER

BY TERESA INGE

"WELCOME TO THE VIRGINIA Wine Shop."

Halee Matthews turned from the task of pouring wine to face her customers entering the store.

"We're here for the wine tasting." Jessie Dalton, a frequent customer, entered the store with two women trailing behind her.

"Find a place at the tasting bar. I'll be right with you," Halee said.

The women joined the other patrons.

"This is Lindsey Taylor, the bride I called you about, and Kayson Prescott, her bridesmaid." Jessie waved her hand toward the women.

"When is your big day?" Halee asked Lindsey.

"June 22nd."

"And will you be ordering wine today?"

"Of course."

Halee placed three sheets of paper, pencils, wine glasses, and a container on the counter. "We're sampling our top ten Virginia wines to learn about specific regions. Plus our customers will receive a discount on all wines tasted today. Ready to get started?"

"Yes," the women said in unison.

"We'll start with whites followed by reds. For each wine, I recommend swirling it in your mouth for flavor then spitting into the bucket." Halee tapped a container on the counter.

"Sounds stimulating," Lindsey purred.

"And don't guzzle it," a striking man with peppered gray hair added.

"Meet Orion Lee, our resident wine critic," Halee said.

"A real wine critic?" Kayson moved closer.

Orion swirled the wine in his glass. "My dear Halee. Must we always discuss my profession in front of novice tasters?"

"He only comes here for the free wine."

Halee set a bottle of Chardonnay on the counter and popped the cork. She placed one finger along the bottom of each glass and poured wine to the top of her finger.

"This is from central Virginia. It's known for its smooth taste."

The women swirled the wine and clinked their glasses together.

"Love the crispness," Lindsey said.

Jessie gulped the entire contents and slid the glass toward Halee. "Fill er' up!"

"Have y'all sampled other wines today?" Halee asked, noticing Jessie's slurred speech.

"Yes, but this is our last stop since we have our driver for only two more hours." Jessie blew a kiss to a man in a white shirt and black pants standing near the door.

Halee nodded toward the driver and made a mental note to check on him later. "Chardonnay is great paired with salmon, fish, or chicken dishes," she continued.

"Needs more substance." Kayson emptied her wine into the bucket.

"Seems I'm not the only critic." Orion rolled his eyes and sipped the wine.

A foursome entered the store and made their way to the end of the bar. Jack Bailey, another wine server, greeted them. Halee grabbed a bottle of wine off the shelf.

"There's bottled water on the counter to clean your palate and glass. And don't forget to rate each wine on the sheet I gave you."

The women rinsed their glasses with the water and emptied them into the bucket.

"Next we have an excellent Pinot Grigio from Southeast Virginia. Kayson, you may prefer this one for its medium-bodied texture."

"It's got a kick." Kayson puckered her lips toward Orion.

"Too many of these will kick my butt." Lindsey laughed.

Jessie turned up her glass.

Orion tapped Jessie's arm. "Nice and slow to appreciate the aroma and texture." The "r" rolled off his tongue as his nostrils flared.

Halee thought it might be a good time to offer more water and snacks.

"Water to clean your palate?" She wiggled a bottle in front of Jessie and refilled the cracker basket.

Jessie guzzled the water.

The group next tasted a Cabernet Sauvignon from Northern Virginia.

"My fave," Lindsey said.

"I love the complex flavors of dried fruit, tobacco, and subtle tannins." Orion held the glass just below his nose.

"You got all that from sniffing your wine?" Kayson grabbed a cracker.

"Orion's sniffer is always on point," Halee said.

Orion winked toward Kayson as she moved closer.

The shop was now filled with patrons sampling wines. Halee held monthly tastings to bring in more business. Sales soared after each event, since customers purchased many of the featured wines. Halee prided herself on offering selections not available in grocery stores and other venues. She had opened the shop on Battlefield Boulevard, a main corridor in Chesapeake, after her husband's passing two years ago. During their marriage, they had travelled to vineyards throughout the world. This location also brought in tourists travelling to the Outer Banks, a popular vacation spot one hour away.

After pouring the last selection for Lindsey and Kayson, Halee grabbed Jessie's glass when she stepped away to the restroom and placed it behind the bar. She noticed the driver had moved from standing near the door to browsing the shelves. She grabbed a bottled water and walked toward him.

"Care for some water?" She extended the bottle.

"Thanks." He twisted the cap and took a long sip.

"I'm Halee, the shop owner."

"George Bordeaux. Great turnout on the tasting."

A group at the bar cheered as Jack uncorked a bottle.

"Yeah, sometimes too much." Halee laughed.

"If you ever need car service, I'm available." He reached into his pocket and handed Halee some business cards.

"Great. And if you ever need wine, stop by." She headed back to the bar to help Jack.

Jessie and Lindsey approached Halee.

"Instead of removing my glass, you should be grateful I referred Lindsey to you." Jessie turned on her stilettos and walked away.

"Don't let her bother you. She has no filter when she drinks." Lindsey paused. "Is now a good time to order the wine for my wedding?"

"Sure. Let's head to the back where we can sit and talk." Halee grabbed her laptop from the bar, and they walked to a table and chairs opposite a stylish couch.

"Have a seat." Halee retrieved the wine and beer list and reviewed it with Lindsey. "What time is the wedding?"

"Four. Reception is at six."

"I can provide bartenders at the reception for a nominal fee. And I have a portable bar to set up that morning."

"The portable would be great on the deck. Can I see it?"

"Sure. It's in the wine room. Where is the wedding taking place?"

"At my house in Chesapeake, by the pool."

"Is there a backup in case of rain?"

"Yes, we can move into the barn."

"Barn?"

"It's not what you think. The building has a spacious party room, kitchen, and bath."

"Great. Our standard package includes a variety of red and white wine, beer, bartenders, portable bar, and set-up. And you mentioned you have liquor, soda, bottled water and mixers?"

"Yes, I have all of that."

"I require a 50 percent deposit today and the remainder one week prior to the wedding."

After Lindsey made the payment, the women walked to the wine room to view the bar, then headed back to the front. Halee eyed Jack talking to George and Jessie cozying up to Orion. Since it was closing time, patrons were making their final purchases. After the last customer left, Jack locked the door, and he and Halee began their cleanup.

"So, you know George?" Halee asked.

"We used to bartend together." Jack pulled the trash bag out of the bin and twisted the tie.

"Does he still bartend?" Halee grabbed three empty bottles of wine and set them in a box.

"Yeah, part time at Big Woody's, a local hangout in Great Bridge, a section of Chesapeake not far from the North Carolina border."

Halee placed wine glasses into the dishwasher while Jay wiped down the bar. She poured herself a glass of Cab and headed to her office to finalize the day's sales.

Thirty minutes later, Jack stepped into her office doorway with a bar towel across his shoulder.

"How'd we do?"

"Here's to another successful tasting." Halee raised her glass.

"Great. I'll lock the door behind me," Jack said.

Halee closed the laptop and grabbed her purse. While turning out the hall light, she noticed the back door was unlocked. She turned the deadbolt, wondering why Jack hadn't locked it. She stopped to close the wine storage door and caught a musky odor. Letting her nose lead the way, she stepped into the room, passing crates of wine. Slipping on a sticky liquid, she fell face first on top of Jessie.

"Omigod!" She flailed at the sight of the corkscrew lodged in Jessie's neck and rolled off the body. She stumbled out of the room and dialed 9-1-1.

Within minutes, the shop was filled with EMTs, police, and officials in blue suits.

One of the suits approached Halee in her office.

"Ms. Matthews?" the man asked.

"Yes."

"I'm Detective Jax Barrett, with Chesapeake Police. I'd like to ask you a few questions."

Halee nodded.

"Do you know the deceased?" He pulled a pen and small notepad from his jacket pocket.

"No. I mean yes . . ."

"Can you elaborate?"

"Her name is Jessie Dalton. She was here for a wine tasting."

"Was she alone?"

"No. She was with a wedding group."

A uniformed officer appeared at the door.

"There's a Jack Bailey at the front door. He says he works here."

The detective turned toward Halee.

"Do you know him?"

"Yes." Halee wondered why Jack had returned.

The officer escorted Jack to the office.

"Are you okay?" Jack studied her face.

"I'm Detective Barrett. There's been an incident in the wine room."

Jack craned his neck. His eyes ballooned at Jessie.

"You know the deceased?"

Jack ran his hand over his mouth.

"She's a customer. What happened?"

"We're trying to determine cause of death. But from the corkscrew in her neck, it appears she bled to death." The detective paused. "Would you know her next of kin?"

Jack shook his head.

"I can pull her friend's phone number from the invoice today," Halee offered.

The detective tapped his pen against the desk. "I'll take that."

Halee jotted down Lindsey's name and number and handed it to the detective. He stepped out of the room.

"What are you doing here?" Halee whispered to Jack.

"I forgot my phone on the bar." He wiggled the phone in his hand.

The detective walked into the office.

"No posting pictures to social media. I have a hard enough time doing my job as it is."

Jack slipped the phone into his pocket.

"Did you contact Lindsey?" Halee asked the detective.

"Yes. I'm curious though. She mentioned you had an argument with the deceased today. Can you provide details?"

"It wasn't an argument. Jessie had been drinking before she arrived, so I cut her off."

"What happened next?"

"She accused me of being ungrateful for the referral."

"And?"

"I got busy with customers and never saw her again."

"You didn't call a cab for her?"

"No, she was riding in a limo."

"Do you know the name of the limo company?"

Halee glanced at the cards George gave her. "By George Limo."

"Did you see Jessie get into the car?" the detective asked Jack.

"No. I was serving wine all afternoon."

"What brings you to the store this evening?"

"Like I was telling Halee, I forgot my phone and came back to get it."

"Do either of you know why Ms. Dalton was in the wine room?"

Halee and Jack shook their heads.

"One last thing. I need to view your security footage."

"Jack handles that." Halee offered.

"Oh, Ms. Matthews. I need you to stay in the area in case I have additional questions." The detective stuck the notepad and pen in his pocket and exited the room.

Halee stumbled out of bed in the morning still shaken from the previous night. She showered and then gulped down bottled water before clicking on the television in her home office. The news flashed a reporter standing in front of the wine shop, which was decorated with yellow police tape.

Omigod! Everyone will think I murdered her. Her thoughts raced to Jessie's body in the wine room. Why would someone kill her? She rubbed her head. Everything was a blur.

Later that morning, Halee nosed her Jeep into a front parking spot at her shop. She ducked under the police tape, unlocked the door, and headed inside. What was once a quaint wine shop was now a tainted crime scene.

Three taps in quick succession led her to the door. Halee found Orion, disheveled.

"I need to talk to you." He pushed past her and walked to the bar.

"Are you okay?"

"I know it's early, but I need something to calm my nerves."

Halee walked behind the bar, popped a cork, and poured Orion a glass of wine, not bothering to measure her one finger standard.

He guzzled the wine.

Orion was all about drinking wine slow and steady. She realized he was really shook-up.

"What happened?"

"Someone tried to kill me last night!"

"How?" Halee poured more wine.

"During the night, someone entered my house and tried to strangle me!" He wolfed down the wine.

"What happened next?"

"I fought back, and he took off."

"Did you call the police?"

"Yes, but they think it's related to a rash of burglaries in the neighborhood."

"I'm glad you're okay." Halee refilled his glass.

This time, Orion sniffed the wine.

"One thing though; the intruder had a distinct scent of roses."

— 🎎 —

Halee and Jack entered the Great Bridge Chapel on South Battlefield Boulevard three days later for Jessie's funeral. After signing the guestbook, they slipped into a back pew next to Orion.

Jack twisted his neck for a better view.

"I see George. Be right back." He shuffled past Halee and made his way to the front of the chapel.

Halee slid closer to Orion.

"How are you doing?"

"Haven't slept in days." He pulled a handkerchief from his pocket and wiped his forehead.

Halee touched his arm. She glanced at Lindsey, who was resting her head on a man's shoulder two rows up. She wondered if the man was her fiancé and how long Lindsey and Jessie had been friends. She also wondered about Orion and Jessie.

"Tell me, did you see Jessie after the tasting?"

"No, why?"

"Just curious. The police asked."

Orion's eyes bulged, and his mouth started to open.

"I'm surprised to see you here." Kayson stood at the end of the pew, dabbing a tissue against her swollen eyes.

"My condolences," Halee said.

"I just hope the police arrest you soon."

"I didn't kill Jessie."

"Everyone knows you had an argument with her and kicked her out of your store."

"That's not true!"

"I personally will never go back there!"

Jack approached the pew and pushed past Kayson.

"The service is starting."

Kayson hurried up the aisle and squeezed into a front seat.

"Don't let her upset you." Jack patted Halee's leg.

Unable to concentrate, Halee scanned the chapel during the ceremony. Do others think she killed Jessie as Kayson suggested?

— 🧑 —

Detective Barrett removed police tape from the shop door, then viewed unclear security footage with Jack. After he left, Halee reviewed the weekly sales report on her computer. Since news of Jessie's death, there was a substantial lull in the business. She closed the file and thought of Lindsey's wedding. She had phoned her several times unsuccessfully. She glanced at the business cards on her desk and decided to pay George a visit at Big Woody's. Perhaps he could help her contact Lindsey.

Once inside the restaurant, she spotted George chatting to a customer at the bar. Halee walked toward the counter and straddled a stool.

"What brings you here?" George dried a wine glass with a bar towel.

"Have you spoken to Lindsey?"

"Why?"

"I'm coordinating the wine for her wedding and can't get in touch with her."

"Let it go, Halee."

"What do you mean?"

George slid the glass into the rack above him.

"She thinks you murdered Jessie."

"But I didn't!"

"That's not how she sees it."

Halee turned and wiped her eyes. She needed to stay strong to clear her name.

"Tell me, did Jessie ride in the limo after the tasting?"

George frowned and leaned in close.

"Look. I don't want any trouble. Plus I already answered that for the detective you sicced on me." He threw the towel on the bar. "But the answer is no. She stayed behind with Orion."

———— 👯 ————

Halee and Jack stocked wine on the shelves. Business remained slow with only a few tourists trickling in on their way to the Outer Banks. She wondered why Orion had lied to her about not seeing Jessie after the tasting.

The doorbell jangled. Lindsey stepped into the shop.

"George said you stopped by yesterday, so here's the deal. You can provide the wine since I signed a contract. But there's one condition . . ."

Halee turned from her task, holding a bottle of wine.

"*You* can't come! Just send your staff, tell them to do their jobs and leave." Lindsey threw a check at Halee and exited through the door.

———— 👯 ————

On the day of the wedding, Halee entered the wine room to box up wine for the reception while Jack and two staff members transported the bar to Lindsey's deck. Walking into the room brought Halee much anxiety. She reached down to grab a box and noticed a tiny bottle of perfume under the shelf. She grabbed the bottle, sniffed it, and stuck it into her pocket.

An hour later, Jack entered the store.

"Is this the wine for the wedding?" He peeked into the boxes on the counter.

"Yes. How'd it go?"

"We set up the bar and left."

"Was Lindsey there?"

"No. But Kayson was directing people to set up chairs by the pool." Jack paused. "One thing though; she said to make sure you didn't come to the wedding."

That afternoon, Jack and the bartenders drove to Lindsey's to serve the beverages. Although business was slow, Halee checked out two tourists who had stopped into the store. She looked at the clock. Quarter past three. She thought about Jessie and how she should have been at the ceremony instead of six feet under. Halee slipped into her black bartender outfit, closed the shop, and drove to Lindsey's.

Halee spotted Jack on the deck when she arrived. She made her way around ushers escorting guests to their seats by the pool.

"What are you doing here? Jack asked.

"I'm here for justice."

Jack stood in front of Halee as the groomsmen escorted bridesmaids along the outdoor red carpet. The wedding march began to play as Lindsey walked to the altar.

Halee peered around Jack, hoping to catch a glimpse of Lindsey. Unfortunately, Lindsey spotted her.

"If looks could kill," Jack said.

"That's what I'm hoping for." Halee muttered under her breath.

After the vows, the wedding party moved to the far end of the pool for pictures while guests flocked to the bar.

"We need more wine from the kitchen pantry," Jack said to Halee.

As Halee made her way to the barn, she saw George talking to Orion.

"Thought you were banned from the wedding?" George smirked.

"I'm just restocking the wine." Halee scooted past guests before entering the barn. She headed into the kitchen just off the doorway, passing hundreds of wedding gifts on the floor. She flipped the pantry light switch several times with no results. With a little help from the kitchen light, she ran her hand along the shelf to guide her through the deep, narrow room. Just as she spotted the wine at the rear, the pantry door closed. Halee turned as footsteps approached.

"I knew you were getting close," a female voice said.

Halee could not make out a figure in the inky darkness.

"What do you mean?"

"Jessie deserved to die. She was always drunk and having affairs. I forgave her for taking what my cheating husband offered." The woman moved closer.

Halee caught whiff of roses, and she thought of the perfume she found in the wine room and of Orion's intruder. "Kayson?"

"But then she had to go after Orion. I told her at the tasting that I liked him, but she didn't care. The bitch."

Halee tried to piece the story together. "You broke into Orion's house?"

"Had to. He was the last to see me and Jessie together as we walked to the wine room."

"You killed Jessie?"

"Yes, and now I'll have to kill you, too." Kayson slipped her hands around Halee's neck and began to squeeze.

Halee couldn't breathe. If she didn't do something, she was going to die. She ran her hand across the shelf, searching for a weapon. She wrapped her hand around a wine bottle and slammed it against the wall, then raked the broken ridges against Kayson's arm. Kayson screamed, and her grasp weakened. Halee pushed her away and ran out of the pantry, tripping over a stray present. Kayson appeared in the doorway, grabbed Halee by the shirt, and threw her to the ground. Halee landed on the presents, her head smacking against the door. Kayson ripped a ribbon from a gift and wrapped it around Halee's neck. As everything began to darken, Halee knew she had only seconds to live. She spotted broken wine glass on Kayson's dress and grabbed it, stabbing at Kayson's leg. Halee scrambled to her feet and stumbled out the door, only to fall forward as Kayson jumped on her back, headfirst into the pool.

Halee surfaced seconds before Kayson, who floundered, sputtering and coughing.

Lindsey and her wedding party gathered around the pool. George, Orion, and Jack emerged from the crowd, followed by Detective Barrett.

Halee pushed her wet hair off her face and looked at the detective.

"What are you doing here?"

"Jack alerted me about additional footage of Kayson and Jessie entering the wine room just before Jessie died." He pulled Kayson from the pool by the back of her shirt and slapped handcuffs on her.

Halee popped a wine cork. Within weeks, business was back on track. She hoped to land more wedding contracts now that the publicity had faded. She promoted Jack to manager since he proved he could handle a crisis situation. She watched Orion at the bar sniffing his wine and flirting with a young woman.

Halee turned as George tapped two fingers against the bar and handed her an envelope.

Puzzled, she opened the envelope as she spotted Lindsey outside waving from the limo. It was a Thank You card.

"She just returned from her honeymoon in the Outer Banks and wanted to make amends for suspecting you," George said.

"I'm sure you had something to do with that." Halee smiled.

"Let me know if you ever need car service. I'll be around." George winked.

REUNION IN SHOCKOE SLIP

BY MAGGIE KING

"TONIGHT THE BODY OF a Nashville man was found in a Richmond motel room. Roger Rucker, sixty-three, was bludgeoned to death at the Good Night Inn on Richmond's Southside."

A photo of Mr. Rucker appeared on the screen. It looked like a standard DMV mug shot.

The news anchor continued.

"The apparent weapon was a twenty-five pound free weight. Rucker was found by his former wife, Jean Rucker of Richmond."

The newscast cut to footage of the motel parking lot: the open door to the room, police cars with lights flashing, the covered stretcher being carried out of the room to the waiting ambulance, the motel's sign with an *o* missing from Good, making it Go d Night Inn.

Mike asked, "Isn't that the guy you had coffee with earlier?"

Unable to speak, I nodded. We listened to the rest of the broadcast but learned nothing more. The report ended with the usual appeal to come forward with any information that would help the police with their investigation.

"I wonder if Jean killed him." I looked at my husband as if I expected him to know.

Mike shrugged. "Well, you said she threatened him with a knife."

"Yeah, that's what he told me. But—but, she used a *weight*." I wondered why I expected consistency in weapon choice. "Of course, she probably didn't bring the knife with her to the motel. And Roger said he traveled with all his weight-lifting equipment."

"So she used whatever was close at hand."

"Sounds like a crime of passion."

— 🐾 —

Earlier that day I'd been signing copies of my latest mystery, *The Berlin Affair*, at the Fountain Bookstore in Richmond, Virginia's historic Shockoe Slip. My face ached from smiling and my hand from writing. A perky woman lingered at my table, wanting to know how I got my writing ideas.

"Be born into my family, and the ideas will never dry up," I quipped.

"Nancy McGregor. It *is* you. You're N.J. Drummond. You haven't changed a bit."

That voice. Gravel infused with Southern drawl. The last time I'd heard that voice was thirty years before in North Hollywood, California. What on earth was Roger Rucker doing in Richmond?

"Roger." I stared at the smiling man before me.

"I was walking by last night and saw your picture in the window with the announcement of your signing. N. J. Drummond. I said to myself 'That looks like Nancy McGregor. Could it be? Here, in Richmond, three thousand miles from where I last saw her?' But I knew it had to be you, the resemblance was too strong. Like I said, you haven't changed a bit."

That was doubtful. Oh, I styled my thick honey blonde hair in a chin length bob, much the same as I had thirty years before. And my face still had what I liked to call the bloom of youth. As for the neck down—well, I won't go into that.

"Neither have you, Roger."

His skeptical look made me realize that he had changed in some ways. The mass of dark curls had gone gray and his bushy dark brows were more so. But his face showed no signs of sagging. I wondered if he'd had work done. The Roger I'd known had been lean and muscular, the result of clocking in many hours at the gym. Was he still fit? Hard to tell under the heavy winter jacket.

"Well, do I get a hug?"

I hesitated for a nanosecond before standing and giving my long-ago lover a hug amid cheers from the many customers.

Roger continued in his sore throat voice.

"I wanted to be the first here for your signing, but I got held up. Any copies left?"

I looked over at Kelly Justice, the proprietor of the Fountain, standing behind the register. Kelly, a tall, attractive brunette, was just finishing with a customer who picked up a foot-high stack of trade paperbacks. Naturally, smiles wreathed Kelly's face.

"Kelly, any more copies of *The Berlin Affair*?" I asked.

"One." She held it up. We'd had a great day. *The Berlin Affair* was surpassing sales of my previous books.

"Sold!" Roger took out his wallet.

While he and Kelly completed his transaction, he regaled the customers with an embroidered story of our long ago love in sunny Southern California.

"How *romantic*," a woman effused, holding her hand over her heart. "It's just like in *As Time Goes By*."

I held back an unladylike snort—as I'm sure Judi Dench and Geoffrey Palmer would have done if presented with such a comparison to their long-running BBC show.

When Roger came back to the table with book in hand, I signed with my usual flourish. "Roger, nice seeing you again. Best wishes, Nancy." Short and sweet.

Customers started taking pictures of us with their iPhones and uploading them to Facebook. Tagging me. I checked my Facebook page on my phone—it was already littered with pictures of me and Roger reuniting. When someone suggested that we hug again, I said playfully, "I have a husband, and he's on Facebook. We don't want to make him jealous." That netted me dismissive hand waves and guffaws.

Roger leaned toward me and lowered his voice.

"I see you're signing until three. Do you want to get coffee at that place on the corner? What's it called?"

"Urban Farmhouse. Yeah, sure." Not only was I curious about Roger's sudden reappearance in my life, but I figured there might be a story in this reunion. I grabbed every opportunity for new material.

Roger sat on a chair, took his phone out of his pocket, and set to swiping at his screen. "Great looking web site." He held up his phone so I could see my home page. He friended me on my Facebook page, then moved on to Twitter where he followed me.

With *The Berlin Affair* sold out, I signed copies of my previous books and chatted with customers. But my mind was on Roger. *What is he doing here?* As I signed, he took pictures of me with his iPhone. I heard him telling a customer about a backup feature he'd enabled that let him automatically upload pictures to Google Plus.

"In fact," he added, "every picture I've ever taken is on Google Plus."

Good old Google—the mega social network had not only taken over our lives, but it let us view them in pictures. Finished with his phone activities, Roger wandered around the store.

"Great place you have here, Kelly."

Kelly was still on cloud nine after such a successful day. Saturdays in downtown Richmond didn't usually draw crowds of shoppers. Roger took in the stamped tin ceiling, wooden shelves, and exposed brick wall that displayed oil paintings created by local artists. Kelly elaborated on the history of the shop.

The number of customers dwindled to two. At three o'clock, I thanked them, shrugged into my coat, looped a long scarf around my neck, and pulled on leather gloves. After Kelly reminded me about another signing event, Roger and I stepped outside to face a cold and blustery January afternoon.

The Shockoe Slip section of Richmond started out as a trading post in the early 1600s. Over the centuries, it has morphed into an eclectic shopping and dining district. Restored warehouses and taverns combined with cobblestone streets and alleyways to create a little of yesterday with a little of today.

At the Urban Farmhouse, we ordered lattes and oatmeal raisin cookies, which we carried to the one available table in the back by the restroom. When we took off our jackets, I noticed that Roger did, indeed, still have that fit body, evident in his custom-tailored shirt. Unlike my own body, ravaged by time, gravity, and a fondness for good food. I caught the appraising sweep that Roger's eyes made over my figure. I sat quickly.

"Do you still work out a lot?" I asked.

"You bet. This morning I ran around the track at a high school near where I'm staying. And I have my free weights with me. That's what I do when I travel."

"So what brings you to Richmond?"

"I gave a lecture on Internet safety at J. Sargeant Reynolds Community College—J. Sarge as you locals say. They're having an IT conference this weekend."

"And how did you happen to be at the Fountain?"

"I passed the store last night on the way back to my car. I had dinner with one of the workshop presenters at that Irish pub down the street." He pointed down Cary Street.

I nodded. "Sine's." I pronounced it *Shin-ay*.

We talked about what had brought us to the East Coast: the pull of family in both cases. I was from Virginia and Roger from Tennessee. He'd inherited the family homestead in Nashville and had moved back five years before.

"When did you start writing? You didn't write when I knew you, did you?"

"I started back in the nineties." I told him about my Christian-flavored mysteries that featured a travel writer who goes around the globe, finding murder wherever she goes. "I just finished my twelfth book in the series."

"And if they're Christian, I take it there's no sex?"

"No sex and no profanity. Violence is okay, though." We chuckled over that one.

"So, Roger, tell me more about your work."

When I knew him, I had been at loose ends, and his ends were even looser. I supported myself with temp work and went to computer school. He worked construction—sometimes. I had a weakness back then for bad boys and taut bodies, and Roger fit the bill.

"Oh, I teach. Web design, Photoshop, Internet safety, social media, you name it."

Photoshop. That's right. Back in the day, he was a budding photographer with a whoopdy-do camera. I remember him snapping pictures at every opportunity.

"I have another reason for being here this weekend."

His ex-wife Jean and ten-year-old son Cameron lived in Richmond. He and Jean were battling over custody and visitation rights for Cameron. He claimed that his wife was mentally ill. He showed me a picture of her and Cameron. His son sported a baseball cap and looked miserable. Jean was a hefty-looking woman with platinum blonde hair and milky white skin. The blue of her eyes was so pale they almost appeared white as well. The whole effect was that of a post-nuclear linebacker—one that I recognized.

I smiled. "I think I can guess where you two met."

"Yes, that AA meeting in North Hollywood. The same one where I met you. You know Jean?"

"I've seen her at meetings. Never talked to her though."

I didn't explain that her fierce look didn't invite friendly overtures.

"She's not the friendliest person in the world," Roger said, as if he had read my mind.

I kept my thoughts about Jean's friendliness—or lack of—to myself.

"I hate to air my dirty laundry, but . . ." He shot me a rueful look that signaled a dirty laundry airing.

"I was over there this morning, and Jean came outside waving a kitchen knife at me. Totally unhinged. Right in front of the neighbors, too." He pressed his lips together and shook his head. It was then that I saw the strain around his eyes. "At least there were plenty of witnesses to testify if she ever does kill me."

"I'm so sorry . . . So how long are you staying in town?"

"I'm heading back tomorrow. I'm holed up at this motel near where Jean and Cam live. I—*damn!*" Roger bit his lower lip and shook his head. "I shouldn't have told Jean where I was staying." Then he waved a hand, either dismissing the subject or swatting at a bug. "So . . . back in the book store you said you were married?"

"Yes, I'm married."

When I didn't elaborate, he picked up his phone and accessed my Facebook page.

"You said he was on Facebook." This guy didn't miss a thing. He scrolled until he found Mike Drummond. "Hmm. Nice looking guy." I smiled and nodded. Salt and pepper hair, green eyes peeking out from bushy brows, gleaming white teeth—it all added up to make Mike one nice-looking husband.

Roger put the phone back on the table.

"You two have children?"

"No children."

"And your family? Wasn't your daddy a preacher?"

"Still is."

Daddy. Perpetually in a suit and tie with perpetually pursed lips showing his disapproval of just about everything. He held the congregants of his Northern Virginia megachurch spellbound with his fire and brimstone sermons. He extended his authority to his three children by constantly threatening to disinherit us if we stepped out of line. His wealthy parents had left him a fortune. I was already a black sheep because of being a mainstream Protestant.

"Is he still anti-porn?"

"Still anti-porn," I laughed.

Daddy was on a crusade to rid the world of porn. I guessed that keeping us in line had something to do with porn. Did he really fear that we'd take up acting in blue movies?

"You know, Nancy, I was disappointed when you just up and left me all those years ago."

"I had to, Roger. You'd started drinking again and smoking weed. I didn't want to jeopardize my own sobriety."

"I understand. But I still hated you for running out on me."

After an uncomfortable pause, he said, "Well, I don't drink anymore."

"Good."

"We were together for quite a while." I caught the edge in Roger's voice.

I shrugged. "Three months?" Maybe three months seemed like a long time to him.

Not liking the path this conversation was taking, I took out my phone and checked the time. "Well . . . I have to get going," I said, trying to look regretful.

"I was hoping we could have dinner. I'd like to meet Mike."

I struggled to maintain the look of regret plastered on my face.

"We have plans. We're going out of town for the weekend. Maybe some other time."

I bit my lip to keep from laughing at the very thought of a meeting between Roger and Mike. Back in the day, Roger had been a die-hard liberal, given to soap box speeches. Not a good combination with my Rush Limbaugh-loving husband. I could just see the two of them facing off over Obamacare.

"Okay, but let me give you the number of my motel room . . . just in case."

He jotted the number down on a napkin that I stuffed in my purse.

"I'm staying at the Good Night Inn." A third—make that fourth-rate—motel on one of Richmond's main drags. Any number of murders, solved and unsolved, had been committed on the premises. I guessed that J. Sarge wasn't footing the bill for Roger's lodging. Couldn't a man who sported custom-tailored shirts secure better accommodations for himself?

We pulled on our cold weather attire and stepped outside. Roger's Honda Civic was parked a few cars up from the café. The Obama-Biden stickers from 2008 and 2012 confirmed that Roger and Mike were best kept apart.

"Nancy, I have a confession. When you broke up with me, I wanted to kill you. Seriously."

I stared. That's the first time someone had shared that particular urge with me.

He laughed. "You should see your face. Oh, don't worry, I don't want to kill you anymore. Now Jean . . . she's another story." His face went from mocking to thunderous.

Did the man always need a woman to want to kill? No wonder Jean shielded herself with kitchen knives. But even without weapons, I think she'd be a good match for Roger. He may be fit, but she had size and fierceness going for her.

Still, it was only right to warn her.

―――🎎―――

I could hear Fox News blasting when I got out of my car. I walked into the house that I shared with my husband on Richmond's Southside.

Mike turned off the TV and listened attentively as I told him about the signing and how I ran into someone I'd known in L.A. "We had coffee at the Urban Farmhouse."

"You mean the guy on Facebook? Who's he, an old boyfriend?"

While Mike would never admit to being jealous, his tone suggested otherwise. And so I kept things vague.

"Not really. We went out for a while, nothing serious." Angelo, our orange and white Manx cat, jumped in my lap. "His ex-wife lives in Richmond." I petted Angelo as I relayed the story about Roger and the knife-wielding Jean. I omitted the part about Roger wanting to kill me or his ex-wife. "I've seen Jean at AA meetings."

Mike shook his head. "I hope you don't get involved with these people."

"Not to worry," I assured him. "He's staying at the Good Night Inn."

"Even more reason not to be involved with him."

"I'm not getting *involved*."

I worked at my computer for a while, posting on my blog, checking social media, and returning e-mail. Angelo helped by walking around on my keyboard. But I couldn't shake the vision of Roger killing his ex-wife. If he succeeded, would he remember that he'd given me a heads up by telling me about the knife incident? Would he then come after me to shut me up—permanently? Had he deliberately put me in that position? But why? After all this time did he still want to kill me? Or was it that he wanted to be able to plead self-defense in his ex's killing and planned to call on me to back up his story? Were the knife and the neighborhood witnesses even real? If he intended to kill Jean, it made sense that he wanted to create a scenario.

I'd seen Jean at the Saturday AA meetings at the church off of Chippenham Parkway. Hopefully, she'd be there tonight— else I'd have to hunt her down online. Sometimes that worked, sometimes it didn't.

"Do you want to go to Italian Delight?" Mike called.

"Sure, good idea."

It beat cooking and having the inevitable wrangle over who was going to clean up. We enjoyed pizza in the unpretentious Southside neighborhood restaurant on Jahnke Road.

Back at home, my friend Darla called, and we chatted for a bit. I had some time before I had to leave for the meeting, so I did more computer work, including my weekly backups.

I found Mike in the family room doing a crossword puzzle.

"I'm going to an AA meeting." I kissed him and said I'd be back in a while. "I might go out for coffee with some of the others afterwards."

"Okay. See you later."

———— 🎎 ————

At the meeting I spotted Jean immediately. Not difficult with her nuclear glow. I sat on the other side of the room, planning to buttonhole her during the break. That would give me more time to summon up the courage to approach her.

I had no idea what was said, or who said it, during the first half of the meeting. During the break, I found Jean outside in the freezing cold, smoking. I stood a distance away, assessing her while I exchanged small talk with another smoker. Had Roger's ex expanded in size since I'd last seen her? Not only did the woman look fearsome, but the news I had to deliver wouldn't have been easy even if she was friendly. I started wavering. Did Roger even mean what he'd said about killing her? Was it just a figure of speech? Was I overreacting? Really, it was hard to fathom that the woman couldn't hold her own against Roger. I felt sure that he had more to fear than she did.

But no, I couldn't take chances. It was my moral duty to warn her. I soldiered on.

As I drew closer, I found myself looking right into those spooky blue eyes.

Nope, can't do it. The woman was too scary.

I arranged a smile on my face and came out with a cheery "Cold, isn't it?"

She scowled, not responding to my inanity. I turned and walked away.

Quickly.

———— 🎎 ————

When I got home later, Mike asked me about the meeting. We sat and talked for a while. I said nothing about the frightening Jean.

"Oh! I was supposed to send Darla some information about a new quilting group that I heard about. Let me do it before I forget."

I got up and ran upstairs to my den. Once there, I brought up my Facebook page. There I was—in all my glory. My profile and cover photos showed me wearing come-hither smiles and nothing else.

I thought back over the past few hours since Darla had called and told me about a strange picture on my Facebook page, posted by one Roger Rucker. When I checked, I groaned—there I was in the all-together. Thankfully my artful placement of a silk scarf over my head partially obscured my face and identity. But *I* knew it was me—I remembered Roger taking those pictures in his budding-photographer days. And I already had a slew of likes and comments, "Is this you?" being the most frequent one. Roger had duplicated the photos on Twitter. Stunned and furious, I reposted my original photos and made sure that I unfriended and unfollowed Roger.

An e-mail from him warned that "next time I'll post more identifiable pictures unless you agree to my terms. On your website, too. Believe me, I can get into it."

Next time? Terms? What did he mean by that? And my website? Oh dear. I had to face it—Roger was an Internet safety expert—and likely that meant he had the know-how to hack into systems. And he intended to put his hacking skills to use by posting nude photos of me. I set to backing up my site so I could restore it if necessary.

Why was Roger doing this? Had he seen an opportunity to get back at me after all these years? For what—breaking up with him? Had he been that obsessed with me? Or had the threat from his wife unhinged him? What did he want from me? Was this blackmail? I had to find out. But first things first—I had to find Jean and warn her. We could both be victims of Roger's apparently psychotic mind.

As I sat and stared at the pictures, I continued to rewind through an evening that I'd give anything to forget.

I hadn't returned to the meeting after my aborted attempt to warn Jean. Instead, I beat it over to the Good Night Inn. A quick check of Facebook on my phone showed that Roger had re-posted the pictures of me wearing only the sinuous scarf. I parked on the street and walked through the motel parking lot that was littered with broken beer bottles. Bass music blasted through open doors. Party revelers, unfazed by the low temperature, spilled out of the rooms, whooping and cheering. Belatedly, I wished I'd thought to bring along a weapon to this hotbed of crime. No telling what the motel denizens might get up to. And Roger might still want to kill me. Would anyone hear my screams? Would they even care? Likely not. Probably everyone screamed in this place.

But if Roger wanted to blackmail me, wouldn't he want to keep me alive? You didn't kill your income source. As for the raucous guests, I prayed that they'd limit their offenses to disturbing the peace.

"Roger, please delete those pictures." I said without preamble when he opened the door.

He laughed. "Oh, ho. I thought you were going away for the weekend."

"We had a change of plans."

"No, you didn't. You *lied*," he guffawed again.

"*Please* delete those pictures, Roger," I repeated. I hated begging.

"What will you do for it?"

The gleam in his eyes unsettled me and made me want to flee. But I pressed on.

"What do you want?"

"What do I *want*? Why, I want *you*. We used to be good together. I have lots of those photos on Google Plus. I can show the world how beautiful you are. Were, rather." He gave me the once over and snickered. "You've spread out a bit, haven't you? I noticed that at the Urban Farmhouse. Sooooo . . . I might just have to settle for money." He punctuated everything he said with that evil laugh.

Roger had set up his laptop next to a stack of twenty-five pound weights on a desk with a scratched and peeling faux grain. He sat and started a slideshow of the images. Were there that many? I remembered that rainy day in L.A. when he took them. I had hammed it up with the wanton looks and the Playboy centerfold poses.

"I'm sure you don't want hubby or daddy to see these pictures, beautiful as they are. And your Christian readers? I don't think so. Tell me, my dear . . . what's it worth to you to keep these photos away from their eyes?"

"Why, Roger? *Why*?"

The laugh turned maniacal. I sensed his frenzied excitement. Was Roger going mad? Was he always this nuts and somehow I hadn't noticed? Maybe Jean had put him over the edge.

Roger continued the slideshow. I'll never know what made me pick up that weight and bring it down on his head. Was it the blackmail threat? The insults? The laugh? The weight seemed light as a feather—was I really that strong, or did the adrenaline surge empower me?

I thanked my lucky stars for the gloves that protected my fingers from the January cold—they left no prints in the motel room; and for having the presence of mind to grab Roger's laptop and iPhone. I'd have to figure out what to do with them. My trunk wasn't the ideal place. Had any of the partiers noticed me arriving and leaving? Probably not. Women my age were invisible.

When I got to my car, I could barely open the door for my trembling. I sat and shook for the longest time. When Jean pulled into the motel parking lot in a monster SUV, I ducked in my seat. A few seconds later, I peeked over the dashboard and saw her turning off her lights. She had parked under the Good Night Inn sign with the missing *o*.

Not a good, or god, night for Roger.

For the second time that evening I considered approaching Jean. And just what would I say?

Hi Jean! Lovely evening, isn't it? If you're here to kill Roger, I saved you the trouble. But you'll still take the rap for it. So sorry. Surely the police will zero in on a very angry ex-wife. Plus your neighbors will remember you coming at Roger with a knife. Unless that was a trumped-up story—who knows with Roger?

But you could plead self-defense. You could say he tried to whack you over the head with one of his weights, and you wrestled it away from him. But if you end up in prison, you'll fare far better there than I would. Remember, orange is the new black.

Needless to say, I stayed put and watched Jean stumble and nearly fall as she climbed out of her vehicle.

She lumbered off towards Roger's room.

I started my car.

Now I could delete the pictures, and Roger wouldn't be undoing my efforts.

I looked again at my image. Hmm. Roger was right . . . I looked pretty good. The thirty years-earlier me had no cellulite; my stomach was smooth and flat, my breasts perky. Nothing sagged. Nowadays all parts headed south, melting and drooping like candles.

Mike yelled from the den, "Hon, come here. You won't believe what's on the news."

Oh, yes I would. "Be there in a sec, sweetheart."

A COLONIAL GRAVE

By Kristin Kisska

LAURYN SAT BACK ON her heels to wipe the grimy sweat from her brow. She was long past caring whether or not Virginia's red clay was smeared on her face. It was everywhere. Behind her ears, under her nails, in her ponytail. No posting a selfie today. Hell, none of her sorority sisters would even recognize her.

Four weeks of the Field Methods course were under her belt. Only one more to go, then her summer vacation could *really* begin. All she had to show for her scraping, sifting, and brushing through the subsoil were flat knees and a single shard of glass that may or may not be a portion of some eighteenth century oil lamp.

No Colonial Williamsburg visitors stopped to observe the archaeological dig behind the Thomas Everard House today. Too damn hot. Too damn humid. The smart people were inside eating ice cream in air conditioning—not watching the students move dirt under the scorching sun. Not today.

In the distance, horses clip-clopped as they pulled carriages full of tourists along the Palace Green and Duke of Gloucester Street.

"Daydreaming about your upcoming nuptials, Miss Battenburg?"

Lauryn bristled at the sound of Dr. Keating's hoarse voice and whipped around to face him. How had he figured it out? She and Sean were keeping their engagement secret until they bought a diamond ring. *Crap.* As if she needed any other strikes against her.

"No, sir. Sorry."

She bit the inside of her lip to refrain from saying anything else. Why was she still apologizing for a mistake made so many weeks ago? It was just that—an unintentional mistake.

Dr. Keating glared at her until her cheeks tingled from what she knew was a telltale blush creeping over her freckled cheeks. Professor Davenport, her College of William & Mary Field Methods instructor, approached them to run interference, thereby breaking the standoff.

After both older gentlemen turned around, Lauryn slipped off her Claddagh ring and shoved it into her shorts pocket. She sharpened her trowel with her file. Leaning over, she prayed for a breeze as she continued excavating.

Scrape. Sift. Brush.

Though he was the Director of Archaeological Research, these past few weeks had been awkward under Dr. Keating's co-direction. He was snippy with all the students, but especially so with her, ever since the first day of Field School when he'd guest lectured about the three periods of archaeology at Colonial Williamsburg.

After the lesson, the students were invited to wander around his office and view his display of collected artifacts, dig site photographs, and archaeological tools. She'd had the nerve to pick up his trowel. The flat metal had been polished with one edge straight and the other scalloped. Dr. Keating had been so offended, he broke into a hacking cough while admonishing her to override her childish impulses. Lauryn had left wondering if she should resign from the course.

Or maybe he should add a Do Not Touch sign!

The only person who dared confront him was Professor Davenport. And they bickered. A lot. Lauryn and the other students nicknamed them *The Odd Couple.* Her professor was Oscar to Dr. Keating's anally retentive Felix.

Scrape. Sift. Brush.

She sliced her trowel through the baked earth, flattening the surface of the soil as she dislodged a layer just millimeters thick.

Thud.

"I think I've found something!" A thrill of excitement tingled.

"Stop!" Professor Davenport rushed to her side. "Don't pull, Lauryn. Excavate."

The dozen or so other William & Mary classmates taking the practical archaeology course with Lauryn stopped their digging and crowded around behind her to watch. Using her wooden pick and brushes, she painstakingly scraped her way through dirt packed around a slim white fragment stuck at the bottom of a tall cliff of soil. The edge of the artifact was smooth and curved.

The Tarpley Bell tolled, summoning worshipers to service at Bruton Parish Church. It was quarter to noon, but taking a break was the last thing on Lauren's mind. She no longer felt oppressed by the heat.

What could her find be? A piece of a ceramic kitchen bowl? Maybe a china plate? She worried at a tough knot of stubborn dirt packed around the edge. Some loose piece of metal. Maybe a ring of some sort.

"Oh my God!" Lauryn sprang up. Covering her gaping mouth with her hand, she looked from Professor Davenport, to Dr. Keating, then to the students all staring back at her expectantly. She pointed her brush at the fragment emerging from the soil.

"Is that a finger?"

— 🧑 —

I got off work early from the silversmith shop tonight to surprise her. It wasn't easy. The Bicentennial celebration is a big deal everywhere around the country. Colonial Williamsburg has been crazy-busy all season. But July 4, 1976—two hundred years after the signing of the Declaration of Independence—it's packed to the max. Can't walk anywhere without hearing cannons shot or running into mobs of tourists—I mean, guests.

She doesn't see me. But God, she's so foxy! Not that her traditional colonial middling woman's outfit is. A burlap bag couldn't be much uglier than the costumes they make us wear for this colonial gig. But Mindy's face glows in the light of the oil lamp inside the shop.

She's helping three kids push a lever to dip wick strings into a vat of melted beeswax. Every time they raise the wooden arm, the amber candles take shape and her smile grows brighter as the kids get more excited. One of the boys says something that makes her tilt her head back and laugh. She reaches behind him into a glass jar and hands him a peppermint stick.

I could watch her all night. Most evenings, I do.

Didn't plan on staying in Williamsburg this summer, but Mindy's worth it. So I'm taking a morning anthropology lecture at William & Mary, then I change into a leather apron and old-fashioned britches and head over to the silversmith shop. I pump bellows, polish tools, and sell our souvenir silver trinkets. Brainless work. But it's good dough, and if it's not too busy, the silversmith lets me work on my own tools. He even taught me how to engrave.

And I get to see Mindy.

The velvet ring box is burning a hole through my pocket. It's my grandmother's. She brought it with her from Ireland. I'm going to propose to her tonight, under the fireworks.

And by this time next year, we'll both have graduated from William & Mary, and we'll get real jobs. Professional jobs, not this tourist stuff. Maybe we'll start a family, and we'll laugh about those college summer days when she made wax candles, and I apprenticed as a silversmith. Far out.

Say yes, Mindy.

—— 👧 ——

Lunch break came and went, but not Lauryn. Her classmates clustered around her while she excavated the hand under the intense afternoon sun. They took pictures with their cell phones and posted them to Facebook and Instagram. She hoped they were tagging her, since she was the one who actually discovered the bones. Should make for one hell of a research paper next semester.

All the Field Course students had found this summer were bits of colonial-era metal, glass, and ceramic. Nothing intact. The Everard House, adjacent to Colonial Williamsburg's Governor's Palace, was the old magazine owner's house. It was located nowhere near a known cemetery, so finding eighteenth-century bones in the backyard was a shocker.

Some staff archaeologists arrived to consult with Dr. Keating and Professor Davenport, to record and document the position of the bones. Lauryn was surprised *The Odd Couple* hadn't rushed in to take over unearthing the finger.

She took a deep breath and steadied her trowel.

Scrape. Sift. Brush.

Little by little, the rest of the hand emerged from the soil. The fingers were curved into a loose fist. The bones were fragile, so she took great care to excavate slowly. Maybe the entire skeleton was buried. Williamsburg's archaeology staff would analyze these bones to study people's diets two hundred years ago.

The ring was delicate and had a tiny diamond. Left ring finger. She'd been in love. Her hand seemed about the same size as Lauryn's. Maybe a bit smaller.

As she brushed particles of red clay away, Lauryn wondered about this young woman's life. Probably not too different from the women who re-enacted colonial life in Williamsburg today, except that two hundred years ago this woman couldn't have gone home to air conditioning, television, and Wi-Fi.

Poor thing! How did this woman die? Why wasn't she buried properly in a cemetery? Did she know Thomas Jefferson when he was a law student at William & Mary, or better yet, when he lived in the Governor's Palace next door?

Chestnut-brown threads of the frayed fabric began to brush off with the dirt. Lauryn slowed and worked extra-carefully, so as not to unravel the clothes, whatever condition they might still be in. Within the cuff seemed to be the end of a rough cotton blouse sleeve. It was probably once cream-colored, though now barely a shade off the red clay around her.

Scrape. Sift. Brush.

At this rate it could take weeks to unearth the colonial woman, but Lauryn would only be around for one more week.

The next sweep of her brush revealed a small crumpled ball of paper between the woman's cuff and wrist. Careful not to dislodge it, Lauryn bit her lip as she gently stretched the wax-lined paper to determine if it was a note of some sort.

She suddenly stood and jumped back as if the bones were an unexploded landmine. Her classmates stopped talking and leaned in closer.

"Lauryn, what is it?" Professor Davenport rushed to her side and knelt. Only the cicadas' maraca call and the shuffling of feet could be heard.

But then he saw it too.

"Somebody. Call the police!"

"Johnny, what are you doing here?" Mindy pauses mid-step while descending the front stairs of the Everard House.

I hop out from behind the crepe myrtle and offer her my hand to help her walk down the rest of the way. I'm still dressed in my leather apron and craftsman costume. Maybe I should've changed. Then again, she's wearing her colonial getup, too. We match.

"The Bicentennial fireworks start at sundown. It's gonna be bitchin'!"

When she smiles, the top of her nose crinkles, and the dimple on her right cheek flashes. All I can think about is kissing her and unlacing the ribbon of the straw hat she's wearing to set loose her straight brown hair. I hate those white ruffled caps they have to wear. Like, did the colonial cats really think they were foxy?

"Oh..." She scans the Palace Green behind me. "...I'm sorry. I have plans tonight."

I glance behind me and see pockets of tourists—I mean, guests—milling up the gravel drive, laying blankets on the stretch of grass, and chilling in front of the Governor's Palace. Kids wearing black tricorn hats are playing with toy wooden muskets.

"So meet your friends later. Come out with me."

I step quickly to keep up with her as she walks around the side of the house, shuttering windows. Dusk is fading into darkness. Her navy skirt appears black against the white siding of the house.

Reaching into my pocket, I rub my thumb over the velvet box. She's going to love the ring. It's not a diamond, but hey, I'm in college. Besides, it's been in my family for generations. Someday I'll have the dough for a real engagement ring.

"I can't." She bites her lip, then continues to the back side of the house.

The oil lamps lighting the walkways disappear from our view. She stoops to pick up a used ice cream cone wrapper littering the grass. When she stands upright, she sighs and shakes her head.

"Look, Johnny, we have to talk."

I smile. Yes, we definitely need to talk. About our future. It's quieter back here, away from the crowds. The tunes from a fife and drum corps fade in the distance as they march toward the Governor's Palace.

As we turn behind the house, the moon casts a shadow. Mindy stops in the yard, her face glowing in the moonlight as if illuminated by a halo. She gazes at me with soulful eyes and takes a step closer. My muse.

Perfection.

"Mindy," I whisper as I lean towards her. "I love—"

"Don't say it, Johnny."

She looks down at her black shoes with large pewter buckles, so my kiss lands on her forehead instead of her lips. Her words stop me, and I hover, not sure I heard her correctly. Hoping I hadn't.

"I'm sorry. It's over."

"What?" I don't understand. What's over? I reach for her shoulder, but she pulls away. "You can't mean that, babe."

She twists the paper wrapper in her hand, pausing as if to select her words carefully.

"I've been...seeing someone else."

— 🎎 —

Scrape. Sift. Brush.

Only this time, it wasn't Lauryn excavating. In the exposed subsoil, a team of forensic archaeologists had taken over exhuming the bones. The procedure had been tricky as the soil packed above the body was riddled with a network of roots from large shrubs or small trees cut down years ago.

But contrary to Lauryn's initial assumption, this young woman had not lived during the colonial era.

Caught in the woman's jacket cuff at the time of death was a used Nutty Buddy ice cream cone wrapper. A report just came back from the forensics lab. The label had a faded expiration date of September 27, 1976. The police were able to trace the lot number to a bulk ice-cream order signed in at a receiving warehouse three months earlier and sold later in a convenience shop in Merchants Square.

Strips of yellow *Crime Scene Do Not Enter* tape encircled the dig. Hundreds of visitors clustered outside the barricade. A dozen folding chairs aligned the bluff overlooking the excavation site so the Field Method students could observe. A front row seat was saved for Lauryn, but it remained vacant.

For the past three days, the students sat vigil as the skeleton of an adult female, draped in the remnants of a dark blue woolen skirt, cream linen apron, and brown waistcoat, was exhumed. Professor Davenport believed the students would benefit academically by observing the efficient work of experienced archeology professionals in action.

Rumors circulated the body was Melinda Jameson, a summer employee—a candle maker—of Colonial Williamsburg, who disappeared sometime during the Bicentennial celebrations. A cold case. And judging from the jagged gash in her skull behind her ear, she'd been murdered.

A professional photographer documented the exhuming process. Samples of the fabric, her hair, and the surrounding soil were collected in small bags for evidence analysis. Her head was turned sideways, jaw open.

Lauryn, standing in the shade of the Everard House so she could read her phone screen better, scrolled through archived newspaper articles from *The Virginia Gazette*. There'd been a large coordinated search to find Melinda, and the police had even sent divers into the James River and a nearby reservoir. With no trace of her body or weapon, they'd eventually called off the search and hoped Melinda had run away for the summer. But when she didn't return to William & Mary for the fall semester, she was presumed abducted.

She glanced over at the body, now almost entirely unearthed, and shivered. If this body were in fact Melinda, she'd have been the same age as Lauryn when she was killed. A college senior, engaged, with so much life and promise ahead of her.

The detective had already taken Lauryn's statement about excavating the woman's hand and was now interviewing Dr. Keating under a nearby tree. Though she couldn't hear him clearly, he was obviously irritated his precious archeological site had been taken over by those not under his control. It was refreshing not to be the only one receiving his outrage.

Commotion rippled through the crowd of onlookers as an older gentleman pushed his way up to the yellow tape. He seemed familiar. Lauryn had seen several photos from the articles of Melinda's fiancé, Henry Thorough, who'd initially reported her missing. He'd run a missing person poster campaign and had organized many of the volunteer search efforts through nearby woods after the police investigation slowed. And at one point, he'd even been named a *person of interest* in the investigation.

Tears welling in Henry's eyes reflected the dig as he mopped his balding forehead with his sleeve. In his other hand was a tattered Polaroid photo. The past forty years had not been kind.

Lauryn swallowed a lump in her throat. She couldn't fathom what this poor man was suffering, the horror of finally having an answer—the worst kind of answer—after all these decades of hoping and searching. But even worse, both Melinda's parents had passed away without ever knowing what had happened to their only child.

Out of the corner of her eye, a sliver of metal caught Lauryn's attention. She edged closer to Melinda's body to get a better view.

—— 👧 ——

"No."

My pulse throbs in my ears. Mindy must be confused. She loves me. I know it. That's why I stayed in Williamsburg this summer. It's why I changed my major. She's my future.

A boom sounds from the first fireworks of the night.

"Johnny, stop!"

She cringes as she steps out of my embrace and rubs her shoulder. Even though she's in the Everard House's lunar shadow, her face dazzles with white, blue and red flashes from the Bicentennial explosions in the sky. Radiant.

But she's making a mistake. A forgivable mistake. I kiss her again, to remind her what we mean to each other. That she loves me.

"Don't kiss me!"

This time, Mindy pushes me away. Hard. Her shaking voice slices through my heart.

I can't think. "But... but..." Heat creeps up my neck. I reach into my pocket for the velvet box. Mindy's ring. Maybe if she sees it, she'll know I'm crazy about her. She'll reconsider. I grip the box, drawing power from it. This ring is the key to reminding her of our relationship.

She takes a step back, mumbling something I can't hear. Her perfect rose-shaped lips move, flashing a glimpse of her dimple, but no sound escapes.

"What?" I'm yelling, so I move closer, trying to hear her over the explosions. Sounds like the whole goddamned Revolutionary War is being reenacted in the sky.

Stepping back toward the white siding of the house, she hangs her head.

"Henry and I are engaged."

I rip the white cap off her head, sure that the ruffles must have distorted what I think she just said.

"Look at me and tell me you love me!"

Mindy yelps and glances around. Colors dance on the whites of her eyes. Eyes that used to close when I kissed her. Eyes that drowned my soul when she pleaded "don't stop" the one exquisite night we spent together.

Eyes that refuse to meet mine right now as she slowly shakes her head.

She loves me, not some other low-life, girlfriend-stealing cat. We're here together. Us. Johnny and Mindy. Forever. She promised. My push is light. Her head snaps back, hitting the wall as she shrieks.

Shit! Stop screaming. Someone could hear us, you know? She tries to run, but we can't part like this. Not now. I haven't given her the ring yet.

I shush her and apologize. Why won't she stop screaming? She struggles out of my hug, so I tighten my grip. *Stop yelling, Mindy!*

Covering her mouth with my hand, I hold her against the house. "It's okay. I'll let go. Just be quiet."

Though her brow is furrowed, she shuts her eyes, and then nods. I remove my hand. Gently. But the second her mouth is free, she peels a scream that makes me want to cover my ears. I clamp my hand back over her mouth. Tighter this time.

With a muffled whimper, Mindy tucks the crumbled wrapper into her cuff, digs into her apron pocket and then slips a ring on her finger. She holds up her left hand and shows me a small diamond ring.

"No," I whisper. She's lying. She's just trying to make me

jealous. I step back, staring at her hand as if it were a coiled snake. She can't be engaged to someone else. The diamond ring must be fake. A joke.

"Johnny. . . " she groans. The ache in her voice is raw. What did she expect? That I'd like the news? That I could just walk away from us? I love her. We love each other. She promised.

"No." The velvet ring box stings against my leg, but I can't give it to her. Not now. Not my grandmother's ring. This memory would be too painful. I swipe my hands around my other pockets. Something hard is in my apron. A tool. The one I'd been polishing earlier. I grab it, for support. For strength.

"No!" Now I'm the one who can't stop yelling.

She dashes to the side, and I swing out to stop her. But I've hit her. In the head. The thud is sickening. Fireworks burst in a constant percussion of lights and booms. The grand finale.

She crumples to the ground as the fireworks die in the sky. In the distance, applause ripples through the crowd. But here, in this empty yard behind the Everard House, moonlight laced in sulfuric smoke creeps toward earth and envelops us.

What have I done?

I collapse to my knees next to her and hold her in my arms, begging her to wake up. Her face relaxes, and she closes her eyes. If it weren't for the blood matting her hair, I'd have thought she was sleeping like a baby.

Oh God, sweet Mindy! Please open your eyes!

But she doesn't. Instead, her arm drops and her head lilts back. I rock her slowly, absorbing every little fiber of life left in her.

A ribbon of smoky moonlight illuminates her angelic face. So silent.

I kiss her eyes. Her dimple. Her lips.

Mindy!

Lauryn inched her way around the dig site to get a better view of Melinda's head. Something was there. It was too small to be a barrette. She needed to get closer to the skull to check it out. Oh, if only she could crawl under yellow police tape to get a better view. But she couldn't risk contaminating the crime scene.

One of the forensic archaeologists was taking a water break. He was youngish. And thank God he was standing far away from the detective, who was busy interviewing Professor Davenport.

"Hi." She smiled as she approached. "First body?" Doesn't every archaeologist secretly channel their inner Indiana Jones?

He smiled back. Good sign.

"Nope. Have a couple dozen on my resume."

"So, what happens next?" She feigned rapt attention as he waxed on about documenting the body and evidence on a grid map, admitting the body to the coroner's office, examining dental records to identify the victim, and performing tests used to determine the cause of death. God, this guy could talk forever.

"Won't the slice through her skull be a solid clue for cause of death?"

Indy chuckled as he nodded. "Yeah, it's the smart place to start." He handed Lauryn a cup of water from the massive orange beverage cooler she usually saw at football games.

Together they strolled up to the crime scene tape and observed the three archaeologists still excavating Melinda's body.

She whispered, so only Indy could hear.

"So—hypothetically speaking, of course—what if a Field Methods Course student only has one day left at this dig site, and she probably won't get to see the body removed? And let's say this student might like to follow the reports on this victim closely, you know, for academic purposes. But after she leaves here tomorrow, her access will be limited to newspaper articles."

"Well... this *hypothetical student* could take pictures."

She coughed a little, hoping no one else could hear her, especially the detective.

"She probably already has, but with the crime scene tape blocking her, she might not be able to get close enough to see much."

"Hmmm, I have crime scene clearance. I could probably snap a few pictures of the body to help this *hypothetical student* with her college project. But I couldn't interfere with the investigation."

Lauryn doused her grin. Fishing out her cell phone from her

pocket, she asked Indy to make sure to take a close-up shot of Melinda's head wound.

— 🎎 —

I stayed in Colonial Williamsburg all these years. Nearly four decades now. How could I leave her—my Mindy?

And every year, I watch the Fourth of July fireworks with her. We're all alone, she and I. But our fates will always be tied together. And every time I lie on the ground above where she lay, I think back on that Bicentennial night and apologize. This wasn't how I thought we'd turn out.

But I know she's forgiven me. I feel it in my soul.

That night, I left her behind the Everard House and kept watch from beside the Governor's Palace for hours. The tourists trickled home after the fireworks. But no one crossed the white picket fence and went behind the house. Sometime after midnight, I sneaked into the silversmith shop and found a shovel, then buried her right where she fell.

As morning dawned, I realized the fresh dirt would attract someone's attention. So I replanted some shrubs from a few fields away over her. Figured it would appear as if the landscapers had been busy. Then, I crept back to my dorm and slept for ages.

A few days later, when I returned to work, I heard that Mindy was finally reported missing by her goddamned fiancé. I'm the one who loved her, but he gets credit for being her almost-spouse. The rest of the summer and the next school year at William & Mary, I expected the police to turn up at my dorm room. They searched everywhere, but they never found her.

On graduation day, I wore my grandmother's ring in Mindy's honor—her memory—so that she and I could graduate together.

Mindy's fiancé—yes, I kept tabs on the schmuck through the years—never gave up searching and never married. He gets to wear his heart on his sleeve, and I'm the one who has to suffer and love her secretly.

But she's mine. She always has been.

Years ago, I had a close call. Landscapers removed the English boxwood bushes I'd planted over Mindy because they weren't historically original to the Everard House. I thought for sure they'd find her body when they dug out the roots.

But now things have changed. I must not have much time left. My doctor doesn't run many lab tests anymore; he just asks about my comfort and then spends the rest of our appointment inquiring about my research. I purchased a double grave plot in a nearby cemetery for us.

Soon we'll be together again, my Mindy and I.

Forever.

———— 🎎 ————

Lauryn stood in the shade of an overgrown tree, scrutinizing the enlarged photo on her phone screen. The forensic archaeologists must have seen this sliver of metal wedged in Melinda's skull. Why hadn't this evidence been sent off to the lab with the other samples? Perhaps they needed to keep it in place for the coroner to officially rule on the cause of death.

The metal piece had an unusual, yet oddly familiar shape. It reminded her of something, but what?

She glanced across the dig. Professor Davenport and Dr. Keating were bickering again, hands gesticulating, voices escalating.

Oh my God. The trowel.

Lauryn turned away and covered her mouth, choking back a gag. How could he have killed her and gotten away with it all these years? Though he might be a well-respected professional in the archeological community, clearly he's also a very, very good actor. But what could've been his motive? And why in God's name did Dr. Keating allow the excavation to go on if he knew Melinda would be found? None of it made sense.

The detective was finally standing alone for the first time since the investigation began three days ago. Now was Lauren's moment—but she hesitated.

What if she were wrong? Just because she knew the murder weapon didn't mean she knew unequivocally he murdered Melinda. She could destroy his career and his reputation by falsely accusing him of murder. Not to mention, a mistake of such magnitude could ruin her final year at William & Mary.

Lauryn's toes crested the edge of the dig. Only a few dozen feet away lay the remains of a young woman who didn't deserve to die. Melinda's life had been stolen from her. She never had the chance to say goodbye to her parents or her fiancé. She was robbed of the chance to graduate from college. She never walked down the aisle and said *I do*. She never even had a funeral.

She owed a dead girl this one posthumous opportunity for justice. It could be Melinda Jameson's only chance. Come what may.

Under the guise of moving back to her saved seat, she inched closer to *The Odd Couple*. Their voices were clipped. One was arguing that his students' course had been interrupted, and they'd lost valuable field experience, the other complaining that first the students, then the police had overrun a historical treasure trove, and who knew what colonial artifacts would be lost in the chaos? Couldn't they just cut the drama and get along, for once?

As she sidled closer to them, a flash of silver on a hand caught her eye. A signet ring. But not just any ring, she recognized the crown, the heart, and the hands. It was the traditional Irish Claddagh ring, just like the one Sean had given her as a promise ring.

Of course. How had she not noticed him wearing it before?

Dr. Keating had recognized what the average person would've overlooked. Worn on the ring finger of her left hand with the heart facing out meant she was engaged. But the heart on his, even though the ring was on his pinky finger, faced inward, which meant he was married.

Committed.

A moment later, she scrolled through a Google search result on her phone, confirming that Jonathan A. Keating, PhD from Williamsburg, Virginia, was not, and had never been, married.

She opened the photo of the skull gash Indy had gallantly snapped for her. Ignoring her racing pulse, she quietly reintroduced herself to the detective and showed him the photo.

"In Dr. Keating's office, you'll find a broken trowel displayed on one of his shelves. The sliver of metal still wedged in Melinda's skull should fit perfectly along the tool's edge."

The detective stopped jotting notes and examined her phone screen. He glanced in the direction of *The Odd Couple*. Dr. Keating was so worked up, he was coughing into a linen handkerchief.

"Really?" Skepticism laced the detective's question. "So you suspect a nationally renowned master of archaeology murdered a college student forty years ago?"

Lauryn nodded, tentatively at first.

The detective held his transmitter to his mouth but then paused, searching her eyes before dispatching police officers to obtain a warrant to search Keating's office for the murder weapon.

"Well, Ms. Battenburg, or should I call you *Nancy Drew*, let's assume you're right. What was his motive? Why do you think he did it?"

"It was a crime of passion. He loved her..."

She let out a deep breath as she gazed over at the older, ailing archaeologist, who was wearing his commitment ring like a banner to those who understood its meaning. But he had no idea his twisted secret was on the cusp of going viral.

Then she glanced at the object of his warped affection, who after all these years was finally unearthed.

"... he always has."

DEATH IN THE GREAT DISMAL

BY C.B. LANE

THE SHRILL SONG OF a cardinal awakens me on Tuesday morning at three. It's my cell phone. Questions burst in my mind like defective fireworks while my heart makes that tapping sick feeling. I roll over and pick up the phone.

My husband sits up, mumbling, only half-awake, probably waiting to find out if it's a family disaster, a problem at work, or a wrong number.

It's work, specifically Kamil, the federal officer I supervise at the Dismal Swamp Wildlife Refuge, headquartered in Suffolk, Virginia. I swipe my finger across to answer, and then launch myself to a sitting position on the side of the bed. His voice is calm.

"Hi, Antonia. Sorry to call you in the middle of the night, but I've received a report of a deceased person at Jericho Lane parking lot."

Kamil is tall and fit with olive skin and dark curly hair. His family came from Iran a few decades ago. On his first day at Dismal, in his first hour, he used an app on his cell phone to get the direction to Mecca. He prays several times each day when he can. It took the staff a little while to get used to it, but now they don't take much notice.

"Okay," I say. "I'm on my way." I'm still not awake mentally, though my body is on high alert.

"I'm almost there," he says. "Can you call the Zone Officer and get the serious incident report going?"

"Of course." I hate to call her in the middle of the night. Stationed in northern Virginia, she has the responsibility of overseeing the law enforcement operations on all the refuges in Virginia and West Virginia, so she has to be in the loop on something this serious. Not to mention unusual. We haven't had a body on the refuge in nearly forty years—at least, none that we've known about.

"Sorry to call you at home," I say.

I'm on autopilot, and it's not until I speak the words to her that it starts to hit me; someone has died, their body out there in the dark on the refuge. Did they drop dead of a heart attack? Is someone waiting for them to come home?

The Zone Officer sounds instantly attentive, reassuring and courteous. She says she'll take care of notifying all the people up the chain of command.

I dress in my uniform and kiss my husband who, relieved that it's not a family crisis, lies back down, but he keeps shifting and changing position, as if he can't quite relax. Probably his heart hasn't stopped pounding yet. I know mine hasn't.

About ten minutes later I arrive at the Jericho trailhead parking lot on the north end of the refuge. The place is alive with blue and red lights and radio chatter. Suffolk Police and Fire are here. It's a rainy night in early April, balmy, with several species of frogs singing, and a light breeze stirring the still mostly-bare branches. I approach the police tape, and Kamil comes toward me.

He's been at Dismal only a few months, fresh out of thirty-one weeks of training, but he's done a couple of tours in Afghanistan, so he isn't green. Though he's not quite thirty and I'm in my late forties, we've already built a strong level of trust and respect—as his supervisor, when something goes bad, he has to know I have his back. And vice versa, of course.

"It's Karen MacBride," he says.

"Karen MacBride?" I echo. I'm stunned. How is that possible? Karen volunteers with us, or rather, volunteered with us, helping with everything from bird surveys to teaching kids archery to greeting visitors. She was about forty, attractive and outgoing.

"Blunt trauma to the head and a railroad spike through her heart," Kamil tells me.

Succinct.

I fight down the nausea and look up to the heavens for comfort. One would think that two miles into the depths of the Great Dismal, the stars would blanket the firmament, but the lights of Suffolk have ruined the night sky despite the so-called ordinances that are supposed to mitigate their effects. The nearby cities of Portsmouth and Norfolk don't help either.

I rack my brain, trying to think of a reason why someone would want Karen dead and realize that, in all the hours I've spent with her, she's never mentioned anything about her personal life except the time she had to put her dog to sleep. Unlike some of our volunteers who share everything, from their favorite recipes to their grandchildren's potty training progress, Karen was one to listen rather than talk. At least around me.

Suffolk PD has taken the lead on the investigation. They're sharp, well trained, if underpaid, and professional. They ask Kamil and me a few questions about access and regulations, and what we know about Karen. We answer. They take notes. They turn us loose.

"Any leads so far?" I ask Kamil.

"I didn't see anything obvious that screams who did it," he answers. "But that railroad spike through the chest—that seems pretty personal. Like someone considered her a vampire."

"Some sort of ritual slaying?"

"Maybe."

"Who reported it?"

"A prostitute and her client called 911 and Suffolk PD called me." He smiles a little, hitches up his duty belt, his slim waist and hips not shaped to support its bulk very well. "I spoke with her a few minutes ago. She's one I've met before. She said they were afraid they might get accused of it since they were at the crime scene, and might have left some evidence behind."

I try not to think about what that evidence would be.

"I thought that stuff had settled down up here," I say. Kamil has hit the practitioners of the oldest profession hard, and they've stopped using the Jericho entrance as a place of business—or so we thought.

"We need a gate up by White Marsh Road instead of two miles inside the refuge," he says. "Stop all the after-hours traffic."

"Good idea," I say.

Kamil doesn't let things go. Already, in his short time here, I've seen that he keeps picking at problem areas until he has them cleaned up. He's a good officer.

We both get texts from the Zone Officer asking for an update. I leave it to Kamil to go to the office and call the Zone and type the report into LEMIS, the web-based reporting system.

I return home hoping to get some breakfast and a little sleep before the regular workday begins, but by the time I eat, it's seven o'clock and my husband is up and the dogs are baying for their morning meal. My husband has a foxhound and a beagle, the last two of many with which he and his friends used to hunt deer and rabbits.

In the last few years, many city people have moved into the area, complaining about slow tractors and gunshots and hunting dogs and wanting everyone to change to suit them, and it's become too aggravating to hunt the traditional ways. Of course, it hasn't helped the neighborly relations when some of the guys let their dogs run in the spring, chasing pregnant does, killing turkey polts, and harassing Yorkie-poos. Having grown up in the suburbs of Newark makes the whole thing foreign to me anyway.

"What's the latest?" my husband asks.

"There is, indeed, a dead body at Jericho."

"Who is it? Drug related?"

"They don't know yet." Not until Suffolk releases the details can I tell him it was Karen. Not that he would tell anyone else, but there it is. I hug him long and hard, grateful to have him, grateful he's alive and healthy and happy. I go back to work comforted, ready to face whatever comes.

When I walk into the office at eight o'clock, most of the staff is at the front desk, wide-eyed and curious, firing questions at me, quoting the morning news, exchanging speculation.

"I can't tell you anything right now," I say. "Not until Suffolk releases the information. Sorry."

None of us have ever been through anything like this; we've always operated as a tight-knit team, but now we're separated into the information-privileged and the left-out. I'm sorry for the rift that is already beginning, and I wonder how deep it will go.

During the morning, radio stations call, and newspaper and TV journalists show up on the doorstep for some "background information," making small talk, trying to slip in leading questions, but I have nothing to tell them. They wait around for a little while socializing with each other, then give up and leave, probably headed back to Jericho to film detectives and crime scene techs coming and going.

Around noon, two detectives want to talk with me. In the conference room, they're distracted by the display of photographs of plants and wildlife of the Dismal Swamp submitted to our Wildlife Festival photography contest. We browse the images of deer and dragonflies, ladies' slippers and trillium, and they ask questions laced with surprised interest in the diversity of life in the Great Dismal. People often come to the swamp on business and find themselves fascinated, asking for brochures and trail maps, planning to bring their families back.

Then they ask me about Karen. How well did I know her; what did I know about her home life, or her family?

"Nothing," I say. "Just that she had to put her dog to sleep last fall." It was a beagle. I feel unsettled when I think how little I knew the details of her daily life.

"Was she married?" they ask.

I squint, trying to remember if I'd met a husband.

"Yes. At least I think so, but she never talked about him, and I never met him." I shake my head. "She never talked about her personal life to me. Just about the swamp and what was on the news, that sort of thing."

They start up the small talk again. Then back to the questions.

"When's the last time you saw Karen?" one asks. He stares at me as if he expects me to confess to seeing her last night, just before I brained her.

I shake my head, tighten my lips. "We can look at the volunteer register," I say. "That will tell us when she was in last."

They look at each other. They keep asking, and I keep shaking my head.

"What about your husband?"

This throws me. "My husband?"

"When was the last time he saw her?"

"I have no idea." Why are they asking about him?

"How well did he know her?"

"Not very. He only saw her at events and meetings when we were all involved."

My legs are crossed, and I have to concentrate to keep the dangling foot from bouncing. What are they suggesting?

"Does he volunteer for these events?"

"Sometimes."

They are silent for several beats. I out-silent them. Is he a suspect? Am I? How much does a criminal lawyer cost? We need a new roof, my car is leaking oil like a colander, and the washing machine only does the gentle cycle. We can't afford a lawyer. Surely they're just fishing.

"Can you explain why her cell phone has quite a few outgoing texts to your husband's cell?"

A wave of heat flushes my face, and my vision narrows to a spark. I can't breathe. I feel faint. I stare. They wait.

"What?" I say.

"Texts like: 'Miss you.' 'When can I see you?' 'Will you be home this afternoon?' Over the course of the last few months, starting in mid-January."

I was gone for a week in mid-January, away at training. We had a minor disagreement before I left; he said I traveled too much and obsessed over work when I was home. The first night I called home, but he didn't answer or call me back. The other nights, he answered but didn't want to stay on the phone for more than a couple of minutes. Normally, when I travel, we talk for at least twenty minutes every night at bedtime.

"Any replies?" I ask, though I already know the answer. Chances are he never saw any of the texts, much less responded. He's not very tech-savvy, my husband. At least I don't think he is. And he would never cheat on me.

They don't tell me.

"Were you jealous?" one asks, leaning toward me, looking sympathetic. "I know I'd be upset if my wife was getting texts like that."

More games. They ask me where I was yesterday evening. I can't believe it was only last night she was found. They badger me with the same questions, but I only shake my head. Then I no longer speak, no longer respond, just gaze out the window at the newly emerging leaves shining from the trees, and the birds flitting through them, snagging bugs in mid-air. Can this be happening?

They depart, thanking me for my cooperation. I sense a little sarcasm. I stay in the conference room for a few minutes, focusing on work, making myself forget about the detectives and those texts, getting myself composed. I wonder if my husband has heard. Have they questioned him yet? I'd like to go right home and see him, but then again, I wouldn't. Will he suspect me, too? He was out at a hunt club meeting last night, so he can't give me an alibi, nor I, him.

I look out the window. In the parking lot, the detectives are still beside their car, and they watch Kamil drive up and get out of his truck. He stops and talks to them, glancing at the office and nodding. When they leave, he stands there a moment, unmoving, and then gets back into his truck and drives away. What did they say to him? Did they tell him I'm a suspect? Am I a suspect? Is my husband?

I go to my office and stand in the doorway. Everything looks alien.

I consider calling the Zone, but before I do, she calls me.

"Hey, Antonia. I just spoke with Kamil. I think under the circumstances, until all this is cleared up, I should be his supervisor of record. That'll free you up to focus on your staff and volunteers."

"What? Why?"

"I think it's the right thing to do at this time."

I don't argue. She's courteous and reassuring, and I feel like everything will be okay while I'm talking to her; she has that sort of demeanor. Then she hangs up, and I feel completely adrift.

At the end of the day, I don't want to go home. But I do, and when I turn into the driveway, I see my husband on the front porch with the dogs, just sitting there, my husband who never sits still; my stomach hurts. What will this do to us? My marriage is the most important thing in my life, the only thing that is solid.

I hope it's solid.

I get out of the car and walk slowly to the porch, greeted by the dogs baying joyfully, their entire bodies wagging, leaping down the steps to meet me. I pet them and crouch so they can lick my face. I'm delaying. I have no idea how to talk with my husband. I kiss him and sit down in a rocking chair.

He is quiet for a few minutes, then says, "Shame about Karen.

I can hardly believe it."

I nod. I don't want to talk about her, but I have to know how he found out it was her. "Was it on the news?"

"Not that I know of. The detectives were here."

Neither one of us says anything further. I go inside and fix scrambled eggs and salad for supper, unable to concentrate enough to cook anything more complex. I spend a long time in the kitchen, cleaning the counters, scrubbing the toaster and the electric can opener, and getting the grease out of the crevices on the stove.

Then it's bedtime, and we kiss good night and lie there. I get up, take a slug of NyQuil, and then fall asleep, only to wake up at three o'clock and fidget until the alarm goes off at five.

— 👧 —

At the office, the volunteers are gathered, exchanging information about Karen, their voices hushed and eager, sad and excited all at the same time.

"Her divorce was final two weeks ago, but I bet she didn't changed the beneficiary on her insurance," says one.

"You think her husband did it?" asks another.

"It has to be the nephew; he gets her house and her bank accounts," a third one says.

"I heard she had an affair with Tommy, the guy who used to take care of the butterfly garden, and his wife found out. That's why he hasn't been back to volunteer."

So that's what happened to our butterfly garden. The comments kept coming.

"What about her boyfriend, the doctor?" says the first one. "I heard he messed up an operation and the patient, a woman, died, and her husband's out to get him. Maybe this was a revenge killing."

"How do y'all know all this?" I ask.

"Are you kidding?" one of them says. "She talks non-stop. She's a walking soap opera. I mean, she was."

"She told you all that stuff?"

"Oh, yes. She never stopped talking."

Evidently, Karen did talk to people about her personal life— just not to me. Was that because she was after my husband?

Do these volunteers know this? Do they wonder if she and my husband had an affair? Do they discuss it when I'm not around?

Kamil comes in, and the volunteers surround him, asking for news. I smile at him, but he gives me a long, appraising look. I stare back, wondering what he's thinking. He says nothing to me, and my throat is too dry to speak. Does he think I did it? What happened to the trust, the "I've got your back? What did the detectives tell him?

"Sorry, folks. I don't have any news for you," he says. He retreats to his office, closing his door.

Back at my desk, I try to focus on timesheets and useless reports and all the mandatory training I haven't yet completed. I have two reports due, reports populated with pointless data that the web-based world makes possible. I used to wonder who stayed awake at night to dream up the need for this information, and what they did with it. Now I'm just resigned.

The day winds to a close, and I consider excuses to stay late. I don't want to go home and face my husband's silence. I don't want to talk about Karen. I don't want to see anything in his eyes like grief. Or suspicion.

I stay until eight-thirty. I don't even call to tell him I won't be home at the usual time.

When I get there, he's sitting in front of the TV, watching an ancient re-run of Batman. I kiss him. "Did you get enough supper?" I ask, as I have almost every night since we've been married.

He nods. I see an empty can of soup in the sink, soaking. No pan. He must have eaten it right out of the can.

I go to bed.

Several more days pass, and the weekend arrives. The detectives don't return. My husband and I avoid each other. We go to Mass, sit side by side but not touching. We don't joke with each other or talk about anything except the grocery list, and we don't snuggle at night. I feel bereft, numb, afraid of what's happening to our marriage. Did he have an affair with her in January? Did it last longer than that?

—— 🎎 ——

On Sunday afternoon, wearing loose sandals, I rummage around in the garage in search of oil for my car. My husband is off somewhere. I stub my toe hard on a sledgehammer on the floor. I scream, full-bodied and primal. I pick up the thing, ready to hurl it across the garage and smash things, but then I notice how the head looks rusty, and I freeze. Is it rust? Or something else? Now it's got my fingerprints on it. Should I wipe them off? I hide it behind a pile of lumber, my throat so dry I start coughing.

The next week, things are seemingly back to normal at work. Visitors come and go. The staff churns away at their assorted tasks: travel vouchers, reports, annual plans, and occasionally even wildlife management or environmental education when time allows. We continue preparations for the upcoming Wildlife Festival, wondering if we should cancel it or have a moment of silence or something.

At home, I fix supper, tidy the kitchen, and talk with my husband only to coordinate tasks or add things to the grocery list.

On Thursday, a little over a week since she was killed, the medical examiner releases her body, and the nephew and the ex-husband schedule a memorial service for the following Tuesday. They're having her cremated, because the ex hasn't been able to get his insurance check yet. Or so the volunteers tell me.

The night before the funeral, I sit with my husband in front of the TV.

"Are you going to the memorial service?" I ask.

He nods, but he doesn't look my way.

"So am I," I say. "We should go together."

He nods again.

The next day at the service, I don't look at his face, but I'm alert to every movement. He seems to shake a little during *Amazing Grace*. Guilt? Grief? Pity? I'm wracked with grief, but not for Karen. I'm afraid for my marriage. I've lost connection with my husband, and I want it back. No matter what.

After the service, I go to the office. The admin assistant stops me.

"What's up with you and Kamil?" she asks. "Y'all don't talk

to each other. Heck, you don't talk to anyone. You just work. Are you all right?"

"It's all just a strain not knowing who killed her," I say. "It's so weird that someone did."

"The police will figure it out. My money's on the nephew, Matthew," she says.

"I just wish they'd hurry up with it," I say, groaning. "I know they're doing their best, but this is horrible. What if the killer's someone we know?" What if it's my husband? I force my thoughts off that road.

"They'll get him."

She hugs me, and the comfort I feel catches me by surprise. We're like a family – when one of us is stressed, it affects every one of us, and this murder has us all on edge.

That night, after we're in bed, my husband says, "I didn't realize you were so close to Karen."

I frown, confused. "I wasn't."

"You seem so upset about her death," he says. "You're so quiet and withdrawn."

I study his face. I still have my lamp on, and he is lying on his side, facing me, but his expression is blank, as in carefully blank.

"She texted you," I say.

"I know. She must have wondered why she never got a response." He watches me, his eyes hopeful, a little scared maybe.

"She probably did," I agree and turn over, my back to him. I can't believe what I'm starting to think. What if it were him? I take in a deep breath and let it all out in a rush. If it was him, he had good reason. I begin to rebuild my marriage in my mind on that shaky rock. Maybe he made a mistake. We all make mistakes.

I roll back over and put my hand on his shoulder. He reaches for me and pulls me tight against him, and we lie there for some time, not talking, then fall asleep.

———— 🐼 ————

A little more than a week later, on the last Thursday in April, the Wildlife Festival begins. Visitors, volunteers, and staff mill around the front desk. I go back and forth between the front desk and my office. I've gotten a little behind on things, what with all that's been going on, and I have more reports to complete. I haven't talked with the Zone in a while, and she hasn't relinquished supervision of Kamil yet.

Kamil taps on the doorjamb. "You have a minute?"

I smile, relieved. He's talking to me again. It's a start.

He doesn't smile back. "They arrested Matthew, the nephew," he says.

"Really?" I say. "Do you think he did it?" I'm babbling, just happy it's finally over, glad they've caught the killer.

He stares at me a few seconds, shrugs, and touches his gun. Then he walks away, looking over his shoulder at me as if he's watching his own back.

I feel like I'm sinking. He doesn't believe the nephew did it. Why?

He won't let it go until he's unearthed every clue. He's a good officer.

But he'll never find that hammer.

WAR AND MURDER
AT NIMROD HALL

By Vivian Lawry

POUNDING RATTLES THE FRONT door. I follow as Rebecca opens it to Capt. Daniel A. Stofer, Assistant Provost Marshal. After throat clearing and foot shuffling, he says, "I'm right sorry to bring bad news—more bad news." Bath County's been under martial law since early 1862, so he could be here about anything. "But a body's turned up on your farm. Dr. Tilden says he's Samuel Cecil, a soldier who's been recuperating here. When did you see him last?"

Rebecca frowns. "Three mornings ago, I believe."

I feel faint. "Sam Cecil is dead? But he just left!"

"And who are you, ma'am?"

"Clara . . . Bruce." Why not? One name's as good as another.

"When, exactly, did he leave?"

"Two mornings ago."

"That's the last time you saw him?"

"No, I saw him last the night before, when we returned from the Warm Springs Baths. While we were gone, Rebecca—Miz Wood—received word of her husband's death. She was distraught. Sam retired. I stayed with Miz Wood. When he didn't come down the next morning, I went to his room. His things were gone. I found a scribbled note, saying he'd imposed long enough and was rejoining his unit."

"Do you have that note?"

"I threw it in the tinderbox."

A thorough search of the tinderbox turns up no note.

Capt. Stofer eyes me from under bushy brows. "You were the last person to see him alive. You claim he left a note. Nobody else saw that note, and nobody saw him leave." The captain rubs his chin. "You ain't from around here. How come you to be in these parts?"

—— 🌣 ——

Major Bruce's uniform and the letter from General R. E. Lee ordering him to report for duty in the west got him a railway pass. He wheedled a seat for me, claiming I was his wife. The last leg of our journey was by Virginia Central Rail from Gordonsville to Millboro Depot.

So here I stand, hot and dusty in the August heat. The small wooden building nestled against the hillside seems largely abandoned. Two soldiers stand casual patrol, nominally guarding dozens of loaded railcars that crowd the sidings. The Major looks down his nose at the man in charge. "Sir, this laxness is indefensible!"

The depot hand spits into the dirt by the step. "Well, now, Major, I reckon it might look that way to regular army. But truth be told, there ain't much military action 'round here. And iff'n a body took a mind to steal the niter or corn or such like, he'd have to haul it away by wagon, 'cuz we ain't got but the one working engine what brought you in, and she's on her way back soon as we turn her around."

"Huh." The Major looks like thunder, but after a few seconds he says, "Where can we get rooms around here?"

"Well, now, there's the hotel yonder. But betimes it's used as a hospital, and then most of the rooms're commandeered." He pushes back his cap and scratches his bald spot. "Then there's the Wood place, 'bout three miles up the road—used to be called the White House, but now it's called Nimrod Hall. It's a big farm on the Cowpasture River, and sometimes Miz Wood'll take a boarder." He sends another stream of tobacco juice in the Major's direction and shifts his chaw to the other cheek. His eyes skitter sideways, and he lowers his voice. "Course, there's some respectable folk don't even speak to her, let alone stay there. Her husband's off fightin' for the cause, leaving her on the farm with four little uns—and she goes and gets a bean up the spout . . . The thing is, that didn't accord with her husband's last home leave. When her time come, she went upstairs alone and closed the door. The next morning she produced neither a baby nor an explanation." He glances expectantly at me, but I hold my tongue and my countenance. He shrugs. "It was some months back. And I hear she sets a good table."

The Major draws me aside. "A mother alone, surely she needs money. And if there's a mite of scandal, maybe she'll not question us, as long as the rent's paid."

I nod and we set off afoot, our baggage tied onto his horse.

Nimrod Hall is a handsome log house. It sits atop a hill overlooking rolling pastures and fields sloping away in all directions, with glimpses of the Cowpasture at the bottom. Two stories, with glass in the windows and porches on two sides, it speaks of prosperity and peace. It looks like the sort of place to suit me well.

Miz Wood is neat and pretty but for the drawn look about her eyes. She has a toddler on her hip and a little one hanging on her skirts. Two bigger children, I'd guess six and eight, stare at us, big-eyed.

She listens in silence as the Major introduces himself, adding, "And this is my wife, Clara. We need a place to stay." He hands her enough money for two rooms for a week.

She eyes me up and down—bonnet to walking shoes, blond curls to ringless ring finger —but her only comment is, "Kindly come this way." She shows us to upstairs rooms at the front of the house. None of us mentions the connecting door. I reckon Miz Wood and I'll get along just fine.

At morning light the Major rides off to the Depot, and I wander around the main downstairs room. I run my fingers along the golden stone fireplace, 1783 carved into the chimney, and pace the broad plank floors, looking for something to do. Eventually, I offer to help with the mending. "I've always been good with a needle."

"There's no need," Miz Woods says. "You're paying your way."

I cock an eye at the overflowing wicker basket by the window. "It looks like you could use a hand—and I got nothing better to do."

She nods. "Whatever we can do while the light's still good and the little ones're asleep." I take the rocker beside hers, and she hands me a blue flowered dress, a three-cornered tear in the skirt. "I swear, there never was a girl so hard on clothes as

Mattie. Bad as her brothers, she is." She ties a knot in her thread and cuts a look at me. "So why did you decide to travel with the Major? Isn't it dangerous?"

I notice that she didn't call him my husband. "He was heading west and I wanted to." I look at her straight on and cock one eyebrow. "Let's say he was my way of getting here."

"Why would you be wanting to come here?"

I laugh. "I didn't want to come here so much as leave there. There's too much war around Richmond. And the sheriff took against me."

I can see questions in her eyes, but she only shakes her head. "You can't get away from the war—not even here. Union raiding parties steal supplies stored at the depot and plunder farms. Whenever I hear they're coming, I get the children and the livestock and whatever valuables I can carry to the mountains." She sighs. "Frank volunteered for the Bath Grays right after secession, for a year. But he was still in the Army at harvest in '62. He was right worried, wrote to me about how to get scarce supplies. I tried to hire a replacement for him—not one to be found anywhere—and since Gettysburg, he's been in a Yankee prison at Fort Delaware. I've got to run the farm on my own till he gets home." Her voice is low and level, but I think I hear a note of desperation. Two days after this conversation, the Major takes his leave. "If I get back this way, I'll surely stop by."

I neither know the nature of his orders west nor wonder. For me, this bloody war is background to my usual life. I sometimes wonder how many feel likewise. He is scarcely over the mountain when we hear gunfire and pounding hooves from the direction of Millboro Depot. I look to Rebecca.

She's pale as moonlight. "We had no warning!" She scrambles to put silver under a loose plank in the floor. She shouts to Mattie and Lewis, "Loose the stock! Drive them toward the river!"

It being too late to flee, we gather the children at the table. "Eat hardy, now. We don't know what's coming," Rebecca says.

So we all fall to, shoveling in stew, slicking butter onto cornbread, gulping milk. Then we wait. While Rebecca nurses the youngest, I recite nursery rhymes and fairytales to the older children.

By nightfall, all is quiet. Rebecca and I sit through the night together. In the morning, concluding we've been passed by, Rebecca dispatches the older children to round up the livestock and chickens. She tosses a rope over a tree limb and ties one end around the middle of each of the littlest ones, allowing them to toddle around. We leave for the Depot for news.

Halfway there, we find a soldier shot through the chest and right shoulder blade. He moans. I turn to Rebecca. "We can't leave him."

"He's good as dead."

"But not dead yet!" Our eyes lock in silent contest. When she shrugs, I strip off my skirt. Rebecca looks aghast. I grin and roll the man onto my skirt. Together we carry him to the house—uphill all the way—stopping to rest every few yards.

Death usually comes from infection; I know that much. I wrap a clean silk handkerchief around a knitting needle and pass it through his body to remove debris. It comes through fine, bits of dirt and metal caught in the folds. He moans. "Nothing to do now but bandage him up."

Rebecca nods. "Not that different from farm wounds." She returns carrying spider webs, vinegar, eggshell membrane, oiled silk, several strips of cotton, and a small bowl containing egg white.

I dab diluted vinegar around the wounds, put the spider webs and egg membrane over the holes to help stop bleeding.

"I haven't had time to render glue for. . . oh, a right long time," Rebecca says. "The best I could do is some egg white. But maybe it'll help keep things in place."

We cover the wounds with oiled silk to keep things moist, crossing the silk with cotton strips, the ends damped in egg white.

"Now it's up to him. He'll heal or he won't." I wipe my face with my apron. "But I'm gonna walk down to the Depot. If they've made the hotel a hospital again, might be I can bring back a doctor."

The hotel in Millboro Springs is indeed a hospital again. I meet Dr. Jacob Tilden, a good-looking man of thirty or so. His crooked smile reveals slightly crooked teeth. They're white, testifying to his frequent use of tooth twigs. I like that. As my gaze sweeps his figure, I admire his manly form as much as his cleft chin. He has broad shoulders and a tapered waist, so as he eyes me from head to toe and back again, I'm hopeful that the slight bulge in his britches reflects more than a carefully tucked shirttail. It's been too long since anyone buttered my bun—that not being part of the Major's pleasures, which were best met by looking and smelling. I always ask for payment in silver or gold, which I stitch into the hems of dresses and petticoats. I came prepared, but I've been paying my way with Rebecca since Major Bruce left. I need a little companionship—not to mention income. "Please come, Doctor." I use my purring kitten voice. It's always worked before. "He may be in dire need of your skill."

I flirt with him shamelessly on the three-mile walk back to Nimrod—smiling, batting my lashes, touching his arm at every opportunity—trying to let him know without actually saying that I'm rentable for riding. He cuts sideways looks at me, blushes, and helps me over minor rough places.

While Dr. Tilden examines him, the soldier wakes. He says his name is Samuel Cecil. "Shot three times, three times lucky. In June, it was my right ankle joint. In July, my left leg. Now this minnie ball. Three red badges of courage. They must've thought I was too far gone to take prisoner and left me to die." His voice is thready. "But you, my angels of mercy, put paid to that."

"You ladies've done a right fine job," Dr. Tilden says before turning to Sam. "But you're not out of the woods by a long shot. I won't lie to you. If infection sets in, I can't do much. I mean, there's nothing to amputate. You take it easy, and do what these good ladies say."

As I walk him to the door, he says, "I'm impressed. Where did you learn nursing?"

"I've no formal training. But I worked some at Sally Tomkins' hospital in Richmond." The lie hurts no one. I see no reason to talk about houses of sin I've known, the beatings, diseases, abortions, births, and deaths I've seen. I learned things.

"Well, I'd surely welcome your services at the hospital." I agree to come the next day.

Help being so scarce, no one questions my qualifications. I learn quickly. The continuous suture is already familiar; the interrupted suture and cross suture are easy. Even the double-needled suture takes only a couple of trials. The needles aren't that different from those for sewing, embroidery, or quilting. I need only adjust to the texture of flesh versus linen. Dr. Tilden admires my small stitching exceedingly. I admire Dr. Tilden.

Rebecca and I wash and dress Sam's wound daily, feed him broth and gruel, and comfort him with cool cloths on his forehead. Returning to strength, he turns talkative. He plucks at the quilt across his chest. "You know, I hate to say so, but I was shot by one of our own. I had a good horse, and he had none. He shot me sure as sure, took my mount, and hightailed it over the mountain. I'd swear he wasn't rejoining our unit."

I report this conversation to Dr. Tilden.

"Unfortunately, there've been traitors in every war ever fought. Human nature will out," the doctor says. He dips his chin and looks at me from under his brows, clears his throat, and tugs at his collar. "Before he left, Major Bruce gave me a card." He withdraws a small rectangle from his waistcoat pocket.

I immediately recognize it as my carte-de-visité. The card bears a picture of me, naked, facing a blank wall on which I am drawing a picture of a butterfly. A red heart tattoo on my right buttock, the heart pierced by a blue arrow, advertises the general nature of my specialized services. When Colonel Levereaux and I established the Butterfly League, these cards were passed among men of good character, and given to me as a sort of reference. Jacob clears his throat again. "I understand you're amenable to providing . . . special pleasures."

I nod and smile. "What do you have in mind?" And thus I learn that the good doctor likes to be wrapped up like a mummy.

"Put me in my death shroud," he says, and hands me a picture. He dons pajamas and brings forth a crate of roller bandages. "I'll stand by the bed. Start at my feet. I'll guide you." He gives me a tube. "When you wrap my head, I'll use this for breathing. I won't be able to speak clearly, but any noise I make three times is the safe signal. Can I trust you to cut me free?"

"Why would I not?" I smile.

And so I wrap him toe to head, eyes, ears, and all. When his time's up, I cut him free with surgical scissors and we share a jolly celebration of his return from death. We settle into quite a pleasurable routine, using his room in the hotel hospital when we aren't medically engaged.

One evening over supper I say, "You know, Jacob—Dr.

Tilden—thinks there's a Union plan to destroy mills, grain fields, provender of every kind. Leastwise, that's what our officers say. The Union wants to leave the valley so bare a crow crossing would have to carry his provisions."

At this, Rebecca harrumphs. "If our government leaves anything for the raiders!" She's concerned that the tax-in-kind will leave her barely able to subsist. Since July, she—along with all the other farmers—must pay one tenth of her crops to the Confederate Government.

It's Sam's first meal at the table. "Do tell." He takes another biscuit. "How would the Union know anything about anything— enough to plot something like that?"

"Dr. Tilden says we—our officers—think there's a spy ring operating out of Warm Springs."

"Surely not!" Sam says.

Rebecca pauses in tending the children. "I can believe it. In 1860, we had strong feeling here against separation of North and South. At a meeting in Red Holes we adopted a resolution ordering our representative to do everything in his power to prevent Virginia's succession. Of course, after the vote went the other way, most people supported the Dominion. But early as '61, counties over the mountains started agitating to separate from Virginia. West Virginia's officially Union now." She sounds so agitated, I wonder just how closely she's tied to the Union. "Why, look at the Terrill family right here in Bath County— their place is in the hills overlooking Warm Springs village, as a matter of fact. Old William Terrill and three of his sons side with the Confederacy. But his daughter and her husband live in West Virginia, and Young William went Union. I hear he's a Brigadier General now, disowned by his father and brothers. Believing there's no pro-Union sentiment around here would be foolhardy."

I'm not political, and I'd as soon give a ride to a Union man as Johnny Reb. In my experience, it isn't where he's from that makes a good man or a bad one. I'd guess one soldier in this war is pretty much like another, fighting for a cause he believes in— suffering and dying—missing wife or girlfriend and home. But I see no need to say any of that.

—— 🐾 ——

After some weeks, when recovery seems complete, Sam makes advances. He starts with compliments, then holds my hand while he gazes soulfully into my eyes, thanking me for nursing him. "I've saved my pay. How better to spend it than on a pretty little lady like you?"

"No better way at all!" I say.

In his room that night he says, "Call me Boots," and I soon discover the source of his nickname: he bids me parade around wearing nothing but his hat and fine boots, occasionally tapping his riding crop against the glossy leather, until he's greatly impassioned. I'm sure Rebecca suspected my relationship with Jacob early on, even though I never bring him to the house. With Sam, she's too smart not to tumble to it, even though we take care, never doing anything till after the children are abed. But Rebecca doesn't ask. I don't tell.

What with keeping the farm going and caring for the children, Rebecca and I become something of a team, sharing everything from cooking to gardening to hauling water from the spring at the head of the pond up to the house. A yoke of oxen pulls the two-wheeled cart—but we still have to fill the water barrel! Laboring together, I start to think what it would be like to have a sister.

Over the bread making one day, Rebecca says, "I didn't kill the baby, you know." She cuts a look at me. "I know you've heard the stories. Folks think the worst. But the baby was stillborn. I buried her down by the river, a nice peaceful place near a little fall in the Cowpasture. I don't know what will happen when Frank comes home. He'll surely hear the rumors. But at least there won't be a public grave in the family burial plot."

"Why didn't you get rid of it? Early on, I mean. Lots of women do."

"I tried," she says, her laugh bitter. "The newspapers are full of ads for patent medicines by mail order—everywhere from Louisville to New York City—to . . . treat my condition. But nothing around here, leastwise nothing I could find. I came across a brochure describing Doctor Andrus's Medicines, and I sent two dollars to an address in Ohio, that being closest. Nothing ever came. Maybe it wouldn't have worked anyway. Eventually I heard that this so-called doctor was a private in the Union Army and was tried for disloyalty, desertion, and correspondence with the enemy. That's me, I guess. And then . . . once I felt the baby quicken, I didn't have it in me to try anything. But when she was stillborn, I counted it a blessing."

I pat her hand. "If you have a need, I can give you some French letters."

"French letters?"

Her puzzlement embarrasses me, and I look aside. I'd forgotten I was talking to a lady. "It's a . . . barrier . . . made of India rubber, gutta percha, or lamb skin. A man wears it when . . . to. . . um . . .you know. They come in paper envelopes, and if you wash them carefully, they last a long time." I feel a bit defiant when I add, "I use them all the time. You must've guessed my usual trade. I can't risk being left high in the belly—or diseased. Some of my clients object, say it's like taking pleasures in galoshes, but I say, 'No protection, no pleasures at all.' Given the proclivities of the Butterfly League, they nearly always comply."

"The Butterfly League?"

And so it all spills out. "I've been on my own since my parents died, when I was twelve. There was no family to take me in. Maybe you think I should take honest work. A spindle operator gets eight dollars a week! A scullery maid gets room and board and a dollar a week. A . . . lady of easy virtue . . . can get three or four dollars a go. But it's dangerous. Most women in my line are dead by age twenty-five." I suppress a shudder and grin instead. "Plying my trade among men with special interests is safer than run-of-the-mill prostitution. I let them paint my body with chocolate, cover me with jewels, tickle me with feathers, make love on pianos or in coffins. I don't do whips or chains or knives, nothing worse than satin ribbons as ties. And here I am, alive and well."

Rebecca's complexion turns ruddy but she shrugs. "Who am I to judge? You do what you gotta do."

I often wonder about her dead baby's father. Is he local? Is he still around? Did he know? How did it happen? Does Rebecca care for him? More than for her husband? I ask none of those questions. Who am I to judge?

That night as Sam and I rest after our endeavors, he says,

"How did you come to be here anyway?"

I'd just made him happy in all the ways he likes best. I settle my head on his shoulder and trace circles on his bare chest. "There was this dead body in Hollywood Cemetery in '61, not long after First Manassas. Nothing to do with me directly, but Sheriff Coltrain thought otherwise because the dead man was wearing women's pink satin underwear. Even after I found out who did it and why, he eyed me like he was a robin at a wormhole. I knew that if I so much as poked my head up in Richmond again, he'd snip me in half and eat me raw. That's when I came west." I roll over onto my side and curl up. Just thinking about the sheriff gives me goosebumps.

"You know, Clara, the Seven Days Battles, Harpers Ferry, Antietam—just to name a few—tell us this here war's gonna be long and bloody. I say that's all the more reason we should have a little fun." Sam props himself up on his elbow. "Warm Springs ain't all that far." He drops one big calloused paw onto my shoulder. I don't shrug it off, so he snugs up behind me.

When he licks the back of my neck, I wriggle away. "Cut that out." I speak softly, and put a smile in my voice. "You got what you paid for and then some. Now, what kind of fun do you have in mind?"

"Well, there's pools of healing waters there, spring fed. Jefferson himself partook. The men's bathing house is older, and completely separate from the ladies'—even fed by separate springs, so it's safe as Christmas. No worry about picking up anything because of run-off from the men." He nips my shoulder.

I box his ears—and agree to taking a jaunt to the baths.

Sam hires two horses from Rebecca, and on the next fine day we make the trek to Warm Springs, about fifteen miles across the mountains. The road is rough and dusty, but turning trees all along the way keep the trip beautiful, and the crisp fall weather saves us from sweltering.

We arrive midday and decide to take the waters before our picnic, both to avoid the potential for cramping and for the general refreshment of it. The buildings appear quite similar, both made of white painted wood with roofs open to the elements. Beside the door to the Ladies Pool House a small plaque announces it was built in 1836.

I leave my clothes in one of the alcoves around the pool provided for the purpose and slip into the water. A dozen other ladies are taking the waters, most in bathing shifts. I surprise myself by feeling self-conscious. I've taken my clothes off more often than a hound scratches fleas. I guess what makes the difference is that it's women eyeing me. I look as good as any, better than most. I rally, smile and nod—no talking above a whisper allowed in the pool in any case—and relax into water the temperature of my body. After a bit, I hear some of the whispers are about me. I realize that my heart tattoo is clearly visible through the crystal water. I blush. But shrinking isn't my nature. I give a little tail wiggle and a dazzling smile and settle onto my back. Tiny bubbles kissing me here and there, I watch wind-driven clouds float across the open roof and forget whispers, forget there even is a war.

By the time I meet Sam for our picnic, I've shaken the dust from my clothes and braided my hair atop my head. I'm hungry enough to eat a mule, tail and all. Sam has spread the blanket and laid out food. He's propped up on his elbows, ankles crossed.

"Good gracious! What happened to your boots?"

Sam chuckles, his cheeks a dusky tan. "Pretty disreputable, huh? I guess I shouldn't have left my fine boots so visible in the clothes alcove. I was the last one out of the water, and these were the only boots left." He waggles his eyebrows at me. "Perhaps a little variety will be good for our pleasures?" My giggle seems to be response enough.

We're both relaxed as wet ribbon, and speak little. The ride home is mostly comfortable silence. We arrive as the moon hits zenith. While Sam tends the horses, I walk to the house. As I open the door, I hear muffled sobs. "Rebecca?" I follow the sound of weeping and find her face-down on her bed, fully clothed. I lay a hand on her shaking shoulder. "Whatever has happened?"

"He's dead. Frank died of dysentery in that damn Yankee prison—on October 2, and I didn't even know! What's to become of us? How can we keep body and soul together?" She again muffles her sobs in her pillow.

When I hear Sam come in, I step out of Rebecca's room to tell him what's happened. He pats my shoulder. "Your place is with Rebecca." He grins. "Not that I won't miss your pleasures, but now isn't the right time." I kiss him soundly on each cheek and return to Rebecca quicker than quick.

By morning, Rebecca is again her stoic self, only a little sadder around the eyes. "Your daddy's died in that Yankee prison," she tells her children over breakfast. "You must always remember him, and what a brave hero he was."

The littler ones start to blubber, and I wonder how much they even remember of him.

"Everything's gonna be all right," Rebecca says. "It will be hard, but we'll make do—just like we been doing." She clears her throat. "Now eat your grits. We got chores to do."

When I realize that Sam hasn't appeared, I go to his room and find a scribbled note: I'm heading over the mountain to rejoin my unit. I should have gone already, but life here's been so welcoming. To intrude on Miz Wood's hospitality longer would be unconscionable under the circumstances. Yours most respectfully, Samuel Cecil.

I think how very considerate of Sam, for Rebecca refused payment from a recuperating soldier, much as she could use the money. "I'd want some kind lady to do as much for Frank, should he be in need," she often said.

Two days later, Capt. Stofer bangs on Rebecca's door, tells us Sam's body has been found on the farm, and asks all those questions. He obviously thinks I'm lying.

"But why would I want to kill him?"

The Captain has no motive to offer. I guess that's why he doesn't take me into custody. Still, I'm a suspect in a murder case—again.

As soon as the Captain leaves, I hurry to the hospital. "The Captain thinks I killed Sam. I know he does. But why?"

Jacob shrugs. "It's a suspicious time. A good-looking woman shows up with an army officer who says he's her husband but leaves her in a house touched by scandal, she keeps to herself but for work at the hospital, and the place is overrun by Union raids. Then you go to Warm Springs Baths, and everyone knows—believes, anyway—there's a spy ring operating there." He shrugs again.

"But I didn't even talk to anyone!" I massage my temples. "You don't think I killed him, do you?"

"Of course not. But nobody's asking me." He scowls. "You shouldn't have gone there—with him. I don't like it one bit!"

Odd, but I hadn't tumbled to the possibility that Jacob might be jealous. "Done is done. You saw the body, though. How did he die?"

"He was knifed several times—maybe tortured. His pockets and knapsack had been rifled, everything strewn about. That's what Capt. Stofer said."

"Can I see his things?"

"I gave them to other soldiers in need. Except his boots. I kept them for myself." He flushes and looks sheepish. "I needed new boots and his are exceptionally fine."

I look at the fine glossy leather encasing Jacob's calves. "Those are the boots he was wearing? But those were stolen! When we left the baths, he was wearing scruffy butternut. Take them off."

Jacob looks startled but does so. Together we examine the boots, inside and out. Jacob says, "Nothing."

"They must be important! How could he have gotten them back?" I turn one of the familiar boots over, inspecting the sole and heel. The heel feels a bit wobbly, and when I twist it, it turns, opening to a small cavity. I remove a paper, folded small. We smooth the page, both bending close.

"It appears to be a list of stores at Milboro Depot, and a schedule of some sort," Jacob says. "Troop movements? Guard duties? Why would he have this?"

"Hidden in his boot? I'd say he was part of that spy ring. The baths are a meeting place, changing boots a way of passing messages. I was part of his disguise!"

"Maybe he was all disguise, even his name. Soldiers have no official identification. They just say who they are. A passel of men avoid Courts Martial by giving fake names." Jacob scowls. "We must tell Capt. Stofer. I've no doubt his spying got him killed."

"He must've met his Warm Springs contact and traded boots again. His killer followed? Knew he was a spy, anyway, but not where he carried the message. Maybe spying's what got him shot 'by one of our own' in the first place! Unfortunately, none of this clears me of anything."

I walk back to Nimrod Hall, thinking I need to leave, wondering how I can. That evening with Rebecca is subdued, my thoughts elsewhere.

—— 🝰 ——

In the morning Lewis and Edward are feverish, coughing and complaining of sore throats. I hasten to fetch Jacob.

"I can't tell yet, but it could be the onset of measles. Keep them quiet. Try to get them to take nourishment, at least broth." When I walk him to the door, he says, "There's nothing to do but watch for the rash and try to keep their fevers down. Don't let anyone in the room. If it's measles, they spread."

Both Rebecca and I've had measles, and you don't get them twice. I convince her to let me tend the boys. "The younger ones need you more, and we shouldn't both be carrying the germs about."

"Germs?"

"It's the latest thinking among medical men about spreading diseases. The best thing is to wash often and keep things clean. And not let more people than necessary in the sick room."

I take a cot into the boys' room to be within call. Rebecca brings food and basins of cool water. A couple of days later the rash begins, first behind their ears and in their hair. When I tell Rebecca, she pales. "Oh, Lord, spare us the pneumonia."

I read and sing to them, try to keep them quiet as scarlet splotches cover their bodies, barely a white speck anywhere. They fuss and throw off their bedclothes, burning with fever. Rebecca carries buckets of water so I can fill a tub and immerse them.

One evening she says, "Capt. Stofer came again today. He has more questions for you. I told him you're nursing the measles, that he shouldn't expose himself, maybe spread it to the troops. He'll be back in a few days."

I nod. I can't leave the boys now.

The splotches recede first from their faces, then their trunks. The worst is over. When their thighs and feet clear, the Captain'll be on me like a bear with a sore head and poison ivy up his butt. As rain drums the roof, I consider ways to convince the Captain I'm innocent. With the war and all, he doesn't need more'n suspicion to arrest someone.

In my room that night, I bundle my five dresses and petticoats, high-heeled shoes and slippers, corsets and stockings, hairbrush and mirror, sewing kit and trinket box into two carpetbags. Lastly, I pack the carefully wrapped packet of French letters, leaving one on the dresser for Rebecca. No note. She's safer not knowing. I sneak out into the night and the rain, hoping I won't be caught in a flash flood.

A HOUSE ON JEFFERSON STREET

By Michael McGowan

THE DUPLEX ON JEFFERSON wasn't Monica's choice. Three months fresh out of college and the only teaching position she had been able to find was ninth grade math at Brunswick County's only junior high. Of course she had tried to find a place to live more local, but in a backwoods like Brunswick the only options were actual houses, which would require things like mortgages and upkeep that Monica couldn't afford. And at thirty thousand a year, Monica made too much money to qualify for federally subsidized apartments, which seemed alarmingly numerous in these parts.

So the last, best option was renting one half of a duplex off Jefferson and Main in Emporia, twenty miles down Rt. 58. Forty-mile commute—everyday.

Monica wonders if it would have been more fiscally responsible to remain unemployed.

First week of her job, she bought relaxation CDs. By the third week, she was spending her Saturday mornings down at the Greenville ABC store, stocking up "care packages" to get her through the week.

By October, she was test-driving a Xanax prescription.

Three blocks of ninety minutes each, twenty-nine or so kids in each class. The demographics says it all. Birth dates indicate that at least half of them should be sophomores or juniors by now. She has two girls who have babies at home and one in her first block who is showing.

Her last class of the day would be three students heavier, the football coach told her, if they hadn't gotten their asses tossed into jail before Labor Day.

It's this class where it all begins.

Two-thirty in the afternoon, the dusk horizon of the Xanax. Weariness comes back. The fear comes back. Just a half hour to bridge on nothing but pure determination.

She tries to wrap up a lesson on quadratic equations to an audience who, based on what she's seen so far, have a good day when they're able to do long division. Glazed looks, heads on desks are her reward. A knock comes at the door. Monica puts down her chalk and answers.

The girl is an eighth grader. That's all Monica knows. Ratty sneakers, faded jeans, ugly purple top. She looks stern and purposeful and hands Monica a folded piece of paper.

Why would an eighth grade teacher have a student courier a note to her?

The answer is obvious too quickly. She unfolds the paper. It's blank.

In that moment, the split second Monica was distracted enough to examine the fake note, the courier has zeroed in on one of her students, one of the baby mommas, and has gone full tilt battering ram, knocking over the table-chair one-piece onto its side, pinning her left leg. The girl's hollering may be coming from that injury, or from the repeated punches the eighth grader lays into her face.

The class, dulled by math, jump from their chairs and circle around. Monica hears someone shout, "Kill that bitch!" Common sense fleeting, she plows her way into the ruckus. She grabs for the intruder, but the girl's thrashing around so hard she feels as if she's got a grip of a different body part at any given time. A shoulder. An arm. Her hair.

Over the noise of thirty-two students, Monica hears the intruder screech with rage. This is followed by a blow to the gut that makes Monica curl up in a fetal position and cry out. By this time the classroom's been invaded by the school's security officer, a burly man in slacks and a turquoise polo. As soon as they see him, the jeering crowd goes dead and gets out of the way. He grabs the intruder by the wrists and drags her out of the room.

Out of the quiet, punctuated by the girl's diminished screaming as she's dragged down the hall, Monica's class begins to socialize, trash talk back and forth. Getting the idea that class is dismissed, they grab their things and exit, leaving their papers and textbooks on their desks, and leaving Monica alone on the floor.

The school nurse cleans Monica up. Bandage here. Antiseptic there. "Not that bad, really," she says. "Nothing you won't survive."

For some reason the nurse doesn't notice that Monica is crying.

Straight from the nurse's office Monica's summoned to see the principal. Closed-door session.

Sit down. Would you like some water? We really need to talk.

The principal begins a litany of concerns. Low grades. Difficulty keeping control of a classroom.

"Why did you open your door for a student?"

Apparently in some reaches of the county there are families engaged in a kind of Hatfield and McCoy scenario with others, and the adults are perfectly content to let the kids play it out in the halls of the school.

"And, for the love of God, why did you step in? You know what kind of a liability issue that could have been?"

He then changes the subject.

"What are your plans for next year?"

Monica returns to the house on Jefferson Street about six-thirty, as it's getting dark. Exhausted, depleted, defeated, and still stinging from that shot to the gut, she's not in the mood to make dinner, so she picked it up on the way home. This wasn't difficult. If there is anything a town like Emporia doesn't lack, it's a supply of joints like Wendy's and Burger King. Sitting smack-dab at the intersection of Rt. 58 and I-95, there's little here that isn't built for the purposes of transience and convenience.

Monica once mused, *I'm stuck in a place where most people only spend thirty minutes at a time.*

When she finally sits, her sadness is beyond the register of her typical bad-day malaise. She doesn't want to read, watch TV, or even get on Facebook and read how her classmates and childhood friends are living lives that aren't running them through the gears. She leaves the fast food bag, unopened, on the dining room table and goes upstairs and goes to bed.

The sound wakes her at two in the morning. Monica's been sleeping since seven, yet her body and mind are languid, and it takes her a minute to wonder if the shuttering sound is real or her imagination. Then, there it is again, a burst of plastic-on-plastic scraping that continues for maybe five seconds, but then repeats five seconds later.

The sound is familiar. When she moved in in August, Monica replaced the dirty curtains downstairs with cheap Wal-Mart venetian blinds. Not artful, barely even utilitarian. But what annoys her the most is the grating sound they make whenever she pulls them up, the slats rubbing against each other.

Plastic-on-plastic.

She grabs for her phone. Her first instinct is to dial 911, but for what? Does she even know what she's hearing? Sounds in the night are regrettably nothing new. On the weekends the parking lot of the 7-Eleven next door becomes an arena for drunks raising hell, so there could be a perfectly logical explanation.

There's the sound again.

Plastic-on-plastic.

She turns on the phone's flashlight app. She searches the upper-floor's other two bedrooms first. An incredible waste of space, but a remarkable bargain. Monica had turned the smallest of the three into an office with a computer table and almost-empty file cabinet, and the other, a kind of makeshift laundry room where her ironing board stands at the ready.

Nothing.

The sound occurs again, and it's most definitely from downstairs.

She takes the stairs one step at a time, sweeping the light this way and that. Nothing moves in her limited field of vision, which makes things all the more ominous. The noise seems to cease.

The first thing she does when she reaches the first floor is check the door. Lock is engaged, deadbolt in place. Windows are closed, blinds appear to be undisturbed as well.

She ventures to the right, slides open the french doors that separate the living room from the dining room, a falsely austere touch to what is otherwise a rather ramshackle living environment, steps through, checking the windows.

Closed and locked.

She should have heard the noise again by now. Perhaps she can be glad that her middle-of-the-night rousing probably scared him off, but just the confirmation that it was someone lurking about rather than some silly flight of her imagination is haunting.

There's one more thing to check. There's a door in the kitchen that leads to a secondary set of steps. The realtor never could find the key to it, so Monica has never used it. In fact, when the weather got colder and she realized that the ill-fitting door created a draft downstairs, she went about duct-taping clear garbage bags over it.

Monica instinctively aims the light in that direction, and then her heart stops. The plastic insulation job limply hangs from the right side of the door. On the left side, the side with the handle, the tape has come loose and just brushes the floor.

Now, Monica thinks. *Time to call the cops. If somebody didn't get into the house, they were obviously trying.*

She sets her hand on the knob and gives it a faint turn. It barely moves. So it's still locked, just the way she left it.

It could be that the breeze slipped in and pushed the plastic sheeting enough that it yanked on the tape.

Monica unlocks the door and slowly opens it.

It opens only about a quarter of the way before it bumps against something at the top of the steps. She shines the light around the door, and the first thing the beam catches is the ratty sneakers the door's pressed against, then the faded juniors-sized jeans, and the eggplant-purple shirt.

Monica shrieks and slams the door shut.

The 911 operator has a devil of a time trying to get the story out of Monica. She sputters it out in breaths that alternately threaten to evolve into sobs or bouts of cardiac arrest.

"There's a body..."

"There's a body, ma'am?"

"Outside my door..."

"Did I hear you right? There's a body outside your door? Has this person been injured?"

Monica realizes she didn't bother to check on the girl's present state. When the most immediate shock had worn off, the details had flooded in.

Ratty sneakers.

Eggplant-purple shirt.

What was this girl doing at her house in the middle of the night? And why was she lying motionless on the kitchen steps?

"Ma'am, is the person by your door injured?"

It comes out in a squeak that in other circumstances would seem comical.

"I think she's dead."

A uniformed Emporia police officer arrives alone, forty-eight minutes later. Monica sits on her couch, rocking back and forth, when the piercing blue and red strobes filter between her venetian blinds. The knock at the door reveals a man with a sandy brown mustache and tired eyes.

"Ma'am, you the one with the complaint?"

Complaint. Interesting way to describe a dead person.

She spins through the whole story, a bit calmer than she was to the dispatcher, but still having to pause to collect herself here and there.

The officer asks to see the body. Monica offers to lead him to it, but he says no.

"Stay in the house until I give the all clear."

While the officer canvases around to the side of the house, Monica thinks about everything that's about to fall into her lap. It won't take long before they make the connection, that this was the intruder who assaulted one of her students and her. And then the questions that seemingly have no answer will begin to crop up.

By the time the first bell rings, she'll probably be on some kind of suspension, a less-than-friendly name for a less-than-friendly state that would have to result when the dead body of a student winds up on a teacher's property.

Nobody will officially accuse her of anything. She didn't do anything, after all, but people will talk.

In a place like this, where hope has been replaced with the

worst kind of vindictiveness, talk is all people do.

She's just about wrapped her head around the extent of this nightmare when the officer knocks on the door again.

"Ma'am, did you move the body?"

"What? No."

"You said it was around the side?" The officer points, general direction of the side of the house where the kitchen door is.

"Yes."

"On top of the steps?"

Now she just nods.

"Ma'am, there's nothing there."

This time, the officer requests that she get some shoes on and show him where she saw the body. She leads the officer around the side of the house, light from his flashlight illuminating the path. When she gets to the side steps, she sees that they are indeed empty.

"I don't understand."

The officer tries to sound as if he's not annoyed, but pretty much fails.

"Is it possible you were just seeing things? Or dreaming?"

"I didn't just see it. It was blocking the door."

She takes the officer inside, pointing out the sheeting that's partially come detached from the wall.

"It wasn't like that when I went to bed," she protests.

"I see." He nods.

She opens the door again. This time, it swings without interruption.

The officer holsters his flashlight. "Have you been drinking this evening, ma'am?"

"What, no."

"Been taking any kind of medication?"

She doesn't mention the Xanax. She hasn't taken one in nearly twenty-four hours, anyway. After this it's a series of denials as the officer ticks off one question after another, all loaded suggestions that Monica is either drunk, high, or a liar.

He tells her he'll write up the report, but since nothing was found, there's little he can do. He tells her to give the station a call back if there are any further "disturbances."

Forty-eight minutes. I'm sure you'll jump right on it.

After he's gone, she drinks about four cups of water straight from the tap to calm down. Maybe she's just tired, jumpy. Maybe the officer was right; maybe it was just a delayed reaction from the chaos today.

She could almost believe that if she had just seen the girl lying there. But the door. That was tactile. She felt it get lodged.

Could she have been partially dreaming?

She lies on the couch, wondering if she'll suddenly wake up in her bed upstairs and realize this was all some kind of nightmare.

She never falls back to sleep.

Because of her fatigue and her rattled nerves, she considers taking a sick day. But everyone will assume that the "incident" yesterday was just too much for her, and they'll talk.

Everyone here talks.

As her morning class files in, she braces herself—for what, she's not sure. A lot of not-good-natured barbs about getting decked in her own classroom. Probably some gossip. No surprise if the assailant isn't in school today. No one would expect to see her here again for the duration of a two-week suspension, but back in the neighborhoods, who knows if someone, a cousin, an aunt, an uncle, noticed that she never came home last night.

Or maybe she did.

As Monica is passing out quarterly tests, it dawns on her that she never stopped to check on the girl, never stopped to see if she was breathing. She suddenly pictures the girl, in her ratty shoes and ugly shirt, dashing away from the house after Monica slammed the door, laughing the entire time.

Sure showed that bitch-ass teacher what's-for.

A total inferno erupts. Monica realizes that her entire class is silent (the rarity is enough to get her attention) and is staring at her with confused and, in some cases, frightened expressions.

And then she notices the pain caused by the tip of the pencil that she's driven into her palm and the blood dribbling out from it.

This idea, this notion she's concocted, it's not something Monica cares to take to anyone in the administration. She'd sound crazy, but the more she thinks about it, the less crazy it seems. The girl got one of her high school cousins to drive her out to Emporia in the middle of the night to play this sadistic little prank.

It's the only thing that makes sense.

At the end of the day, she stops by to see the security guard who dragged the girl out of her room and left Monica on the floor, and asks for the girl's home address.

Just want to have a sit-down with the parents, she says. Talk about what happened.

The security officer sneers, as if this is a foolish idea and as if she's a fool for even attempting it, but gives her the address anyway.

The girl's neighborhood is a trailer park northwest of Lawrenceville. A collection of double-wides, none newer than ten years old, surrounded by broken, rusting fences, and accessible only by gates that are, in many cases, hanging half-off their hinges.

The security officer's silent judgment is probably right. There's plenty of folly in what she's about to do, but Monica is too incensed, too humiliated to care. Driving here and pointing an accusing finger at the little bitch right in her home, she hopes to dish out the same comeuppance.

—— 🝖 ——

Monica's hopes are dashed a bit by the absence of any vehicle out in front of the trailer. Undeterred, she marches through the gate and knocks on the door. A pit bull chained to a post along the side of the trailer howls.

She knocks a few more times and tries to listen for any noise inside, although it's difficult to hear over the dog's baying. After a good five minutes she gives up, *at least I tried,* and starts to walk down the steps.

At the foot of the steps, off to the side a bit, the girl's ratty sneakers.

Furious, Monica kicks them into a nearby shrub and drives off.

—— 🝖 ——

The sound wakes her at two in the morning. Same rustling, same plastic-on-plastic. Despite being sleep-deprived, Monica's rest has been fretful and, when the noise starts, she's far more alert.

That bitch.

She grabs her phone and thinks about calling the cops, letting them nab that delinquent as she tries to play dead outside. But the cops, thinking she's crying wolf, won't make her a priority, and the girl will be long gone again before they get here.

Monica may not be able to restrain her herself, but she can get a picture. Proof of what this witch is up to.

She tromps downstairs, this time without caution. Right to the French doors. Right to the dining room. Right to the kitchen.

The noise stops, and now the plastic sheet is detached from the wall, lying in a lump on the floor.

Had she repaired it after last night? Maybe not, but it hadn't been like this.

Monica scowls and turns on the camera app on her phone. She swings the door open and doesn't even wait to feel if it gets stopped before clicking on the screen. The flash goes off; in that sudden burst of light she sees the top of the steps, empty.

Her heart falls, and at first she feels defeated, then angry. The girl's wily. She's turning this into a game. Where am I going to show up next?

Monica slams the door closed and turns.

The plastic under her feet is given an enormous pull, and it carries her along with it. She hits the linoleum, rump first, and her cell phone skitters into the dark. A silhouette runs at her, howling, and dives at her, the impact evacuating the air in Monica's lungs. Her arms flail, grabbing at the figure on top of her, but her strength has left her. The shadow grabs for a clump of sheeting, draws it over Monica's head, and pulls down. Monica, her breathing already distressed, finds the air she's now able to pull in to be warm and spent. Her hands now go from trying to dislodge the shadow to trying to remove the sheeting. They're in the way of her face as the first blow lands, her fingers barely making a protective cover for her nose as the shadow's fist rains down.

With each hit, something sprays all over her face, all over the sheeting. It tastes salty, like metal.

The shadow roars like a low-pitched banshee as she delivers one punch after another to Monica's face. Not able to remove the shadow or move the sheet, she lets her hands dance out to find something to help her. Her right hand just touches the edge of her cell phone. By this point, the blood that the beating has unleashed on her nose has pooled up and has begun to slide into her esophagus, and she begins to choke.

Either tired of just face-beating, or realizing Monica is on her way out, the shadow cups its hands around her neck and squeezes. Monica's breathing ceases, and she shudders. Her right hand claws, finally drawing the phone close enough to get a grip.

Losing strength, she puts everything she has into sending it down in one blow on the shadow's head. The phone is hardly heavy, but the shock of it must be enough because the shadow screeches and rolls off of her.

Monica rips the sheet away from her face, feeling the ick smear along her cheeks and her ravaged nose. She takes in air in panic gasps, no longer dying, but too weak to do much else.

The cell phone sits on the kitchen floor. When she slammed it down on the shadow's head, she must have woken it up, because now everything at cabinet level is bathed in an eerie blue light. At the other end of the light is the girl, the shadow, wearing the same eggplant-purple shirt, the same faded jeans.

She crouches, animal-like, on bare feet.

The girl barely looks human. Her eyes are wild, her lips curl into a snarl as she pounces on her again, wailing. This time Monica is ready and catches the girl's hands by the wrists before she can use her nails to claw her eyes out.

"I hate you, I hate you, I hate you!" the girl screams.

Monica twists one of the girl's wrists and lets go to backhand her in the face. The girl rolls back again, and Monica tries to make it to her feet. But she's also on her and lunges at Monica, pushing her against the counter. The girl tries for her throat again. Monica kicks at her legs. One gives and they roll. This time, Monica shoves the girl against the countertop and plants one hand on the girl's face, uses the other to grab a twist of the girl's greasy hair, and pushes and pulls once, twice, three times, driving the girl's head into the counter each time.

As the girl's body fails, it feels as if her muscles turn into poorly inflated balloons, and she's less a person than a half-filled sack of grain. Monica grabs the girl by the neck and squeezes . . . Until she realizes what she's doing, that she's about to end the life of a child. She can no longer see the girl's face, but the head and arms hang.

She's done. It's over.

Monica starts to loosen her grip when the girl's arms dash out again, and an epicenter of the most intense pain she has ever known blossoms in her chest. She stumbles back, the girl not following, there in the dark savoring her victory.

Monica realizes there's something foreign that's part of her now. She wraps her hands around it, feels the smooth, curved wood of the carving knife. She sees the light from the discarded phone glinting off what little of the blade isn't inside of her.

The rack of knives, up on the kitchen counter, now one missing.

Monica tries to pull it free, but the pain is too intense. Her knees buckle, and she crumples to the ground, hands still wrapped around the hilt. It's odd. With the knife staying still, things feel safe. She'll die, but with no more pain.

The girl finally steps towards her, kneels, then with an unusually low-pitched grumble says, "Miss, are you okay?" The fighting chants of Monica's students have all died off, and they stand in an unbelieving circle around the walls of the room. The first face she locks onto is that of the security officer, his eyes wide with horror.

"Can you talk?"

She tries to say something; she can't even fathom what, but just wheezes instead.

"Hold on, we've got an ambulance coming," the security officer says.

The stillness is broken as that banshee shriek returns. Monica watches as the girl, ratty sneakers, faded jeans, eggplant-purple shirt, hands coated in blood like gloves, gets pulled out of the room by a custodian and one of the male teachers.

She struggles to move—to breathe—but she lowers her head enough to see the narrow shaft of a switchblade sticking out of her chest and the waterfall of blood cascading from the wound.

She feels cold all of a sudden. She shakes.

"Hurry up!" the security officer screams, sounding a little bit distant now. "Get someone in here!"

There are more faces, more voices, but Monica can't make them out enough to pay much attention. She's floating, sailing through a black void, away from pain, away from disappointment. She turns, and as she's ready to give one more kickoff to send her drifting away from this life for good. She's glad for one thing—she never has to go back to that house on Jefferson Street again.

THE TANGLED WEB

BY KATHLEEN MIX

TRUDY DRIED HER HANDS on her faded blue apron and glanced anxiously over her shoulder to check the time on the kitchen clock. Five minutes before six.

Her heart raced, and dread rippled down her spine. She pushed away an image of Lucien's rage-contorted face. If she didn't have dinner ready and on the table when he arrived home, his wrath would be very real.

She rubbed the skin of her lower arm in the sensitive area of her mended bone, remembering another day. She'd put the roast in the oven on time, but the baby had been colicky, she'd been distracted, and she'd forgotten to start the stove. The spot where her bone had cracked still ached on afternoons like today. Lucien's anger could flare again, and the same, or another, vulnerable bone could break.

The garage door rumbled open, and an engine hummed as a car pulled inside. Tears heated her eyes. *Oh, God.*

Trudy grabbed the colander from the cabinet, put it into the sink, removed the spaghetti pot from the stove, and dumped the contents to drain, wondering once again how a man who'd seemed so gentle and loving before their marriage could mutate into such a monster.

As Lucien opened the connecting door and stepped into the kitchen, she wet her lips and forced a smile. "You're early, darling."

He stopped, looked around the room, and narrowed his eyes. "What have you done?"

"Nothing. I swear, nothing. It's just..." she gulped. "The power was off for twenty-five minutes. I couldn't start heating the water for the pasta. Dinner isn't on the table. Yet. But it will be, in just one minute."

"I don't want your feeble excuses. I want you to do your job. A decent wife would have her husband's meal ready when he got home—no matter what."

She braced for a slap or punch, but neither came. Relaxing marginally, she said, "I'm sorry. It won't happen again."

Faster than a cobra, he lashed out and slapped her hard across the face. "Have you forgotten how to beg my forgiveness?"

Ignoring the sting in her cheek and the hatred in her heart, she fell to her knees. "No. No, darling. Of course I haven't forgotten." She bent her head. "Please forgive me. I'm stupid and worthless and don't deserve to be married to a wonderful man like you."

He pushed her aside and strode toward the dining room. "Leave the little brat in his room tonight. I'm not in the mood to watch him drool while I eat."

"Drooling is perfectly normal. He's teething."

"I don't care why he does it. It's disgusting. Keep him out of my sight."

Trudy nodded as she got to her feet and covered her bruised cheek with her hand. "Anything you say, darling. You're the boss."

As soon as Lucien left, she placed the precise amount of spaghetti he liked on his plate, spat on the middle of the pile, covered her gift with meat sauce, and headed for the dining room. With a demur smile, she served the man who considered his own son disgusting the disgusting dinner he deserved.

— 🐱 —

At precisely eight-forty in the morning, Lucien parked his red Lexus in his reserved spot and entered the office building Trudy had inherited from her father. He smiled and puffed out his chest as he walked under the sign over the door where *Lucien Doyle, Investment Broker* was emblazoned in two-foot-high letters.

His secretary, Marge, sat behind her desk and immediately flashed him a bright smile. The sight of her breasts straining the buttons on her blouse caused an instant reaction. A little recreation before his first client appointment suddenly seemed like a fine idea.

He raised his eyebrows and flashed Marge his most charming grin. "As always, you're a beautiful sight and the perfect way to start my day. Come into my office before I die a painful death aching for you to touch me."

The line worked the usual magic. She stood and followed him into his office, closed and locked the door, and slipped off her blouse and skirt.

He chuckled to himself. She was nothing but a cheap tramp. But he had her trained like a dumb puppy anxious to please and could have anything he wanted, anytime he wanted. Why limit himself to his prissy little wife when a looker like Marge couldn't get enough of him?

He removed his suit jacket and hung it neatly on the back of his desk chair. "We have to be quick. My nine o'clock will be here soon."

"He cancelled. We have all the time we want."

Lucien grinned and feigned relief. "Perfect."

He rushed to finish by nine, regardless. He didn't need or want extra time, and he certainly wasn't going to pay Marge to be away from her desk any longer than necessary. After all, time was money.

Later, as he straightened his tie and combed his hair, he took a few minutes to ensure she'd be available in the future. "You're the best, honey buns. I don't know how I'd survive without you."

"Is Trudy mistreating you again?"

He put on a distressed expression. "No more than normal. I had to fix my own dinner again last night and then spend the entire night taking care of the baby. She neglects him worse than she neglects me. He's teething, and the poor boy needed someone to comfort him."

She squeezed his hand. "Oh, Lucien. Please don't keep doing this to yourself. Leave her. I'll leave Rob, and we can be together."

He hesitated a second before he thought of a stroke-of-genius excuse. "You know I desperately wish that were possible. But I can't leave. She's vicious and vindictive. She's threatened that if I ever cheat on her, she'll kill me. I don't want to even think about what she'd do if I asked for a divorce."

"Kill you?" Marge gasped. "You can't be serious!"

He slumped his shoulders and played the part of a man trapped in an unhappy marriage, putting sorrow and fear in his voice. "I'm dead serious. As much as I love you and want us to be together, I can't risk asking for a divorce. If it were just my own life at stake, I'd gladly die for the chance to be with you forever. But I'm a father, and I have to think of my innocent son. What would happen to him if I was dead and she went to prison for murder?"

———— 🎎 ————

As lunchtime approached, Marge recalled Lucien's words and still felt sick to her stomach. He could be killed. The thought chilled her blood.

She propped her elbows on the edge of her desk and sighed in dismay and frustration. As much as she wanted Lucien to get a divorce and marry her, she couldn't fault him for being a loving father. She had no doubt he'd be brave and face Trudy if the situation was different, but the poor man had to think of his child's welfare. Of course he couldn't risk destroying a baby's life.

Regardless, her heart ached for Lucien. He was miserable, and something had to change. There had to be a way for him to safely escape his abusive wife and his awful marriage. She pondered the dilemma all afternoon and, shortly before five-thirty, suddenly had an idea.

Yes, it could work. She'd get her foolish husband to help.

An hour later, when Rob came home for dinner, she gave him a big hug at the door and pretended interest in his dead-end police department career. "Did you catch any interesting cases today?"

"Same old dumb perps."

"Have you asked the new Head of Detectives to assign you the next big case?"

Rob shrugged. "Yeah, but everything is based on politics. Martell and Stone get the good assignments."

"You and Bert are a great team. As good as Martell and Stone. Probably better. How are you supposed to prove you deserve a promotion unless you're given a chance to show what you can do?"

"We can't, unless you know of a way to change the system."

She took a deep breath. "Suppose you made an important arrest on your own?"

"We'd have to catch the case."

"I know of a case. I mean, it's not a case yet, but it could be. My boss, Lucien Doyle, has a terrible witch of a wife. She's threatened to kill him. You could arrest her."

"It's not that easy. I can't just arrest a woman for something she might have said during an argument."

"This is way more serious than a lover's spat." She smiled suggestively and laid a hand on his chest. "I'm sure you know a lot of methods to trap criminals. Couldn't you pretend to be a hit man and get her to hire you to kill her husband? Then you could charge her with conspiracy or solicitation to commit homicide and throw her into prison before poor Mr. Doyle became her innocent victim. He's well-known in town, and saving his life would earn you a lot of credit."

He rubbed the back of his burly neck. "Are you sure she's trying to kill him?"

"Positive. The man's scared for his life. He can barely work he's such a nervous wreck."

"What if she doesn't want to hire a hit man?"

"Talk her into it. Tell her he's cheating on her and get her angry. Offer to kill him for her, so she won't get into trouble. She has a baby. She won't want to risk going to jail and being separated from her child. I'm sure you can be persuasive and get her to incriminate herself without your part sounding like entrapment. Remember, you'd be taking a dangerous woman off the streets."

Rob pursed his lips. "I suppose arresting her for conspiracy to commit murder could work. And pulling off a sting like that might look good on my record . . . Yeah, it's a good idea, babe. I'll talk it over with Bert in the morning. We can always massage the evidence a little if need be. If the two of us come up with a good story and testify to the same thing, we can fabricate an airtight case against her with no sweat. "

—— 👧 ——

The note someone taped on Trudy's back door a few minutes after nine in the morning said: *Your husband is having an affair.*

She almost laughed. Right. He was always having an affair. What else was new?

The call came at ten sharp.

"Good morning Mrs. Doyle," a male voice said.

"Who is this?"

"Someone who can help you with your problem."

"I don't have a problem. And I'm not buying whatever you're selling." She shifted the phone away from her ear, intending to hang up.

"You have a husband problem."

She moved the phone back up to listen. "Go on."

"If you want your problem resolved, meet me at the Virginia Aviation Museum, on the access road to Richmond International, at one. I'll be out in front, on the lawn by the nose of the big black plane, the sleek looking Intruder. I'll be wearing a yellow shirt and a Squirrel's baseball cap."

The line went dead. Trudy's hand shook as she hung up the phone. Did someone know about Lucien's abuse? Was someone willing to help her escape? She'd dreamed of running away for years. At least once a day, she wished she had the courage to walk out on the bastard and go to a shelter. Was this her chance?

But who was this man on the phone? And why was he offering to help?

She chewed her bottom lip, wrapped her arms across her chest, and stared toward the baby's room. She could survive Lucien's mistreatment. After all, she had stayed with him while his physical and verbal abuse intensified. Leaving was a scary thought. She had no job or job skills, no money to support herself. But she had someone beside herself to worry about now. What if some day he started in on the baby, hitting him and causing him pain? Her stomach quaked at the idea of Donny being hurt. She couldn't let that happen, not if there was the slightest possibility that she could get away.

She grabbed the phone and dialed her elderly neighbor. "Hi, Helen. Would you do me a favor and watch Donny for an hour or so if I bring him over at around twelve-thirty?"

Rob watched the woman with hair the color of burnished copper walk toward the nose of the retired military jet then stop and look around. He nodded to his partner stationed nearby and pretended interest in the mechanics of a wing as he spoke into his hidden mike.

"Start the tape, Bert, looks like our target has arrived."

The redhead walked to within a few feet of him and surveyed the area around them. "Who are you? How do I know you're not a serial killer?"

He chuckled. "Come a little closer so no one can overhear, and we'll talk, Mrs. Doyle. It's nice and public here. You're safe."

She shifted her purse strap on her shoulder, scanned the area again, and then took two steps closer. The scent of herbal shampoo sweetened the air. She met his gaze with a skeptical stare. "Do I know you? Why did you call me?"

"You don't know me, but I heard about your situation from a concerned friend. You don't know her either, but she's heard about your problem and wants to help."

"How? What can you do? And why do you care?"

"I can take care of him for you. For a price."

She frowned. "Are you talking about beating him up?"

He gave her a twisted grin and waited for the roar of a departing 737 to fade before answering. "I usually arrange something more permanent."

"Usually?" Her eyes widened. "You've done things like this before?"

"Dozens of times."

"But how?"

"Any number of ways. Drowning. A fall in the shower. It can look like an accident. His car runs off a cliff. Splat, he's dead."

She sucked in a breath. "Dead? Oh my God. Are you talking about murder?"

He leaned forward and lowered his voice. "Let's lay out our cards here, Mrs. Doyle. Isn't that why you're here? Isn't that what you want done? For me to do it for you, take him out of the picture permanently."

"I . . ." She moistened her lips, stared into space for a few seconds.

"Think about your son," Rob said.

She hung her head. "How much would you charge?"

"Five thousand. Half now, half when he's cold."

"I...I don't know," she said, eyes darting right then left. "This is so sudden. I have to think. He controls our money. I'd have to . . . I don't know."

He looked up at the nose of the plane, pretending to be a curious tourist. "You have twenty-four hours. Meet me the same time tomorrow on the other side of Williamsburg Road. The Dominion Motel. Room 105. Bring the down payment, and we have a deal. I kill him. You pay me the balance. No one will be the wiser."

"Can't we meet here again?"

"Privacy and secrecy are important. No one sees me take the money. Got it?"

"I guess you're right."

Rob touched the lip of his ball cap in a mock salute. "Have a nice day." Then chuckling to himself and mentally praising his performance, he strutted toward the parking lot where his partner was sitting in his personal car, recording and waiting.

— 🀄 —

Trudy stood by the front window in the morning and watched Lucien's Lexus move away from the house. As soon as it disappeared from sight behind the boxwood hedge at the street corner, she made a call.

"I hate to impose, Helen, but could you watch Donny again today at about the same time and for a few minutes longer?"

"Of course, dear. I love that sweet boy like my own. You're doing me a favor by letting me be a substitute grandma."

"Thanks, Helen. You're a lifesaver."

At the allotted time, Trudy drove to the motel and parked near Room 105. She shut off the engine and took several deep breaths to calm her frazzled nerves. A breeze skidded an empty Marlboro package along the blacktop, a garbage truck rumbled by on the road leaving a stench in its wake, but no people were around. A jetliner roared low overhead, aimed at a Richmond International runway.

She chewed her bottom lip and thought about the man behind the hotel room door. He probably didn't realize she'd recognized him from a photo taken at his police academy graduation. Lucien's secretary, Marge, used to keep the photo on her desk when she was first hired—before she started sleeping with her boss.

Discovering Marge's husband moonlighted as a hit man had been quite a surprise. But a cop moonlighting as a hit man wasn't as much of a surprise as Marge being the friend who'd told her police officer husband about the abuse. Did that mean Lucien's affair with his current secretary was over? Had he dumped her for someone else, making her angry enough to want him dead?

Trudy closed her eyes and blew out her breath. The situation raised so many baffling questions. Maybe she shouldn't go through with this. Maybe she should just turn her car around and go home before anyone saw her.

She heard a short blast of a car horn and opened her eyes. A red car had pulled into the far end of the parking lot, taking the stay-or-go decision out of her hands. Trudy grabbed her key ring and pushed the car door open. She couldn't sit here exposed any longer.

She slid out of her car, rushed to the motel room door, paused to wipe her sweaty palms on her jeans, and knocked. The car and the eyes of the driver witnessing her actions were closer.

The door to Room 105 opened. She squared her shoulders.

"Welcome, Mrs. Doyle. Glad to see we have a deal."

She stood facing the rogue-cop-turned-hit-man but hesitated to step through the doorway.

"Come in." He moved aside.

She gathered her courage, slipped by him. He grabbed the door to push it shut and she said, "Leave it open a couple inches, please. This will only take a minute."

He stood by the cracked door. "Did you bring half the money?"

She took a deep breath and stalled a few seconds before answering. "No, I didn't. I just came to tell you I'm not taking your deal."

Footsteps outside. Her pulse accelerated. As the door burst open, adrenaline shot into her veins, and she dove to the floor. A shot rang out. She bit on her bottom lip to keep from screaming and wiggled under the bed.

Another shot. A grunt. A heavy body fell.

Running feet. A door opened close by. More running. Another door opened, farther away.

Trudy shivered with cold fear, like a child awakening from a nightmare.

"Henrico Police. Freeze! Drop the gun. Hands on your head."

The same voice shouted, "I need an ambulance, 2343 Williamsburg. Dominion Motel. Officer down."

A radio crackled. *Roger.*

"Get down on the ground. Hands behind your back."

Lucien's voice. "That bastard was screwing my wife. I couldn't let him get away with touching something that was mine."

"No, shithead. You got it wrong," the cop said.

"But I got a note. It said they'd be here together."

"Notes can lie. If you want the truth, here it is: you'd better start praying my partner lives. If he dies, you get a one-way ticket to death row."

Trudy swallowed hard and tried to make connections in her numb brain. The hit man had a partner? This other cop sounded legitimate. Was the would-be hit man a good cop or a rogue cop? If Marge's husband wasn't trying to earn extra cash by killing Lucien, why had he been sneaking around here and at the Air Museum? Why the charade and the offer to commit murder?

Uncertain if she should feel remorseful or not, she sent a silent thought to the man who most likely was dying. *If you aren't really a killer, I'm sorry. But how was I supposed to know?* She couldn't feel pity for his scheming and cheating wife but hoped he wasn't leaving behind any innocent children.

A minute passed. Or an hour. Sounds came and went, lost in a jumble and competing with the thunder of her pulse at her temples. Sirens blared. Multiple voices. Shouting. Shuffling feet. Trudy stayed motionless, riveted to the floor by fear, hardly daring to breathe.

"I'm not getting any pulse or respiration," a woman said. "Looks like he's gone."

"Yeah, from the size and location of the hole in his chest, I'd say the bullet ripped into his aorta," a man said. "He never had a chance. I guess we call in this one and leave the body for the medical examiner."

Trudy sucked in several deep controlled breaths to force oxygen to her screaming nerves. Reassuring herself that she could do this, she crawled cautiously out from under the bed. She peeked toward the doorway. At least a dozen people in uniform milled around the body and the waiting ambulance. Several police cars were parked, lights flashing. If she tried to go out that way, she'd be seen.

A door in the middle of the wall opposite the bed stood open. Looking through, she saw two queen size beds with a nightstand between them. An adjoining room. She got to her feet and sprinted. The adjoining room was empty, but a computer drawing a series of jagged sound waves on the screen was set up on a dresser. The nearby noises and voices were being recorded. Suddenly her meeting with the cop pretending to be a hit man made sense.

For a split second, she considered shutting down the computer or deleting the file. She decided not to tamper with the recording. Maybe it could be used as evidence at Lucien's trial.

On tiptoes, she crept toward the outside door, which, like the one to Room 105, stood open. Through a crack in the drapes, she scanned the area outside the room. Several people were clustered close by. She held her breath and waited for the proper moment. Sweat slid between her breasts and down the side of her face. Another police car and a medical examiner's van pulled up. Under cover of the renewed commotion, she bolted out the door. Without slowing, she ducked behind a tangle of vehicles and headed for the red Lexus.

She reached the car, checked that no one was looking, opened the door and grabbed her carefully worded note off Lucien's front seat, and stuffed it into her pocket. Then she stepped away, waited a minute for her breathing to slow to normal, and called Helen.

"Something terrible has happened, and I'll be a few minutes late picking up Donny."

"Are you hurt?"

"Oh, no. Don't worry, I'm fine. Better than fine, actually. I'll explain what I can when I see you."

Trudy smiled, and her feet seemed to float over the ground as she made her way to her own car. She had plenty of time to get to the bank before it closed. In a matter of minutes, she'd empty out all their joint accounts. Without cash or her signature on a loan using the house equity as collateral, Lucien would never get out of jail, even if the public defender he'd be assigned could convince a judge to set bail.

She bounced her shoulders and sang *Because I'm Happy* as she started her car. There was no question that Lucien had shot and killed a police officer. He would be tried and get the punishment he deserved. As far as the law was concerned, she'd done nothing wrong.

Maybe she'd pick up the baby, pack, buy plane tickets to somewhere far away, and leave town tonight. After all, she never had to worry about dinner being late again.

IT'S WINE O'CLOCK SOMEWHERE

SOMEWHERE

BY JAYNE ORMEROD

"WHAT IN THE *HELL* is *that*!"

I cringed at the comments coming from the garage. My buyers, Skip and Tammy Eaton, were what we call in the real estate business *PITA clients*. That stands for Pain-In-The-Ass. And the Eatons were about the PITA-iest people I'd ever worked with.

At this point we had toured seventy-nine houses in the greater Yorktown, Virginia, area, and not one had been their forever-and-ever-amen home. Something as minor as a chipped kitchen cabinet caused them to walk out of the house in disgust. But I had high hopes for this 1960s Dutch colonial tucked deep in a desirable community and nestled on a small pond. The house itself had been gutted inside and out and redone with highest-end everything. We'd been inside for thirty-five minutes and not one complaint throughout the twenty-five hundred square feet of living space. In fact, the opposite had happened. The two gushed—literally gushed—about how great the house was, with its open floor plan, earth-tone color scheme that matched their décor, and double sinks and spa shower in the master bath. But any good Realtor knows that checking things off the must-have list doesn't matter a hill of beans unless there was also an emotional connection to the home. That happened when Tammy spotted the original wide-plank, heart-of-pine floors. Seems they reminded her of the barns where she'd spent her formative years. Now who'd a thunk the meticulous forty-something woman would want to be reminded of her stall-mucking days? But far be it from me to point that out.

Finally, I'd found them the perfect house. My palms itched

as I ran the commission calculations in my head—enough to take a trip to Pensacola to visit my son.

But a bucket of ice-cold Chardonnay was dumped on my fantasy when I heard Skip say, "I can't live with that."

What was it my mother had always said about not counting one's chickens? I shouldn't have mentally spent the money I hadn't earned yet, because judging by the disgust in my buyer's voice, there was an oil spot the size of a pinhead in the garage, so this deal was dead.

"There is no way I want *that* in *my* house!" This high-pitched nasal screech came from Tammy.

Yup, they'd found an oil spot.

I put on my best happy-real-estate-agent face and headed for the garage.

"I've got a guy who can fix—"

I stopped dead in my tracks when I spotted a structure that looked like a large Lego project, only this one was seven-foot-square constructed out of cinderblocks. It had a corrugated metal roof and a four-inch-thick wood door. An old thumbtack held a hand-scribbled note that read, "*SHELTER IN PLACE! Walls are concrete block reinforced with rebar and tied to the garage floor. Built to withstand a bomb blast. Use at your own risk.*"

I'd seen a lot of crazy stuff in my days as a Realtor, but nothing even remotely as bizarre as a homemade bomb shelter.

So the Eatons wouldn't be buying this house, but I could get a lot of mileage out of it for my next *You Won't Believe This* real estate blog. In the name of research, I needed to see this thing from the inside. Fingers crossed I didn't find some sort of wildlife cowering in the corner. I'm not a big fan of wildlife, inside or outside of a house.

I put my hand on the door and pushed. It opened halfway. I poked my head through the crack and two eyes stared at me— not wildlife eyes, but human eyes. And not just eyes, but a whole human body. A little old man, dressed in jeans and a plaid shirt, sat on the bench looking as startled as I felt.

"Oh," I said aloud, then paused for a moment for my heart to slow to a pace below Mach one. It's not uncommon to find homeowners puttering around vacant houses, putting a little spit-polish on the place, but I sure hadn't expected to find one resting in the bomb shelter.

After five deep, calming breaths, I spoke in my confident Realtor voice.

"I'm just showing the house to my clients." I fished in my pocket for my business card and pushed the door open further so I could hand it to him. In doing so, I bumped the man's legs, causing the man to slump forward and crumple into a heap on the floor.

"Yikes," I said, before giving in to a nervous giggle. I cleared my voice and steadied my nerves and then called out to Skip and Tammy, "Can one of you please call 911? There's a man in here, and I think he's suffering from heat stroke." A logical conclusion, considering the temperature of the garage had to be in the nineties and the man was dressed for a fall duck-hunting excursion.

I squeezed through the opening and bent to offer limited medical assistance. I'm not a doctor but had worked my way through college as a lifeguard, so I was versed in CPR basics. I put two fingers on his wrist—no pulse. Two fingers on his carotid artery—still nothing. I put my ear to his chest in hopes of hearing a faint but steady thump or feel the rise and fall of breathing. Nothing.

I raised my head and looked the man in the eyes. It was then I recognized the bulging gaze of a man who had been strangled.

Then reality hit me. I was stuck in a tiny airless bomb shelter snuggled up to a dead man.

So I did what any Southern-raised woman of a certain vintage does when confronted with a situation such as this—I closed my eyes and screamed my fool head off.

Nine-thirty-eight a.m. and my cell phone dinged. I checked the screen.

Being associated with a murder investigation is bad for business, my boss texted, *therefore I'm reassigning all of your clients until this blows over.*

What? Until what blows over?

I quickly switched over to the web and Googled myself. Sure enough, pages of reports of how I'd found the body. The stories were peppered with words like "suspicious" and "possible link to the killing."

Me? A murder suspect? The detective who'd taken my statement yesterday hadn't hinted at anything like this. But I had nothing to worry about, right? I had no connection to the deceased. I have no criminal history whatsoever, not even a speeding ticket. And I'm sure one of the counter clerks at Mickey-D's would remember me and give me an alibi. My name would be cleared in no time, and I had faith the police would find the killer and justice would be served. But how long would that take? More importantly, would I still have any clients left by the time it did?

There was one person in my life who always had answers to everything (usually in the form of a good strong drink), so I texted my best friend to meet me ASAP at the new trendy restaurant in the York Riverwalk District. They made the best Sangria this side of the Mason-Dixon, light on the fruit and heavy on the alcohol.

I arrived before her and settled on a comfortable stool on the outdoor deck offering view of the York River. At the same time I pondered my life.

Me, a suspect in a murder. Me, with no clients. Me with no income to make the payments on my new chic condo or my red BMW convertible or even to purchase the Lean Cuisines I scarf down at the end of a long day of selling houses. And there isn't a damn thing I can do about it.

I took another sip of Sangria and almost spilled it when an arm slipped around my shoulders. I looked up and into the concerned face of my dearest friend in all the world, Binnie Babcock. We'd met in the sandbox back in pre-school and had been inseparable ever since.

"I came as soon as I got your text," she said, sliding onto the stool across from me. She's a tiny girl who carries a big purse, which she shoved onto the empty seat between us. "What's up?"

"I'm guessing you haven't heard any news this morning?"

"Nope."

"My boss just reassigned all my clients because according

to the news reports, Detective Willy Watson says I'm suspect *numero uno* in the murder of that man I found yesterday."

"What? Do you want me to call this Detective Willy Watson and tell him you didn't kill anybody? Just because you found a dead man in a bomb shelter doesn't mean you're guilty of murder. What's Willy's number? I'll call him right now." She pulled her iPhone 6 out of her blue Fendi satchel.

I took the phone from her hand and laid it next to me, where she couldn't reach it.

"No, Binnie. That won't help. Willy's got facts on his side."

"What facts?" Binnie finger-quoted the word. I can tell when she's pissed off about something because the finger quotes start flying. "A dead body is not a fact." Finger quotes. "The only fact," finger quotes, "I know is you did not kill anybody."

"I know that and you know that, but Detective Willy Watson doesn't. And it's more than me just finding the body of Joseph P. Ballentine. That's the dead man's name. Apparently real estate agents stumble across dead bodies in vacant houses more often than you'd think."

"So what's the problem?"

"The problem is I used my Realtor key to open the lockbox to access the key that opens the front door. Then the Eatons called and said they were running late, so I locked up the house but, instead of putting the key back in the lockbox I tucked it in my pocket and headed to Mickie-D's for a Diet Coke and fries." I held up a finger. "Don't judge. I needed some sustenance before dealing with the Eatons, and wine was not an option on account of I was driving."

Binnie still judged me with her eyes and arms crossed across her middle. I sipped my Sangria then finished my story.

"So after I had my monthly quota of grease and caffeine, I went back to the house to meet my clients. That was about an hour later."

"Is it illegal to keep the key?"

"No. But the lockbox can tell I accessed the key at one-thirty. The man was last seen alive at about that time. He was strangled and left in that shelter while I had the key in my pocket. Hence, Willy says I have means and opportunity. He's determined to find a motive."

Binnie reached across the table and patted my hand.

"What's it gonna take to get you off that suspects list?"

"Find the person who really killed Joseph P. Ballentine."

"I'm a hairdresser," Binnie said while fluffing her mop of curls, "not a detective, but I'm game if you are."

I about choked on my Sangria. "You want *us* to track down a killer?"

"Who do you think is more motivated to keep your butt out of the hoosegow, you and me or that wimpy detective?"

She had a point. "But I wouldn't even know where to start."

"Fortunately I read all hundred and seventy-five *Nancy Drew Mysteries,* so I have something to talk to my niece about. I consider myself somewhat of an expert on crime-solving."

"I've watched all thirteen seasons of *American Idol,* but that doesn't make me a singer."

"Singing takes talent. Detecting doesn't."

"Says who?" I asked.

"Says me. Now listen, this will be easy. We start by asking a lot of questions."

"On *Castle* they carry guns and get shot at."

"I still have that gun Daddy gave me when Terry got out of jail," Binnie offered helpfully.

"How do you know the gun even works? That was six years ago, and Terry hasn't been around since." Terry was Binnie's ex. It had been an unhappy marriage and an even unhappier divorce after he'd tried to run her over with his rusty old Gremlin. "Besides, a gun wouldn't do me any good unless I'm willing to pull the trigger. Which I'm not."

"But I bet you could if—"

Our conversation was interrupted when a waitress delivered a plate of the house specialty: fresh calamari soaked in buttermilk and deep-fried to a golden brown, then smothered in caramelized onions, tomato, and baby kale. "Chef Carlo sent this out to you, sugah," she said. "No charge. It's not often we get a local celebra-teee in heeayh."

Maybe I should have the waitress talk to my boss about my celebrity status being good for business.

"Thanks," I said to her, then turned my attention to the plate of calamari that smelled sooooo good I couldn't wait to dig in.

Binnie waved off my offering of food (really, she doesn't eat enough to keep a gnat alive). "Time to get to work," she said. "And we're lucky because we have something ol' Nancy Drew didn't, the World Wide Web." She stretched all the way across the table, grabbed her cell phone, and let her fingers do the sleuthing.

I ate and drank with gusto, and thought about maybe taking a drive down to the Outer Banks of North Carolina, just to get away for a few days until all this blew over. Plus long walks on the beach would work off the calories I was consuming right now. But Binnie had other ideas.

"Ever been to Yorktown Victory Center?" she asked.

My mouth was full of calamari so I shook my head in answer. I'd lived in the area for thirty-five years but had never visited. I'm not much of a history buff, and wars are just too sad all the way around, so it had zero appeal to me.

"Joe Ballentine's neighbor is someone by the name of Carla Schneider. Boy, some people don't know how to set their privacy settings." Binnie scrolled through her phone. "According to this woman's Facebook page, she's scheduled to work at the Welcome Center from eight to four today. Your first assignment, if you choose to accept it, is to go talk to her about Ol' Joe."

I wiped my fingers on my napkin then used a clean spot to wipe the grease off my lips. That was the best thing I'd tasted, ever.

"And what, pray tell, are you going to do?" I asked.

"I'm gonna go buy me some bullets, then head over to the shootin' range and make sure my gun still works."

"You think we're going to need it?" I asked, unable to suppress the fear in my voice.

"Would you rather have it and not need it, or need it and not have it?"

She had a point.

— 👧 —

Like I said, I'm not a history buff but had paid enough attention in Mr. Granger's American History class to know that Yorktown was the battlefield where the allied American and French forces won the decisive battle of the American

Revolution. What I didn't remember was that it all took place in 1781. The brochure promised that the exhibit would chronicle the entire Revolutionary period, from colonial unrest to the formation of the new nation.

I must be growing up, because it sounded very interesting. I looked forward to exploring what the Yorktown Victory Center had to show me, but only after I completed Binnie's assignment to find out what I could about Joe Ballantine.

It was easy enough to spot Carla Schneider behind the ticket counter, thanks to her curly red, Lucille Ball-style hair. Binnie had shown me a Facebook picture of a much younger woman, but the hair hadn't aged with the rest of her. Carla stood about five-foot-two and was almost as wide. I'd put her in her late sixties based on her skin, but maybe she'd smoked all her life. That was the reason I'd quit. I hadn't been worried about cancer, but I sure didn't want my skin to look like gray, crinkled rice paper.

"One, please," I said and handed my VISA card over to Carla.

"Hey, you look familiar," she said.

I get that a lot. I've spent a lot of money putting my face on billboards, bus benches, and bulk mailings in hopes that people will think of me when they want to buy or sell a house. So while I'm not quite a household face, people occasionally recognize me.

She narrowed her eyes and studied me.

"You're that real estate agent that found Joe's body, aren't you?"

Why is it that in all my real estate training they'd never mentioned that being a suspect in a murder investigation gives exposure that all the money in the world can't buy?

"I am," I said, then on the fly decided that Carla seemed like the type of person who would respect honesty. "In fact, I was wondering if I could ask you a few questions. I'm curious why anyone would want to kill him."

"I know why," she said. "But I don't want to talk about it here."

We agreed to meet at her house at seven so she could share with me the lurid details of that dirty rotten scoundrel—her words, not mine—Joe Ballentine.

"Oh," she said as I turned to head into the exhibit. "Bring a bottle of your favorite merlot. I talk better with a glass of wine in my hand."

I'd found a kindred spirit in Carla.

— 🎎 —

It was a warm late spring—pre-mosquito season—evening and we settled around a weathered picnic table in Carla's backyard. We were halfway through our first glass of Goldschmidt Merlot and had just about exhausted the topics of weather and traffic congestion on I-64.

During a lull in the conversation, Carla used her pinky to dab a dribble of wine from the stem. She licked her finger, crossed her arms, and then looked me straight in the eye.

"My money's all going on Red Two."

"Huh?" Was she talking about a new kind of wine?

"Red Two was Joe's second wife. About six months after I moved here, they moved into the house he's selling. The one where he was murdered. I already had the nickname Red, so when she moved in, somebody dubbed her Red Two and it stuck. That was so long ago I don't even remember her real name. Wait. It was somehow connected to a Rod Stewart song."

I sipped and waited for her memory to scroll back through the annals of her personal history.

"Maggie Mae. That's it. And she didn't take too kindly to Joe moving in with Nina Ingram a few years back."

"Wait, you mean Nina Ingram, the real estate agent?"

"Yup. She lives in that sprawling white-brick mansion at the other end of the street."

"Huh," I said. Nina was legendary in the business and was often referred to as Nut-Cracker Nina. She'd retired a few years ago. I'd never spoken with her but had passed her in the halls of the Realtor's Association often enough, and she'd always had a fierce scowl on her face. I had a hard time putting her in the role of a paramour.

"Let me get this clear; Joe left Red Two to be with Nina?"

"Yup. And Red Two wasn't too happy about it. Not at all. She's got quite a temper. But then that's the curse of us redheads." Carla patted her vermillion curls.

"When was all this?"

"About ten years ago, and boy, won't nobody on this street ever forget that day." Carla settled her forearms on the table and leaned in towards me. "One sunny Saturday afternoon Joe rolled his suitcases down the street and moved right in with Nina. Next thing you know, a Disabled American Veteran's truck rolls up and hauled all the furnishings away from his old house. Red Two had been down in Atlanta visiting their daughter and came back to an empty house. Even the dirty underwear she'd left in the laundry basket was gone. She hightailed it back to Georgia to live with her daughter, and I haven't seen her since."

"But he still owns the house?"

"Joe and Red Two still own the house. It's been a rental for a long time, but after the last tenants moved out, Joe and Nina gave it a complete face-lift. I didn't expect him to ever sell it, considering Red Two's last words to Joe, yelled from the backseat of a cab as she headed for the airport were, 'Joseph Peter Ballantine, if you ever try to sell my house, I will kill you!'" Carla reached for the merlot and tipped the bottle over her glass. Not a single drop dripped out.

How had that happened? My first glass was still half-full.

"I'll go get some more. Be right back." Carla got up from the table and headed inside.

I pulled my cell phone from my pocket and sent Binnie a text. *First suspect: Maggie Mae Ballentine. Joe's second wife. Can U find out anything?*

Ooohhhh...a thought popped into my mind...could Joe have done something to anger Nut-cracker Nina? She could have easily followed him down the street and strangled him in the safe room. I texted Binnie, *Check Nina Ingram out, too.*

I seemed to be a natural at this detecting stuff.

Carla returned with a bottom-shelf merlot, the kind that costs less than five bucks. If I were to be honest, after the first glass, it all tastes the same to me.

With goblets refilled, she launched her second theory.

"Theory two. Rocko Lusardi," she said. "Gambino mob out of South Jersey. Joe's been in the witness protection program for almost half a century. He always said Rocko would find him one day. Maybe he finally did. Rest in peace, Joey Boy."

She clinked her glass against mine, took a big healthy swallow, and then swiped a lone tear off her cheek.

"Did you tell the police this?" I asked.

"Sure did. That's when they called me crazy."

Maybe they knew something I didn't.

We—correction, Carla—finished two more bottles of wine and called it a night. When I got home, I sent Binnie an email giving her all the details of my conversation with Carla. Then I climbed into bed. Even Jessica Fletcher slept occasionally.

———— 🎎 ————

My cell phone rang at four-forty-five the next morning. I answered it.

"Somebody better be dead." I am *soooo* not a morning person. Binnie, on the other hand, is.

"Well, good morning, Merry Sunshine."

"You calling to tell me Maggie Mae killed Joe?" That's all I wanted to know.

"No, the opposite. There is no way wife number two killed Joe because she's been in a wheelchair for the past five years. Suffered a broken back when her SUV was hit by a drunk driver."

"She could have hired someone, though." Ever the optimist. That's me.

"I doubt it. For the past three years she's been living in an Alzheimer's facility. My source says she doesn't even remember her daughter, let alone that sometime last decade she threatened to kill Joe if he ever sold the house."

So much for that theory. "How about Nina?"

"She was on the schedule to teach a class at real estate school."

"Oh, yeah. Her class was titled *The Fine Art of Negotiating*. I was registered to take it, but then the Eatons wanted to see the house, so I skipped it."

"Can you make a call to confirm she was teaching?"

"Once the sun is up. Sure." I was starting to wake up, and something that Binnie had said sparked another idea. "Hey, Maggie Mae was wife number two. Any chance wife number one had motive for murder?"

Binnie laughed. "I'm one step ahead of you there, girlfriend. Sad to report she died of breast cancer years ago. Long before Maggie Mae came into the picture."

No wonder the police were happy to put me on the suspects list. I looked like the best option, even to myself. "That leaves us with the Gambino connection. Probably not much on Google about them."

"I tried to find something, but public records show Joe lived in Yorktown his entire life. I don't know how he would have hooked up with a South Jersey mob."

"Keep looking. It's all we have."

"Maybe you could go talk to Carla and get a little more information."

"Carla only talks under the influence of merlot, and it's four-forty-eight in the morning."

"Hey, it's wine o'clock somewhere," Binnie said before disconnecting.

— 🎎 —

By ten thirty that morning I had confirmed Nina had an airtight alibi teaching a real estate class. That left a conversation with Carla as the only unfinished item on my To Do list for the day.

Unsure as to what kind of donuts paired well with merlot, I picked up a dozen assorted, and, thus armed with breakfast and a goodly supply of Carla's beverage of choice, I headed for her house.

"Hey, friend." Carla opened the door wide, so I could maneuver myself and my food and drink offerings into the house.

Carla must not be a morning person either, or even an almost-noon person, as she was still dressed in a pink chenille robe whose front edges barely met across her massive middle. The color clashed horribly with her red hair, which stuck out in every direction. I felt overdressed in my navy blue T-shirt, white Capri pants, and strappy sandals showing off toenails painted a stunning coral color.

Carla waved me to follow her as she stumbled down the hall towards the small, helplessly outdated kitchen. It occurred to me that she'd already been hitting the bottle this morning. Or maybe she hadn't stopped from last night.

"What brings you by?" Her slurred words confirmed my suspicion.

"I felt the need to talk about Joe a little more. I hope I'm not inconveniencing you."

"Nope. Glasses are in the cupboard."

She plopped herself down at a small wooden table.

I put the donuts within her reach, then started opening cupboards looking for suitable goblets. Inside the one next to the fridge I found an eight-by-ten glossy of Carla taped to the inside. A much younger and thinner Carla, but I recognized the hair. She wasn't alone in the picture—a very dapper man (think Ward Cleaver in weekend attire) had her wrapped in his arms. It wasn't a friendly embrace, but more of a lover-ly one, with the two gazing into each other's eyes.

"That's my Joe," she said.

"Joe Ballentine?" I hadn't recognized him with life in his eyes.

"Yup. We had quite a thing going."

I'm guessing the picture was circa 1970s.

"So that was before Maggie Mae?"

"Before, during and after."

"What?"

"Yeah, we were hot and heavy for thirty-five years, me and Joey B. Gawd, I miss that bastard."

Wow!

Wine goblets in hand, I returned to the table and poured a glass for Carla. I slipped it in front of her. She took a healthy sip. I poured a splash in my glass and offered up a *salud*. I took a healthy sip myself. I sure as heck hadn't seen the Carla-Joe love connection coming. But the lone tear and wistful words last night should have clued me in. Some sleuth I am turning out to be.

Carla reached for the donut box and selected a chocolate éclair. It was gone in two bites and washed down with merlot.

I sat twirling my goblet and waited for her to speak.

"Me and Joe met at the clinic while Janet, that's wife number one, went through chemo." She paused to sip her wine. "Painful death, that was." Sip. "Painful for her, and painful for Joe to watch." Sip. "Never complained, though. Neither one of 'em."

Big sip and a pause.

I reached for a donut and picked off the rainbow sprinkles while waiting for the rest of the story.

"I helped him work through his grief. Lance, my husband, never knew. He was a long-haul trucker and gone a lot. Made an okay living, but his daddy was richer than Midas, and if I divorced Lance, I wouldn't get a dime of that pile of money. Truth be told, I didn't want to marry Joe anyway, I just liked the fooling around part."

I shifted in my chair. This was getting to be too much information from someone I'd just met yesterday. But it did explain how she knew he was in the witness protection program.

"Joe wanted a wife to do his cooking and cleaning so he married Red Two, but I would always be Red One. He bought the house across the street to be near me. We managed to get together, just the two of us, pretty regular. Lance died in a trucking accident, and his daddy gave all the money to the Wounded Warrior Project. I got zilch." Carla drained her glass and poured some more.

I waved off the splash she tried to pour for me.

"So Joe left Maggie Mae," Carla continued. "But he didn't come to me. Instead he moved further down the street. Since I didn't have Lance's daddy's money, Joe went looking for a cash cow and found Nina. But he and me kept on as we'd done." She paused to eat another donut, a simple glazed one. "But last month Nina found Joe and me together. Threatened to leave him penniless if he didn't break it off with me. If I couldn't have him, I sure as hell didn't want that rich bitch to have him." She took another long sip of wine. "So I killed him."

What? Had she just told me *she'd* killed Joe Ballentine?

Either Carla was in a weird state of alcohol-induced delusion, or she was a cold-blooded killer. The look in her eyes told me it was the latter.

My heart pounded in my chest. *BOOM! BOOM! BOOM!* Sweat dripped from my underarms and slid down my side in some sort of crazy Chinese water torture. *DRIP. DRIP. DRIP.*

I needed to get out of here, but panic held me hostage. The only thing that I could move was my eyes as they followed Carla as she shuffled over to the kitchen counter and opened a drawer.

I swear, time stood still as I watched her pull a butcher knife from the drawer.

And yet I still couldn't move.

"I probably shouldn't have just told you that." She turned the butcher knife over in her hands.

She's not thinking about using that on me, is she? No, of course not. People don't slash up people they drink wine with.

Carla shut the drawer and strolled back towards the kitchen table, the overhead light glinting off the steel blade. She looked me right in the eyes and said in a low, raspy, maniacally calm voice, "Cuz now I'm gonna have to kill you, too."

Holy crap! I swallowed hard and tried to convince my heart it didn't need to pound so hard in my chest. It distracted me from formulating a plan as to how I was going to get the hell out of here. Carla—and the knife—stood between me and the door. Oh, how I wish I had Binnie's gun right now because I would definitely be able to pull the trigger if it meant saving my life.

I stood with the intention of making my escape. Carla slashed the knife in my direction and moved closer to me. I stepped backwards until the table stopped me. She kept coming forward and leaned in until our noses were touching. Her merlot-tinged breath wafted across my cheek. She stared at me for a moment before swiping the tip of the blade across my right cheek.

I felt a sting, and put my finger to the spot she had touched. When I pulled it away, I saw blood. *My blood.* The coppery smell filled roomy nostrils.

Carla outweighed me by at least a hundred pounds. But I had age—and sobriety—on my side. She might get a good swipe at me with the knife, but I could get past her and down the hall to the front door.

Before I could move, she spoke, in a soft way that scared the beejeezus out of me.

"You never should have come asking so many questions, you nosey bitch. I could tell you figured it out last night when we were talking. I should have killed you then."

"But . . . but . . . but . . ."

"It's a real good thing you came back this morning so I didn't have to go chasing you all over Yorktown." The point of the knife inched towards my eye.

I leaned away from the knife, as far away from her as possible, until I was almost prostrate. My hand slid across the table for balance and brushed against the bottle of merlot. Suddenly I had a plan. I wrapped my hand around the bottle's neck and with one swift movement I smashed it over Joe's killer's head.

Carla crumpled to the floor in a puddle of pink chenille.

An adrenaline surge had me shaking like a Chihuahua hyped up on Red Bull. I stood there until my inner voice screamed at me, *What in the hell are you doing? Get out! Now!*

No need to tell me twice. I rolled off the table, leapt over Carla's body, raced out the front door and scampered to the house next door.

"Call 911," I screamed while banging on the door. "Call 911."

Then I collapsed in a crying, shivering heap in their pansies.

— 🎎 —

"Hey, girl," Binnie said as she walked into my cubicle at the emergency room.

Turns out the cut on my cheek had been deep enough to require five stitches. And I'd have a scar, but that's why God invented makeup, right?

"You are so famous, people in every dining establishment in Yorktown will be buying you a glass of wine for the rest of your life. You're trending on Twitter with hashtag whackakiller, and WAVY-TV is waiting outside to interview you. I'm just so proud of you." She bent down to hug me, and I saw a tear in her eye. "And so thankful that Carla bitch didn't cut you up into itty bitty pieces."

We hugged, good and tight.

"Yeah, me too," I said. "I don't think I'm cut out for this sleuthing business."

"I'm sorry I got you into this mess."

"Hey, all's well that ends well, right?"

"Yup. Carla confessed to the cops, and she'll spend the rest of her life in jail." Binnie picked up her big purse and slung it over her shoulder. "And Joe B. wasn't ever in the witness protection program. That was a lie he'd used when they'd first started dating to make himself sound more adventurous. He kept the lie alive for all those years. Sad, huh?"

I nodded.

"Come on, I'm breaking you out of here." Binnie lifted her satchel over her shoulder. "We'll slip out the back door and avoid the crowds. There's plenty of time to tell your story tomorrow. Right now I need a quiet chat with my best friend over a glass— or three—of wine."

I'd lost track of the day after I escaped from Carla's house. If I had to guess, it was the wee hours of the morning. At least it felt that way to me.

"What time is it, anyway?"

Binnie fished her iPhone out of her satchel.

"Well, waddayaknow," she said as she turned her phone so I could see the screen. It displayed an image of two wine glasses clinking together. Splashed atop that was a message in big, bold, burgundy-colored letters.

"It's wine o'clock!"

Lucky for me, it's always wine o'clock when Binnie's around.

THE CAPE CHARLES COFFEE CAPER

BY YVONNE SAXON

THE FIRST TIME I WENT to Cape Charles, it was by accident. Someone else's. I won't say I'm caffeine-addicted, but if I'd gotten my usual double-shot, handcrafted cappuccino that morning, I wouldn't have been driving over the Chesapeake Bay Bridge Tunnel to the Eastern Shore in a coffee service van that I wasn't exactly authorized to drive, delivering coffee for people who didn't actually employ me—*yet*. Or maybe never. Being considered as a "person of interest" in a bank robbery probably wasn't going to help me at the job interview.

I'm not a morning person. It's hard to think things through in a sleep and caffeine- deprived state. So when Jeb—the guy-friend who suggested I apply for the job—called early-early saying he had a problem or something, could I help him deliver coffee up to eastern something, *yada yada yada* . . . I kind of missed the details. My brain heard *coffee? Deliver coffee? No one should go without coffee!* So, I rose to the challenge.

Next thing I knew, I'm dressed in the coffee service logo jacket, struggling to hold the van steady while the wind tries to blow me off the Chesapeake Bay Bridge.

Sometimes I surprise even myself. I managed to get all the way past the wildlife refuge on the Eastern Shore without having any coffee. Who knew? Sea oats and sky and highway stretched for miles in front of me without a coffee shop in sight. I told myself I could make it. But by the time I saw a lighthouse in the distance, I knew I had to stop at the first place I saw. I was in serious caffeine withdrawal.

A sign pointed me in to *Historic Cape Charles*. The next sign I saw through my coffee-headache squint was *Aunt Rosie's Café Pie and Coffee*. I was sliding out of the car with the money in my hand before I put it in park.

Inside, my focus—what little there was left of it—was on finding coffee. Maybe the woman sitting in the back could help me.

"Menu?" I whimpered, looking around.

The woman got up and walked behind the counter near the cash register. Late 50s, with streaks of gray in her dark hair and her mouth set in a hard line, she eyed me over her glasses, saying nothing.

"Pie and coffee?" I asked hopefully.

"You get your drink first and then order." She pointed to a sign taped to the cash register that said that and then to an alcove where I could see my much-needed rescue—a coffee machine with two pots.

Steam was rising out of the pot with the green handle. Ugh, decaf. Might as well drink hot water. I grabbed the carafe on the top burner and started to pour. I touched the side. It was cold.

"Did you know the coffee was cold?" I leaned out of the alcove to ask.

"Somebody must have turned it off."

I could have cried into the empty cup.

"I guess you could heat a cup in the microwave," she finally responded.

In Styrofoam? No. Wait. What was this? Beside the coffee machine was a plastic box filled with, well, the only way to describe it was coffee tacos. A dozen or more white filters had been filled with ground coffee and folded in half. Above it, a hand-lettered sign read, *If you use the last of the coffee, make a new pot*. I shook my head in disbelief. Although, for a split second, I thought about wadding up one of those things and sticking it in my mouth. Desperate times, desperate measures.

"I am not going to pay to make stale coffee that's been sitting out here getting bitter, when I have a case of specialty-roasted brands in the van!" I said under my breath. How did this woman stay in business? How could she pay the rent? More importantly, how was I going to survive to finish the day?

"I guess I'll just have pie, then." Maybe food would help. The menu was typed on two sheets of white paper taped to the counter.

"The cherry cheesecake looks good."

"I'm all out of that."

"What about the blackberry cobbler?"

"Blackberries are out of season."

I glanced at the big chest freezer on the side wall.

"What do you have?"

"One slice of coconut cream pie."

She wasn't happy about breaking my fifty to pay for the pie, but I told her it was all I'd been given for expenses. Cheery red and white tablecloths, stuffed bunnies, and plants on shelves were inviting, making Aunt Rosie's feel homey, but the signs on the walls made me wonder about this place. And her. I ate my cold pie under the placard that said:

Dinner Rules: 1. Take it 2. Leave it.

One up by the cash register proclaimed: *You can't have it your way, you'll have it my way or you can go somewhere else to eat.*

When a couple came in and ordered biscuits, she treated them like she was doing them a favor. Did she know it was called food *service* for a reason? She didn't even say "thanks for coming" or "have a nice day" when they left. Rosie's attitude bothered me. Here she was in a great tourist location; there were enough regular residents to support a little café even in the off-season, and she acted like she was just biding time. She was sitting on a gold mine here! Maybe she just needed a little help. Mine.

Is cappuccino withdrawal a valid defense in a court of law? I hope so. How else can I explain what happened? All I tried to do was show her the different types of coffee products we offered. Rosie wasn't interested.

"There's nothing wrong with my coffee," She told me. "I don't need you to bring me that fancy expensive stuff; my son brings a case every time he visits."

I kept trying, talking faster.

"What about a better machine? Or a grinder? There's nothing like a cup of coffee from freshly ground beans."

Opening a bag of medium-roast Costa Rican beans and holding it out for her to sniff, I said, "You can buy them in bigger quantities—it's less expensive that way— and they'll keep for a month in the freezer here."

I opened her freezer to make the point. Rosie's eyes widened and she yelled, slamming the lid down on my hand. The pain jolted me into flinging the sample bag of beans into the air. I popped the heavy lid back open so fast that it clocked Rosie on the chin. Her eyes rolled back and she lost her footing, slipping on the oily beans scattered all over the floor. She was out cold before I could reach to break her fall. Something told me I wasn't going to get this account.

I looked around the empty café. Would anyone believe it was an accident? Who had to know? I put the closed sign on the door and tugged Rosie out of sight behind the counter—just so no one looking in the window would call 911 before I figured out what to do. The coffee beans had rolled everywhere! Grabbing a broom, I swept beans frantically. From behind the counter, I heard Rosie groan.

Tearing off a length of wax paper from the roll on the counter, I placed it halfway under the freezer. Then I dragged Rosie back in front of the freezer, placing her foot where it would look like the wax paper had caused her fall—not me.

The paramedics took one look at that wax paper under Rosie's foot and didn't question my story a bit. As they loaded her into the ambulance, she was mumbling and pointing my direction. Uh oh.

"Yes, ma'am, Ms. Rosie, I'll be happy to lock up for you," I yelled from the doorway. "Hope you feel better real soon." She passed out again.

I ran back behind the counter looking for her keys. Rosie's purse, in the cabinet under the cash register, fell out and dumped the contents when I opened the door. I grabbed the keys and

. . . now that's interesting. I picked up a photo of Rosie and Jeb in front of a cake that said "Happy Birthday Mom." So Jeb was her son? I stuffed almost everything back in the purse and took it out to the ambulance.

When it left, I made coffee—one of our brands—and it was hot, fresh, and strong. With my headache clearing, I locked Rosie's and ran to my van; I still had deliveries to make.

— 🔯 —

Coming back from Exmore, I noticed the police car behind me. Route 13 on the Eastern Shore can be pretty desolate, so I felt more secure. The news on the radio sure didn't give security. On the Virginia Beach-Norfolk side of the Bay, the Southside, there were two fires, a murder and another bank robbery. The FBI was even offering a twenty-five thousand dollar reward for information about this latest string of bank heists. *That would buy a lot of cappuccinos!* I let myself daydream. *With that much cash I could start my own little pie and coffee shop!* I reached into my jacket for my phone to let Jeb know I'd made all the deliveries. Oh, no. I still had Rosie's keys. Now I had to go back.

— 🔯 —

When I pulled up to Rosie's, two squad cars pulled in behind me.

"May we ask you a few questions?" One of the uniformed policemen asked when I rolled down my window.

"Yes—I can explain about Rosie—it was an accident— didn't mean to take the keys—I was bringing them back . . ."

One of them held up a hand to stop my babbling.

"How long have you worked for this company?"

Uh-oh. "Today's kind of my first day."

He stared at me.

"Really? Seems a long way to send you on your first day."

I nodded and wished I had a sip of rich dark espresso to steady me, then told him about my morning.

"So, you never drove a route before today, and you drove straight over here after picking the van up?"

Maybe this guy needed an afternoon shot of caffeine to wake

him up because I'd already told him that. I explained again how I'd come to be here and gave them Jeb's phone number.

"How do you know Jeb?" His voice was firm, and a little scary. I swallowed twice before I could answer.

"We run into each other at a Virginia Beach coffee shop a lot. We talked. He said since I liked coffee so much, I should apply for the coffee service job. He even brought me the application and took it back in for me."

They looked at each other.

"He told me he cleared it with the coffee service." Then I remembered. "I tried to call him, on my way back here, but he's not answering."

"Why did you come back to Rosie's?"

"To return these." I held up the keys.

Then they asked me to tell them about Rosie's fall. Really? Again? I did, the whole story, skipping the wax paper bit.

The policeman looked at me quizzically.

"Ma'am, Ms. Rosie says you knocked her on the head and tried to steal her money."

"No, I was trying to show her . . ."

He interrupted me. "There was a bank robbery in Virginia Beach yesterday, ma'am. We received an anonymous tip that this van was involved. According to the company, there's no job application on file for you. They don't know who you are. So you're a person of interest in this case."

"Jeb didn't turn in my application?" I asked, shocked.

He continued. "You have a complaint against you for assault and attempted robbery by the owner of this restaurant. And you admit you left the premises with her keys. What do you have to say?"

"I didn't, I . . . I only came back to give her . . . All I wanted was a decent cup of coffee!" I wailed. Could it get any worse?

They waited until I stopped crying to hand me the search warrant for the van.

They let me sit inside Rosie's. Outside, onlookers gathered to watch the police tear apart the van. It was a little chilly, so I offered to make some coffee while I waited for them to send me to prison. Would they let me have a bag from the van? Of course not. I was stuck with the coffee tacos. Please, no. Maybe she had something fresher in that freezer.

"Officer?" The uniformed cop who was sitting with me turned in response. "I found some fresher coffee in the freezer but I can't seem to get the lid open." He walked over to the big chest freezer and looked in.

"She has quite a few cans here, doesn't she?" he said, looking down. I'd piled food to one side and the bottom of the freezer was covered with store brand coffee cans.

He struggled with the can I handed him, gave me a look, and then went behind the counter to find something to help open it. Using real force, he pulled the lid off as coffee grounds and bank notes spurted out. We stared at each other in surprise.

"So that's why she didn't want me looking in her freezer!" I told him. Wait. Did Jeb know about this? If he was her son . . . and she said her son brought her coffee . . . What had he tried to drag me into?

The second time I went to Cape Charles was after Rosie and Jeb's arraignment two months later. Sipping my extra foamy cappuccino at a table in front of a gourmet coffee house near the beach, I thought how close I came to being framed for the bank robberies. Jeb's heists were sealed inside regular coffee cans; his delivery job was the perfect cover for transporting the cash to his mom's café. No wonder she didn't care whether she had customers or not! Jeb knew he was being watched the morning he called me, so he set me up. That anonymous tip? He called it in. But thanks to my coffee habit, I stumbled into Rosie's and led the police right to the money. I was exonerated. It helped that investigators found my job application crumpled up in Jeb's apartment. But I didn't get the job with the coffee service. That's okay, though. Twenty-five thousand dollars was going to buy a lot of handcrafted cappuccinos.

ARTIFACTS OF A FRIENDSHIP

By Rosemary Shomaker

Leeds, England, 1879

AN OLD WOMAN WITH impossibly askew grey hair sat straight-backed on the edge of a blue upholstered loveseat. Her scrambled coiffure together with her gray-blue eyes and the alacrity of her perch bespoke alertness and movement. The four-year-old child next to her dropped the old woman's hand and darted from window, to desk, to table, and to fireplace, and then back randomly among these, all the while humming. The plainly dressed child glanced from the old woman to the papers, vases, books, and other items on the furniture she circuited.

The woman's clear eyes followed the child's route. "Oh, my sweet Butterfly!" she said, "To see the New World as I did—its cities, forests, towns, and mountains—inspired my young life. The edge of the ocean met a shore that lay soft and beige as far as I could see. I'd run along the shoreline to a point far away, and still the coast continued, with waves crawling up the sand, reaching for the sea grass, and then receding in an endless unbroken vista. The oceanside held a vastness and tranquility as God caressed the land with His tides. You could be everywhere and nowhere in that eternity.

"As an old woman now, I feel the peace of that, but when I was young with Mother, Father, and Henry on our American journey, the varied rivers held excitement and entertainment. The wide expanse of the James River flowed into the Chesapeake Bay at Hampton Roads. The choppy narrow Appomattox River west of Blandford coursed over rocks and sprayed freshness into the air.

"Indeed, in Virginia, the Carolinas, and Georgia, we were hosted along these rivers. I viewed grand houses through green clearings that interrupted the forested riverbanks. Roads and paths to the water from plantation lands culminated in riverside mills, docks, ferries, and settlements. The Skipwith home on the Roanoke River had all of this in 1811. My father's cousin Sir Grey sent us from England to Prestwould to visit his father's grave, honor his mother's memory, and convey renewed condolences to Lady Jean Skipwith, Sir Grey's aunt and his father's second wife. Papa had the additional duty of accompanying Sir Grey's merchandise shipments to Virginia."

"Great Gran, is this where your friend Lettie lived? Tell me again about Lettie and her leather bracelet!" Beryl pleaded.

Tessing Langforth Eastman became young again as she relived her adventures, telling her great-granddaughter about chasing chickens, collecting wild blackberries, and tossing pebbles into the river with Lettie.

"These are old memories, my Butterfly. Lettie was goodness and nature herself."

"I've an idea, Beryl. Let us together record these stories," Tessing said with a jolt to her back and widening eyes. "I'll write words as I tell the story. You draw pictures of what you hear."

Prestwould, Mecklenburg County, Virginia, 1811

Lady Jean and her black house servant Jusset stood watching pale Tess and nut-brown Lettie skip and run over grass and through flowerbeds. The British child of privilege and the slave child played, mindless of any distinction in their stations, simply glad of camaraderie.

"No farther than the wall, children," Jusset called to prevent the girls from going through the gate and down the river path.

Tess spent most mornings inside the sandstone plantation house attending her mother, whose delicate condition limited her outdoor exertions. In the mornings Tess' mother insisted on attendance to studies and quelled Tess' protestations of her brother Henry's absence. Tess tolerated the mornings so she could enjoy the freedom of the afternoons. As she ran to the stone wall, she considered her earlier words with her mother.

"If Henry avoids this book drudgery, so should I," Tess complained. "I want to be outside with him."

"Dear, your brother's duty is to inspect the farm's properties with Father and Overseer Cunningham," Tess' mother explained. She handed Tess a small leather pouch. "Lady Jean made presents to us from the goods we delivered, so I've a new sewing set. Take this old worn one to play with."

Tess opened the stiff case, and finding it empty, shoved it into the seam pocket of her muslin dress. "Thank you, Mother," she said absently.

Feet still flying, Tess resolved to forgive her mother and Henry and to revel in her slice of Prestwould that Mother and Henry didn't share—these gardens.

After garden chores, Lady Jean and Jusset allowed Tess and Lettie to go down the river path to see Madro, one of the slaves who tended the plantation's water commerce. With joy on his face Madro said, "Hullo, Tiny Beet!" to Lettie as the girls appeared at the river. Their similar wide set large eyes and pointed chin left little doubt that Madro was Lettie's relation, yet Lettie's eyes were pale green and not Madro's deep brown.

"Missy Tess! What mischief are you two about?" Madro asked.

"Mama sends herb drink and a biscuit for you," Lettie said as Madro lifted and twirled her in the air. Once Madro set her down, her arms encircled and squeezed his waist. She said, "We'll go straight back to the garden, though."

They would return up the path, but before seeking out the coolness of the summerhouse cellar, they'd sit beneath a special maple tree—special because of its shade and the view of the river—special also because of their collection of playthings in a cavity under its shallow roots. The hollow held small smooth rocks, tiny freshwater clamshells, acorn caps, broken buttons, a marble, cloth ribbon pieces, feathers, mica flakes, and other natural and man-made detritus.

"Lettie, what would you put in a secret cache?" Tess asked. She picked up a pink rock, the largest shell, a black button, and a blue jay feather, and held open her hand. "I'd pick these."

"What's that word, Missy Tess? You mean 'cash' alike to money?"

"*Cache*. C-A-C-H-E. It's a word from the French language that means a hidden storage space," Tess said as she drew the letters in a cleared dirt patch among the maple roots. "France is a country near my home in England."

Lettie considered the new word and Tess' items as her fingers entwined the tan leather strip at her wrist.

"I add these," she said, and she gathered a robin's eggshell fragment, broken chandelier prism, tiny carved wooden cat, homemade peach pit button, and freshly planed cedar shavings, and placed them in Tess' hand.

"We've got a treasure cache! Now where shall we hide it?" Tess said after loading her dress pockets.

"First, we best return to the garden before Jusset frets," Lettie said as she placed sticks and moss over their storage hollow. "Bring the cache, and we'll find someplace."

"There—I'd put it there!" Lettie whispered at the cellar doorway to the white frame summerhouse. The cool air relieved her sweaty skin. She pointed to the earthen floor inside where the south and east sections of the block foundation joined.

As Tess freed their treasures from her pockets, she pulled out the damaged sewing case as well.

"We can use this," she said, and she began inserting the items.

Lettie rummaged around the cellar.

"Use this with it," she said smoothing out a torn square of burlap sacking. "It'll protect our cache—and mask it."

Tess saw Lettie was right. When the treasures were in the leather case, wrapped in burlap, and laid under a few cool clay clods, the package was disguised.

"Let's dig a little deeper. We'll bury it."

On a still, cloudy day a week later, Lettie and Tess sat on the packed earth of the summerhouse cellar. They'd not run and played as usual, and Tess was somber.

"Lettie, my sojourn here has ended."

"*Sew-jern*? What does that word mean, Missy Tess?"

"It's another word taken from French. S-O-J-O-U-R-N. A sojourn is a period of time when you stay in a place as a traveler or guest. I'm going with my family to visit more relations. Mother will give birth in Savannah, and within a few months we will sail for home on a ship with big sheets of fabric that catch the wind and blow us across the ocean."

"Missy Tess, you can come back. See the Roanoke River? Madro can row and pole across it—not just to one of them islands—in a boat and be back soon. So can you."

"No, Lettie. To cross the ocean to England, a ship sails for weeks and weeks. Once I'm on the ship, the moon will grow full, get thinner to nothing, and then expand halfway to full again before I'm home. A trip across an ocean and back will happen only once in my life. I won't make the journey to Virginia again."

"To go home is good, Missy Tess." Lettie continued, "Sew-jer-nin'. Stayin' a while somewhere when on a journey. Not being home. My mama, Madro, and most in the quarters talk about journeys, good and bad—mostly bad. I think my people are sew-jer-nin' like you, Missy Tess. We make do here, and Lady Jean is good to us, but many feel far from home—like somethin' is missing.

"Your stories and words to me, Missy Tess, are my voyage. You tell me of big worlds. You show me the words to reach them."

"Lettie, you show me cherished little worlds—the fields, the woods, the earth itself. The truth of what is around me. Thank you."

"You take your trip, Missy. I'll be here, and I'll keep at my voyaging, learning words with Lady Jean's help, I honor. I'll teach my babies about sew-jer-nin' and about words, just as I'll show them the here and now in the fields," Lettie finished.

Tess' gloom broke, and with happy agitation, she said, "We must add to our secret cache to mark my departing." Tess left for a moment, visited Lady Jean in the office above, and returned with paper on which she'd written: Langforth Family Prestwould Sojourn 1811. Showing it to Lettie, she said, "I'll add this."

Lettie removed the leather strip she wore as a bracelet and placed it in Tess' palm. "I'll give this." Both heads bowed, sheltering the treasure, as Tess gently felt the length of the band, turning it over and back.

Tess threw her arms around Lettie. "Yes. That completes the cache."

— 🎎 —

Prestwould, Mecklenburg County, Virginia, 2014

Professor Joseph "Joe" Hardesty stacked another beige stone and then stood upright as the silver two-door Chevrolet Cruze rolled slowly towards him down the plantation's carriage lane.

"Yep, it's a rental car," he said. Such a small vehicle in this pickup truck-populated rural area wasn't utilitarian, and yes, the license plate sported the telltale orange registration sticker.

A British-accented "Hello, boys," sounded from the driver's side as the car passed Joe's crew of stone slingers.

"Back at ya, Lady. Can we sit in the air conditioning with you?" The driver's giggle sounded genuine to Joe. She did not reply but gave them a delicate wave. The movement of that slim white hand distracted him from reprimanding his dallying workers. He stood sweaty, disheveled, and covered in sandstone dust, staring at the gauzy bleached fabric covering the ivory arm extending from the window. The driver gave Joe a tiny wave also, but he merely stared, the pert smile on her lovely fresh face further addling him as she drove by.

"I need some water," Joe said. "Come on over, guys. That woman's cool expression, her breezy sleeve, and even the ice color of her car all have me sweltering."

"That's not why your overheated, Professor Hardesty," commented one of the workers, and then he had to duck as a potato-sized rock whizzed near his head.

— 🎎 —

After Jocelyn parked the rental car, she approached Prestwould's landside entry and followed the *Tour Entrance* signs to the mansion's west-facing basement door.

"I'm Jocelyn Bernard Simpson from Great Britain, reporting for the eleven o'clock tour," Jocelyn said to the small white-haired woman at the tour desk in Prestwould's English basement. "My family is related to the Skipwiths. I emailed the director informing him of my intention to visit to follow up on some family lore.

"My sixth great-grandmother was Tessing Langforth Eastman. Tessing's father was a Skipwith cousin, and she, her mother, father, and brother visited Prestwould in 1811."

"Oh, yes, Miss Simpson! Very nice to meet you," the diminutive docent said. "I'm Mrs. Betts. I'm told that Lady Jean Skipwith's records substantiate both the visit by relations and the arrival of the British goods."

"Our family has Tessing's lifelong journal. Fragments of it recount her visit," Jocelyn said.

"Well, my! Transcripts of these would be welcome in the Prestwould archive," Mrs. Betts said. "Four others are waiting for the tour. Let me gather the group. Please make yourself comfortable."

Jocelyn ambled in the cool darkness, noticing the rough rafters of the basement's eight-foot ceiling.

"The mansion's dimensions are roughly sixty-eight feet by fifty-two feet," a tall young woman with a sketchpad said. "The transverse width rafters are said to be cut from one massive tree." She extended her hand in introduction. "I'm Trisha Elkins, a decorative arts intern from the College of William and Mary here at Prestwould for the summer. I couldn't help overhearing that you are a Skipwith family member. Nice to meet you— brings history alive to meet a descendant."

"Yes. I'm Jocelyn. I'm expected on the tour now, but may we talk later? I need some advice before I meet your director."

"I'd like that. The grounds are not on the tour proper. Perhaps I can show you some of the outbuildings?"

"Brilliant," Jocelyn replied.

At the end of the tour, Jocelyn thanked the docent, and then retreated towards the larger basement area to find Trisha.

"Shall we walk outside now?"

"Sure. Let me tell Mrs. Betts where I'm going."

As they crossed the south lawn, Trisha pointed to the mansion.

"How was the tour? Don't you just love the lobby-like entry hall and the wide central staircase? The first floor's twelve-foot ceilings create such a feeling of openness . . . Even the grounds are spectacular. Here, we've come to the Occoneechee Oak. It predates the mansion. The native Occoneechees would gather here for important meetings."

"Perfect," Jocelyn said. "Shall we sit?"

Settling on a bench, Jocelyn began.

"I'm attending a couture conference in Atlanta—I design gloves for several international fashion houses. I added a few days to my trip to come to Prestwould." She reached in a dark blue tote bag, pulled out a drop front document preservation box, and removed a leather-bound book. She opened it to a page showing girls running amidst flowers. She flipped through pages displaying drawings of girls chasing chickens, sitting on stone walls, and sorting through a tumble of small objects while sitting under a maple tree.

"What do you think of these?" Jocelyn asked.

"These sketches are compelling—really strongly drawn but simple," Trisha said.

"This is an intergenerational journal of sorts. My grandmother Grace's great-grandmother Beryl was seven when her great-grandmother Tessing died in 1882. When Tessing was in her seventies, the energetic and scattered Beryl became her charge. According to family stories, Beryl was Tessing's *Butterfly* who flitted from toy to toy, idea to idea, chore to distraction. Most adults thought Beryl disobedient since she rarely followed instructions. 'Beryl's lack of focus is troubling,' they'd say, but Tessing knew. 'That is the child's nature. Send her to me,' she directed. Beryl's energy renewed Tessing, and, in exchange, Tessing captivated her with stories, both feeding Beryl's imagination and settling the girl."

Jocelyn stood and laid the book on the bench. She gestured east.

"That's the summerhouse, right? Let's walk that way."

As Trisha rose to follow, Jocelyn continued.

"Beryl was the journal's artist. She became a painter, and her boldly colored works with their simplified lines and dramatic brush marks are categorized today as Fauvist," Jocelyn said.

"I've studied that! *Fauve* means wild beast in French," Trisha exclaimed.

"Our ancestors no doubt considered Beryl wild," Jocelyn continued. "I think Tessing may have unlocked Beryl's expression. The colors in Fauvism relay a spiritual, emotional quality.

"The journal came to my hands from Grandmother Grace. She told me the stories of Tessing at Prestwould as her great-grandmother Beryl had told and shown her. My own mother has an eighteen-by-twenty-four oil painted by Beryl of a white frame building, with lawn, trees, and a gated stone wall in the background. That's what I see now," Jocelyn said as they stopped fifteen yards from the summerhouse.

"You've got a real connection," Trisha said.

"That's not all of it. There's more. Let's go back to the bench. I need you to read a few pages of the journal."

— 🧸 —

Leeds, England, 1993: Langforth Family Lore Recorded by Grace Overton

While at Prestwould in 1811, Tessing's father and brother were occupied with the male pursuits of touring the Skipwith properties to assess crops and livestock with the plantation's overseer and to evaluate the plantation's remaining breed horses.

After the midday meal Lady Jean brought Tessing to the gardens. One slave, Jusset, accompanied Lady Jean on her garden tasks. Realizing Tessing's separation from her brother, Lady Jean allowed Jusset's daughter, eight-year old Lettie, to serve as a Tessing's companion. When first in the garden, the girls would run to the stone wall and back. Tessing, with her coltishly long legs, would win and then turn with a smile to receive a briskly trotting Lettie into her arms in supportive congratulations.

Lady Jean allowed no indolence, however, and Tessing and Lettie completed garden tasks before they could play. They pulled weeds and plucked spent flower heads side by side with Lady Jean and Jusset, all the while subject to Lady Jean's botanical lectures and Jusset's simpler plant lore as Lady Jean selected flora to draw, study, and preserve.

The afternoon routine would end in the summerhouse cellar with the girls examining stem, leaf, and flower specimens from

Lady Jean's funaculum. Tessing and Lettie would huddle over upended old crates, placing the plant pieces on paper that Lady Jean would stack and press in a book.

Jusset would return with shrubs and biscuits from the kitchen, and they'd all have some refreshment. Lady Jean enjoyed the vinegar and sugar drinks Jusset prepared with fruit or herbs. As she refreshed, Lady Jean worked with Jusset and Lettie on their spelling and letters, using the cool mud floor as a tablet. Tessing took up the cause with Lettie, always explaining and writing out new words.

Lady Jean would pour an extra glass of tonic and mount the southern steps into the summerhouse proper, where she withdrew to research the botanicals, chronicle the plantation's business, and write letters. Her white octagonal-frame hideaway, outfitted like the plantation house with wainscoting, plaster walls, and a cornice, served as her office. Designed by Lady Jean, the elevated room, bright with four nine-over-nine paned windows, reflected the refinement and illumination of its designer.

Jusset had other gardening duties and had to be on hand to attend Lady Jean, so she stayed within calling distance of the summerhouse. For Tessing and Lettie this was their free time, and Jusset let them run down to the river to see Madro at the ferry. His strong arms rowed or poled the boats and rafts from the north bank to Skipwith's Island, the location of crop and pasture fields and animal pens, as well as of the Upper Quarter where Madro resided. Often he navigated the watercrafts across the Roanoke River to the southern side, where more fields lay. Jusset and Lettie lived in the Home Quarter with the other house servants near the plantation's sandstone block Georgian mansion.

— ✿ —

Prestwould, Mecklenburg County, Virginia, 2014

Closing the book, Trisha exhaled slowly.

"Wow. Beryl's early drawings and Tessing's words about her and Lettie are magical. Your own grandma's journal entries on family stories round out the tale."

"I think it is more than a tale," Jocelyn said. "This may be just a whim, and I cringe at the layers of review necessary if I sought official channels. The journal tells of items buried by the girls in the southeast corner of the summerhouse cellar."

Trisha leaned toward Jocelyn and whispered, "You want to dig under the summerhouse?"

Jocelyn's pale lips curved in a slight smile. "Yes, but I get the distinct impression from the docent that my scrabbling around in the summerhouse would be frowned upon."

"Oh, yes," Trisha agreed.

"Well, I have an idea," Trisha said. "Stop by the old office with me, and we'll pick up some jugs of lemonade. I know someone you must meet."

Joe Hardesty stopped and sat on some stones as the women approached. Even in the shade, sweat drenched his T-shirt and cargo shorts and ran down his bare legs, soaking his white cotton socks all the way into his boots. Joe wearied of repairing, and in many sections rebuilding, this stone fence—until he lifted the next stone and felt the surge of history.

That energy had captivated him since his first visit to Williamsburg and Jamestown in 1990 with his sixth grade class. They'd stayed overnight at the John Yancey Motel. The recreated Jamestown fort cemented his interest in reviving history. On his desk he still kept a photo of himself at age eleven in replica armored helmet and breastplate.

Now he captained Prestwould's stone fence repair. These fences paralleled the carriage lane from Prestwould Drive to the gate of the stone-walled mansion grounds. He'd written the grant that secured the money to repair the fences, or at least the fence sections immediately leading to the mansion from the Route 1601 dogleg. Stone fences also lined much of the Route 1601 approach to Prestwould from Route 15, but he'd have to find additional funding, staff, and time for a project expansion to repair those sections.

The 18th century quarrying of ashlar stone blocks for the mansion left quarry rubble, and that, along with fieldstone, was used to build the fences. Skilled masons, both paid and enslaved, constructed the dressed sandstone block walls of the main house. Repointing twenty or more years ago stabilized that stonework. Over the years, the rectangular wall cordoning the plantation house saw more repair than the stone fences, but not all repair was sensitive. Patching did more damage than mending since cement mortar retained the damp and hastened decay. Lime and sand mortar, Joe learned, served better.

The dilapidated fences he rehabilitated now presented a hodgepodge of stone rubble, cement, and other media, even bricks used to patch holes. Joe's proposal to construct mortarless, dry-laid, stone fences won Prestwould Foundation approval. Deconstruction of sections of the old fencing and artful restacking of stones constituted his summer.

"Professor Hardesty, this is Jocelyn Bernard Simpson from Leeds, England," Trisha said.

"Hello, ma'am. Please excuse my condition—a condition for which I see you have a ready remedy," he said indicating the lemonade jugs in their hands. Hardesty called over the two younger men working on the fences with him and made introductions. They all drank, he and the two men from plastic liters each, the women sharing a liter and drinking from plastic cups.

"This is not proper Prestwould etiquette or refreshment, Miss Simpson. I am sorry," Joe said. He reclined half on stones, half on the grass while the ladies, amazingly fresh and much less bedraggled than he, perched more ceremoniously on stacks of stones.

Trisha explained that she and the two young men were here this summer from Williamsburg under Professor Hardesty's care for three months.

"We stay in a bunkhouse at Occoneechee State Park just down the road," one of the male interns said. "Professor, we're going to the main house's basement for a break, if that's okay?"

"Sure," Joe responded. As his crew walked away, he added, "I may follow you." He looked at the women to judge their intent. They made no move toward the cool basement. Instead, they looked at him expectantly.

"Okay, what is this really about?" Joe asked.

"Miss Simpson's six-times great-grandmother was the daughter of one of Sir Peyton Skipwith's nephews. They visited

Prestwould in 1811."

"Impressive," Joe said.

"We do know a cool cellar we'd like to explore," Trisha said, and, with words cascading from her like cold lemonade, she told Hardesty about Tessing and Beryl's journal and the essence of the mystery.

"Can we look? Dig a bit?" Jocelyn asked.

Protocols registered in Joe's mind, as did images of fruitless digging and tedious work that broke the morale of interns. And of professors.

He'd always held that discovery was paramount, often uncontrolled and serendipitous. The place for procedure and detail, in his opinion, was post-discovery, to protect, examine, and document the revealed artifacts.

Joe considered that minor digging in the summerhouse cellar would disrupt nothing, not even be noticed, and be cool work in the company of these two ladies on a hot afternoon. With a smile and a swipe at his sweaty brow, he agreed to a minimally invasive digging foray on which they'd spend no longer than twenty or twenty-five minutes. After that, he'd tidy up what they disturbed and then return to the stone fence repair.

Joe let Trisha and Jocelyn skim away the damp earth with trowels he'd brought from the fence repair site. The journal pinpointed the southeastern-most joining of the octagonal walls, so that's where they focused their digging.

Joe leaned on a shovel, wondering how deeply two girls in the early 1800s dug to bury their treasure and how much foot traffic or other disruption this cellar floor may have seen since. Unknown, he surmised. Prestwould had the fortune, or the curse, of being off the beaten path, ignored by most tourists, protected, or obscured, by its location far from urban centers. Nearby Clarksville residents proudly touted that the area's annual three-day Virginia Lake Festival in July attracted approximately seventy thousand visitors, but Joe doubted many of the festival revelers visited Prestwould. He'd seen only a few score of visitors in the past weeks, but the summer had been uncomfortably hot and the plantation open for tours during limited hours. He'd have to ask Mrs. Betts. In any case, Prestwould's attendance was a pittance compared to Monticello's estimated annual four hundred fifty thousand visitors and Colonial Williamsburg's eight hundred thousand.

Trisha and Jocelyn were wrenching up clods of dirt bigger than his fist. Enough, he thought, alarmed that their interest had not waned. In two minutes he'd stop them and use the shovel to fill in and tamp down their excavated areas. When Jocelyn and Trisha found tattered bits of burlap in the damp earth, Joe's plans changed.

"Look!" Jocelyn cried. Joe focused on Trisha holding a pliable, mud-colored fraying bundle. He knelt beside them as Tricia held the bundle out for Jocelyn to unwrap.

The three of them babbled to an irritated and then delighted director seated behind his desk in his 18th century office. The ragged burlap lay unwrapped over archival paper, the leather sewing case opened, and the contents displayed. Pieces and smashed bits were separated from identifiable items. Trisha busily sketched the peach pit button, broken prism, small carved wooden cat, large shell, pink rock, and the crumpled paper with faded writing. The vacant spaces of long departed letters confirmed Jocelyn's family lore: L NGFO TH FAMILY PREST LD SOJOURN 18 1. Trisha made a larger, separate drawing of the leather strip inked boldly with Lettie's proclamation: I am Lettie. Tess is my friend.

The director called experts, sent press releases, and convened the Prestwould Foundation Board to share and authenticate the finding. Jocelyn changed her travel plans to attend a hastily arranged Prestwould tea with historic, academic, and other professionals who linked her with United Kingdom peers who would arrange for the examination and preservation of her sixth great-grandmother's journal and interview Jocelyn's family to record the oral family lore.

Trisha's summer continued with her decorative arts renderings but was highlighted with the publication of her sketches of Tessing and Lettie's stash.

Joe enjoyed the find, felt vindicated about his discovery-is-paramount philosophy, and returned to the repair and restoration of the carriage lane stone fences. Two weeks later as the excitement waned, Joe received this email from Jocelyn:

> *Professor Hardesty,*
>
> *Your fence project will not escape rewards. Examination of Tessing's journal and interviews with my family uncovered further time capsule frenzies by Tess and Lettie. Apparently, maintenance of the carriage lane fence was a constant task. Lettie and Tess would run along the fence tops, often falling, often dislodging rocks, and always earning reprimands from both Jusset and Lady Jean. My great-aunts remember stories from their elder relatives of how the girls would giggle about this; they knew where the fences were stable and unstable. The girls knew the fence holes and crevices quite intimately.*
>
> *I've got some rather specific information for you on spaces between stones where Lettie and Tess secreted small items: a thimble, another small wooden carving (attributed to Madro), a heart-shaped stone, metal and bone needles, several marbles, and the like. I don't know if the landmarks or measurements will help you now, but...*

With a whoop, Joe hit reply, attached a map of Prestwould's grounds and his own fence restoration diagram, and began typing:

> *Jocelyn—*
>
> *Tell me they hid items near section C; that's our next area to restore.*

DOWN BY THE RIVER

BY ROSEMARY STEVENS

I'D BEEN PLANNING TO tell my story, but I had to build up my courage, you see. Although I'd had great success with my twenty-two Miss Hope Mystery novels, writing down the old secrets was a greater challenge. Tonight, as I did so many nights, I looked out over the James River from my veranda. Under the full moon, my old friend, the River, glistened as it seemed to stand still in anticipation. I picked up my pen.

Everyone's story begins in childhood, I suppose, but I can't recall much of mine until my father left when I was seven. Then it was just me and my mother, Doris Harold, in the large house in Bon Air. After moving us down to Richmond, Virginia, from upstate New York, my father had left us for his secretary whom he'd impregnated. A cliché by today's standards, but in the mid-1960s my mother was branded a divorcee and later considered crazy when she unraveled from depression.

She was admitted to psychiatric hospitals half a dozen times, taken by ambulance with all the neighbors watching from behind their curtains. These periods when Mom was "away" never seemed to help her, though I kept hoping they would. Part of me felt her illness was my fault. This feeling was made worse by the fact that even when she was home, Mom often seemed to be away in her mind, not speaking to me for days on end, perhaps not really seeing me. I learned to be very quiet as I sneaked down to the kitchen from my bedroom for a peanut butter and jelly sandwich and a glass of milk. Over the years, I escaped the overwhelming sadness that pervaded the house by reading books and listening to music, two great loves that would last my entire life.

As for my father, I never saw him again.

In the middle of June, 1972, I was almost seventeen and between my junior and senior years of high school. I was reading the new horror novel, *The Exorcist*, and mourning the breakup of the Beatles, consoling myself with everything from The Allman Brothers and Led Zeppelin to the Grateful Dead. Awkward and shy, I kept to myself and had no close friends except Chad.

The previous autumn, I had started working after school at Richmonders, a small, exclusive department store located just across the River from my house. Chad worked as an assistant pharmacist at the drug store next to Richmonders. We'd met at the drug store's Formica lunch counter the previous October. He talked about his fiancée, Debbie, who was attending college up north, and I listened, wondering if one day I would have a boyfriend.

On a Tuesday morning, I walked downstairs to the pink kitchen, already dressed in an orange and yellow paisley print blouse, brown vest and skirt, and gold hoop earrings that were almost hidden in my long, dark hair. My Mom sat at the kitchen table, a black headband pulling her short, graying hair away from her face, her white slip pulled up to reveal her thigh. She spoke in a low voice.

"I made you scrambled eggs, Melody, and I'll pour you some juice after I give myself this shot."

Mom had been seeing a different doctor who advised vitamin B-12 injections for her depression.

"That's okay, I can get it myself."

She looked up, large glass syringe poised, an angry look pinching her features.

"Shut up!" she yelled. "If I inject this wrong, I could die!"

I froze, afraid to say a word.

Mom was like that. Her moods changed on a dime, anger the only one that stuck around like sugar ants, invading and ruining everything sweet.

After she'd injected the vitamin and put the syringe onto the table, she slumped in her chair with a heavy sigh.

"I'd be better off dead anyway after what your father did to me."

I'd heard her say this many times, but that didn't make it

any less terrifying. Adopting a soothing tone, I said, "No, Mom, that's not true. Here, I'll get us both some juice. You sit there and let the shot take effect."

The injections didn't do any good, at least not that I could tell, but maybe this time there'd be a change. If only I would hurry and finish school, get a job in New York, and take Mom back there, maybe she'd get better.

"You working all day at that fancy store?" she asked.

I got my eggs and set the glasses of orange juice on the table.

"Yes. We got a new shipment of ladies sportswear. We have to unpack it and put everything on a display."

"I hope those high-falutin' women from Windsor Farms come in and buy expensive clothes and the store gives you plenty of hours. You need to make your own money since your father won't send anything for you once you turn eighteen. We'll probably have to sell the house. I can barely hold on to it with my alimony and child support."

"Don't worry about that now, Mom. It's over a year away, and I've been saving most of the money from my paychecks. Come on; let's turn on the radio while we drink our juice."

I reached over and turned the dial to WRVA. Alden Aaroe, the announcer, was talking about the beautiful weather, but I was thinking about my plan to discuss my future with Mrs. Nelson, Richmonders' manager, on my lunch break.

I hopped into my old VW bug, rolled down the windows, and opened the sunroof. Sunlight warmed my face, and the wind blew my hair as I made the ten-minute trip through our neighborhood across the Huguenot Bridge to Richmonders.

"Good morning, Melody," Mrs. Nelson, a tall, handsome woman in her fifties with a bouffant hairdo said. "Janet, you and Amy come with Melody and me."

She led the three of us back to the storeroom, where a long rack with clothes still in their protective plastic hung. "Unwrap these. We'll hang them from a round rack in the center of the women's department."

"Red, white, and blue! Patriotic for the fourth of July," Amy, a student at Westhampton College, enthused.

Janet, who'd just graduated from Westhampton and whose family was one of the First Families of Virginia, rolled her eyes.

"That's right, now be busy bees while I get the rack ready," Mrs. Nelson said as she walked off.

"Do you have to be such a suck-up?" Janet asked Amy. Janet was blonde and tall, easily five-nine, and she looked down at Amy's five-four. "I got you the job because you're a sorority sister. You don't have to keep selling yourself."

"I'm not! I just like to be positive. What's wrong with you, anyway? Did you have a fight with Ted?" Amy prodded.

Janet's hands stilled on a red blazer. She glared at Amy.

"Ted and I are getting married in two months. Nothing is going to change that. Nothing!" She turned and stalked out of the room.

Amy flipped her frizzy brown hair and giggled.

"I don't know what's bugging her, Melody, do you?"

I didn't, and even if I did, I wasn't going to gossip with Amy. I didn't particularly like her. She couldn't pass any of the mirrors in the store without primping and preening.

"She's probably hassled by all the wedding preparations. You know her parents want her to have a big wedding."

"Of course they do, and so does Janet. Every girl wants a big wedding, don't you?"

I smoothed a white, pleated skirt and took the plastic off a matching blouse. A big wedding? When we had no money? I hadn't even thought about it.

"People nowadays get married on the beach."

Amy pulled a face. "You've got to be kidding. Maybe if you actually had a boyfriend, you'd understand."

I grabbed half dozen hangers, willing myself not to cry. *Boyfriend?* I'd only been out on one date and had been so nervous I'd barely spoken. I walked away saying, "I'm taking these to the Boutique."

The Boutique contained juniors and women's clothing, lingerie, and jewelry, and was my favorite place in the store. There I could admire the soft materials and expert sewing of the clothes I couldn't afford but hoped to one day purchase for department stores all over the country.

At the beginning of my lunch break, I sat on the other side of Mrs. Nelson's desk. She listened as I told her my ideas.

"Melody, I think you have the potential to be a terrific buyer.

You're a good worker, smart, and have a creative eye and a sense of style."

Hope and excitement rose inside me.

"Thank you. What advice do you have? I mean, how exactly do I become a buyer?"

Mrs. Nelson looked at me for a long minute.

"You should move to the downtown location of Thalhimers or Miller & Rhoads and gain the experience of working in a big department store. I know people at both stores who would be happy to have you."

"Gosh, I don't know what to say."

Mrs. Nelson held up a hand. "Experience at that level is necessary, but what's equally important is that you get a college degree. Richmond Professional Institute—I'm sorry, I keep forgetting it's now Virginia Commonwealth University—is downtown near both Thalhimers and Miller & Rhoads. I recommend you attend VCU so you can stay employed while working toward your degree."

At the mention of college, my gaze dropped to my shoes. The one conversation I'd had with Mom about college was brief. We had no money for such a luxury.

"Melody?"

I stood. "Thanks again, Mrs. Nelson. I'd better go."

"Your home situation doesn't make it easy for you to go to college, correct?" Mrs. Nelson pressed.

"My mother—she's not well," I whispered. "My parents are divorced."

"I see. I don't know, Melody, a girl, from a broken home. Well, I can make some phone calls to the stores on your behalf. I never can keep girls at this store anyway. Would you like me to call Thalhimers?"

"Yes, ma'am," I said, feeling the familiar shame wash over me.

I grabbed my purse from the employee room and hurried next door to the drug store. I hadn't budgeted money for lunch, so, when I sat at the counter, I ordered a small Coke.

"Hey, Sugar Magnolia," Chad said, sliding onto the red stool next to me. His sandy-colored hair was just short of being too long for his job, and his eyes were an intense blue.

"Hey."

"What's got you down?"

I thought about telling him. Although his dad was a country vet with a practice way out in Powhatan, Chad had told me the family didn't have much money. He'd understand.

"I told Mrs. Nelson about my big plans to be a buyer and got a dose of reality."

I told Chad everything, and, as usual, he listened intently. He really was a good friend and, at twenty-seven, like an older brother.

"Did she talk to you about getting a scholarship, so you can go to VCU?"

"No. Aren't scholarships hard to get?"

"Nah. You get good grades already; just keep that up. When the fall semester starts at VCU, go down and talk to a counselor. They want kids like you; you're smart and have a goal in life."

"You're making it sound easy. Even if I get a scholarship, there are bound to be other expenses. Mom will freak."

"And you're making it harder than it is. You can get more than one scholarship; you need to apply for a bunch of different ones. Plus, say you get a job at Thalhimers. They'll love you. I'm positive that they give scholarships to their promising employees."

"Really?" I asked, my heart racing.

"Sure. You can do it, Sugar Magnolia, if you're determined."

"Mom says I should be a secretary like she was."

Chad shook his head. "That's not what you want, and you know it. Listen, I'll even help you fill out the scholarship forms when the time comes."

My spirits lifted. "Thanks, Chad."

"That's more like it. But now you owe me," he teased, flashing his dimple. "You have to let me in on your secret spot by the River. How about you take me there on Friday?"

I tilted my head, pretending to think about it.

"I'll bring a picnic basket full of food," he tempted.

"It's a deal!"

"Great," Chad said, getting up and motioning to the cook. "Bring this little girl a burger and fries before she passes out from hunger. Put it on my tab."

Later after my shift ended, I walked out to my car wondering if I should tell Mom about my hopes for a scholarship. I decided I'd better not in case she got upset.

With the key in the lock of my Bug, I heard Janet's voice somewhere nearby.

"You'd better tell me what happened, Chad."

"How can I when I don't know what you're talking about?"

I glanced over my shoulder. They were standing by Janet's car, which was parked four cars down. Even from that distance, I could see Janet's red face.

"I'll talk to Ted," Janet said in a threatening tone.

"Has he noticed any difference?"

"You jerk!" Janet screamed as Chad strode away toward the drug store. Janet almost ran him over in her car in her haste to leave.

What was that all about?

Ten minutes later, I walked in the front door to my house, feeling the usual mix of dread and anxiety. Would Mom be okay, or would she be locked in her room? I entered cautiously. The living room draperies were closed. That was not really unusual— Mom liked to keep the house dark—but there was not a sound to be heard. It was almost six o' clock. If Mom weren't feeling too bad, she'd be fixing dinner about this time. But she wasn't; the blinds in the kitchen were drawn.

I closed the door quietly. Climbing the stairs that led to the bedrooms, I looked up. The hallway was dark. Mom's bedroom door was shut. Many times when I was younger, I'd sat on the floor outside her door begging her to come out, to tell me what I'd done wrong. She never would answer me.

Now, I crept down the hall and listened outside her door. When I heard her moving around, I breathed a sigh of relief and went to my bedroom. I read, washed my face, got a glass of milk, and eventually dropped off to sleep.

— 🯁 —

The next morning, I packed a tuna sandwich for lunch and drove to work. I entered through the employee entrance down at The Boutique and heard voices coming from the main level.

I'd started in that direction when Amy came running down the steps.

"Have you heard?" she asked breathlessly. "Janet is gone. She's not coming back."

"Where is she? What happened?"

"Last night my mother talked to Janet's mother. Ted broke it off with Janet, and she's had a breakdown. Janet's parents are thinking of sending her to Paris for a year to get over him."

"Poor Janet. I wonder why Ted—"

"I think she's been cheating on him," Amy interrupted.

"Janet wouldn't do that."

"Oh no?" Amy said in a sly tone.

"Amy, do you know something about Janet and another guy?"

She shrugged. "I'm not a gossip. I only told everyone what my mother told me. Oh, here comes Mrs. Randle and Mrs. Wilson. Better look busy."

All day I spotted people whispering, and I was sure Janet was the topic. When I had lunch in the break room, white-haired Mrs. Carter from the baby department sat down next to me. We ate in silence for a while.

"Now we've lost Janet. Seems like in the last two years we haven't been able to keep girls at the store," Mrs. Carter said as she got up, brushed the crumbs from the table into her palm and then threw them into the trash. "You girls with your miniskirts. Nothing but trouble."

After Mrs. Carter left, I chewed my tuna sandwich thoughtfully.

That night, Mom cooked spaghetti. We watched the cops catch the bad guys on *Adam-12* while painting our nails with Cutex's frosted pink nail polish. I went to bed happy, thinking maybe the B-12 shot had helped after all.

So when I came home from Richmonders the next night, I was shocked to find Mrs. Smith, our neighbor across the street, in my living room.

My heart pounded. "Where's my Mom?"

"MCV," she answered, referring to the Medical College of Virginia. "Sit down, Melody."

I obeyed automatically.

"In the psychiatric unit?"

"Your mother tried to jump off the Huguenot Bridge earlier today but was stopped by the police. An ambulance took her to the hospital. They called me as your mother had my name and phone number in her purse. I told the nurse to tell her that I'd keep an eye on you while she's . . . away."

I looked down at the patterned rug. The Huguenot Bridge. Mom had been right by Richmonders, yet I hadn't known. Last night she'd seemed okay. I closed my eyes.

"Melody? Are you all right? Do you want to come and sleep in our guest room?"

"No, I'd feel better here." I looked at Mrs. Smith. She had a pleasant face and light short brown hair. Her husband was an executive at DuPont, and they had four children, two of whom were girls around my age. I'd often thought that they were the perfect American family. From my window, I'd seen them pile into the car headed to the beach in summer, rake leaves together in the fall, and string lights along the house at Christmas. I wouldn't fit in with them.

"All right, but I'll be watching out for you."

"Yes, ma'am."

She got up to leave. "I hope your mother is home soon. Our family is going to the beach next week. Oh, I brought over a chicken casserole. It's in the fridge."

"Thank you." I closed and locked the door behind her. I wished I could talk to someone, but there wasn't anyone, really. Then I thought of Chad and the picnic tomorrow. Maybe I'd tell him.

I went into the kitchen, turned on the radio, and heated the casserole. The announcer said a tropical depression had formed off the coast of the Yucatan Peninsula. I ate and then went to bed.

I awoke to darkness, and my hand groped for my glow-in-the-dark alarm clock: 4:47 a.m. The numbness I'd felt when Mrs. Smith told me about Mom had worn off. I went downstairs and called the hospital. A nurse told me Mom couldn't have visitors. I asked if they were giving her shock treatments, but the nurse would only say, "Your mom is resting comfortably."

When I arrived at Richmonders later, I found myself the

subject of curious looks.

"That's a nice sailor dress, Melody. Now, I want your help this morning," Mrs. Carter said. "Two babies were born to my ladies last night, and we're going to make up the layettes together."

"Okay," I said, seeing Miss Young and Mrs. Wilson with their heads together.

"Don't worry about them," Mrs. Carter said sharply. "They like to gossip. Just between you and me, how is your mother?"

Oh, no. They knew. Had the news been in the papers?

"She's okay," I said.

"That's good. Now we have a tiny baby boy that needs an outfit to wear when he goes home. Let me show you what to do."

The morning went by quickly. I didn't get away to the drug store until after one-thirty.

"Sugar Magnolia, I was beginning to think you forgot me."

"Are you ready? Can we please just go?"

Chad stared at me for a long moment. "Go wait for me by my car."

A few minutes later, he opened the door to his white Pontiac Valiant, put a wicker hamper in the back seat, and then held the door for me. He turned the ignition key.

"Okay, you promised to take me to your secret spot. So give me directions."

"Go across the bridge to the Rocks."

"The Pony Pasture by the River? No secret there."

"Just drive. I'll show you."

We drove in silence until we got to the Pony Pasture. From Riverside Drive, we could see girls in bikinis sunbathing out on the Rocks and boys in cut-offs smoking pot and drinking beer. Music drifted on the warm summer air.

"Park at the very end. There's a place behind those trees that's really private."

Chad carried the hamper as he followed me, past some thick bushes into a tiny clearing carpeted with grass and a few wildflowers. He laid out a plaid blanket, retrieved chicken salad sandwiches, chips, and Coke bottles from the hamper, and handed me a napkin. Then he pulled out a transistor radio and turned it on WLEE just loud enough for us to hear the music.

I managed half a sandwich and was leaning back on my

elbows, my face to the sun, when he said, "It was in the newspaper this morning. About your mom, I mean. I'm glad she's getting help."

I told him how the doctors never helped her, how I couldn't see her, how Mrs. Smith wanted mom to hurry and come home so she and her family could take off to the beach. Chad listened.

"So you're staying alone at your house? No one will be there when you get home?"

"Yeah, but it's okay. I'd rather be there by myself than be at the Smiths'. I can't be perfect like them!" At these words, the tears came. I sat and cried while Chad patted my arm.

Finally, he handed me a napkin, and I dried my eyes.

"Here, drink a little of this," he said, holding a paper cup toward me.

"What is it?" I said, sniffling.

"A little strawberry wine. It'll mellow you out," he said, flashing his dimple at me.

I took the cup and drank it down. "It's kinda bitter."

"You'll make it sweet, Sugar Magnolia," he whispered.

All of a sudden, I felt myself falling back to the blanket.

Chad's face was above me, his blue eyes staring at me intently, his hand pulling up the hem of my sailor dress.

I couldn't seem to move or talk. The sun faded out, and I entered a semi-darkness, images floating in my brain. Pain, a sharp pain between my legs, a weight on me, Chad's face above me—no, it was my father, and we were in my bedroom back in New York.

Then everything went black.

From a distance, I heard someone talking about spilling the wine. I struggled to open my eyes, but couldn't. I couldn't feel my arms or legs. It was like my body wasn't part of me. Still the words came to me about the wine. I realized it was Eric Burdon singing and giggled. Then darkness came again.

The next time I woke, tree limbs were waving above me, thousands and thousands of them floating between me and the blue sky, millions of leaves trailing back and forth.

I slowly sat up. Dizziness threatened to make me faint, and I felt lightheaded. For a minute, I didn't know where I was, then I realized I was at the Pony Pasture, in the secret place where sometimes I came to read on my lunch break, only today I'd brought Chad. *Where is he?* A glance at my watch told me it was after four o'clock. Confused, I struggled to stand and then walked on wobbly legs to where a few cars were parked, none of them my Bug or Chad's Valiant. I had to get back to Richmonders or I'd lose my job.

I walked toward the River. A guy in jeans and a T-shirt and a girl with blond hair were rock-hopping toward me. My gaze went to the water, sparkling and flowing gently on its way. I must have stood there, lost in the beauty of the River, for several minutes because the next thing I knew, the blond-haired girl asked me if I was okay. I told them my friend had left me and bummed a ride with them over the bridge.

I crept to my car, still in the Richmonders parking lot, and got in, my hands shaking. A quick glance in the rearview mirror told me that I looked as sick as I felt. There was a gas station nearby. I drove there and bought a Coke from the cooler. The liquid felt soothing as it went down my throat. I walked to the phone booth and called Richmonders. I explained to Mrs. Nelson that there had been an emergency at home.

"Is your mother all right?" she asked.

"Yes, ma'am, but I can't come back to the store today. I apologize for not calling earlier."

"All right. Will we see you tomorrow?"

I squeezed my eyes shut against the dizziness. "Yes."

Creeping along at thirty miles an hour, I made it home without killing myself or anyone else. I collapsed in bed and slept.

It wasn't until I woke about three hours later, clearheaded, that I saw the blood on my panties and realized the horror of what had happened. The shame I felt from coming from a *broken home* was nothing compared to the shame I felt now. I crawled back under the covers, shivering in the June night, and slept again.

In the morning, the last thing I wanted to do was go to work, but I couldn't lose my job. I forced myself to control my thoughts, but I couldn't prevent Chad's face from flashing through my mind, sending chills of revulsion through my body.

I struggled through the day by staying focused on my

customers until we were getting ready to close. Amy came over to me as I was counting the money in the register.

"Guess what? I had lunch at the drug store today, and that cute guy, Chad, came over and talked to me. His dimple is so adorable! He said he has a fiancée, but I know he was flirting with me. I'll have to think of an excuse to go to the drug store next week so I can see him again."

Dimes slipped from my fingers into the till. "Finish the money, will you? I have to leave." On the ride home, a scream burst from my throat, followed by another and another.

— 🎎 —

Sunday, I showered in the morning, but by one o'clock, I still felt dirty. I showered again, dressed in my bell-bottoms, gathered my wet hair back with a leather tie, and called MCV. Mom was still resting comfortably, and, no, I couldn't speak with her, nor were visitors allowed.

I got a glass of milk and returned to my room. I locked the door, then drew the curtains even though the day was already dark with rain, and lay down on my bed with the radio playing softly. Now it was safe to remember the picnic, to think about Chad and what he'd done to me. What was I going to do? There were no witnesses. Who would believe me? Not the police. Not Mrs. Smith. Not my mother.

I closed my eyes. Suddenly, I remembered that, when I was talking to Mrs. Nelson about going to Thalhimers, she'd said, *I never can keep girls at this store anyway.* Then my mind flashed to Mrs. Carter at lunch; *Seems like in the last two years we haven't been able to keep girls at the store.* Then Amy talking about Chad flirting with her. A terrible realization made me decide that I had to do something, but what?

About seven o'clock the radio announcer's voice caught my attention. "...storm that first formed off the Yucatan Peninsula is off the coast of Florida and has been declared a hurricane named Agnes. The hurricane is moving up the east coast, and showers and locally heavy thunderstorms are expected in the Richmond area tomorrow night. Be prepared for heavy rains, folks, and possibly flooding."

I sat up in bed staring straight ahead. With sudden clarity, I knew what I had to do. I ran downstairs to the bookcase, pulled out an encyclopedia, and began reading.

Monday morning Mrs. Nelson briefed us on plans to move clothing from downstairs to the middle level of the store in the event that the James River flooded badly enough to reach Richmonders. Afterward, she called me aside.

"Melody, I've spoken with the head of ladies sportswear at Thalhimers. She can use you right away. You have an interview tomorrow morning. Can you make it?"

Here was the opportunity I'd wanted, yet I couldn't feel excited. My mind was focused on Chad. "Thank you, Mrs. Nelson, of course I'll be there. May I please take lunch at one o'clock today? I'd like to go see my mother." I let my voice drop. "She's in the hospital, and I doubt I'll be back afterward."

"That will be fine." She looked at me over her glasses. "If you were staying all day, I'd have to send you home to change. That red skirt is shorter than our standards permit."

It should be. I'd shortened it last night. I bowed my head.

"Yes, ma'am. I'm just going to the drug store for some aspirin, then I'll be on the sales floor."

I walked out of Richmonders, into the drug store and directly back to the pharmacy area. I'd unbuttoned two of the top buttons of my white blouse on the way over.

Chad helped a lady at the register. At the sight of him, I had a strong desire to run.

When he finished with his customer, Chad turned to me, his eyes giving me a quick once-over. "Hi, Melody. What can I get for you?"

His voice was bright, but his jaw tense. I smiled, running my painted-red fingernail down the opening of my blouse.

"I'll take this small tin of aspirin." I handed it to him, keeping my fingers on his. Nausea surfaced, but I licked my lips and whispered, "I really came over to see if we could go to the Pony Pasture again today. You don't have to bring food, I just want to, um, be with you."

"Yeah?" He visibly relaxed.

"I told Mrs. Nelson I was going to visit my Mom in the hospital and wouldn't be back after lunch. We have all afternoon if you'd like."

I could see the indecision on his face.

"Please, Chad. This might be my last week at Richmonders. I have an interview at Thalhimers tomorrow, but Mrs. Nelson pretty much told me I have the job."

He drew in a breath. "I'll see what I can do . . . One o'clock?"

"Meet me at my car." I smiled again and took my time walking away from him. Outside, I leaned against the brick wall of the store and gulped air.

By one o'clock, clouds gathered. I sat in my Bug, hoping the rain would hold off. In my side mirror, I saw Chad coming up to the passenger side of the car carrying a brown bag. I steeled myself.

He got in. "Are you sure you want to go? Looks like it might rain."

I started the car and moved my hand to the gearshift, brushing his leg.

"I'm sure. It's bound to be nice and cool by the River with the storm coming. It'll be groovy."

I pulled into the spot Chad had parked his car in on Friday. My heart pounded as we got out of the car. We were almost alone. Two boys were lugging a cooler, ready to leave. I swung my purse over my shoulder, reached into the back seat, and pulled out a floral sheet.

"I brought something for us to sit on."

He grinned, flashing his dimple at me, sure of himself now. He held up the paper bag. "Two Cokes and a couple of burgers."

We walked back behind the trees, through the bushes to my secret place, the one forever tarnished now. My hands shook as I tried to spread the sheet. Chad grinned and helped. I threw my purse on the sheet and sat down next to it, my skirt riding up almost to my hips. I tugged at it and Chad chuckled, dropping down next to me.

"Don't bother," he said, then pushed me down and kissed me.

Kiss him back! My mind screamed. He didn't perceive that anything was wrong, though, as his hand stroked my thigh.

Remember what it said in the encyclopedia! My right hand closed on my purse. My left hand tugged my blouse down.

He angled his head to trail kisses down to my left breast just as I'd planned.

"I knew all along that you wanted it," Chad said.

See it? There it is! Do it now! Now!

In one fluid, fast motion, I pulled Mom's large glass syringe from my purse and jammed it into Chad's jugular vein, pressing the plunger all the way down, shooting air directly into his vein.

I scrambled out from under him and jumped to my feet as he rolled backward, screaming. His eyes bulged with disbelief.

"A venous air embolism, you only have a minute or two to live," I ground out, my whole body shaking with rage. "You drugged me. You put something in that wine. What was it?"

He didn't answer, just stared with that incredulous expression.

"Your dad's a vet, and you work in a pharmacy. That's how you got whatever it was. Didn't you, Chad? You did it to Janet, too. How many others have there been? Tell me!"

"I . . . I ca' . . .can't remember. Help m . . .me, I'm your fr . . .friend." Chad clutched his chest, gasped, and collapsed on the ground. Dead.

I took one last look at him, his eyes open and staring. I pulled the syringe from his neck, wiped it clean on the sheet, and put it back into my purse.

Sitting on one of the rocks, I lost track of time. I was alone. I laid on my side on one of the big boulders, my tears falling into the water, the River swirling around me under the dark clouds.

Chad's body was found after Hurricane Agnes caused historic flooding in Richmond. His death was ruled an accidental drowning.

No one named Debbie came to Richmond for Chad's funeral. Later I realized Chad had never had a fiancée.

As for me, romance was never part of my life. Instead, I focused on my career. At the end of the 1970s, I did get a job as a buyer in New York City and moved Mom back to her home state, but it didn't matter. She took an overdose of Valium and died soon after I turned thirty. Not long after that, I started writing.

I guess writing murder mysteries year after year where in the end the victim always got justice made me decide that Chad needed his justice, even though I believed I was justified in killing him. But there's a difference between justice and justification, isn't there?

It will be an easy death, drowning in my old friend the River, the river that gave me respite from my home life, which watched while I endured my greatest horror, and that flowed on while I took my revenge. Down by the River, I'll finally find peace.

Signed,

Melody Harold

USED

By Linda Thornburg

HAM SETTLED WITH RELIEF into his seat between Celia and Marguerite in the fourth row from the stage. Ten minutes until curtain. The drive down had not been relaxing. An accident blocked both lanes on I-81. He had tried to call but got Marguerite's voice mail and could only hope she got the message. They were to meet up at a coffee shop, but he suggested she go on to the theater. He didn't want to be responsible for her missing any of John's opening night as Don Quixote/Cervantes.

Marguerite, a diminutive blonde with nervous energy, was the opposite of Celia, who radiated calm. Before the curtain went up, she nattered on, gesticulating about the history of the Barter Theater, which Virginia called its state theater, how she and John ended up in Abingdon, what the kids were doing in school, and what her role as costume designer for the theater company involved. Ham learned more about her life with John in ten minutes than he would have in an hour's conversation with her husband.

Man of La Mancha was the perfect vehicle for his old college roommate. Thirty years earlier, John would burst into their dorm room after studying late, singing a tune from *Oklahoma* or *South Pacific*. Ham found the latter particularly irritating, but he had to admit that John had an enormous talent. He was surprised when John, who majored in dramatics, joined the insurance industry. Now he was a full-time member of the Barter Theater equity company and apparently earning a good enough living. A dream come true.

Ham had never seen *Man of La Mancha* performed, although he was familiar with the music. He was impressed with the set. A plank came down from above, and the actors descended into the dungeon where Cervantes was imprisoned during the Inquisition. John held the audience spellbound. Time passed quickly. By the time the inquisitors were calling Cervantes from above at the end of the play, Ham regretted that the production wasn't longer. John was under the descending plank, ready to ascend, when the plank fell on him.

The audience understood immediately that this was not a part of the play. Spectators rose from their seats in alarm. Without thinking, Ham rushed to the stage and climbed the stairs in front to get to his friend. The curtain came down as he reached the plank.

Actresses shrieked. Ham helped seven other men remove the heavy metal and wood. The plank must have weighed more than five hundred pounds. His heart stopped when he saw John's crushed face. A man who said he was a doctor pushed through the crowd and felt for a pulse, then shook his head. He began issuing commands and waving his arms to shoo everyone away.

People moved to the wings, and Ham was swept along. He watched as the doctor took out a cell phone and made a call. A man wearing a T-shirt that said *Stage Manager* asked everyone to exit through the back. Ham found himself in the street behind the theater. He could hear a siren.

He walked around the block to the front of the building and entered the lobby, where he found Celia looking for him.

"Where's Marguerite?" he asked.

Celia shook her head. She was wearing a simple black dress. She looked elegant, but she was scowling.

"How could you just leave us there?" she asked accusingly.

"I'm sorry. I just reacted. Where did Marguerite go?"

"She's on her way to the hospital. Someone told her they're taking John there."

"I don't think so," Ham said. "The doctor who went back stage thought he was dead."

"No, I'm sure that's what the paramedics told her."

Ham felt a surge of hope. Perhaps John would be all right. Then he remembered John's crushed face. No one could recover from that.

"What should we do, do you think?" he asked.

"She'll need support. We should go to the hospital."

Ham pulled out his phone to look it up. There was only one, and it wasn't far. They had trouble finding a parking place. Then, to delay them, the woman in reception gave them the wrong directions, and they ended up in a wing opposite from the wing where John was being cared for. By the time they finally found his floor, a half an hour had passed. Marguerite was sitting in a chair near the bed. John was on life support.

"The doctors say he doesn't have any brain function," Marguerite said softly. "They're waiting for my approval to take him off support."

"What can we do?" Ham asked. An immense sadness washed over him. He felt entirely helpless.

"There is nothing." She shook her head. "I'm just waiting for a neighbor to bring the children to say goodbye . . . You should probably go on home. I'll let you know about the funeral."

"Are you sure?" Celia said. "We'd be happy to stay if you think there is any way we can help."

"I just . . . I just want . . ." She began to cry and couldn't finish her sentence.

"I can't believe it." Ham gave her a hug. "I just can't believe it. I'm so sorry."

She nodded and then turned to stare at John. She wanted to be alone with him.

On the way back to Blue Hill, Ham flashed on his college days. He and John used to pull pranks to alleviate the intensity of their studies. At least Ham's studies were intense. John seemed to have more fun. He remembered panty raids on girls' dorms, dressing like vampires and spooking students after dark as they walked home from the library, late night strip poker, drinking contests, and one wild concert that ended in a fight between John and Ham and some giants from the town. By the time he and John moved off campus junior year, he was as close to John as to any friend he'd ever had. They shared just about everything, including one girlfriend who couldn't make up her mind.

Ham glanced away from the road and at Celia. "How are you doing?" he asked.

She put her hand on his arm. "I'm all right. How are you?"

He shrugged and brought his eyes back to the highway.

"He was such a good friend in college. But I don't really know him anymore. How is it that we can lose touch like that?"

"You move on," Celia said listlessly, as if she knew it was only something to say.

"We've both been through eternities since then. He has two kids, I have one, I'm divorced and with you, he's still with the woman he married fifteen years ago, and now he's going to die. I wonder what Marguerite will do. I guess she could sue Barter for the accident, but she gets a salary from them so she probably won't."

"I doubt if costume design for a theater company will be enough to raise two children," Celia said.

"It seemed like they were happy in Abingdon, didn't it?"

"Yes. Marguerite seemed content, if a bit fluttery."

"Fluttery?"

"Well, you know, like she couldn't settle down. She talked too much and too fast, like she was nervous."

"Maybe that's just the way she is."

"Maybe," Celia said.

— 🎭 —

Two days later, as Ham was looking at his books and wondering what kind of a year 2015 would be, hoping he would exceed his 2014 revenue, which was below predictions, he got a call from Marguerite.

"How are you holding up?" he asked her as he closed the file with his accounts and returned the computer to the screen saver, a photo of Celia with his daughter he had taken last spring.

"I need a favor," Marguerite said.

Ham was surprised. He had seen her only once after her wedding. But he was willing to help if he could. "Tell me," he said.

"The police think John may have been murdered. The plank had been tampered with."

"Oh, no," Ham said.

"Yes, and they suspect a member of the acting company. Her name is Lucy Barastrow. She's fairly new. Someone heard them having a fight a couple of days before the performance."

"Was she in the production?"

"What? No, she was hanging around backstage."

"What was the fight about?"

"Another actor walked into the middle of it. He didn't understand it, but he said they were both screaming."

"What's the favor?"

"Can you come down here and talk to her? Find out if it's likely that she might have done this? I can't collect on his insurance until they determine the cause of death, so, if she's responsible, the sooner the police arrest her the better. They don't seem all that interested yet, even though they think she's suspicious. I don't know who else to ask. I can't ask anyone from the company."

"Are you sure this is a good idea? Why not let the police handle it? I might just make it worse."

"Well, if you don't want to do it, that's that." Marguerite's voice sounded accusatory, as if Ham would be letting John down. "The funeral is on Friday. Come for that and talk to her afterwards. What can it hurt?"

"Well, when you put it that way."

"Good." Marguerite gave him directions to the church. "I'll see you then."

——— 🧑 ———

Celia didn't feel obliged to go to the funeral. She had agreed to accompany Ham to the Barter Theater only because he promised her a spa weekend afterwards, a promise he didn't keep.

"We could go to the spa after the funeral," he said.

"You wouldn't have any fun."

Celia was right, of course. But Ham wished she would go with him to Abingdon. She might get more from Lucy Barastrow than he could.

"I don't think you should get involved," Celia said. "Let the police handle it."

Right again, but still, he had promised Marguerite.

The Episcopal church was full. Ham found a seat in a pew near the back. During the long, melancholy service, he thought about what a good person John was. At college he was both fun and dependable. Ham couldn't remember John ever letting him down. He was surprised to hear from John after all these years. They had not been in touch since shortly after his wedding. He and Marguerite were moving to Atlanta, and he sent his new address. Why hadn't they made more of an attempt to stay in contact? They were both busy, and neither had occasion to visit the city where the other lived, he supposed. Still, he wished now that he had made an effort. Friends like John didn't come along that often.

John had finally been able to fulfill his dream of professional acting. He wanted Ham at opening night for *Man of La Mancha*. He'd called twice to make sure Ham would be there, proud of his role as leading man. Ham was glad he saw John on stage, even if it was his last performance.

After the service, the mourners were invited to John and Marguerite's home. Inside the house, a tiny clapboard that sat back from the street, he was introduced to John and Marguerite's children. Connor, thirteen, had a butch haircut and piercing green eyes, and wore a dark blue suit. He shook Ham's hand.

"How do you like school?" Ham asked, realizing his mistake when Connor merely stared at him. He tried again. "I knew your dad in college."

"What was he like?"

"He was a lot of fun. And he sang, even back then."

Connor pursed his lips. He looked around the room and then hit his little sister with the palm of his hand on the side of the head.

"Get him some punch," he ordered.

The girl, who Marguerite called Ellie, was about two years younger. She glared at her brother and then moved to the other side of the room, returning with a cup of punch.

"Dad was sick, you know," she whispered to Ham as she handed him the cup. "He wasn't much fun anymore." Connor had chosen to make his escape. Ham saw him head for the kitchen.

Marguerite approached with her hand on the elbow of a woman who looked as if she was in her mid-twenties. She was dressed in blue jeans and a sweater, and she wore long bright green earrings that dangled near her shoulders, which her brown hair just brushed. She was strikingly good looking, but something about her was a little off kilter. She didn't look as if she belonged at a funeral. And she was nervous. Her eyes darted around the room suspiciously, as if someone might jump up at any minute to attack her.

"This is Lucy Barastrow," Marguerite said. "Why don't the two of you go out on the back porch to talk?" She steered Lucy with her hand through the kitchen. Ham followed obediently, although he imagined it would be cold on the porch in the early spring weather. He laid his punch cup on the kitchen counter.

Marguerite practically shoved them out the door.

"No one will bother you out here," she said and closed the door.

"Well," Lucy Barastrow said, "that was rude. Even for a woman who just lost her husband."

"People do strange things in their grief. Did you know John well?"

Lucy shivered from the cold and rubbed her arms. "Brrr. If she doesn't want us in there, let's at least go somewhere warm. There is a cafe down the street."

Ham nodded. They walked briskly to the next block. Inside the café, Lucy found a table near the window, and they both ordered tea.

"Now," Lucy said. "Marguerite indicated that you wanted to speak to me. What about?"

Ham cleared his throat. He felt ridiculous and wished Celia were there to help. "It's about John," he said finally.

"What about John?"

"Someone heard you arguing a couple of days before the accident. You've heard that the police think it was murder?"

"You're not suggesting that I did it?" She practically screamed the question.

"Calm down. People are staring. I just want to know what you were arguing about."

"It's none of your goddamned business." She spoke through clenched teeth.

"Fair enough. Let's talk about something else. How did you get to Abingdon?"

"I got a job," she said sarcastically.

"With the theater company."

"Yes, with the theater company. Did that woman want you to find something that would implicate me in John's murder? We just had a fight, that's all."

"Can't you tell me what it was about? It seems like you're hiding something, and that makes you look suspicious."

"John accused me of taking some money. But I didn't. And I didn't like the way he kept hounding me about it."

"Why did he think you'd taken it?"

"He left his wallet in his dressing room. He saw me walking out of there. He said he was missing more than three hundred dollars."

"What were you doing in his dressing room?"

"It's not just his; it's for the male members of the cast. Another actor told me to get something from in there."

"What?"

"Is this really any of your business?" Lucy sighed.

"No, but the police will ask you the same questions if they haven't already, so you might as well tell me. Practice."

Lucy folded her napkin into little squares. "I don't even know you."

"Look, Lucy, I can't make you talk. But I think you're in trouble, and I might even be able to help if you level with me. John was a good friend, and his wife deserves to rest easy. They won't release the insurance money until this is solved. I don't think you killed John, but something you know might tell us who did. So can't you just talk to me?"

"I was having an affair with another actor. Don't ask me who because I won't tell you. He's married. He left me a note on his dressing table about where we could meet." She snapped the words out.

"Wow," Ham exhaled. "I can see why you wanted to keep that to yourself. Who do you think took John's money?"

Lucy looked at him without flinching for almost a full minute before she answered.

"I don't think he had any money." She spoke slowly and annunciated each word for emphasis.

"Why not?"

"I think he wanted to start a fight with me and needed an excuse. When I first arrived in Abingdon, he asked me all sorts of questions. Where did I come from? What I had done? Was I married? Did I have any family? No one else was that nosy. I would see him watching me all the time. Like he was looking for an opportunity to do something. At first I thought he might be interested in me sexually, but that wasn't it. It was as if he was deciding whether he should set me up. That's what I believe. I know it sounds crazy."

"So why did you go to the funeral if you think he tried to set you up."

"I didn't want people talking about my not being there," Lucy said. "Also, I thought maybe I could learn something."

"And did you?"

"Not really. His wife seems all right. She's not crazy or anything."

"Do you have any ideas about who would have wanted him dead?"

"No, but he was acting strange, I can tell you that."

"His daughter said he was ill."

"You should look into that," Lucy said. "Maybe you'll find some answers there. Now, I really have to go." She riffled through her purse, looking for money for the tea.

"That's okay. I'll get it," Ham said.

He stood up when she left. Then he sat down again to think about what she'd said. What if John had somehow arranged to kill himself for the insurance money? He might have been dying. Depending on his life insurance, he could have been covered for accidental death or murder, but not for things like long-term illness. There were insurance policies like that. Maybe he was trying to set up Lucy. But how would he have worked it so that the plank fell when only he was under it? And why did he want Ham there?

Ham paid the check and decided to drive home rather than returning to Marguerite's. He'd learned all he could from Lucy. And he didn't particularly want to tell Marguerite his theory about what had happened. Better to stay out of it and let her sort it out.

On the drive back to Blue Hill he thought, not for the first time, about what a good guy John was. Ham was sure he would do everything he could to take care of his family.

At home, Ham left a message for his insurance agent. When the agent called back, he confirmed Ham's supposition that there were polices that didn't cover lingering illnesses but covered sudden death, even if by murder. Some of these policies did not cover suicide. Ham wanted to get his hands on John's life insurance policy, but he wasn't going to ask Marguerite about it.

He reported all this to Celia the next day.

"It sounds kind of farfetched," she said. "Someone would have to do something to that plank, and John couldn't. He was on stage."

"And Marguerite was sitting with us."

"Lucy could have been lying."

"I don't think so," Ham said. "But that's just my instinct talking."

"You don't even know if he was dying," Celia said. "Your imagination is running away with you."

— 🎎 —

Two days later, he got another call from Marguerite.

"I expected you to come back to the house," she said. "Did you find out anything from Lucy Barastrow?"

"Nothing worth talking about," Ham lied.

"Did she tell you what she and John were fighting about?"

"Something to do with money was all she said."

"Well, I need another favor."

"What's that?"

"Bail money. They've arrested me for John's murder. I'm at the county jail."

Something in Ham screamed, *Don't do it. Tell her to find someone else.* Instead he said, "How much do you need?"

It was a lot for someone he didn't even know. As he drove to Abingdon, he wondered if he'd ever get the money back. But he didn't see how they could have a case against Marguerite, who was sitting next to him when the plank fell. He was doing this for John.

At the jail, he called the bondsman. She was charged with murder. Ham agreed to take her home.

"How is that charge possible?" Ham asked. "You were with us."

"They think I paid someone to do it; they just haven't figured out who."

"But what motive could you have?"

"Insurance money. John was dying of stomach cancer. The doctors had given him less than a year. They think we arranged it together."

"It doesn't sound like they have much of a case."

"Of course they don't," she huffed. "You'll get your money back when they realize what a stupid mistake they've made."

After Ham dropped off Marguerite, he returned to the jail to speak with the sheriff. He asked who he could talk to about the murder charge against Marguerite.

The sheriff gave him the phone number of a detective. He called the man as he drove back to Blue Hill. What he wanted to know, he told the detective, was whether the case against Marguerite was strong since he had just laid down a lot of money for her bail.

"Strong enough," the detective said.

"Can you give me a little more than that?"

"Talk to the insurance inspector," the detective said. He gave Ham the inspector's name and number and hung up.

The inspector told him two things: the policy didn't pay for death by lingering illness, and Marguerite was the sole beneficiary.

"We won't pay out until all this is settled," he confirmed. "But even if she killed him, she is the beneficiary. We'd have a hard time justifying non-payment if she was convicted, but we'd probably deny her claim and then take her to court if she protested."

"I don't see how they can suspect her when she was sitting with us," Ham said.

"From what I gather, there was a chain holding the plank that had been broken by a saw or something like that. It finally gave way in the final scene of the play. It could have been tampered with before the performance."

"Then it was just luck that John was the only one hit by it?"

"My guess is that it would make a noise that warned people

to get out of the way, no matter when it fell."

It seemed that John had chosen to die under the plank.

—— 🎭 ——

The trial date was six months away.

"I'm sorry. I hope you don't need your money back right away," Marguerite told Ham over the phone.

"I'll manage. Did you find a decent lawyer?"

"Yes, I think I have the best defense attorney in the county. He's worked out a payment plan. And he agrees that everything they have is circumstantial. We're asking for a jury trial. He thinks we'll be fine."

"Glad to hear it. Are you still working for the acting company?"

"No, that's too painful. I'm just helping the attorney prepare my defense and spending as much time with the kids as I can."

Ham wanted to ask her if she needed money, but he realized he didn't want to give more than he already had, so he ended the conversation.

"Take care. And let me know how it's going." That seemed noncommittal enough.

That same week, the insurance inspector called.

"I thought you'd want to know," he said. "They've arrested Marguerite's brother for the murder as a co-conspirator. He was in town, traveled all the way from Chicago, apparently something she neglected to tell the police. And one of the actors saw him backstage the day of the accident."

Ham swore under his breath. Marguerite had played him, and so had John. They must have wanted him there to help further their plan to throw suspicion on to Lucy Barastrow. Ham hoped he'd get his bail money back. But more than feeling bad about the money, he felt bad that John had used him. It was something he would have to live with for the rest of his life. He took Celia out to dinner and told her about it.

"It just shows you can't go back," she said. "Maybe John didn't have such warm feelings toward you. Or maybe you did something to him in college that he had been holding as a grudge all these years, and that's why he used you. Or maybe he just didn't care. You were just someone convenient to call on. I guess you'll never know how he felt. I'm sorry."

So was Ham. It was one more surprise in a life filled with them, many of them good, this one disagreeable. "Well," he said, taking Celia's hand, "I'm so much luckier than John was."

SPRING CLEANING

By Heather Weidner

DOUGLAS WEIMER SLAMMED THE second drawer in the filing cabinet so hard that its rattle echoed across the floor of empty workspaces. His cubicle lights were the only ones on except for the glow of the red exit signs over the stairwell door at the end of the hallway. He threw piles of paper into the orange, rolling bin, designed for moving offices. He kicked the trashcan and sank down in his chair. Life was so unfair. He was hired as the records officer for this medical billing firm. When he interviewed, the job was going to be an executive role with all the perks. And here he was being transferred to another team, his fifth move in three years. Each time he slid farther down the organization chart, and the expectations always changed.

Today, his new vice president and team lead, Keith Myers, cornered him in his cube and berated him for not coding a bunch of invoices. It was just routine paperwork.

Everyone in the office heard the VP's tirade. Keith had the nerve to give him two days to pack all his stuff and two weeks to get the invoices organized, an impossible task with no help. So here he was at ten o'clock at night, moving piles of important documents. He needed to go home soon. After checking the time on his cell phone, Douglas set it on the edge of the desk. The cats would be wondering about dinner.

Sweating through his dress shirt, Douglas stripped off his tie and unbuttoned the collar. He tossed the tie on his guest chair, already stacked with articles that he never got around to reading because he spent too much time with the trivial stuff. He kicked the second rolling orange bin. It skidded into the cabinet on the other side of his workbox. Douglas caught himself when he slipped on the papers littering the floor.

He plopped into his chair and stared at the blank computer monitor. This was a crappy cubicle, and now he was going to the other side of the building where there was a view only of other cubicles. Douglas' first office had a view of the huge neon star on top of Mill Mountain. To Douglas, it was his own personal beacon, not the neon sign that overlooked all of downtown Roanoke since 1949. His mother had said long ago that it was his special star. Now he was banished to an area closer to Keith's team with a view of gray walls instead of the majestic Blue Ridge Mountains. The people here just didn't understand the importance of his role. They kept bogging him down with stupid paperwork when he should have been designing strategic plans and organizational policies and telling other people what to do. He couldn't get Keith to listen. Most days, he couldn't even get past that pit bull of an assistant. Douglas scowled and wiped the sweat off his forehead with his sleeve.

After a short sulk, he stood up and reached to grab the stacks of folders on top of the overhead bin, but missed. Douglas wheeled his chair over the papers on the floor and climbed up to reach the files. He wobbled several times before righting himself. Tossing the papers into the bin, he quickly jumped down, huffing at all this unnecessary work.

That was it. He was going to empty one more cabinet and call it a night. Keith would just have to give him more time. And the four bins that Ingrid, the assistant, sent over would never be enough to pack all of his vital files. She would just have to order more bins.

Bending over the two-drawer cabinet, Douglas started sifting through piles of papers that never made it into file folders. When he stood, he felt something pinch and collapse his throat. Douglas panicked and flailed his arms around in the darkness. He tried to swat at his attacker, but he batted only air.

Grasping at what was caught around his neck, Douglas struggled to pull it loose. The cord only tightened. After several seconds, black spots began to swim in his line of vision as the cord constricted. He dropped to his knees and tried again to loosen the thing around his neck. He could feel someone standing over him. He got a whiff of flowers or perfume. And then he couldn't breathe.

— 🖤 —

"Hey, what's going on in Douglas' cube? It looks like it's been ransacked," said Mitchell Banister, the blond marketing specialist, pausing on his way to the coffee station.

"It always looks like that," Annie Hroesko replied. "Keith gave Douglas two days to get it packed and moved. It doesn't look like he made much progress. And it doesn't seem to be his first priority this morning either."

"It looks like a month's worth of work to me. We could speed it up with a match," Mitchell said. "Didn't he just move?"

"Yep. It's the second or third move. I think they put him on Keith's high-octane team to kickstart him. Douglas has two speeds, and neither of them is much faster than tortoise," Annie sniffed as she closed file folders and returned them to her drawer.

"Well, at least, you'll be getting a new office neighbor."

"That'll be nice. I can't take any more stories about his cats," Annie said as she rolled her eyes. "He is the only grown man I know who uses *precious* and *darling*. And he always talks loudly on that stupid speakerphone. I think he uses it because he knows we have to listen to his *important* conversations," she said.

"Isn't he the one who's always clipping his nails?"

"Don't get me started. Between that and the smelly food in his trash can and his sweatiness, it will be, well, refreshing to have someone new around. I just hope Ingrid, Michael, Sabine, and Keith can get him to toe the line. I'm not sure if he'll know how to deal with them. He may have trouble keeping up."

"That team won't like that. They're all a bunch of overachievers . . . Hey, Eric and I are going to the new deli on the corner at noon. Let me know if you want to go. Good luck with the new neighbor. See ya," Mitchell said as he turned and almost walked into Ingrid Peterson, Keith's overly protective personal assistant.

"Oh, hi, Ingrid. How are you?" He took a step back to look her comfortably in the eye. She towered over most of the men at the office except Keith.

"I'm fine," she said as she took a step in Douglas' cube and retreated. "He got himself all worked up into a snit because Keith made him clean up his cubicle and move to the other side of the floor. It looks like he filled one bin, but it barely made a dent. I'm almost tempted to recycle this stuff. It would be years before Douglas missed it anyway. I don't see why he thinks he needs to keep everything he's ever touched. Annie, do you have a few minutes this morning to help me shovel some of this stuff into the bins?"

"No problem," Annie said. "Does it need to be categorized or organized or something? If so, we'll be here for months."

"No, Keith just said to box it and get it out of here. He doesn't care if we're neat or not. We can box Douglas' personal stuff, too. It can go to his new space and wait for him," Ingrid said as she backed out of Douglas' disaster area and smiled.

"Well, that's the last of it," Annie said as she pushed down the papers in an attempt to close the rolling bin. "I didn't think we'd get it all in there. You are a cleaning machine. I can't believe how quickly you tossed all those piles in the bins."

"Hey, we made it fit," the tall assistant said. "I was motivated to get his mess out of here before Douglas gets back. He doesn't know what he has and doesn't have," Ingrid replied as she dusted off her hands. "I have never seen so much paper before. I think Keith needs to look carefully at our records management processes. I can't believe Douglas knows what he's doing, especially if his cubicle is any indication of his organizational skills. How could this guy be the example for records management for our company?"

"I'm surprised that the building floor marshal didn't say something to him. His workspace is a fire hazard. We did our good deed for the week by cleaning it up," the diminutive blonde said as she returned to her workspace.

"Thanks for all of your help with this debacle."

"Hey, I think of it as beautifying the neighborhood," Annie snickered as she returned to her computer.

Ingrid looked up from her desk when Keith Myers raised his voice to the caller. Trying to concentrate on the numbers she was verifying, Ingrid couldn't block out Keith's booming voice. She had to tune him out most days. He never closed his office door.

"I know it's a risk....I know....You're telling me. But I think we can make it work . . . It will affect the team for a while, but I need a little time to turn it around. It's an important effort. Karl, I see it as a challenge. Just give me some time. I will talk to Douglas and the team. I don't think he's a bad guy. He just needs to be focused and to have his expectations defined. Hey, and if it doesn't work out, we'll get someone else who can do the job."

Ingrid fidgeted in her seat. She didn't want Keith to see that she was eavesdropping. He was talking to Karl Boseman, the Chief Operating Officer. Ingrid hated that Douglas was now on their team. That slug's laxness was going to bring down their numbers or cause an audit. They were focused and always exceeded expectations, which meant big bonuses. She didn't want to miss out on a bonus because of Douglas. Keith was wrong about this one. She adored her boss, but he gave too many chances when it came to his staff. He wanted to coach and do everything he could to try to help. This was not good for the team. He should focus his energy on his stars, not the dead weight. Keith interrupted the rant in Ingrid's head.

"Okay, okay. A couple of weeks. He didn't show up again today. I'll get with him as soon as he returns. He'll know that he has a set timeline, and that's it. He needs to get on board with this new team, or he's gone. I'll partner him up with some of my guys to help."

Keith hung up the phone and stepped outside in front of Ingrid's desk.

"Any word from Douglas?"

"No. I've called his home and cell and texted him. He's not on Facebook or LinkedIn. He hasn't called me back," Ingrid said as she stared up at her tall boss.

"Well, go ahead and have the stuff moved to his new space on our side of the floor. He can sort it out when he returns. Also let HR know that he's been out two days with no contact. If we don't hear from him tomorrow, they will have to step in."

"Annie and I packed his stuff this morning. I'll call the movers and HR. It's not like him to not contact anyone," Ingrid said sweetly.

"Thanks for getting this mess cleaned up."

"No problem. I do what needs to be done. You can always count on me," she said, smiling at Keith.

— 🎎 —

Ingrid walked toward the elevators to meet the movers. When the three guys in jeans and yellow T-shirts stepped out with two dollies, she said, "I'm Ingrid. Follow me." She led them through the warren of cubes and file cabinets to Douglas's area.

"Here we are. The three here go to basement storage. That one with the lock goes to the offsite storage. It's full of confidential documents. I tagged it. We have to keep it for fifty years, so find a good place in the back of warehouse for it to rest in peace. Everything should be good to go. All the paperwork is in order."

Ingrid stepped back and scowled as she looked around Douglas' empty workspace.

The first guy nodded and wrote something on his clipboard. When he pointed to the smaller bins, the two guys behind him rolled them out to the hallway.

Annie walked by with a stack of folders. "Moving day?"

"Yep," Ingrid replied. "Cleaning house."

The movers returned and wheeled the locked bin slowly out of the cube.

Seeing their struggle, the guy with the clipboard said, "Get the other dolly. That one is heavier that it looks."

After some maneuvering, they managed to get it rolling down the carpeted hallway.

The mover guiding the pushcart stopped suddenly. "Did you hear that?"

His partner shook his head.

"It's a phone," the first mover said. "I heard a phone coming from in there. I heard *What's New Pussycat*."

Ingrid quickly pulled her cell out of her jacket pocket.

"It's just me," she said as she smiled and waved her phone. She tapped the screen a couple of times. "Thanks for getting this junk out of here so quickly."

"That's funny," Annie said as she stepped into her cube. "You have the same ring tone as Douglas. I didn't know you liked Tom Jones, too."

The clipboard guy nodded and handed Ingrid a pink form. He followed the movers with Douglas' bins toward the elevator.

"Well, Annie, it looks like we're done," Ingrid said. "Sorry for all the ruckus. It should be quieter and less cluttered around here from now on. See ya."

"And it will smell a little better, too," Annie said as she smiled.

BIKES, BOATS AND BERRIES

By Lee A. Wells

HOMEMADE STRAWBERRY ICE CREAM! It was all Allison Mitchell had been able to think about since the berry farm announced it was open for the season. So when Saturday arrived, she dusted off her mountain bike and hit the road.

With the mid-morning sun on her back, she cruised into a convenience store parking lot. Passing a small red and green RV parked at the gas pumps, she chuckled at the personalized license plates, HUMNBRD. *Clever,* she thought.

Across the lot a long-haired man squatted by a low rider Harley. As he turned, Allison noticed the colors and rockers of a motorcycle club embroidered on the back of his leather vest. She had no doubt one of the gang experts from work could rattle off whether it was a weekend warrior club or a 1 percent gang, but it was all Greek to her. Behind him on the grass stood a tall, slender woman dressed in skintight leather pants and a barely legal halter-top, puffing on a cigarette as she watched him work.

Gliding between a pair of parked SUVs and up a small ramp onto the sidewalk, Allison parked her bike next to a faded ice cooler.

Entering the store, she made a beeline for the ATM. Every aisle of the store was crawling with young boys wearing matching white club T-shirts. Opening her fanny pack, she pulled out a bankcard. As she sidestepped several boys running by with handfuls of candy, a leather wallet fell out of the pack. Striking the floor, it opened revealing a gold badge and picture ID.

One of the boys slid to a stop, gawking at the badge. "Cool."

"You like that, huh?" Allison chuckled as she bent to pick up the wallet.

"Are you a cop?"

"Sort of, I work for the FBI." She held the badge out for him to see. "It's okay, you can touch it."

Tracking a fingertip over the badge, the boy's face broke into a wide smile.

"What's your name?"

"Thomas." He answered without taking his eyes from the badge.

"Hello, Thomas. I'm Allison." She held out a hand, and he gave it a firm shake.

"Hi."

"You've got a strong grip there, Thomas."

Grinning, he held out a small paper bag. "Want a jawbreaker?"

"No, thanks. Are you visiting Jamestown?"

"Nah, we just left there. Can I see your gun?"

"Well, I..."

"Boys!" A slender woman outfitted in the same club t-shirt, with a white baseball cap, blond ponytail pulled through the hole at the rear, held the door open. "It's time to load up."

"I gotta go." Thomas waved as he rushed to the door.

"Bye." Allison waved back as she watched him sprint to one of the SUVs.

"Children," laughed an older woman behind her. "I wish I still had that kind of energy." Her voice had a faint twang often found in southwestern Virginia.

Allison laughed as she stepped to the ATM and began punching in numbers.

"I know what you mean."

"Do you have any children?"

"No, do you?"

"Yes, three girls. But they're all grown up now, raising families of their own." she smiled. "I'm Dot by the way, Dot Anderson."

Allison took the money from the ATM and placed it in her pack.

"Nice to meet you Dot, I'm Allison Mitchell."

"Allison, that's a pretty name. So do you live around here?"

"Thank you. Yes, I live in Williamsburg."

"It's lovely here. I told Jerry, that's my husband, that we should bring the Hummingbird here more often."

"Hummingbird? You mean the RV out front?"

"That's my baby." Dot's small frame shook with laughter. "When I saw it on the lot, I said 'Jerry, that looks just like a hummingbird.' And he said, 'It sure does.' So we bought it, and that's what we named it: the Hummingbird."

"I noticed the plates."

"Aren't they darling? Jerry wanted to name it after something NASCAR, but I told him I won't ridin' 'round the country in a rolling man cave."

Allison chuckled with her.

"So where are you from?"

"South Boston. Jerry retired last month, so we loaded up the Hummingbird and hit the road."

"Sounds like fun."

"The places we visit are beautiful, but the driving gets a bit boring." Dot scanned Allison's bike attire. "I noticed all the trails in the area. It must be nice to get out and ride without worrying about getting run over."

"It is, but I'm heading over to Surry, to the berry farm. Unfortunately, there aren't any trails there."

The woman's soft blue eyes lit up. "There's a berry farm in Surry?"

"Yes, College Run Farm, off Alliance Road."

"I'm not familiar with that one."

"It's not hard to find. Once you cross the ferry, head toward Bacon's Castle. But, if you get to the Castle, you've gone too far."

"Well, that sounds easy enough. So the berries are ripe?"

"According to their Facebook page, the strawberries are ripe and ready. Just grab a basket and start picking."

"A pick-your-own farm?" Slender eyebrows disappeared beneath silvery bangs. "I love those."

"Me, too," Allison leaned in, "but I'm actually going for the homemade ice cream."

"Oh, that does sound good."

"Just make sure you bring cash; they don't take plastic."

"Lordy, how do they get away with that in this day and age?"

"I don't know, but it seems to work for them." Allison glanced at her watch. "I need to get going. Don't want them to run out before I get there."

"Can't have that now, can we?" Dot chuckled. "Thank you, dear. Maybe we'll see you at the farm."

"Maybe." With a wave Allison headed for the door.

She pulled the bike onto the pavement and mounted up. At the gas pumps a short man in a checkered, button-down shirt was washing the RV's windshield with a squeegee. *Jerry, I presume.* Fastening her helmet, Allison pushed off. She waved at the man, who tipped his baseball cap in return, as she glided by. From the corner of her eye, she noticed the man still tinkering with the bike; there was no sign of the woman. Reaching the bike trail, she settled into a comfortable pace.

The smell of fresh-cut grass filled the air as Allison cruised the final mile leading to the river. Dogwood trees lined both sides of the road, their branches weighted down with white blooms that shone bright against the green backdrop of the trees behind them. Reaching the end of the line of cars waiting for the next ferry, Allison glided to a stop. Dismounting, she pushed the bike along the dock between the vehicles and the jersey wall. The dock on this side of the river jetted out farther than the one on the Scotland side, affording a nice view of the river.

Spying the ferry churning toward the slip, she smiled. Perfect timing. Even from this distance, she knew it was the *Virginia*, her favorite of the four ferries that serviced the river. Though the smallest, it had an open observation deck that circled the wheelhouse, where the other ferries had enclosed observation cabins.

Leaning her bike against the railing, Allison noticed a faint redness spreading over her pale forearms. Taking a small spray can of suntan lotion from the fanny pack, she coated her arms and legs. Spraying some into the palm of her hand, she rubbed it onto her face, careful to cover her nose and the tips of her ears. Returning it to the pack, she settled against the jersey wall to wait.

Several of the boys from the store were gathered at the railing, laughing, pointing, and shoving each other. Judging by the feathers, toy muskets, and wooden swords they carried, she guessed the Jamestown fort gift shop had enjoyed their visit.

The recreated fort and American Indian village lay in the woods just beyond the dock. When the wind shifted, she caught a faint hint of wood smoke from the re-enactors campfires. Allison remembered when the three ships, reproduced to look like the ones the settlers arrived on, had been visible from the dock. She was just a child then. Over time, the trees along the cove's rocked outcrop had grown to shield them from view.

The clack, clack of wood striking wood drew her attention to two of the boys engaged in a sword fight in the open travel lane. They spun, kicked, and flailed wildly with awkward moves, no doubt mimicking some Ninja or superhero.

"Thomas, put that away!" The woman from the store was striding toward the boys gathered at the railing.

Allison turned from the battle as two more boys rushed to join in.

Armed with a slingshot, Thomas was zeroing in on something bobbing in the clam waters. As she reached him, he released the sling and something hard smacked a plastic crab pot dead center. Grinning from ear to ear, he waved at Allison. Impressed by the shot, she waved back giving him a thumbs up. The woman stopped him as he reached to reload with another jawbreaker. She and two men began herding the boys into SUVs as the ferry bumped against the dock and settled into the slip.

Retrieving her bike, Allison glanced over her shoulder to see a green and red RV stop at the end of the line. She started to throw up a hand in greeting but noticed there was only one person in the front. Even at a distance she could tell it wasn't Jerry. *What are the odds of there being two red and green RVS heading for the ferry at the same time?* It's seemed impossible, but it was a tourist haven, and there were acres of RVs in the area. Shrugging off the thought, she pushed the bike along the dock.

It took less than ten minutes for the ferry to unload and reload. The crew had the process down to a science. Placing her bike under the open stairwell, Allison sprinted up the stairs to stake out a spot on the observation deck.

From her perch she could look down on the loading ramp. The RV was one of the last of the vehicles to board. As it crossed the ramp, she had a clear view of the man driving. It definitely wasn't Jerry. The RV was directed to the inner row next to one of the club SUVs. Behind it, a motorcycle eased aboard and a crewmember directed it to the end of the line on the opposite side of the ferry. A lone figure dressed from head to toe in black leather guided the bike to its parking spot. Even with a mirrored full-face helmet covering the rider's face, the form-fitting attire left little doubt the rider was female.

Once the loading ramp started to rise, the boys poured from the SUVs, weapons in hand, looking as if they were storming the beach. Some headed for the railing, while others climbed the steps to the observation deck. Beneath her feet, Allison felt the engines throttle up, and the water at the stern churned white as the ferry moved away from the slip.

Cruising along at a decent speed, the ferry followed the shoreline, first passing Jamestown. Ashore, groups of children ran along the dock between the sailing ships; several paused long enough to wave at their parents to hurry up.

Two little girls with matching outfits and ponytails rushed to the ferry railing. The younger peered through the wire mesh as the older one's chin rested on the handrail. A young woman holding a toddler, with a plastic bread bag dangling from her hand, moved to the railing.

"Mommie, can we ride the ship across the river?" The youngest girl asked, bouncing against the mesh.

"What ship, sweetie?"

"The big one. You know, the Sarah Conner."

Allison suppressed a laugh.

The older girl turned to her sister. "It's not called that."

"Is too."

"Is not. She's the lady that fights robots."

"Girls, Isabel, don't fight with your sister." She shifted the toddler on her hip. "Elaina, honey, it's named the Susan Constant. Remember, the lady at the fort said the ships were just for show."

"Oh." Elaine pressed her head against the wire mesh.

Eying the small vessels tucked away in their cove, Allison couldn't fathom crossing the river, much less, an ocean in one.

"Isabel, do you know the names of the other ships?"

"Discovery and Godspeed!" The girl announced with a broad smile.

"That's right." Prying her necklace free, the woman kissed the toddler's fingers.

"Look, Mommie, it's the glass house." Isabel pointed at a wooden structure nested in the wood line beyond the fort area.

"Why's it called the glass house?" their mother asked.

"'Cause that's where the Jamestown people made their glass," Elaina replied.

"That's right. Okay, girls, do you want to feed the seagulls?"

Twin ponytails bobbed up and down.

Opening the bread bag, she held it out, letting each girl scoop out a handful of crumbled bread. Isabel tossed her bread over the railing, where a flock of gulls chased after it. Her sister's aim wasn't as true. Bread struck the mesh wiring and bounced off, landing on the deck. The girls gathered the bread, throwing pieces over the railing one at a time until it was gone.

"Mommie, who's that green man?"

Allison followed Elaina's pointing finger to the shoreline. They were coming in line with Jamestown Island, site of the original fort.

"That's Captain John Smith," her mother replied.

Mounted atop his perch, the good captain's green-tinted statue stood watch at the river's edge. Behind him, Allison could make out the brick Memorial church with the Tercentenary Obelisk close by.

"Where's Pocahontas?" Isabel asked as she stood on tiptoes for a view over the railing.

"She's behind the trees," her mother said. "You can't see her from the river."

A seagull swooped within arm's reach, eyeing Allison as it searched for crumbs. Stepping back from the railing, she decided a change in venue was needed. Heading down the stairs, she moved around the rear of the RV, heading for the railing. Glancing at the vehicle's tag, she pulled up short. HUMNBRD.

Moving along the railing, she found a position where she could see the driver. She noticed he seemed out of place behind the wheel of the RV. Large mirrored sunglasses concealed his eyes, while a heavy five o'clock shadow covered the lower half of his face. A dark blue golf shirt strained at the seams over his thick arms and chest. From under one sleeve a sliver of a tattoo peeked out, but she couldn't tell what it was. While everyone else seemed interested in sightseeing, he kept checking the side mirrors, as if he were looking for something or someone.

Dot hadn't mentioned anyone else traveling with them. So who was this guy, and where were Dot and Jerry? Circling the vehicle deck, Allison checked upstairs before returning to her spot at the railing. There was no sign of the couple. They had to be in the RV, but they didn't seem like the type to miss out on enjoying the sights of a ferry ride. Studying the driver, Allison couldn't shake the nagging feeling that something wasn't right. She felt the ferry turning. Spying a green buoy, she realized they were entering the channel. In about ten minutes they would reach the opposite shore.

Reaching into her fanny pack, past keys and the can of suntan lotion, she touched the leather ID wallet. Though she carried the title FBI Special Agent, her true talents had lain in spreadsheets and computer systems. For her the G in G-man had always been more geek than government. During raids she'd been part of the bag-it and tag-it squad, showing up after the big guys with the big guns had done their thing. Her gun was locked away in a safe, buried under a pile of dirty clothes in her closet. As the ferry lined up with the channel buoy, she moved toward the RV.

With a pleasant smile she stepped up to the open driver side window. "So what's her name?"

"What?" The man's head snapped around causing a ponytail to bounce into view.

"Your RV. I know most road folks like to christen their babies."

The man shifted in the seat looking out the windshield. "It ain't got one." His harsh tone didn't match the urban dad outfit he was wearing.

"Well, she's a beauty. With those colors you should call her Hummingbird."

"Nah," He snorted out a laugh. "That ain't happening." He turned back to the windshield.

Allison resisted the urge to rock on the balls of her feet as she debated her next move. There was no way the growling gorilla in the driver's seat was related to Jerry and Dot.

Taking out the ID, she straightened her back. Mustering her most official tone, she held the badge up for the man to see. "Sir, I'm FBI Special Agent Allison Mitchell. I need to search your vehicle."

"What?" Thick eyebrows flexed up and down at the top of the mirrored glasses as he blinked in surprise.

"I said I need to search your vehicle. It's a security concern, sir.

"You got a warrant?"

Allison felt her stomach tighten. Something told her the man's knowledge of legal procedures hadn't come from law school.

"Sir, under U.S. Marine Security Code all persons, baggage, personal effects, and vehicles are subject to screening and inspection." She quoted the large notice sign that had been posted at the dock.

His jaw set as his grip tightened on the steering wheel. A vein in his forehead began to throb, and she wondered if he was going to respond. "Come to the side door." He rolled up the window before she could answer.

Standing at the door, she tried not to bounce as she waited. The summer homes and cottages along the shore were growing larger. Checking her watch, she considered returning to the window when she heard the lock turn and the door opened. The man looked around then stepped back. "Get in."

She hesitated; perhaps she should have notified the ferry crew of her intent. Looking up at the irritated man, she knew it was too late to back out now. Setting her jaw, she grasped the hand railing for support and stepped onto the first step. As she reached the second step, a hard shove from behind sent her sprawling face first on the RV floor. Behind her the door slammed shut darkening the interior.

It took a moment for her eyes to adjust. Rising to her hands and knees, a booted foot struck her hip, rolling her onto her back. She looked up to find the man and the leather-clad biker woman standing over her. The woman's helmet was gone, and Allison was sure it was the same woman from the convenience store. Pale light reflected off the silver semi-auto gun she held pointed in Allison's direction.

"Why did you let her in?" The woman's teeth were clenched, causing the words to hiss out.

"She's a Fed. What was I going to do, say no?"

As the couple argued, Allison looked around the RV; at the rear of the vehicle was a table area with a wraparound bench. On the bench sat Jerry; his baseball cap was gone and a nasty red bump shone on his bald forehead. Beside him sat Dot; both were bound and gagged with duct tape. Fear shone in their eyes as they silently pleaded for help.

"So what are we going to do with her?" the man asked.

"Get the duct tape, and tie her up." The woman motioned toward a set of cabinets with the gun.

Dread settled in the pit of Allison's stomach as she felt the ferry slowing. They were leaving the channel.

The man moved to the cabinets and began opening and slamming doors.

"You shouldn't have tried to rob the RV in the parking lot," he said to the woman.

"How was I supposed to know the old man would come back so soon?"

"You could have just hit him and run." He slammed the door and moved on to the next one.

"We've been talking about stealing an RV to live out of. This one is perfect."

Digging through the cabinet, he looked over his shoulder at her. "What are we going to do with a hot RV?"

"It's only hot if someone reports it stolen."

The man paused to stare at her. "You wanna kill 'em?"

"Shut up." The woman glanced sideways at the couple.

Easing a hand up, Allison unfastened her helmet strap.

"You didn't say anything about killing anyone."

"I don't hear you coming up with anything better," the woman said.

"Have you gone crazy, Tina? You're talking about killing a Fed."

"Don't use my name, you idiot."

"Hey!" Slamming the cabinet door, he took a step toward her, pointing a grease-stained finger. "Don't call me that. You know I hate that."

A bright red flush had settled in Tina's cheeks as she waved the gun in his direction.

"We don't have time for this. Find the tape and tie her up."

Allison shifted her weight, drawing her legs under her. Her mind raced through her academy defensive tactics training. She cursed herself for blowing off combat classes for computer tech ones.

Opening another door, the man slammed it shut. "Where's the damn tape?"

"How the hell should I know? You used it last."

Mumbling under his breath, the man knelt, opened a door, and began rummaging through the cabinet.

Holding the bike helmet by its strap, Allison swung it at the woman's hand. Tina let out a squeal as she watched the gun leap from her grasp to land in the driver-side floorboard. Bouncing to her feet, Allison held the helmet with both hands and struck the woman across the face, drawing blood. Tina staggered back against the passenger seat. Charging in, Allison struck her again. The force of the blow sent the woman head first into the cab area. She landed face down in the floor with her legs pointed skyward. She made no move to get up.

"You little. . . "

Staring at the fallen woman, Allison had forgotten the man. His fingers squeezed painfully into her arm as he jerked her toward him. Allowing her momentum to carry her forward, she brought the helmet up, slamming it into his face. There was an audible crack, followed by a strangled cry as he stumbled back releasing her.

In two strides she landed on the bottom step, grabbing for the doorknob. She struggled with the lock, as her hands shook. Then it released with a click, and she threw the door open. Bright sunlight greeted her. Biting back a cry of relief, she moved to jump to the deck. Something caught her ponytail, jerking her head back at a painful angle. She fell back against the man's solid chest as a muscular arm wrapped around her throat. The sleeve had ridden up, and a tattooed red-eyed snake resting in a skull eyehole stared at her. Holding the doorframe with one hand, she clawed at the arm with the other. He tried to pull her back, but she refused to let go. Standing on the step above her, he was safely out of kicking range. She couldn't twist enough to bite him. Clawing and pinching only caused his grip to tighten.

Balling her hand into a fist, she swung back, hoping to strike his groin. Her hand bounced harmlessly off his thigh. Trying to reach back for another target, her hand brushed against her fanny pack. Grasping for the pack's zipper, she fumbled with it before managing to open it.

The pain in her neck dulled as her lungs began to ache. Spots dotted her vision. Digging into the pack, her fingers brushed against cool metal. As she pulled her hand free, her ID wallet fell out, bouncing off the bottom step to land open on the deck. Closing her eyes, she reached back waving her arm from side to side, spraying the suntan lotion in what she hoped was the man's face.

With a startled yelp, he released her. Pulling herself forward, she tumbled out onto the deck, gasping for air. Inside the RV she heard cursing as the man stomped down the steps toward her. She tried to stand, but her legs refused to work. Something whizzed over her head, followed by a muffled crack, then a dull thud rocked the RV. Through the doorway she could see the bottoms of the man's boots hanging over the edge of the steps.

"Hi."

She looked up to find Thomas hanging out the SUV window, slingshot at the ready, smiling at her. With a teary smile she gave him a thumbs up.

The ferry bounced lightly against the dock, then came to a stop. She saw the yellow shirt of a ferry crew member rushing toward her. Relaxing against the RV, she closed her eyes and breathed a sigh of relief.

— 👧 —

Settling onto a plastic picnic bench, Allison watched as the club leaders attempted to corral the boys, wooden weapons in hand, running around the parking lot. She hardly noticed the evening heat as a cool breeze passed through the open-ended garage that doubled as a storage space and picnic area for berry pickers and store customers.

After hours of questioning by local and state authorities,

Allison had given up on her quest for ice cream, but her newfound friends would have none of it. An impromptu parade of minivans, sheriff department and state vehicles, led by the red and green RV, besieged the berry farm.

Folks in the fields stood to watch the line of vehicles roll into the parking lot. More than a few rushed to the store to either pay for their berries or see if they could pick up some juicy gossip from the group.

Hailed as a hero, Allison had been deposited at the picnic table as the group mingled around the store area of the farm. Several jumped in line for ice cream as Jerry and a deputy sheriff were eyeing a large strawberry pie in the glass display case.

The bench shifted as a state trooper settled in beside her with a Styrofoam cup of vanilla ice cream. Allison's mouth began to water as she eyed the cup.

Trooper Myers scooped up a spoonful of ice cream. "Thanks to you, we're going to be able to close about a dozen larcenies and at least two assaults in the area."

She watched with envy as he placed the spoon in his mouth.

"Those two idiots have been preying on tourists in the area for the past year, breaking into vehicles, mugging travelers, basically stealing anything that wasn't nailed down. Facing kidnapping and attempted murder charges, they've turned on each other like wild dogs. They can't throw each other under the bus fast enough to save their own butts."

"Glad to hear it."

"Here you go, sweetheart."

A board smile spread over Allison's face as she reached for the heaping bowl of strawberry ice cream Dot held out to her. "Thank you."

"Do you need anything else?" Dot hovered at the ready.

"No, thank you. How much do I owe you?"

"Oh, please," Dot waved her off with a tsk. "After what you did for us, the least we can do is buy you some ice cream."

Dot patted her shoulder and then moved to a nearby table where Jerry had settled with a slice of strawberry pie a la mode. A blue ice pack poked out from beneath his ball cap.

Allison lifted a spoonful to her mouth, pausing to inhale the sweet smell of fresh strawberries. The table shifted as Thomas settled onto the bench opposite her. He held a large cup of ice cream.

"Hey, Sureshot, what flavor did you get?"

"Strawberry." He held the cup up for her inspection.

"Good man." She touched her cup to his in salute.

Taking a bite, she closed her eyes to savor it, letting the sweet cold confection settle on her tongue as it slowly melted. "This is so good."

Across the table Thomas giggled. "It's just ice cream."

Opening her eyes she arched a brow at him. "No, my boy, this," she poked the spoon at the creamy scoop, "is heaven."

Everyone in earshot laughed.

Taking another bite, she smiled. Bikes, boats, and berries, it was a good day.

WITHIN THIS CIRCLE

By Ken Wingate

IT WAS A WARM Saturday evening as the Panoptic Financial Investments annual corporate gala began. The attendees gathered in the atrium of the Virginia Museum of Contemporary Art for cocktails before dinner. PFI had used MOCA in Virginia Beach for its yearly celebration for over a decade.

Charles Worthington stood by the doors leading into the Price Auditorium. He gazed disdainfully across the hall at his coworkers. Standing there was Paul Cummins, newly promoted Director of International Investments, the position that Charles believed should have been his. Paul was conversing with Michael Prescott and Gregg Orloski, the two key associates who had aided Paul in snatching the directorship out of his hands. Paul would tap them for his personal assistants, leaving Charles limited in his international travels and answering to others for his scheduling. He felt he had been cheated and had expressed his anger to everyone.

Charles watched as a server came from the kitchen to present Paul, Michael, and Gregg the three mugs of Crown Ambassador Reserve beer. Paul had discovered the beer on one of his trips to Australia. The beer was Paul's only request of Mr. Schwartz, the CEO.

As the server approached Paul, Michael, and Gregg, Charles's wife Danielle wrapped her arm around his and escorted him into the Price Auditorium.

"Charles, your scowling is disturbing everyone here," she whispered. "You've got to get past this anger and accept what's happened. We still have our lives to live."

The Chihuly centerpiece hung majestically from the ceiling as they entered the Rodriquez Pavilion. Charles looked into

Danielle's eyes and replied, "This was supposed to be my day! I've spent the last three years working for this, anticipating the recognition I deserve and being promoted to my rightful position where I wouldn't have to answer to anyone but Mr. Schwartz. What others think, how they may feel doesn't matter to me. This was supposed to be my day of celebration, not Paul's! If people have an issue with my anger, let them come to me and tell me to my face!"

"Charles!" Danielle exclaimed, "I don't understand why you are acting this way. What has changed you? You were so much happier when we had so much less. Your thirst to gain power has hardened you and made you into a person I don't know. Why?"

Just as Charles was about to answer her, screams of horror and panic were heard throughout the hall. Danielle and Charles rushed to the atrium. Everyone had gathered in the corner where Paul, Michael, and Gregg had been standing. Charles pushed his way through the crowd to see the bodies of the three men lying on the floor. Their wives were kneeling over them in anguish.

Associates began appealing for everyone to step back and make room for the medical professionals who were in attendance. Charles was told that the police and paramedics were on their way. He grabbed Danielle by the hand and led her over to a chair. She was visibly shaken with tears streaming down her cheeks. The atrium was still in chaos when the police and paramedics arrived.

The police immediately directed the guests away from the bodies so that the paramedics could have room to set up their equipment. The police divided the crowd into groups: Mr. Schwartz and the managing officers, the guests, and the catering company employees. The wives of the three victims were led into the gallery with some close friends while the medical crew tended to their husbands. After twenty minutes of CPR, the paramedics pronounced all three dead.

Detectives Tony D'Angelo and Jack Taylor were standing by their desks when the captain of Virginia Beach Homicide rushed in. "Tony, Jack," he spoke firmly, "we have three dead men at MOCA. A crowd of three hundred people in attendance witnessed them suddenly collapse. It's going to be a long evening for you and your team. This involves some very high profile citizens and a major financial investment firm from our city. It's a real mess. Be thorough. Good luck. Get moving."

D'Angelo and Taylor were homicide veterans and knew by the captain's tone that this was no ordinary investigation. As they sped toward the scene, they discussed strategy. The crime scene crew had already arrived and was canvassing the atrium when the detectives' car pulled into the parking lot. As they entered the building, they were briefed by the responding officers. They looked at each other and breathed deeply. The captain was right. This was going to be a very long evening.

— 🎎 —

It had been a stressful three days. D'Angelo and Taylor had a major homicide case on their hands, and it was clear that city officials desired results quickly. The chief of police had received the city officials' directive to use all of the police force necessary to close this case. Since Saturday night, another related homicide had occurred. This fourth homicide brought to light a person of interest who became the target of the detectives' investigation.

It was early Tuesday afternoon when D'Angelo, Taylor, and an investigation team arrived at the Bay Colony residence of Charles and Danielle Worthington. Danielle answered the door. D'Angelo spoke calmly.

"Mrs. Worthington, we have a warrant to search your home and your husband's car. You'll find the details here." D'Angelo handed the search warrant to Danielle as he and the crew entered.

Charles came down the stairs. "What's going on?"

As the crew began searching the house, D'Angelo answered.

"As a part of our investigation, we're canvassing homes and questioning selected employees and managers of PFI concerning the events of last Saturday evening."

One of the investigative crew interrupted D'Angelo.

"There's a secured room at the other end of the house we are unable to enter."

"That's my office," Charles said to the detective. "There's nothing in there but my desk and computers."

"We need to enter it for our records. Open the door, so we can have a look inside," insisted D'Angelo.

Charles hesitated but then relented and led D'Angelo to the room. He entered the security code on the keypad and opened the door.

As the crew walked in, they noted that the office was soundproof. Achievement awards hung on the walls. Centered on top of an elaborately designed oak executive desk was a desktop computer with a microphone headset. A laptop was positioned to its right. A locked briefcase leaned against the right side of the desk. Charles was asked to set the briefcase on his desk and unlock it for the crew to view its contents. He complied and walked out of the room. D'Angelo followed.

Charles found Danielle seated on the sofa in the sitting room. He joined her there. D'Angelo sat in a chair across from them.

"Mr. Worthington, would you mind telling me where you were yesterday evening?"

"Is there any particular reason you need to know?"

"Just answer the question, Mr. Worthington."

"I was home most of the day, as our office was closed due to what happened. I left here around five-thirty in the afternoon to go by the caterer's office. I met the manager there and gave him the balance of what we owed for their services. I left there and went jogging down the Boardwalk, which is my routine every Monday, Wednesday, and Friday evening when I'm home."

"How long were you at the caterer's office?"

"Just a little while."

"After your jog, did you come straight home?"

"No. I stopped by Catch 31 and had a few drinks."

"We were having a disagreement concerning his trip to Thailand this Thursday," Danielle said. "He knew I was upset and wanted to give me time to think things out."

"Why did the trip cause a disagreement?" D'Angelo asked.

"Danielle believes I should stay in town for the funerals. I reminded her that this trip was one of the most important I'd ever arranged in my career. It would be disastrous to put it off now."

"I disagree," Danielle was adamant. "I feel your leaving is wrong. The deceased were associates important to Mr. Schwartz and your company. They should be shown the respect they deserve."

"Let's stay focused on the matter at hand," D'Angelo said.

Just then, Taylor stepped into the room and motioned to speak to his partner. They walked down the hall and began whispering. After a few moments, D'Angelo returned.

"I need to make a phone call. I'll be back in just a moment."

Danielle sat on the sofa, deep in thought. She was disturbed that Charles wanted to leave town during such a horrific time. She felt it was a slap in the face to Mr. Schwartz and his company, but knew that Charles would not change his mind.

The two detectives returned to the sitting room. D'Angelo spoke directly to Charles.

"As per the search warrant, we're removing your computers to have our investigators search them more extensively. There's no need for us to hold your car. We'll be in touch."

Danielle and Charles watched from their door as the investigation crew drove off. Danielle could tell Charles was upset.

"What's going on, Charles? Is there something you need to tell me? Are they going to find something I need to know about?"

"No," Charles replied sharply. "It's nothing that concerns you." Charles paused and looked away from Danielle, "I'm going to the office. I have some loose ends to tie up before my trip."

Charles walked out to his car and drove off.

Danielle stood on the front steps of their home. The sun was making its way toward the western horizon. She turned, went back inside, and closed the door.

It was early Wednesday morning. The aroma of freshly brewed coffee filled the house. Danielle sat at the kitchen bar as the sun gleamed through the windows. Charles entered the kitchen. He had returned home late the night before. He did not look at Danielle or speak a word. He was dressed for work. The silence was broken by the ring of the doorbell. Danielle stepped down from her stool and proceeded toward the front door while Charles poured himself a cup of coffee. Danielle opened the door to Detectives D'Angelo and Taylor.

"Good morning, Mrs. Worthington," D'Angelo said. "Is Mr. Worthington home?"

"Yes," Danielle replied as she opened the door to allow the detectives to enter.

"We need to speak to him."

"I'll get him. He's in the kitchen."

Charles made no attempt to conceal his annoyance. "What do the two of you want now?"

"Mr. Worthington, we need to question you more extensively concerning the events of the past few days. We'd like for you to come with us to the station. It's to your benefit that you do so voluntarily."

"I'm beginning to feel that I need my attorney."

"You have that right."

"Danielle, call Allen and let him know what's happened. Tell him to meet me at the station. I don't want to delay my trip to Thailand. Let him know that. I'm sure this will be over soon. I'll call you when I'm on my way home." Looking at D'Angelo, he said, "Let's make this quick."

Danielle immediately went to the phone and called Allen Jacobson, Charles's attorney.

———— 🎎 ————

Charles had been sitting in one of the interrogation rooms of the Virginia Beach Homicide Division for a couple of hours when his lawyer joined him.

"I got here as soon as I could," Jacobson announced. "I had a hearing this morning that I had to attend. Are you okay?"

Charles replied, "What's going on? I need to get out of here. I still have a lot to do before I fly out tomorrow."

"Charles, this is a major homicide investigation. The heat's coming all the way down from the mayor's office to make an arrest. You have become their primary person of interest. You need to keep yourself calm and not be so intent on this trip. Get your name cleared first. If the authorities see you rushing to get out of town, it will only make you look more suspicious."

"What are you saying, Allen? Are you telling me that they think I murdered Paul, Michael, and Gregg?"

"Charles, the detectives have statements from witnesses and PFI associates, security video footage, and strong circumstantial evidence that provide them with motive and opportunity, not just for the deaths of Paul, Michael, and Gregg, but also for the manager of the catering service you hired for the gala."

"Jesse?" Charles asked with a shocked look. "Jesse is dead?"

"Yes, Jesse. His boss found his body at the office Monday night. Jesse was supposed to meet him for an appointment with one of their clients. When he didn't show or answer his cell, his boss drove to the office and found Jesse stabbed to death."

"They think I had something to do with that?"

"They have video footage of you entering and leaving through the front door of the office. You came in carrying a duffle bag. When you left, you were still carrying the duffle bag, but you were wearing your jogging clothes. You were there during the time of Jesse's death, according to the coroner."

"Allen, when I left Jesse, he was alive. I dropped off the balance of the money PFI owed the company; we had a beer and talked. I used the back bathroom to change into my jogging clothes." Charles paused for a moment. "That's why Detective D'Angelo wanted to know where I was Monday night."

"What did you tell him?"

"Exactly what I just told you."

"Charles, they also know you were planning to serve Danielle with divorce papers this Friday while on your Thailand trip. They know about your three-year affair with Mai from that country. They've spoken to her and taken a statement from her about your relationship. You're in serious trouble. You need to give me an accurate account of all these matters in order for me to prove your innocence."

Feeling his throat tighten, Charles looked at Allen.

"What are you saying? What have they done? What did they tell Mai? How did they find out about her?"

"They found all of your correspondence to her on your computers. They also found all of the messages for the procurement of the cyanide they believe was used to kill Paul, Michael, and Gregg. The evidence is stacked against you, Charles. They are confident you are guilty of the murders."

"I must speak to Mai. I have to let her know I love her. Once she knows that this is all a mistake, she'll be fine."

"Charles, you cannot speak to Mai. She's told them everything about your relationship. She told them that you had an engagement ceremony planned during your visit to Thailand over the next three weeks. Her family and friends had planned to be there. She's very upset and has made it clear that you're not to contact her. She said you have disgraced her and her family. Charles, you've got to focus on what's happening right here, right now. Get her out of your head. If we don't prove you are innocent, you won't ever see the light of day."

At that moment D'Angelo and Taylor entered the room. "Mr. Worthington, I gather your attorney has filled you in as to why you are here," proclaimed D'Angelo.

"You!" bellowed Charles. "You have turned Mai against me by telling her lies!" Charles glared at Allen. "You must contact Mai and tell her that I am going to fix everything. You have to tell her that I am innocent and that it will all be okay. Let her know we'll be together once I've fixed this mess. Allen, I need you to do this for me. Contact Mai and tell her I love her. Tell her it will all be okay."

Charles was so distraught that he did not hear Taylor read him his rights. He did not feel the handcuffs tighten around his wrists behind his back. He was aware only of the words that Allen had spoken to him: Mai did not want to hear from him again. He continued his pleas to Allen to contact Mai as he was escorted out of the room to his holding cell.

The deputy directed Danielle to her visitation terminal at the Virginia Beach City Jail. Once seated, her video monitor came on and Charles's face appeared. She stared at the man before her. He was not the man she had known. He was disheveled and expressionless. His eyes were bloodshot from lack of sleep. His hair was uncombed. He was looking at her but not seeing her. He was empty of any emotions.

Although Danielle was shocked by Charles's appearance, she did not show it. Her thoughts went back to the young man she knew who wooed her many years ago on the campus of the College of William and Mary where they had met. She remembered the young man who refused to take "no" for an answer when he asked her to dinner. She remembered the young man who had professed his eternal love to her on their wedding day. She remembered that young man. The man that sat before her now was someone she did not know.

Danielle reached for the handset and placed it to her ear. She watched as Charles reached for his. His hand was shaking. He took a deep breath.

"What happened?" Danielle asked. "What did I do to deserve this? I have stood beside you and supported you throughout your career. I didn't ask for anything from you but your love. You were the one driven to have the nicer cars, a bigger home, and more money. I never asked for any of it. I never required you to provide it for me. All I wanted was your love and devotion. Why did you betray me? What could she do for you that I could not?"

"I love her," said Charles, staring at her and never changing expressions.

"Enough to kill for her? Enough to destroy all that we have together?"

"My innocence is irrelevant. They've turned her against me. I need to talk to her. I need to make her understand that I'm going to fix all of this. I just need to talk to her, and it will all be okay. That's all that is important right now."

Danielle was enraged. His speech and actions had become so irrational and careless. Didn't he understand all that was happening? Had he lost all sense of reality? Didn't he understand the severity of his situation?

"You sit here professing love for a woman halfway around the world while I, your wife, am sitting here in front of you. Do you know what she's doing right now? She's making the most of the spotlight cast on her by this mess. She's all over the news and media shows, sharing how much shame you have brought to her and her family. She's openly discussing the anger you expressed over losing the director's position to Paul. How you would fix it all so that the plans you made with her would still work out. She's digging a grave for you with her words, yet you sit here and profess your love for her."

"She has been lied to and has believed the lie. It'll all be better once I talk to her. Everything will be fine. I just have to talk to her and let her know I love her, and all of this will be fine. I'll fix it. All I need to do is talk to her, and she will believe me and know I didn't do this."

Danielle had nothing more to say. She knew the man who sat before her was not the man she had fallen in love with and married. In his place sat another man, one who had allowed his obsession with a younger woman to destroy him. She quietly pushed her chair back, stood up, and walked out of the room.

The trial was a blur to Charles. He sat motionless and emotionless during the whole process. The only time he showed any expression was while he viewed the video of Mai's deposition.

The prosecuting attorney, Barry Samuels, painted a picture for the jury of the events that had occurred. He presented to them statements from PFI associates of the reckless proclamations Charles had made. He shared how Charles had told everyone that Mr. Schwartz had made a serious mistake and would regret appointing Paul Cummins to the position of Director of International Investments. He paraded one PFI associate after another onto the witness stand to corroborate all of the statements that Charles had made. During their testimonies, some of them described Charles as "self- indulgent," "cocky," "arrogant," and "an ambitious egotist with aggressive behavior."

Samuels presented to the jury the statement that had been obtained by the detectives from Jesse Hammond before his death. Jesse had told the detectives that Charles came into the kitchen, opened the bottles of beer, and poured them into the mugs himself. He had huddled over them in the corner of the counter, so Jesse could not see what he was doing. Upon topping them off, Charles placed them onto a tray and into the refrigerator to ensure they would be cold. He instructed Jesse to serve them to Mr. Cummins, Mr. Prescott, and Mr. Orloski within thirty minutes. Charles left the kitchen.

Samuels provided several catering employees and gala attendees as witnesses. All confirmed seeing Charles with the beer and talking with Jesse.

The partially filled bottle of cyanide that had been found at the bottom of one of the trashcans in the kitchen of MOCA was presented into evidence by Samuels. He presented to the jury screenshots from the laptop computer belonging to Charles of inquiries for and the procurement of that cyanide.

Samuels then turned the jurors' attention to that following Monday evening. He shared how Charles had arranged for Jesse to meet him at the catering company. The security video showed him entering the facility with a duffle bag in tow. It showed him leaving through the same door wearing his jogging outfit fifty-four minutes later, duffle bag still in tow. He told how there were two bottles of beer sitting open in Jesse's office. One of them contained Jesse's DNA; the other contained Charles's DNA. Mr. Samuels presented to the jury the statement given to Detective D'Angelo by Charles admitting his meeting with Jesse. Samuels stated that it was during this meeting that Charles murdered Jesse. Samuels provided evidence of the knife used in the murder, along with a bloodstained waiter's jacket. The knife had been found wrapped in the bloody jacket inside of a garbage bag that had been tossed into the dumpster by the back entrance of the building. Both were covered in Jesse's blood. Samuels called Detective D'Angelo and the head crime scene investigator to the witness stand to confirm these findings.

Finally, Samuels played the taped deposition from Mai concerning her three-year affair with Charles. She shared how Charles had promised her that when he was promoted to his new position, he would be free to visit her more often. When Charles did not get the promotion, he expressed anger. Charles promised her he would fix it all. He told her to make plans for an engagement ceremony that would take place during his next visit to Thailand. He promised her he would have his wife served with divorce papers during this same visit. After the taped deposition, Samuels presented a copy of the divorce papers into evidence.

In his final remarks, Samuels surmised that Charles believed he would be out of the country by the time the police had realized what had happened. With the financial resources available to Charles and his contacts in Thailand, he could easily get lost there and never have to return to this country.

Jacobson was unable to find anyone to act as an effective character witness for Charles. He had no one to refute any of the accusations against Charles. He had no one that could provide him with testimony that would even bring a slight hope of swaying the jurors' opinions of Charles's guilt. Charles had burned all bridges with friends and associates on his quest to become the Director of International Investments. Jacobson had nothing, and when he expressed his concerns to Charles, his answer was always the same. "Allen, we need to contact Mai. If we do that, it'll be okay."

The parade of witnesses, statements provided by associates, and the abundant evidence the police had gathered stacked the deck heavily against Charles. The prosecuting attorney had done an effective job of closing all avenues for reasonable doubt. For those reasons, it did not surprise Jacobson when the jury came back with a guilty verdict. Charles continued to sit motionless as the verdict was read.

Charles remained emotionless throughout the sentencing. He showed no remorse or empathy toward Hillary Cummins, Karen Prescott, and Greta Orloski, the widows of the deceased, as they stood and expressed their pain over the loss of their loved ones. Nor did he show any emotion when the judge sentenced him to four life terms in prison. He was focused on only one matter, contacting Mai.

It was on a Friday night when Danielle's doorbell rang. It had been three months since Charles's sentencing. The eleven o'clock news was beginning as Danielle passed through the sitting room. She opened the door, and her guests quietly entered. Danielle led them down the spacious hall, through the kitchen, and into the sunroom. A bottle of Château Lafite Rothschild Red Bordeaux sat centered on the coffee table. Four Vera Wang crystal wine goblets surrounded it, glistening from the ambient lighting in the room.

Danielle began to talk. She spoke barely above a whisper. Her voice was strained from the emotions she had experienced over the past few days. "I received word Wednesday afternoon that Charles was found dead in his cell. The guards found him with a bag over his head and a zip tie tight around his throat. He had left a note to Mai expressing his unequivocal love for her.

"The prison official told me that Charles had been caught

trying to contact Mai on one of the library computers. He'd received permission to use the computer to communicate with Allen concerning his appeal. Instead, he tried to contact Mai. When confronted by the guard and told that his computer access had been revoked, Charles fell into a state of deep despair. The official believes he obtained the bag and zip tie from another inmate. He performed the act sometime during the hours between the final bed check and the morning wake-up call."

Danielle sighed deeply. She had experienced so many emotions during the past few days; she had no more to release. She continued, "They'll be bringing the body back to Virginia Beach tomorrow. I'll have him cremated and his ashes scattered over the ocean."

Danielle sat up straight. She cleared her throat, took a deep breath, and spoke with renewed strength.

"He was a fool to think that I didn't know about Mai. I could smell her on his clothes. I could see her in his eyes when he looked at me. When he said, 'I love you,' it was for her, not me. His heart had turned away from me to her. I knew that, but I never let him know. Even knowing that, I was still surprised when I found out he had planned to serve me with divorce papers. I don't know why I was surprised, but I was."

Danielle lifted the bottle of wine and began to pour it into the four crystal goblets. She quietly passed each of her guests a full goblet, careful not to spill any of the precious wine.

"It's the same road all of us were headed down," Greta said calmly. "It's the common truth which brought us together. Those papers would've come sooner or later for all of us. The writing was on the wall. I, for one, wasn't about to settle for fifty percent or less. I'd put too much into our marriage to accept that agreement. The affairs come with the territory of promotions and unbridled power, but I wasn't about to let a younger woman enjoy the fruits of my labor. I knew Gregg was beginning to take his last affair more seriously. I could tell she meant more to him than the others had. I wasn't about to be pushed aside."

"The things that men with power will do," said Hillary.

"Yes, but better are the things that women can do with the power they have," Greta responded as she took a sip from the goblet cradled in her hands.

"Michael," Karen interjected, "had so many affairs I'm sure many thought we were in an open marriage. I played along with the game. I kept the leash loose, knowing that I could tighten it when I wanted. Though he thought he was getting away with his affairs, I knew about them all. I always knew where he was and who he was with."

Greta spoke up, "Let us give credit where credit is due. We have Charles to thank for providing us with the perfect scapegoat and Danielle to thank for her willingness to allow him that honor."

A slight smile graced Danielle's face as she nodded her approval to Greta.

Greta continued, "A salute to Hillary for her excellent computer skills and knowledge of all things technical."

"Figuring out Charles's pass code to his office security pad and planting all of the messages concerning the cyanide on his computer were child's play," boasted Hillary. "I could've done all that in my sleep. I say the highest praise should go to Karen and her fascination with the macabre. It was her willingness to perform the dirty deed that made this all work."

"Agreed," chimed Danielle and Greta in unison.

Karen stared intently at the light reflecting from the deep red Bordeaux in her goblet. Hearing the words of Hillary took her back to that evening. A shiver ran through her body as she reflected on that moment. "I must admit," she spoke softly "my fling with young Jesse was one I will never forget. He played into our plan so very well. He did and said all that I had asked of him. It's a shame he got caught in friendly fire. We both had been laughing at the fact that I would be hiding in a hallway closet as Charles came by to visit that evening. Jesse thought I'd be providing him some pleasure after his meeting with Charles. As soon as Charles left, I came out of the closet wearing nothing but the waiter's jacket. He was so completely distracted by what was under the jacket that he never noticed the knife in my hand. It was over before he knew it. That moment was an adrenaline rush like I had never experienced before. Poor Jesse was a necessary sacrifice for our purpose. Tossing the garbage bag, with the jacket and knife inside, into the dumpster was the final touch to a perfect evening."

A moment of silence enveloped the room as the women took in all that Karen had shared. Greta broke the silence.

"We need to continue playing the part of grieving widows for at least another nine months. Then, we can move on with our lives as we each see fit."

"It's a lot easier pretending to be Paul's grieving widow than it was pretending to be the happy, supportive wife of a misogynistic jerk," Hillary said.

"You can say that again," Karen said.

Danielle leaned back into the soft cushions of her loveseat. "It's over," she whispered.

Greta sat erect. "Yes, it's over," she expressed. "But it'll always be known within this circle. It's within this circle that this secret must stay. Always be aware of that truth. Agreed?"

"Agreed," they said in unison.

Greta then raised her goblet.

"A toast. Here's to the good life...our beautiful homes...*all* of the money *and* investments . . . and four deceased husbands."

Acknowledgments

The authors would like to thank Judy Morgan and Mary Miley for their time and talent. We appreciate your attention to detail in proofreading and editing our manuscripts. We would also like to thank the Mystery by the Sea and the Sisters in Crime – Central Virginia chapters for their support.

Virginia is for Mysteries Authors

Meriah Lysistrata Crawford

Meriah Crawford is a writer, an assistant professor at Virginia Commonwealth University, and a private investigator. She has also been a horseback riding instructor, library page, programmer, graphic designer, technical editor, software tester, and has even been paid to put M&Ms into baggies  for bingo. Meriah's writing includes short stories, a variety of non-fiction work, and a poem about semi-colons. Her most recent publications include a story about kids, death, and art set in 17th century Germany, and the real explanation for the Virginia earthquake. Meriah also co-edited the anthology *Trust & Treachery: Tales of Power and Intrigue*. Visit Meriah on Facebook, Twitter, and www.meriahcrawford.com.

Adele Gardner

Adele Gardner goes by her middle name to honor her father and mentor, Delbert R. Gardner—poet, scholar, and WWII veteran— for whom she's literary executor. Adele's Sherlock Holmes mystery, "The Adventure of the Hidden Lane," appears in *A Study in Lavender*. She's had over 325 short stories,  poems, artwork/photographs, and nonfiction published in *Daily Science Fiction, Legends of the Pendragon, The Doom of Camelot, American Arts Quarterly, The Cape Rock, and Magill's Choice: 100 Masters of Mystery and Detective Fiction*. Her poetry collection, *Dreaming of Days in Astophel*, appears under the byline, Lyn C.A. Gardner. Visit Adele on Facebook and www.gardnercastle.com.

Debbiann Holmes

Debbiann Holmes is the author of the modern day pirate series, *Unforeseen Circumstances, Compromises,* and *Surrender.* She resides in Virginia Beach with her husband. When she isn't writing, she to spends her free time at the beach. Follow Debbi on Facebook, Twitter, and www.debbiannholmes.com.

Maria Hudgins

Maria Hudgins lives in Hampton, Virginia. For thirty years, she taught high school sciences, including biology, earth science, oceanography, and chemistry. Maria is the author of five travel mysteries set in exotic locations, two ebook mysteries, and short stories in *Ellery Queen's Mystery magazine* and *Virginia is for Mysteries.*

Visit Maria on Facebook, Twitter, and www.mariahudgins.com.

Teresa Inge

Teresa Inge grew up in North Carolina reading Nancy Drew mysteries. Today, she doesn't carry a rod like her idol, but she hot rods. She assists two busy executives and is president of the Sisters in Crime Virginia Beach Chapter. Teresa is the author of "Shopping for Murder," and "Guide to Murder" in *Virginia is for Mysteries*, "Fishing for Murder" in the *FishNets* anthology and has coordinated anthologies. Visit Teresa on Facebook, Twitter, and www.teresainge.com.

Maggie King

Maggie King is the author of *Murder at the Book Group*, published by Simon and Schuster, and she contributed "A Not So Genteel Murder" to the *Virginia is for Mysteries* anthology. Maggie is a member of Sisters in Crime and the American Association of University Women. She has worked as a software  developer, retail sales manager, and customer service supervisor. She lives in Richmond, Virginia, with her husband and two cats. Visit Maggie on Facebook, Twitter, and www.maggieking.com.

Kristin Kisska

Kristin Kisska, a native Virginian, used to be a finance geek, complete with MBA and Wall Street pedigree. A member of Sisters in Crime, Kristin is now a self-proclaimed *fictionista*. Her short mystery story, "The Sevens" was included in Bouchercon's anthology, *Murder under the Oaks* (October  2015). When not writing suspense novels, she can be found tweeting *@KKMHOO* or on her website~ *about.me/kristin. kisska*. Kristin lives in Richmond with her husband and three children.

C. B. Lane

C.B. Lane grew up in Virginia Beach. After college in Blacksburg, Peace Corps in Senegal, and work in Northern California, she settled in Suffolk, where she lives on a farm near the Great Dismal with her husband and two wiener dogs who bark at everything that moves. C.B. received her  MFA in Writing from Spalding University and is a member of Sisters in Crime. She has written short stories, is a frequent student at the Muse Writer's Center in Norfolk and is working on a novel set in southeastern Virginia just after the Civil War. C.B. blogs at cblanewrites.wordpress.com.

Vivian Lawry

Vivian Lawry is a founding member of the Central Virginia Chapter of Sisters in crime and served two terms as chapter president. She writes mysteries, historical fiction, magical realism, and memoir-based prose. *Nettie's Books* was a finalist in the Best Unpublished Novel Contest sponsored  by James River Writers and *Richmond Magazine*. Her short stories have appeared in more than four dozen literary journals and anthologies, from *The Alembic* to *Xavier Review* to *Virginia is for Mysteries*. She coauthored two Chesapeake Bay Mysteries, *Dark Harbor* and *Tiger Heart*. Her most recent book, *Different Drummer*, is a collection of offbeat fiction. Vivian collects carved wooden Santa's, dictionaries, and Depression glass. She lives and writes near Richmond, Virginia. Visit Vivian on Facebook and read her blogs at vivianlawry.com.

Michael Sean McGowan

Michael Sean McGowan is a teacher and the author of two novels *Pawns* and *The Shadowlands*. He also contributed to the original *Virginia is for Mysteries*. He lives in Virginia Beach. Visit Michael on Facebook and Twitter.

Kathleen Mix

Kathleen Mix is a multi-published author who writes stories with a thrilling mix of romance and suspense. Her latest book, *Sins of Her Father*, was released by Entangled Publishing in September 2015. Two more books, *Impossible Ransom* and *Willing Target*, are slated for release in 2016. After earning a B.S. in Computer  Science and Engineering, Kathleen worked as a software engineer, consulting on applications ranging from submarine combat systems to biological research databases. But as an avid sailor and licensed charter boat captain, Kathleen prefers sailing to sitting in an office. She has traveled extensively on her boat, exploring the US coastline, Bahamas, Caribbean, and north coast of South America. To learn about her books and her travels, visit Kathleen on Facebook, Twitter, Goodreads, and www.kathleenmix.com.

Jayne Ormerod

Jayne Ormerod grew up in a small Ohio town and attended a small Ohio college. Upon earning her accountancy degree she became a CIA (that's not a sexy spy thing, but a Certified Internal Auditor). She married a naval officer, and off they went to see the world. After fifteen moves, she realized she needed a more transportable vocation, so she turned to writing. Jayne writes cozy mysteries about small towns with beach settings. Learn more about Jayne and her stories at www.JayneOrmerod.com.

Yvonne Saxon

Yvonne Saxon lives in Chesapeake, Virginia with her family and the cat. A former English and history teacher, her love of books led her into a high school librarian's position, then into writing. When she's not homeschooling her son, she's writing mysteries and drinking lots of coffee at her local coffee shop. Visit Yvonne on Facebook and Twitter.

Rosemary Shomaker

Rosemary Shomaker writes about the layers beneath seemingly ordinary happenings. She's an urban planner by degree, a government policy analyst by practice, a fiction writer at heart, and a member of Sisters in Crime. Rosie's short stories populate several anthologies. "Death in the House" appeared in *Virginia is for Mysteries*. Follow Rosie on the Sisters in Crime, Central Virginia Facebook page.

Rosemary Stevens

Rosemary Stevens was raised in Richmond, Virginia and took home the trophy for Vocabulary Student of the Year in high school. She went on to study marketing at Virginia Commonwealth University. An early career selling cemetery plots was perhaps a portent for a life-long love of detective fiction. Rosemary is the author of eleven novels and has won the Agatha Award for Best First Mystery and the RT Reviewers Choice Award also for Best First Mystery. She lives in the Shenandoah Valley with her family and two Siamese cats. Visit Rosemary on Facebook, Twitter, and www.rosemarystevens.com.

Linda Thornburg

Linda Thornburg is one of two authors of the *Cool Careers for Girls* series, fourteen books written to inspire career exploration in teen and pre-teen girls. The books are used in schools throughout the United States. She manages the website memoriesintostory.com, which offers advice and vignettes from the memoir genre. Linda has been a writer and editor for thirty years and is working on her first full-length mystery.

Heather Weidner

Heather Weidner has been a mystery fan since Scooby Doo and Nancy Drew. Originally from Virginia Beach, Heather lives in Central Virginia with her husband and pair of crazy Jack Russell terriers. When she's not reading and writing, she enjoys kayaking, photography, and visiting the beach as much as possible. She is President of the Sisters in Crime, Central Virginia Chapter. Heather's story "Washed Up" appeared in *Virginia is for Mysteries*. She writes the blog *Crazy for Words* and is a guest blogger for a variety of sites. Visit Heather on Facebook, Twitter, Goodreads, and www.heatherweidner.com

Lee A. Wells

Lee A. Wells is a native of Southeastern Virginia and resides there with her husband. Raised on a hardy diet of Agatha Christie, Alfred Hitchcock, and Stephen King, she loves a good mystery, especially if there is a dash of horror tossed in for flavor. She is a member of Sisters in Crime, Central Virginia Chapter. Find Lee on Facebook, Twitter, Tumblr, and flyingmeerkatcreations.wordpress.com/events/.

Ken Wingate

Ken Wingate writes short stories, poems, reflections, and songs that are shared in performances, recordings, and messages. Ken worked in the music retail business for thirty years and returned to his hometown of Portsmouth, Virginia to focus on writing. When not creating in his writing room, Ken enjoys movies, music, and red rock mountains. Ken would like to express his deepest gratitude to Judy Morgan for believing in him then and now, for being his greatest inspiration, and for encouraging his creative nature. A toast, to a most perfect and ideal love! Follow Ken on www.kenwingate.com, Facebook, and Twitter.

CPSIA information can be obtained at www.ICGtesting.com
Printed in the USA
LVOW08s2122240316

480671LV00001B/71/P